MY KIND OF LOVE
MARIAN OAKS

ZEBRA BOOKS
KENSINGTON PUBLISHING CORP.

ZEBRA BOOKS are published by

Kensington Publishing Corp.
850 Third Avenue
New York, NY 10022

First Printing: October, 1994

Printed in the United States of America

With love and thanks to my wonderful agent, Joyce Flaherty, and my incomparable editor, Ann LaFarge, who helped to make this book possible, and to Georgia Romance Writers, who have given me their love and comfort and support, not just in my writing, but in my life.

MOVING ON

People will tell you, "Let go of the past."
But that's wrong.

The past is part of you.
Yours to keep forever.

It's the future you have to let go . . .
    Hopes and dreams that can't come true,
    Might-have-beens that will never be.

Because,
    Until you let them go,
    You can't build new hopes and dreams and
    You can't take hold of

The bright new future that waits for you.

—Marian Oaks

One

Joanna Blake moved briskly around the office, collecting the last of the personal possessions that had accumulated over the years and packing them neatly in the cardboard box on her desk. There wasn't much left. She'd been clearing things out a little at a time since she'd shocked her staff two weeks ago by announcing abruptly that she had decided to retire.

Now, glancing around at the nearly bare room that had been her home-away-from-home for so many years, she felt a moment of doubt. She shrugged it off irritably. Her decision had been sound and the result of much deliberation. Her work no longer gave her the satisfaction and sense of accomplishment it once had. It was time for a change, a new challenge to shake her up and put some pizzazz in her life.

Still, she was going to miss this place, this

business that she and Robert had built from the ground up: Efficiency, Incorporated— We Bring Order to Your Chaos! Not a multimillion-dollar corporation, by any means, but it had made them a comfortable living and let them put something aside for the leisure years they had planned with such loving care.

What they hadn't planned was that Robert would die before they could carry out those plans, and she would spend her leisure years alone. She sank into her chair, overwhelmed for a moment by the depression and sense of futility that had plagued her recently. Since Robert's death, she'd survived by living one day at a time, not realizing that it was the same day, over and over again.

But no more. She squared her shoulders and sat up straighter in the chair. It was time to start moving forward again, time to begin carrying out the plans she and Robert had made.

"Promise me," he'd insisted when they finally understood that he wasn't going to get well. "Do the things we planned. Find someone to do them with if you can, but if not, do them anyway. I can't bear to think of you sitting at home in a darkened room grieving for me while life passes you by."

So she'd promised, and now, finally, she was going to keep her promise.

She checked the desk drawers one more time, found them empty, and took a last look around the room before she taped the cardboard box shut. She was ready to leave, and thank heavens she'd had the foresight to veto any sentimental farewell parties, where she'd probably make a fool of herself and leave everyone believing their efficient, organized boss lady had finally lost it.

She stood up, grabbed her purse, tucked the box under her arm, and started for the door.

It swung open as she reached for the knob and Helen, her longtime assistant who would be running things from now on, and Trudy, her irrepressible but indispensable young secretary—Helen's secretary now—came in carrying a plate of decorated cupcakes, a bottle of ginger ale, paper cups, and party napkins.

Joanna made her voice brisk and businesslike. "I thought I told you I didn't want any fuss over my leaving."

"You did," Helen agreed with determined cheerfulness, "but you aren't the boss anymore."

"Oh, Joanna," Trudy said, "we're going to miss you so."

"No more than I'll miss you," Joanna admitted. Her voice came out gruff and a little shaky. She cleared her throat and tried again. "I'm not dropping off the face of the earth, you know. I'll still be coming by from time to time, to check on things, collect the profits, and see how you're doing without me."

"And to let us know what's happening to you," Helen said. She twisted the cap off the ginger ale and filled three paper cups. "We'll want to know all about the things you do, and the places you go."

"And the tall, handsome men you meet," Trudy added.

"Men?" Joanna accepted the cupcake and napkin Helen handed her. "Trudy, believe me, it's a vast wasteland out there."

"How do you know?" Helen demanded. "You haven't even looked."

"I have too many other things to do to spend my time looking for men. Besides, I've already had a man, the best. He'd be a hard act for anyone else to follow."

"What are you going to do first?" Trudy asked.

"I'm going to broil the steak I took out of the freezer this morning. And after that? Who knows? I haven't had time to make up my mind yet." She set the cupcake down, untasted, and hugged first Trudy, then Helen. "But right now, I'm going to get out of here before I decide to stay after all."

She gathered up the box and her purse, blew kisses to both, and was out the door before they could stop her.

Driving home, she admitted to herself that she'd had plenty of time to make up her mind what to do; she just hadn't had the heart. Perhaps it was a side effect of the general malaise she'd been suffering lately.

Or more likely was the cause of it. If she'd got busy and kept her promise to Robert, instead of sitting around feeling sorry for herself, she'd probably be driving into Atlanta right now for a concert or play, or she might be in the middle of a wonderful ocean cruise, surrounded by Trudy's tall, handsome men vying for her attention.

She grinned at herself. She knew perfectly well she wasn't going to find any tall, handsome men out there, and certainly not vying for her attention, but at least there'd be new people, new experiences, and more important, the knowledge that she was no longer drifting, but had taken charge of her life again.

She'd begin with dinner. Instead of simply broiling that steak, she'd grill it over charcoal and eat on the patio tonight. With a baked potato, salad, and perhaps a small glass of burgundy, it would be the kind of simple but elegant dinner she and Robert had shared so often, and a good start to her new life.

She sat up a little straighter behind the wheel, and drove a little faster. For the first time in far too long, she was looking forward to a meal.

Benjamin Walker drove his grandchildren home after the first day at their new school. Next week they could take the bus, but today they were coping with enough change in their lives. He wanted to spare them as much anxiety as possible.

The mess the movers had left in their new living room didn't bother him. The unnaturally subdued manner of the children did. They'd hardly spoken on the way home, and now they stood just inside the doorway, looking so lost and forlorn that a wave of guilt hit him. He'd been so wrapped up in his own grief and need to cope that he hadn't paid sufficient attention to the shock they were going through.

He cleared his throat and drew a deep breath. "Well, kids, here we are, in our new home. It's a mess, isn't it, but . . ." He let his voice die away as he realized how phony his cheerfulness sounded. The children deserved better than that—and so did he.

He dropped into the nearest chair and pulled them to him, settling Joey on his lap and putting his arm around Becky's slender shoulders. He was surprised to find that their closeness eased his own hurt a little, and made it easier for him to say, "I know how hard it is for you to have everything in your lives change, all at once. Losing your mama and daddy hurts me, too, but I know they'd be happy that you have such a nice new school, and such a great place to live."

"It's very nice, Grandpa," Becky told him. The stiff, adult tone of her voice tore at his heart.

"And they'd be glad we're together," he added, "helping each other, and learning to be happy again."

"Grandma Spencer said we must be very good, and do what you tell us," Becky said.

"And Grandpa Spencer said we should be brave," Joey added. He rubbed first one eye and then the other with the back of his hand.

Damn! Ben thought. He'd gone to pick up the children as quickly as possible after the accident that killed their parents, but instead of the shocked and grieving children he'd expected, he'd found little automatons—no tears, no outward signs of grief, just self-contained quiet. He'd thought at first they were still in shock but during the last few days he'd begun to wonder what other nonsense his late daughter-in-law's parents had stuffed into their little heads. They were strange people who seemed to substitute arbitrary notions of right and wrong for common sense and compassion. For all he'd loved Jennie, he'd never gotten along with her family, or even understood them. No wonder Ben and Jennie had wanted him to be the children's guardian.

He held Joey a little closer and told him

quietly, "You don't have to be brave if you don't want to be. I know how much you miss your mama and daddy. I miss them, too." He took a deep breath and added, "Sometimes I miss them so much I cry like anything."

Both children looked startled. "Grown-ups don't cry," Joey said after a minute.

"Oh, yes they do, too," Ben said. "They just don't like to admit it very often, but when you're very, very sad, it's okay to cry. Sometimes it makes you feel better."

The scratching and thumping sounds he'd been hearing from the garage became louder and more frantic. He released the children and told them, "Bernie feels strange in his new home, too, and he's been lonesome while you were at school. Why don't you take him outside for a good romp while I see what I can do about cleaning up some of this mess?"

He ushered them through the kitchen and opened the garage door, then stepped out of the way as a young, exuberant, and very large Saint Bernard bounded into the kitchen, slipping and sliding on the vinyl floor and rattling the windows with his welcoming *woof!*

Within seconds, children and dog were twined into one joyous, hugging, petting, tail-wagging, face-licking love-in. Ben gave silent but fervent thanks as the dog accomplished what he had not, then sent them all out to play in the spacious backyard with the lush, thick hedge that was one of the reasons he'd bought the house. The only way out of the yard was through the house or garage. He didn't have to worry about the children wandering off, or Bernie terrorizing innocent neighbors.

He watched through the kitchen window for a few minutes, then turned his attention to the task ahead. Between his own familiar belongings and the things he'd kept of the children's, the house was a jumble of furniture, toys, miscellaneous and unidentifiable boxes and barrels, and the luggage and loose clothing he'd brought in the car. It was going to take weeks to establish any kind of order.

He sighed and reminded himself that this house was spacious and comfortable, at a price he could afford, and most important, available when he needed it. He shuddered at the thought of spending even one more day with the children and

Bernie—good old Bernie!—in his small bachelor apartment.

First things first, he thought. He needed to find and unpack clean clothes for tomorrow. They'd be with the things he'd brought over from the apartment himself. And he'd had the foresight to include towels and washcloths so the kids could bathe tonight.

He had no idea where in the clutter the bed linens were, but Becky and Joey could spend one more night in their sleeping bags. The linens would probably turn up tomorrow. Or the next day. Dishes and kitchen utensils presented another problem, but they, too, would turn up eventually. Until then, there were restaurants and delis.

For tonight, he had plastic plates and forks, and they could heat their hot dogs and canned chili in the microwave.

Maybe he'd be able to muddle through this business of being a single parent after all.

Joanna shed her tailored suit in favor of a pair of comfortable white slacks and a candy-striped blouse, then went downstairs to start the charcoal burning in her small hibachi. She scrubbed a potato to bake in the microwave, and made a tossed salad while she waited for the charcoal to burn down.

Now and again, she glanced toward her desk, at the small, framed picture of Robert that seemed to watch her as she worked. "You'd be proud of me," she told him. "Look at how well I've learned to grill only one steak, and bake only one potato."

Still, she admitted wistfully, as she set a single place at the table, it would be nice to have someone sharing her dinner besides Tinkerbell, her plump and matronly Siamese cat.

She pushed the thought aside and carried her T-bone outside. The coals were glowing nicely, and she was about to lay the steak on the grill when Tinkerbell, squalling and spitting, burst through the hedge at the rear of the yard a scant foot ahead of a Saint Bernard that looked big enough to saddle and ride.

The Siamese skimmed past Joanna's ankles and took refuge in the top of the dogwood tree. The Saint Bernard, less maneuverable, crashed into Joanna and catapulted her through the air. The steak flew off the fork and sailed in another direction as the dog skidded to a stop under the dogwood.

Joanna added her scream to Tinkerbell's ear-splitting yowls. The Saint Bernard glanced from one to the other, tongue lolling from grinning lips like half an acre of wet red felt. Then he threw back his head and joined in with a joyous *"Woof!"* that rattled windowpanes and set the charcoal dancing in the grill.

Before Joanna could draw enough breath for another scream, the dog dashed to the patch of clover where she sat, slurped the half-acre of felt once around her face, snatched up the steak from another patch of clover, and disappeared back through the hedge.

Joanna wiped her face with both hands and told Tinkerbell, still teetering in the top of the dogwood tree, "The next time you want to bring someone home to dinner, I wish you'd check with me first."

She climbed painfully to her feet, brushed at the seat of her pants, and tried to remember if her refrigerator held the ingredients for a Denver omelet.

The sound of another commotion in the

shrubbery sent her leaping for the security of the patio, where she peered at the hedge from behind one of the wrought-iron standards that supported the patio cover.

Instead of the Saint Bernard, two children emerged from the hedge, made their way hesitantly across the lawn, and stopped in front of her. The girl—Joanna was no good at guessing children's ages, but thought she might be nine or ten—held out the bedraggled steak, now full of tooth marks and covered with leaves and grass, and asked timidly, "Is this yours?"

Joanna regarded the mangled remains of her dinner and shuddered. "It used to be," she conceded after a minute.

"We're awfully sorry." The girl's voice trembled a little. "Bernie didn't mean to be bad."

"I'm sure he didn't," Joanna said hastily, hoping to ward off the tears that seemed imminent.

They seemed to relax a little. "We can wash it off for you if you want us to."

Before Joanna could think of an adequate answer, the hedge crackled and rustled again. They all turned and stared at it. This time it was a man—white-haired and fair-skinned, with blue eyes and rosy cheeks that inexplicably made her think of the Kewpie Doll she'd had as a child—who pushed his way through the hedge. "Becky? Joey?" The worried frown that creased his forehead disappeared as he spotted the children. "Oh, there you are. What are you doing over here?"

As he came closer, she realized that he was only an inch or so taller than her own five feet seven inches, and not roly-poly, as she'd first supposed, but solid and stocky, with an aura of male authority that immediately banished the Kewpie Doll image.

He eyed the steak with a mixture of curiosity and distaste. "What on earth is that?"

The little boy—Joey?—found his voice suddenly. "Oh, Grandpa, Bernie was bad and stole her dinner. We brought it back."

The girl added, "We asked if she wanted us to wash it for her, but she didn't tell us yet."

The man studied the steak again, then glanced at Joanna, his blue eyes alight with obvious amusement. "Well? Would you like them to wash it for you?"

She brushed futilely at the grass stains

on the seat of her pants and said quickly, "I, uh, no. No. I'm sure, ah, Bernie wants it more than I do."

"More than likely," he agreed with a hint of laughter in his voice. Then he sobered. "I do apologize for Bernie's behavior. Fortunately, we were just about to cook dinner, too. Since Bernie ruined your meal, the least we can do is share ours with you. Don't go away. We'll be right back."

Before she could protest or assure him he was under no such obligation, he had urged the children back through the hedge and disappeared after them, leaving only his warm, slightly husky baritone voice lingering in her ears.

"Heaven only knows what *they're* planning for dinner," she murmured, "but I'll bet it isn't steak." Something soft and warm twined around her ankles. She glanced down at Tinkerbell. "Don't look so pleased with yourself. I hope they bring *you* a bowl of dog food."

Tinkerbell said, *"Wowr?"*

"Yes, *dog* food. And kindly stop grinning at me like that. You're Siamese, not Cheshire."

Although, she couldn't help adding to

herself, the whole episode had a kind of Alice-in-Wonderland madness to it. Maybe, with a little luck, she'd wake up, like Alice, and find she'd only been dreaming.

But of course she didn't. She was still staring sadly at her now-useless bed of glowing charcoal when the hedge shivered and the three of them—no, four; Bernie was with them—pushed their way through the hedge again.

The man carried a tray covered with—surely not a kitchen towel, she thought; it had to be a bath towel—which he whipped off to reveal a package of hot dogs, and not just ordinary hot dogs, but hot dogs obviously destined to nestle in fluffy, cottony, white buns under indigestible mounds of the chili and cole slaw that took up the rest of the space on the tray.

She glanced in horror at the jar of pickles Becky carried, and stifled a groan at the bag of potato chips Joey was clutching to his breast. Clearly, her stomach was about to go slumming.

Her self-invited guest set the tray on the table beside the grill and grinned at her. "You've probably figured out by now that we're your new neighbors. May I present my granddaughter, Becky, and my grandson, Joey? And I'm Benjamin Walker, sober, solvent, sexy, *single* senior citizen."

"Good heavens," she exclaimed. "Should I curtsy, or simply ask for your autograph?"

"Neither." He studied her with obvious male approval that should have been offensive, but somehow, was not. "Just tell me you're single, too. Please, tell me you're single."

The word jolted her as if she'd received an electrical shock. She'd faced the fact that she was now a widow, but so far, she hadn't let herself acknowledge that being a widow meant being single as well. Nor had she felt single, until this moment, under Benjamin Walker's frank and amiable scrutiny.

She felt the heat rising in her face and squelched it through sheer willpower. "I'm Joanna Blake," she said, "and yes"—she was pleased at how cool her voice sounded— "I'm single. My husband died several years ago."

"Oh. I'm sorry. I didn't mean—"

"Of course not," she said quickly. She smiled at the children, standing close together behind their grandfather, was rewarded by two shy smiles in return, and changed the subject firmly. "I knew someone had bought the house, but I didn't expect anyone to move in so quickly."

There was nothing shy about his smile. It lit his whole face and brought a sparkle to his eye. "We didn't have much choice," he admitted. "Can you imagine sharing a one-bedroom apartment with two children and a Saint Bernard?"

"I don't even want to try," she said honestly. "But how did you happen to be . . ." She broke off, suddenly aware of her rudeness. "Sorry. I didn't mean to pry."

He picked up the fork she had used on her steak and placed the hot dogs in precisely spaced rows on the grill, then took the pickles and potato chips from Becky and Joey. "Go home and wash your hands. And don't take too long. Dinner will be ready in a few minutes."

Obediently, they pushed back through the hedge, and he turned to Joanna. "The children came to live with me after my son and his wife were killed in a car accident recently." His voice was quiet and matter-of-fact, but his grief and pain were obvious.

"I'm so sorry. Was he your only child?"

He nodded. "And I missed most of his childhood after his mother and I separated, so this business of being a parent is still pretty new to me."

"Oh." She immediately forgave him for the hot dogs and chili. After a moment's thought, she included the white buns and pickles.

"But we're learning," he added. "The children are learning how to be orphans, and I'm trying to learn how to be father, mother, and whatever else they need. But it isn't easy." He rotated the hot dogs a quarter turn. "That's one reason we barged in on you like this, for which I sincerely apologize. I was praying desperately for some way to get us all through this first meal in a strange new home, and then, like a miracle, there you were."

"Oh," she said again. "I don't believe I've ever been the answer to anyone's prayers before. Glad to be of service."

She studied him unobtrusively while he tended the hot dogs. "Sober, solvent, sexy, *single* senior citizen," he'd described himself. The wonder was that some enterprising woman hadn't latched on to him by now. She grinned, remembering how she'd told

Trudy a couple of hours earlier that, as far as men were concerned, it was "a vast wasteland out there." Now, this one had dropped almost into her lap. He was not quite one of the tall, handsome men Trudy had described, but she couldn't deny that he was much more interesting, and uncommonly attractive, in his own way.

He had the same masculine self-confidence she'd liked so much in Robert, and the ability to size up a situation quickly and take appropriate action. He was going to need it, she thought, with two lively youngsters to raise. He seemed properly concerned at the prospect, but not at all intimidated by it, and except for his grief over the loss of the children's parents, if he was distressed at the way his life had suddenly turned topsy-turvy, he didn't show it.

He gave the hot dogs another quarter turn. They were browning nicely and beginning to smell the way they ought to taste, but somehow, Joanna thought, never quite did.

Tinkerbell came out from wherever she'd been hiding and rubbed against Joanna's ankles. She stretched her neck up to sniff deeply in the direction of the grill, and her sharp, imperious *"Mrow!"* indicated clearly that she approved of hot dogs even if Joanna didn't.

Her timing was bad. Bernie and the children chose that moment to push through the hedge again. Bernie spotted Tinkerbell and bounded toward her with gleeful exuberance. She fluffed her fur and arched her back, but this time she was on her own turf, and held her ground. Bernie hunkered down with his rump in the air and his chest and chin on the ground in front of her and woofed gently.

Tinkerbell took a dainty step forward, lifted one paw, and smacked him sharply on the nose. He yelped, jumped, and somersaulted backward away from her.

Joanna grabbed for Tinkerbell and managed to catch the end of her tail. Tinkerbell howled and spat. Becky cried out, "Oh, Bernie!" and Joey broke into tears.

Ben laid down the fork and knelt to examine Bernie.

"I'm so sorry!" Joanna cried.

"No harm done," Ben said. "Don't cry, Joey. Bernie's all right."

"But she scratched him," Becky said.

She glanced at Joanna as if expecting her to defend Tinkerbell.

Ben got to his feet again. "No, she didn't. She only smacked him. He isn't hurt, but he'll be a bit more respectful toward her from now on."

Joey's sobs quieted, but his voice was quivery as he said, "Bernie wouldn't hurt her. He just wanted to be friends. Nasty ole cat."

Ben started to speak, but the distress in Joey's voice was more than Joanna could take. She gathered Tinkerbell into a firmer grip and dropped to her knees in front of Joey. "Tinkerbell wants to make friends, too," she explained, "but Bernie is bigger than she is and might hurt her accidentally. Smacking him was just her way of telling him to be careful. She really is a nice cat. Would you like to pet her?"

Joey studied the cat with apprehension, but Becky reached out and stroked her, tentatively at first, then, as Tinkerbell arched her neck and began to sing, with pleasure. Joey watched, then took one cautious stroke, and then another.

Delighted by so much attention, Tinkerbell wriggled free of Joanna's arms, rubbed against Becky's ankles, and butted her head into Joey's lap. Bernie, one forepaw still pressed protectively over his insulted nose, watched in disbelief as his children lavished their affection on someone besides himself, then lifted his muzzle and howled softly but with obvious anguish.

The children froze into shocked immobility, until the adults burst out laughing, then they laughed, too, and ran to pet and hug Bernie.

Joanna turned to grin at Ben and was startled to see his eyes gleaming with moisture.

He smiled, a blissful curving of lips that lifted him from uncommonly attractive to almost irresistible, and said simply, "They haven't done much laughing lately. I owe you, Joanna Blake. Big. You and Tinker-bell."

The warmth in his voice and on his face flustered her, but seemed to call for an answer. She blurted out the first thing that came to her mind.

"Your hot dogs are burning."

Two

Ben held his coffee cup out to be refilled for the third time, well aware that it was long past time to go home, but reluctant to leave the comfort of Joanna's lounge chair, even more reluctant to leave the greater comfort of Joanna's presence. He'd never believed in guardian angels, but she was clear proof that someone, somewhere, was looking out for him.

And for the children. They'd been as drawn to her as they were to Tinkerbell—not because of anything special she'd done, but on some more primitive, instinctive level that he understood all too well. She had the same effect on him.

"Wonderful meal," he declared. "The company was delightful and the food couldn't have been too bad. The kids haven't eaten that well since I've had them." He resisted the urge to let his smile turn into a grin, remembering that Joanna had eaten well, too, despite his distinct impression that she'd originally been less than thrilled about his choice of a menu.

He shifted his gaze to the center of the yard, where Joey sprawled comfortably against Bernie while they both watched Becky drag a long piece of grass across the ground for Tinkerbell to chase. "They haven't had that much fun, either. The truth is, I've been worried as hell about them. They don't laugh, they don't cry, they don't misbehave. They're like little robots."

She set the coffeepot down, picked up her own cup, and slipped into the other chair. "They're still in shock."

"Maybe. Or maybe I'm just not coping well enough."

"Don't be so hard on yourself, Ben. There's a limit to what you can do." She cradled her cup in both hands and watched the children over the rim of it. "It takes time to recover from a hurt as big as they've suffered. And they're scared, too. They've not only lost the two most important people in their lives, they've learned that everything they counted on could be snatched away from them without warning. Right now, the most important thought in their heads is that it happened once, it could happen again."

"I hadn't thought of that," he admitted, "but it makes sense." He studied her profile in the gathering dusk, then added, "Thanks for the input. Somehow, I have a lot more faith in the future knowing you're so close at hand. I think Becky and Joey do, too."

"No." Her response was quick and firm. "Don't count on me for help. It isn't that I don't want to, it's just that . . . I don't know anything at all about children. Robert and I never had any."

"Was that by choice?" he asked, "or . . ."

She shrugged. "It just turned out that way, I guess. We spent our first few years together getting a business started. Then, when we were ready for children, we simply didn't have any. By the time we realized we weren't going to, we discussed seeing a doctor, or adopting, but somehow, we never seemed to get around to it."

He couldn't tell from her tone of voice if she was glad or sorry, but after a minute, she added, "It's probably just as well. By then, we were pretty well settled in our ways, and children . . . well . . . they're a big responsibility. I'm not sure that we could have done right by them."

"That's how it was with me, after my divorce," he said. "I kept thinking that someday I'd find somebody else and marry again, but somehow, I never did. And that's probably just as well, too."

He glanced back across the lawn at the children just as Joey yawned hugely and let his head droop down to rest on Bernie's broad back.

"It's way past their bedtime." Reluctantly, he levered himself out of his chair. "Come on, kids," he called. "Time we were getting home."

Joey climbed to his feet and waited for Bernie to stand up and provide a place for him to lean. Becky carried Tinkerbell over and put her in Joanna's lap and asked shyly, "Do you think Tinkerbell might have kittens anytime soon?"

"Not if she knows what's good for her," Joanna muttered under her breath, then told Becky, "It's not very likely."

"Why do you want to know?" Ben asked.

"My teacher's cat had kittens and she had to find homes for them. I wanted one, but Momma said Bernie hadn't got his clumsies under control yet, and she was afraid he might hurt a kitten." She leaned over to press her cheek against the top of Tinkerbell's head. "I don't think Bernie would hurt a kitten, especially not Tinkerbell's kitten. Do you?"

Joanna glanced at Ben, a startled and somehow uncertain look on her face. "Uh, no. I'm sure he wouldn't. But I don't think you'd better count on Tinkerbell for kittens."

Becky sighed. "That's too bad." She put her arms around the cat and hugged her gently. "But I love her anyway. Can I come back and play with her again?"

"Well . . ." Joanna hesitated, and Ben was afraid she was looking for a polite way to say no. Then she smiled at Becky and said, "Tinkerbell would like that, but it's really up to your grandfather."

He forestalled Becky's eager plea by ruffling her hair and telling her, "You have to leave before you can come *back*. And if we don't take Joey home pretty quickly, he's going to fall asleep right here."

He ushered them to the hedge, pleasantly aware that Joanna had put Tinkerbell out of her lap and was walking with them. At the hedge, he told the children, "Go on in and start getting ready for bed. I'll be along in a minute."

He waited until the hedge closed behind them and turned to Joanna. "You're a good sport and a great hostess, letting us descend on you the way we did."

"No problem," she told him cheerfully. "The truth is, I enjoyed myself tonight more than I have in a long time." The slight note of surprise in her voice told him she meant it; she wasn't just being polite.

It was time for him to go, past time, but he stood as if he'd put down roots, studying the sweet, pretty face in front of him and wishing like hell the kids were old enough to put themselves to bed. The faint evening breeze shifted suddenly, bringing him a whiff of her light perfume mixed with a hint of smoke and slightly scorched hot dogs. The combination was almost unbearably erotic, and before his brain realized what his body was going to do, he'd moved toward her, folded her into a warm embrace, and found her lips with his.

Despite her slimness, her body was delightfully rounded and soft against him.

The feel and taste of her were even more arousing than her scent, and the kiss he'd expected to be little more than a quick brushing of lips became something totally different.

She was going to pull away any second, he thought, and slap the hell out of him, and it was going to be worth it.

But she didn't pull away. She stiffened for half a second, then relaxed in his arms and seemed to flow against him, her lips parting, her body meeting and matching his in a one-to-one correspondence that made him feel sorry for tall men kissing short women.

It took every ounce of willpower he had not to take advantage of the situation. He wanted to slide his hands up and down her back, cup her slender but shapely behind in both hands, and press her hard against him, and then— He cut the thought off before his body could translate it into action.

Their lips separated finally, but he continued to hold her close, relishing the warmth of her cheek against his, savoring the soft fullness of her breasts against his chest, and realizing belatedly that even if he wasn't clamping her against him, she was still close enough to feel his burgeoning arousal against her.

It was time to let her go, before he offended her or tormented himself any further. He dropped his arms and stepped back. "Good night, Joanna. I had a wonderful evening."

"Good night, Ben." She hesitated, then added the words that followed him all the way home. "I did, too."

He pushed his way through the hedge and paused to collect his wits and give his body time to settle down before going in to face the kids.

It occurred to him that if they hadn't been waiting for him, and if Joanna had been wearing a skirt instead of slacks, he'd have explored a whole lot more than just her lips, and the evening might very well have had a completely different ending.

He pushed the thought away quickly. It was demeaning to Joanna to make such assumptions, and he was only making his physical discomfort worse.

But even as he willed himself back to normal, the thought persisted that Joanna was exactly the kind of woman he needed—

warm, friendly, intelligent, and not intimidated by the children or Bernie. So what if she claimed to know nothing about children? Women were born with maternal instincts. She could learn.

She was uncommonly attractive besides, and seemed to like him as well as the children. She might not realize it yet, but he intended to make her an important part of his life. He promised himself that the day was not far off when they'd share a whole lot more than just a kiss.

Joanna watched the hedge close behind Ben and remembered, with wry amusement, that it was her stomach she'd been worried about tonight.

Her stomach was fine. The rest of her . . .

Watching Ben Walker all evening, she'd thought he was just a bit pudgy, but she'd been wrong. He was firm and muscular and masculine, and her body had reacted to his in ways she'd thought it had forgotten forever. Somehow, in her grief over losing Robert the person, she hadn't realized how much she missed Robert the man.

She fought down a wave of regret as she remembered how she'd melted into Ben's arms, enjoyed the warmth of his body against her breasts, shamelessly pressed herself against him.

The regret wasn't that she'd done it, but that it was over, and nothing had come of it, nothing *could* come of it. She liked Ben Walker, liked him a lot. He was a warm, vital, attractive man, young for his years, patient and loving with the children. He clearly found her attractive, too, which she had to admit was no small part of his charm.

But the timing and circumstances were all wrong for them. The children had just turned his life topsy-turvy, and she was about to embark on a new phase in her life. What a shame they hadn't met sooner, or later, or anytime except *now*.

Ben's unconcealed interest in her was flattering, but misplaced. They were neighbors. Perhaps they could also be friends. But that was all. Even if she'd wanted a new man in her life right now, Ben wouldn't be that man.

She had things to do, plans to carry out. It might be different if he were free to share in them, but his first priority had to be the children. And if he wanted a woman in his life, or in theirs, she couldn't be that woman. She wasn't qualified.

Still, she thought wistfully, *it might have been fun.*

Ben threw back the light covers and rolled out of bed, Joey's terrified scream still echoing in his ears. He grabbed his robe from the foot of the bed and shrugged into it as he ran.

As quick as he was, Becky was there before him, dodging Joey's flailing arms as she tried to get close enough to shake him awake. "Joey, wake up! You're having a bad dream."

"Let me have him," Ben said. He sank down on the edge of the bed and pulled Joey into his arms, holding the rigid young body close and murmuring wordless sounds of comfort until the flailing ceased and the screams gave way to heartbroken sobs.

Between sobs, Joey managed to choke out, "Bernie! Bernie! I told him not to. I told him."

"Told him what?" Ben asked.

"I told him not to run across the street. I told him a car would hit him."

"Joey, Bernie's all right. You were dreaming."

"No. The car hit him, and he's dead."

Ben glanced up at Becky standing beside them, her eyes mirroring the sense of helplessness he felt. "Bernie's all right," he repeated. "Don't you remember? He's down in the garage, in his own bed."

"No, he's dead. The car hit him. Oh, Bernie."

Ben drew a deep breath. "Becky, go downstairs and get Bernie. Bring him up here where Joey can see for himself that he's all right."

She nodded, and as she turned to go, he added, "Be sure to turn on the hall light so you don't fall on the stairs."

While he waited for Becky to bring the dog, he cradled the sobbing child in his arms, rocking back and forth in a rhythm as old and instinctive as breathing. Some of the stiffness went out of Joey's body and his sobs quieted to deep, shuddering breaths and an occasional hiccup.

It seemed forever before Bernie galloped up the stairs and down the hall. He skidded to a stop outside Joey's door, managed to turn himself ninety degrees, and bounded across the room to place a front paw on the bed on each side of Ben and nuzzle first Joey's hand, and then his face.

"Bernie!" Joey threw his arms around Bernie's neck and pressed his cheek against the dog's muzzle. Bernie twisted his head enough to reach Joey's face with his tongue, and began to lick away the tears. Joey sighed blissfully. "Bernie, you're okay. You aren't dead!"

"I told you it was just a dream," Ben said. He continued to cradle Joey with one arm while he pulled Becky to him with the other for a warm hug and a kiss on the cheek. "You okay, sweetheart?" At her nod, he told her, "Then maybe you'd better go on back to bed. I'll stay with Joey for a while."

She returned his hug and kiss. "Okay, Grandpa."

"And Bernie," Joey said. He slid off Ben's lap as Bernie clambered up onto the bed beside them. "I want Bernie to stay, too."

"Well . . ." Ben studied the dog and the boy, so twined together it was hard to tell where one left off and the other began. "For a little while, anyway."

He tucked Joey back into bed, started to order the dog back onto the floor, then thought better of it. He sat with them until Joey fell asleep cuddled against Bernie, gave the dog a grateful pat on the head and tug on the ear, and went back to his own bed.

As he waited to drift back to sleep, he remembered what Joanna had said earlier. "They're scared. It happened to them once, it could happen again." He hadn't completely understood what she meant—until now. Suddenly, he was scared, too. Just being a good single parent wasn't going to be enough. They needed more, and he wasn't sure what it was or how to give it.

He fell asleep with the comforting thought that Bernie knew. And he was willing to bet Joanna did, too, whether she realized it or not.

Joanna woke sometime during the night, aware that she'd been dreaming, but unable to remember the dream. *Strange,* she thought. For most of her life, she'd been a prolific dreamer, but since Robert's death, she seldom dreamed at all. Maybe Ben's hot dogs were getting to her after all.

Something tickled her cheek and she reached up to brush it away. Her hand came away wet, and she realized she'd been crying in her sleep. She hadn't done that since the first few weeks after Robert's death. Obviously *something* was getting to her.

The children, most likely. They'd been so quiet, so subdued, not at all like most of the children she knew. She understood what they were going through. How well she understood it! And there was so little anyone could do to help them. They had to work through it for themselves, just as she had done.

She wiped the tears from her cheeks, then rolled over and reached for the soft furry shape curled up beside her. "Oh, Tinkerbell," she murmured as the cat's rich, warm purr filled her ears and vibrated against her, "what would I ever do without you?"

Ben waved at the rear of the departing school bus, wistfully aware that Becky and

Joey were doing their best to pretend they didn't know him. He sighed as the bus disappeared into the distance, then he turned and went back home.

The house was still in a mess, even after a weekend of cleaning and unpacking. He wandered into the kitchen, where the breakfast dishes still sat on the table, and poured himself a second cup of coffee, torn between his desire to set his home to rights, and his knowledge that once he did, he wasn't going to have much to occupy himself during the day.

It was beginning to dawn on him that he might have been a trifle hasty in taking early retirement, but he didn't know what else he could have done. The children deserved better than day care or after-school activities, and he sure as hell wasn't going to let them become latchkey kids.

The house seemed uncommonly quiet with the kids gone. Funny, he'd lived by himself for years and never minded the quiet before. Now, it made him feel lonely.

He carried his coffee over to the sink and stared out the window into the backyard and the thin spot in the hedge.

There was, of course, his delightful new

neighbor. He'd enjoy seeing her again, without the children this time, but he couldn't think of an adequate excuse to do so. If he descended on her every time he felt a little lonely, he'd wear out his welcome in no time.

He grinned as Bernie sniffed his way from one end of the hedge to the other in obvious hopes of finding Tinkerbell. Too bad he couldn't send the Saint Bernard to work his magic in reverse and bring Joanna over here.

Maybe he could.

He went upstairs to Joey's room, found a small red sneaker, and took it out to the backyard. By now, Bernie had abandoned his search for Tinkerbell and had flopped down on a bare spot in the lawn to stare dejectedly at the house. He stood up when Ben stepped out into the yard and came toward him in a drooping, semisideways gait that shouted "poor, abandoned, lonely, unloved dog," and was clearly intended to overwhelm Ben with guilt.

"Sorry, old boy," he said cheerfully. "The kids won't be home until this afternoon. Meanwhile, let's see if you can do something to earn that ton of dog food you pack away every day."

He braced himself as Bernie leaned mournfully against him, his hindquarters sliding slowly down Ben's legs until his rump encountered Ben's feet. Ben held out the sneaker.

Bernie stared at him as if he'd lost his mind, but finally took it into his mouth.

"Good boy," Ben said. He pointed toward the hedge. "Go," he said firmly. "Take."

The tip of Bernie's tail moved tentatively. Ben tried to take a step closer to the hedge and found that Bernie had his feet pinned to the ground. "Damn it, dog! Stand on your own four feet and get off mine." He hauled irritably at the loose skin across Bernie's rump until his feet were free, then lined the dog up with the sparse part of the hedge and pushed.

Bernie turned his head to look at Ben, which turned him sideways to the hedge, so that he slid past the hole instead of through it. He dropped the sneaker and let his tongue hang from his mouth in a grin that seemed to say, "I don't know what kind of game we're playing, but it's sort of fun, and sure beats being ignored."

Ben cursed under his breath, heaved at the dog until he had him lined up facing the hedge again, stuffed the sneaker back in his mouth, and gave him another shove. This time, either Bernie got the idea, or caught the scent of cat, and wiggled through willingly.

Ben watched the hedge close over the dog's rear end, then told himself he was an idiot who had just thrown away half a pair of expensive sneakers. He had no more reason to think Joanna was at home than he had to believe Bernie would deliver the sneaker. He doubted she was a full-time homemaker. She'd mentioned the business she and her husband had started. And she was surely too young to be retired. He couldn't think of any other reason she'd be at home on a Monday morning.

"There's no fool like an old fool," he told himself, "unless it's an infatuated old fool." With a wry shake of his head, he turned and went back inside.

* * *

Joanna lingered over another blueberry muffin and a second cup of coffee until she heard the groan and wheeze of the school bus stopping at the corner. She offered the last bit of muffin to Tinkerbell and brushed crumbs from her fingers. "Time's a-wastin'," she said firmly.

She rinsed her cup and saucer at the sink, tossed her paper napkin into the wastebasket, and took a minute to scan the assortment of notes and clippings cluttering the front of the refrigerator. Other women covered their kitchen appliances with cute or clever "fridgies"; she covered hers with lists and memos. She smiled, remembering how Robert had always insisted their refrigerator was better reading than the newspaper.

Occasionally, she'd surprised him by posting an impulsive love note, and he'd responded with an invitation to dinner or the theater, fresh-cut roses from the garden, and occasional small gifts, like the engraved pen she still used for jotting down her notes.

She swallowed past the sudden ache in her throat and closed her eyes until the threat of tears had passed, then lifted the pen from its holder and took it to her small desk under the window. Tinkerbell murmured her approval of this departure from normal weekday routine, and hopped up to sun herself on the windowsill.

Joanna sat down and stared unhappily at the stack of file folders, manila envelopes, and notebooks she'd put there the day before. She hadn't opened them since Robert's death, and barely remembered what was in them, only that it was her whole future—the future she and Robert had planned together, but that she would carry out alone.

She picked an envelope at random and dumped the contents out. For a few minutes, she riffled through them—newspaper clippings mostly, travel articles, advertisements, a few sheets of notebook paper, slightly yellowed, covered with her small, neat handwriting, or Robert's bold, precise printing. Tinkerbell watched lazily, occasionally stretching one paw down to pat Joanna's arm or bat at the papers on the desk.

After a few minutes, Joanna gathered everything together, stuffed it back into the envelope, and glanced with dismay at

Robert's photograph. "This isn't going to work," she told him. "These things are meant for two people, not just one. Besides, everything here is at least three years out of date. I'm going to have to start all over again from scratch."

She held the envelope in both hands, feeling not just the weight of the papers it held, but all the hours, and days, and years that had gone into it. She couldn't help feeling that, when she put it down, she would be letting go of a part of Robert as well.

After a moment, she forced herself to lay it on the corner of the desk, and went to find the travel section of the Sunday paper.

When she came back, Tinkerbell had given up lounging on the windowsill and was standing at attention, switching her tail back and forth and uttering small, plaintive cries as she stared out the window.

"What's the matter, baby? Birds teasing you again?" She glanced out the window and felt her spirits lift at the sight of Bernie, tongue lolling from the side of his mouth as he grinned up at them. Tinkerbell pawed at the window, then jumped down and ran to scratch at the door.

"Shame on you," Joanna scolded. "Do

you want him to think you're easy? You only met him a couple of days ago. Besides, we aren't going to get involved with him, or his children." She hesitated and added, "Or his master. We have other things to do."

Tinkerbell scratched at the door again and demanded imperiously, *"Mrr-o-ut. Now!"*

"Oh, all right. I suppose it's too nice a day to keep you cooped up in here." She opened the door, inhaled deeply of the fresh spring morning, and decided she didn't want to be cooped up either. She followed Tinkerbell outside.

Bernie gave a yelp of joy and bounded toward Tinkerbell. He lowered his head so they could rub noses, then stood with his tail cutting circles in the air and his tongue lolling from the corner of his mouth in a picture of perfect canine bliss as Tinkerbell stood on tiptoe and twined herself around his front legs.

Watching them, Joanna felt an unexpected twinge of envy. As if sensing her feeling, Bernie stepped carefully over Tinkerbell and came to sit on Joanna's feet, leaning back to look at her over the top of his head. His eyes glazed in ecstasy as she scratched him between the ears. After a moment, he blinked and stood up, as if he'd suddenly remembered something. He woofed politely, picked up a small red sneaker, and offered it to her.

Trying not to laugh, she took it from him and laid it on the window ledge, intending to return it to Ben the next time she saw him. She gave Bernie a last pat and turned to go back inside, then stopped. Joey might need the sneaker today. And it really was too nice a day to be cooped up inside, making lists and plans.

She picked up the sneaker again and started for the thin spot in the hedge, trying not to trip over Bernie or step on Tinkerbell as they frolicked alongside her.

Three

Ben piled the dirty breakfast dishes in the sink, emptied a box of kitchen utensils onto the table, and pawed through them halfheartedly. He resisted the impulse to dump them all into the nearest drawer and move on to something else. There had to be a logical way to go about this, but damned if he wanted to spend all morning trying to find it.

He compromised by leaving them where they were and clearing a spot on the counter where he opened the next box. This was silverware, and probably ought to go into the sideboard in the dining room, except that he didn't intend to use the dining room that often. The kitchen was more comfortable for one man and two children, and he wasn't likely to be doing much entertaining.

On the other hand, his stainless didn't

have to be polished; the sterling did. He closed the box and pushed it to the back of the counter to worry about later, and moved on to the next one, which held pots and pans. He sighed with relief and began transferring them to the cupboard beside the stove.

It wasn't until someone tapped lightly at the back door that he remembered Bernie and his mission. He abandoned the pots and pans and ran to the door.

Joanna Blake stood outside, dangling Joey's red sneaker from one finger. "Bernie strikes again," she said.

"Bless Bernie!" He took the sneaker from her with one hand and drew her into the kitchen with the other, while silently vowing to gift Bernie with another steak—a big, juicy one. "Look, the kitchen's a mess, but I've just uncovered the coffeepot. Why don't you come in and have a cup?"

He didn't blame her when she hesitated. The disorder in the kitchen was enough to daunt anyone. But she let him close the door behind her and glanced around, her eyes widening as she surveyed the clutter. She seemed particularly fascinated by the jumbled pile on the table.

"Sorry about that," he said cheerfully. "I spent most of the weekend trying to get the kids' stuff unpacked and their rooms in order. I'm still trying to decide what to do with these things." He pushed them to the other side of the table and pulled out a chair for her. "The trouble is, I'm not sure what half of them are, much less where to put them."

She looked surprised, and he added, "This stuff didn't all come out of one small bachelor kitchen; most of it belonged to my son and his wife. I kept it and most of their furniture because I knew I'd be moving into a house and would need it, and because I thought it would be better for the children if they could still have familiar things around them."

"That makes sense." She continued to study the assortment on the table. "I take it you're not a gourmet cook."

"You take it right. My field of expertise is electronics, not food. Except, of course, for eating it." He grinned and added shamelessly, "I'll bet you could help me figure out what everything is, show me how to use it, and tell me where it should go."

She ignored the chair he was still holding for her and gave the kitchen another once-over. "You'd better believe it. Now you're talking about *my* field of expertise."

"Cleaning kitchens? You sound a lot more enthusiastic about it than most women do."

"Not just kitchens," she told him sternly. "Ben, you're looking at the co-founder, owner, and until Friday, CEO of Efficiency, Incorporated. 'We bring order to your chaos.' This is my *professional* expertise— helping people organize their kitchens, their paperwork, sometimes even their lives."

"Oh-oh. My mistake. And my apologies," he said, then added, "What happened Friday?"

She drew a deep breath. "I retired."

He studied her face, sensing that her simple statement covered something far more complex. "You seem awfully young to be retired," he said carefully.

"So do you."

"But I have the children to worry about. What's your excuse?"

The question seemed to startle her. After a short pause she shrugged. "I suppose I just decided that, after years of removing chaos from other people's lives, it was time to put a little back into mine."

He sensed that there was something behind that statement, too, but he decided not to pursue it. Instead, he swept his hand around the room. "Well, you've certainly come to the right place. I have enough for both of us!" His conscience prodded him and he added soberly, "Joanna, as much as I'd like your help, and even more, your company, I don't want to impose on you."

She rubbed her hands together briskly. "Don't be silly. I haven't had the chance to get my hands on a challenge like this in years, not since I got trapped behind a desk. I can hardly wait to get started. Uh, I don't suppose you have any shelf paper or drawer liner?"

"I'm afraid not. Will newspaper do?"

She grinned and shook her head. "Not unless you want everybody who comes in here to know when you last cleaned your cupboards."

The lady had a sense of humor—another point in her favor. He returned the grin.

"I don't expect to have a whole lot of traffic through my kitchen," he assured her. "Besides, you know the old saying, 'Those who matter don't mind, and those who mind don't matter.'"

She laughed and rolled up imaginary sleeves. "All right, then. Newspaper it is."

I must be out of my mind, Joanna thought. *If I don't have time in my life for this man, why am I spending my day organizing his kitchen for him? I ought to suddenly remember a "previous engagement" and take myself back home where I belong.*

But she didn't. As she unpacked, sorted, organized, and generally brought order to Ben's chaos, she found herself feeling productive and needed for the first time in months. She liked the feeling, and she liked the admiration and growing respect in Ben's eyes as the kitchen began to shape up.

Now and again, he tried to help, until she told him, "Ben, you're a lot better at creating chaos than at getting rid of it. Why don't you just hand me things as I need them, and carry the empty boxes outside?"

"You make it look so easy," he told her.

"It is easy," she told him. "Compared to some jobs I've tackled—successfully, I might add—just organizing a kitchen is child's play."

"For you, obviously, but if I'd had to do this, it would have taken me weeks. More likely, I'd have gotten disgusted halfway through and tumbled everything into whichever drawer was handiest, and I'd never have been able to find anything. But you're going to have this mess turned into a functioning kitchen in time for me to fix us some lunch. When you said 'expertise,' you weren't kidding."

"Thanks." She stepped up onto a small stool to line the last section of cupboard with newspaper, then added wistfully, "It reminds me of the days when Robert and I were just a couple of consultants, doing all the work ourselves, before we grew into a company and I got stuck behind a desk." She gestured toward a box beside the door. "I'm ready for those dishes now."

He set the box on the counter beside her. "Is that why you retired? The work got boring?"

She transferred dishes from the box to

the shelf while she thought about it. "Not boring, exactly," she said finally, "but it wasn't a challenge any longer. Or even very interesting. Organizing the company, getting it up and running—that was a challenge, and I enjoyed it tremendously. But lately . . . I woke up one day to realize I was just doing the same things over and over again, all routine, nothing new, no changes, no crises to cope with."

"Which was great for the business," he said, with the quick understanding she was coming to expect from him, "but no good for you."

"No good at all," she agreed. She closed the cupboard door and glanced around the kitchen with satisfaction. "Well, it isn't finished, but it's close enough you should be able to manage the rest by yourself."

"I can manage lunch right now," he said. "And just in time. I'm starving. Can I interest you in a couple of sandwiches and a bowl of soup?"

She started to say no thanks, that she had work to do at home, but then realized that she was hungry, too, not just for soup and sandwiches, but for a meal with a companion and conversation, and the sight of Ben's cheerful grin across the table. "Sounds wonderful," she admitted.

"Gourmet cooking it's not," he acknowledged cheerfully as he put the soup on to heat, "but it's quick and easy, and I've grown accustomed to the taste."

"It's fine," Joanna told him. "I'm an expert at quick and easy. Also at piecing and snacking, frozen dinners, and meals from the deli." She squelched the impulse to ask if she could help, and sat down at the table to watch him as he worked.

He was well worth watching. He moved with the grace and precision she usually associated with taller, slimmer people, or with athletes and dancers. She felt a rush of warmth as she remembered from the kiss they had shared that his stocky body felt as good as it looked.

But it was something beyond the merely physical that accounted for much of his appeal. He put together their simple lunch with the care and flair of a master chef preparing a banquet. She thought wistfully that he probably managed his whole life with the same zest and expertise. She envied him. The zest had left her life longer ago than she cared to remember.

"What are you going to do now?" he asked. "I mean, now that you're retired?"

For the first time since she'd followed Tinkerbell out the door, she thought of the newspaper's Sunday travel section, lying neglected on her desk. "Oh, do the sort of things Robert and I were planning to do before he died. Travel, I suppose. See the world. I shouldn't have any trouble keeping busy."

Ben set the platter of sandwiches in front of her, poured hot soup into mugs, and sat down opposite her. "You don't sound much more enthusiastic about 'keeping busy' than you did about sitting behind a desk."

It was one thing for her to feel that way, and another thing entirely for him to notice and comment on it. She told him, "That's probably because I haven't been very enthusiastic about anything lately, and because I'd expected to do these things with Robert. But I can't, so I'll do them alone. Most of them, anyway. I don't really have much choice, do I?"

He grinned and reached for a sandwich. "You could stay here and help me raise Becky and Joey. And I can think of dozens, maybe hundreds, of things you could do with me. I'll bet I could raise your enthusiasm level to unprecedented heights."

She was willing to bet he was right, but since she intended to take charge of her life, not let him do it, she answered only the first part of what he'd said. "They're lovely children, Ben. Really they are. But I've already told you. I'd make a lousy grandmother."

"The kids and I don't agree with you. Becky's comment was, 'Mrs. Blake said she doesn't know anything about children. Maybe that's why she treats us like real people.' Joey was more succinct. He simply said, 'She's pretty, isn't she, Grandpa? I like her.' And I . . .'' He leered goodnaturedly. "I have to agree with Joey."

"I treat them like real people because they are real people," she told him. "And as for Joey, I can only compliment him on his good taste."

"On his behalf, I thank you. So tell me," he added, "are there any teenagers in the neighborhood?"

The abrupt change of subject startled her. "Teenagers?"

"Babysitters," he explained. "So we can find new and better ways to keep you busy, and so the next time we enjoy a meal together, I can take you out and do it properly."

She studied him warily, trying to decide if he meant it as an invitation, or was already trying to take charge. "That's very thoughtful of you, Ben, but it really isn't necessary."

He looked startled at first, then amused. "I'm not being thoughtful, Joanna. I'm asking you for a date."

"Oh." That was worse, somehow. First, he'd made her feel single again. Now he wanted a date. She drew a deep breath. "I'm sorry, I don't . . . that is, since Robert died, I haven't—"

"I can't tell you how glad I am to hear that," he interrupted. "I was afraid you might be involved with someone."

"I— No. I'm not."

"High time you were, then." He reached across the table to take her hand. "High time we both were."

She moved her hand out of his reach and shook her head. "I told you, I'm going to be busy."

"There's no reason we can't be busy together, is there?" His voice dropped to an intimate murmur and his eyes sparkled with mischief as he added, "I have chaos you haven't even seen yet."

She knew better than to think he was talking about the rest of his house. "I'm sure you have, but I think I'd better stick with my own plans. Lunch was delicious, Ben, but there are things I need to do at home."

She slipped out quickly, in case he had any ideas about another kiss. His soft laughter followed her, and she scolded herself for being so transparent.

At home, she riffled through the papers still spread on her desk, then gathered them up and put them in the desk drawer. Robert seemed to stare at her reproachfully.

"I'm just not in the mood today," she explained. "Organizing Ben's kitchen has me fired up to make some home improvements of my own. I'll get back to these later."

Ben watched Joanna until she disappeared through Bernie's hole in the hedge. Bless Bernie! Bless his guardian angel! Bless the power or powers in charge of scheduling the events in human lives, because their timing was perfect. If Ben and

Joanna had met earlier, he'd still be a workaholic, too busy to consider anything but the most ephemeral of relationships. If they'd met later, she might already be involved with someone else.

He wasn't worried about her plans to keep "busy." He intended to keep her busier and offer her more challenges than any amount of travel could do.

Life was definitely looking up. He couldn't remember when he'd enjoyed himself more.

The downside was that now the house seemed emptier than ever. And there was another downside, one he'd been refusing to face, until Joanna talked about no longer finding any challenge in her work.

Unlike her, he'd loved his work, lived for it, particularly since Fran had decided she and Joel would be better off without him. Giving it up was going to put a hell of a big hole in his life.

He wandered restlessly from room to room, making a mental list of the work still to be done, but unable to work up an interest in doing any of it, until he heard the school bus wheeze to a stop at the corner.

He resisted the impulse to go meet the

children. They'd been polite that morning, when he walked them to the bus, but he had an idea that walking them home would embarrass them beyond endurance. He stood at the window and watched instead as they came slowly toward the house.

He'd hoped they would come bouncing home, full of enthusiasm for their new school, for the new friends they'd made. Instead, they seemed so listless and forlorn that he could have wept for them.

To hell with the hole in his life, he thought. It was the hole in their lives he should be worrying about. Besides, helping these beautiful children turn back into the happy, carefree youngsters they used to be should be challenge enough for any man.

And if it wasn't, he decided, with a touch of smugness, there was Joanna. Something told him she was going to be challenge enough for any man, too.

Joanna spent the rest of the week and half the next one using her expertise on her own behalf. With more energy than she'd had in months, she cleaned out drawers and cupboards, threw away what seemed like tons of accumulated clutter, then started on the bedroom. She went through her wardrobe and discarded things she no longer wanted, promising herself a shopping spree to replace them.

After a week of cleaning and organizing, she'd built up enough momentum to clean out Robert's closet, add the usable items to her own discards, and donate the whole lot to a local church-operated thrift shop.

As she drove home, she became aware of a heady sense of freedom and liberation, and knew it had nothing to do with having a clean and orderly house. It was because she had, symbolically, at least, let go of the past. She was free now to move into the future.

But at home, it occurred to her that she might as well wait for Sunday's paper and start planning her future with an up-to-date travel section. Besides, it was too nice a day to spend at her desk when the yard needed attention as much as the house had.

Outside, Tinkerbell looked up from her sunny spot on the patio, gave Joanna her favorite "don't you feel sorry for me?"

look, and muttered something unintelligible but unmistakably grumpy.

Joanna stifled a laugh. "Poor baby. Did Bernie stand you up today? Well, don't feel too bad about it. It probably wouldn't have worked out anyway. Ships that pass in the night and all that. Bernie has a life of his own, and responsibilities to worry about. Besides, I haven't seen Ben since last week and you don't see me mooning around, do you?"

But she couldn't help wondering why she hadn't seen him. Somehow, she hadn't thought he'd be so easy to discourage. As she pulled on her gardening gloves, she told herself firmly that she wasn't disappointed, just surprised.

She'd barely begun to pull weeds from her kitchen herb garden when Tinkerbell gave a joyful cry of welcome and streaked across the yard toward the hedge. Joanna glanced up, expecting to see Bernie, but it was Becky who came through the hedge, scooped Tinkerbell up into her arms, and buried her face in the cat's soft fur.

Joanna watched the pair for a minute, then realized that although Tinkerbell was ecstatic, Becky looked more like someone desperately seeking comfort. She wasn't quite in tears, but she seemed so unhappy and forlorn that Joanna pulled off her gloves and followed Tinkerbell across the yard. "Becky? Are you all right?"

Becky glanced up at Joanna as if she expected to be scolded. "I was lonesome, and I came to talk to Tinkerbell. Is that okay?"

"Of course it's okay. Tinkerbell and I are glad to see you. But why are you lonesome? Where are Joey and Bernie?"

Becky relaxed and cuddled Tinkerbell a little closer. "Joey didn't feel good this morning. He had a stomachache. Grandpa said if he was too sick to go to school, he was too sick to get up and play, and Bernie doesn't want to come out and play if Joey can't."

Joanna hesitated, torn between amusement at the child's aggrieved tone, and the need to do something about her very real distress. "Well, you can stay here and play with Tinkerbell as long as you like. Does your grandfather know where you are?"

"He does now," Ben said as he came through the hedge. As always, he looked completely masculine and in charge, but he also looked a little worn around the edges. Joanna wasn't sure whether it was from worrying over a sick child all day, or simply the normal stresses of parenthood. Either way, her respect for him went up another notch or two.

He smoothed Becky's hair with the palm of his hand in a loving gesture that brought a lump to Joanna's throat. "Becky, you can come over here anytime it's all right with Mrs. Blake, but let me know first, okay?"

Becky relaxed and let Tinkerbell pour through her arms onto the ground. "Okay, Grandpa. Thank you. Come on, Tinkerbell. Let's go play."

Joanna turned to Ben. "Is Joey all right? Becky said—"

"Joey's fine. I think he just had a bad case of 'I don't wanna go to school,' because he enjoyed a remarkable recovery as soon as the school bus left. I made him stay in bed anyway—which was harder on me than it was on him." He grinned at her and pantomimed exhaustion. "I've just about run my legs off, fetching and carrying for him."

Joanna felt a wave of relief wash over her. "I'm glad it wasn't serious."

"The stomachache is already history. What I'm more worried about is that he should be getting used to his new school and starting to make friends, and he isn't."

"Give him time, Ben. It's only been a couple of weeks."

"I suppose you're right, and he'll make friends when he's ready to, but at the moment, he's a pretty lonesome little boy." He smiled suddenly, as if he'd just thought of something pleasant, and added, "It would certainly brighten his day if you could find a few minutes to come visit with him."

His words conjured up a picture she found hard to resist. Besides, she suddenly wanted to see Joey again. "I'd love to."

As he helped her through the hedge, he asked unexpectedly, "Whose hedge is this? Mine, or yours?"

"I'm not sure. Why?"

"Because if it's mine, I'm going to take some pruning shears to it and enlarge this hole a bit."

"Actually, I think it's mine, but be my guest. It isn't going to hold up to this kind of traffic very long, anyway."

"Aha!" he exclaimed. "Practical as well as pretty. I like that in a woman."

* * *

Ben stopped abruptly at the door to Joey's room as he remembered, too late, that Bernie was still sprawled across Joey's bed, taking up about twice as much space as Joey. He braced himself for Joanna's disapproval. Most women, he was sure, would not allow even a small dog to share a child's bed, much less a Saint Bernard.

But Joanna only gave Bernie a friendly scratch between the ears and shoved him over far enough so she could perch on the edge of the bed. "Hi, Joey. Your grandfather tells me you weren't feeling well today."

Joey grinned, obviously pleased by her presence. "I had a stomachache this morning, but it went away."

"Stomachaches have a way of doing that," she agreed. She took a quick inventory of the books, crayons, and toys that surrounded him. "But I'm surprised your grandfather hasn't turned you into a lifelong invalid."

"What do you mean?" Ben asked.

"I mean, who wants to be well when it's

this much fun being sick?" She hesitated, then asked Joey, "Does Bernie sleep with you?"

Ben felt his face grow warm. "Uh, Joey was having nightmares, and it seemed to help, having Bernie with him."

Joey looked alarmed and grabbed a double handful of Bernie's fur, as if fearing Bernie might be banished on the spot. "I want Bernie to sleep with me. Please, Grandpa, don't make him sleep in the garage again."

Ben's own doubts about letting Bernie share Joey's bed resurfaced. "Uh, well—"

"That isn't what I mean," Joanna said quickly. "I know just how you feel, Joey. Tinkerbell helps keep away my nightmares."

Joey's eyes widened. "I didn't know grown-ups had nightmares."

She drew a deep breath and nodded. "Sometimes they do. But what I wanted to say was, I think you ought to get Bernie his own bed. You could put it right here beside yours, and reach down and pet him anytime you wanted to."

"But Bernie likes sleeping on *my* bed."

She laughed and rubbed Bernie's head

again. "I know, Joey, but Bernie hasn't got his full growth yet, and—"

"Good grief!" Ben exclaimed. "You mean he's going to get bigger?"

"I'm afraid so. Maybe not taller, but he's got a lot of filling out to do yet, and a lot of weight to add."

"How do you know?" Joey asked.

"I had a Saint Bernard, too, when I was little."

"Filling out to do," Ben murmured, eying the two-thirds of the bed the dog already filled. "Weight to add. Yes, Bernie definitely needs a bed of his own."

He'd thought Becky was still outside with Tinkerbell until she exclaimed, "Grandpa, that isn't fair. If Bernie has his own bed in Joey's room, I'll never get to have him sleep with me. Bernie's supposed to belong to *both* of us, but he won't anymore. He'll just be Joey's, and I won't have *anyone*. It isn't fair!"

She burst into tears and ran from the room, leaving Ben staring after her, too stunned to move.

Joanna hesitated briefly, then patted Joey's hand and told him, "I'll be back in a little while," and went after Becky.

Ben hesitated, not sure whether to go with her, or leave the two alone together. After a minute, he followed them as far as the door to Becky's room.

Joanna, the lady who didn't know anything about children, sat on the edge of the bed, holding Becky in her arms, and Becky, the little automaton who didn't laugh or cry or misbehave, clung to Joanna, her whole body shaking with fierce, soundless sobs.

She wasn't crying about Bernie, Ben realized, but about everything else she had lost and would never have again. Once more, he thought wryly, Joanna and Bernie had accomplished what he had not.

As if sensing his presence, Joanna looked over her shoulder, saw him, and turned quickly back to Becky, but not before he saw the tears streaming down her face, and understood again what a rare treasure he had found in this woman.

He felt almost like an intruder, watching them, but wild horses couldn't have dragged him from his spot in the doorway. He compromised by looking away and noticed for the first time how painfully neat, even austere, Becky's room was. No clutter, no personal things. Just the furniture and, he assumed, her clothes in the closet and drawers.

She had just as many toys and childhood treasures as Joey had, but when he'd started to unpack them, she'd told him she wanted to do it herself. But she hadn't, and in a flash of insight, he comprehended that the almost-empty room was a sign of Becky's refusal to accept the reality of her loss. By putting out her possessions, trying to make the room friendly and welcoming, she would be accepting it as a permanent part of her life from now on. Instead, she kept them packed away, as she'd kept her emotions packed away.

Guilt washed over him, that he hadn't done anything about it, hadn't even realized it until now, still didn't know what, if anything, he could do to help.

He studied the room again. God, it was bleak and unfriendly in here. How could she stand the loneliness? No wonder she was afraid of losing Bernie. If anything, she needed him even more than Joey did.

And then he knew what to do.

He crossed the room swiftly and knelt beside the bed. Some of the tension went out of Becky as he stroked her hair gently, and he thought her sobs were quieter.

"Becky, even if Bernie sleeps in Joey's room, he'll still love you and be your dog, too. But you won't have to be by yourself. Maybe Tinkerbell isn't going to have any kittens, but there are other kittens in the world who need good homes. Would you like to have one of them?"

Beside him, Joanna murmured something that sounded approving, and some of the tension went out of her, too.

Becky's sobs tapered off slowly. After a minute, she lifted her head to look at him, her eyes wide and hopeful. "Can I, Grandpa? Really?"

He reached for a tissue from the box on the nightstand and handed it to her. "Yes, you can. Really. Saturday, when we go to buy a bed for Bernie, we'll find a kitten for you. Not just any kitten, but the perfect kitten. And a bed for him, too."

Becky mopped her face and blew her nose with youthful inelegance. "Not a him. I want a girl kitten, and maybe someday, she'll have kittens. Only I won't find homes for them. I'll keep them myself."

Ben glanced quickly at Joanna, caught

her grinning at him through her tears. He pulled another tissue from the box and handed it to her. "I suppose you think that's funny."

She mopped and blew, as inelegantly as Becky had done. "Hilarious," she assured him.

Four

Joanna kept her promise and went back to Joey's room, but found herself upstaged by Becky's announcement that she was going to get a kitten. The adults left the children eagerly debating what kind of kitten she should choose and went downstairs together.

"You said you didn't know anything about children," Ben reminded her.

His voice held a gentle teasing note, but she answered seriously, "I don't. But I know what it's like to lose someone you love, and to have your whole life torn apart. I think grief is grief, no matter how old you are. And it must be even harder for children because they don't have any experiences to help them handle it."

"No," Ben agreed. "They don't. At least Joey's nightmares give him some outlet, but Becky's been keeping it all inside. I've been terribly worried about her. I was beginning to wonder if she needed professional help."

"It's still a possibility, Ben."

"I don't think so. Not with you, and Bernie, and a brand-new kitten to help her through it." They had drifted into the kitchen, where Ben peered into first the refrigerator, then the freezer. "What would you like for dinner tonight? You can have your choice of hamburgers or hot dogs."

"Lucky me."

"I'm only kidding. This is beef stew night. Beef stew is one thing I do really well. Even the kids like it."

It occurred to her that her vow not to get involved with Ben and his family was getting a little worn around the edges, but what harm could one more meal do? "Well, I really should go on home, but . . . I like beef stew, too."

"Great. Sit over there and keep me company while I cook."

She settled herself at the table and watched while he rolled cubes of beef in flour and dropped them into a sizzling skillet. Robert had cooked, too, as he'd done everything—precisely, neatly, efficiently. Ben had spilled the salt, scattered flour on the counter, and kept misplacing his fork, but he was more fun to watch, probably because he was clearly enjoying himself

And so was she. As complete as her commitment to Robert and their marriage had been, she'd still enjoyed seeing attractive men, the same way happily married men enjoyed looking at other women. She suspected most women did their share of looking—and appreciating. They were just more subtle about it than men.

And Ben, as she had already realized, was well worth watching. His youthful energy and enthusiasm made him enormously attractive, but it was his maturity and self-confidence that made him sexy, and not just sexy, but sexy as hell. On a scale of one to ten, Benjamin Walker was way off the top end.

The room suddenly seemed warmer than the heat of the stove would account for. She drew a deep breath and switched her thoughts elsewhere. "Uh, Ben, we've done a lot of talking about me, but now I'd like to know more about you."

He looked pleased. "That's always a good

sign, except that once I get started, I'm likely to tell you more about me than you ever wanted to know." He lowered the fire under his stew pot and took a bag of carrots from the refrigerator. "What would you like to know first?"

There were a lot of things she wanted to know. She picked the safest. "You said earlier that the children were your excuse for retiring."

"Not excuse, exactly. The reason. The difference between you and me is that I loved my work and would gladly have kept on working until they booted me out, but the kids needed me."

"What kind of work did you do? You said something the other day about electronics."

He nodded. "I wrote how-to books for missiles."

"How-to books for missiles? I don't—"

"Missiles, planes, and whatever other deviltry occurred to the powers that be."

She studied him for a minute, half suspecting he was teasing her. "Why how-to books?"

He finished scrubbing the carrots and began to cut them into bite-sized pieces. "Battle axes and bows and arrows are pretty simple to use, but today's weapons are a bit more complicated. The people who operate them need instruction manuals, which someone has to write. That's what I did."

"How in the world do you get started in a job like that?"

"By accident, mostly," he admitted. "In my case, I came out of the service with a good working knowledge of radar and other marvels of the electronic age, and made a pretty good living with it until I got caught in a layoff during an election year."

He grinned. "There's a lot of unemployment in the defense industry during election years. The outgoing administration no longer has the clout to hand out contracts, and the incoming party doesn't have the authority yet. But I lucked out and found a company that already had a contract to build some pretty sophisticated equipment and needed writers. I thought it would tide me over until something else opened up, but it turned out I was good at it, and I enjoyed it, so . . ." He added the carrots to the meat and gravy bubbling in the pot.

"I can see why. It must have been fascinating. And it must have been hard for you to give it up."

"It was, but I lost one family because I was a workaholic; I'm not about to lose this one or give those children less than my very best."

His tone was gruff, but there was no mistaking his sincerity. Her respect and admiration for him took another leap upward.

After dinner, she stayed to help him wash the dishes, but declined the invitation to help put the children to bed. "Not tonight, Ben. I have things I really need to do at home."

He walked across the yard with her, but as she started to slip through the hedge, he caught her by the hand. "Joanna, wait a minute. There's something I want to talk to you about."

She waited for him to go on, but for the first time since they'd met, he seemed at a loss for words. "Look," he said finally, "I know you're planning to travel and do all the things people do when they retire, but I can't believe you're ready to put yourself out to pasture just yet."

She frowned. "I hadn't thought of it as putting myself out to pasture, exactly."

"I'm sure you hadn't, but that's what it is, exactly. And if you think you're bored and restless now, how do you think you'll feel on one of those cruises, surrounded by all those predatory females hunting for men in an environment where single, desperate women outnumber available men ten to one?"

"It wouldn't be like that at all," Joanna protested.

"Yes, it would. And you wouldn't like it one bit. So, I have a proposition for you— or call it a challenge, if you prefer. You told me the other day that your expertise was in helping people organize their kitchens, their paperwork, sometimes even their lives. Well, you've already organized my kitchen, and I don't have that much paperwork, but how about helping me get my life organized?"

"Ben, I didn't mean that *literally*. I couldn't possibly do anything so *personal*. I only meant—"

He laid a finger across her lips. "I know what you meant, and that's all I'm asking you to do. Show me how to run a household for three, instead of just one. Help me get a handle on things like keeping house, doing laundry, planning meals for the kids, shopping for groceries. Don't you see? The time you save me having to learn those things is time I can spend with the children."

She did see. And she wanted to do it, not just because it did, indeed, present a challenge, but because she'd already begun to care about those gutsy little kids and their sexy grandpa—she dampened that thought as soon as it occurred. She'd spent the last three years trying to extricate herself from a job she no longer wanted; she had no intention of being trapped again by the Walker family, no matter how cute the children were, or how attractive Ben was.

"Ben . . ." She hesitated, trying to find words that would convince him without giving away what she was thinking and feeling. "Ben, that's a big job, and I'm not sure—"

"You said you enjoyed the challenge of getting your company up and running. Well, I'm just asking for help getting my home up and running. How much harder could it be?"

"A lot. A home and a business aren't at

all alike. Business I understand. But a home and family! I wouldn't have any idea of what to do or even where to start."

"No problem. You can start by going with us to the pet store Saturday to help Becky choose her kitten."

She thought of Becky, her face aglow as she tried to pick one perfect kitten, and murmured, "Oh, I'd love to!" She felt her own face grow warm as Ben smiled, and tried to cover her blunder by exclaiming, "A kitten is just what she needs—something of her own to love and care for. I'm so glad you thought of it."

He lifted her hand to his lips and kissed it gently. "Bless you. You're one hell of a woman, Joanna Blake. I owe you more than you'll ever know."

She didn't get her hand kissed all that often. It seemed to go right to her head, like champagne. "And you, Benjamin Walker, are one hell of a man. Those are mighty lucky children." Then, embarrassed by her impulsive words, she added, "You remind me of my own grandfather."

"Good grief! You could have gone all day without telling me that!"

She eased her hand out of his grasp and

laid it against his cheek. "I didn't mean it that way. I meant the caring and understanding, and the love." Impulsively, she caught his face between her hands and brushed his lips gently with hers.

She hadn't meant it as an invitation, but he took it as one. He slid his arms around her and pulled her close as their lips met again, not gently this time, but firmly and warmly. She relaxed against him, marveling at the way they fit together and at the joyous way her body responded to his. She shivered with pleasure as he slid his hands down her spine to knead her buttocks gently and hold her firmly against him, but when he slid them back up her hips and around to cup and fondle her breasts, she finally pulled away from him, gasping. "Ben! The children!"

She inhaled sharply as he caught her in his arms again and lowered his head to rub his cheek against her breasts. "It's all right. They're in the living room, watching television. They can't see us here." His last words were muffled as he worked the top button of her blouse open with his teeth.

His rich, warm laughter followed her as she pulled away from him again and slipped hurriedly through the hedge. "Do I still remind you of your grandfather?"

She crossed the yard as quickly as her shaky legs would let her. Once she was safely inside her own kitchen, she stared at Robert's photo without really seeing it, remembering the feel of Ben's firm, warm body against hers, fully aware that if it hadn't still been daylight, and if the children hadn't been waiting inside for Ben, she wouldn't have pulled away from him the way she had.

Ben held the car door for Joanna, then circled around to the driver's side. He slid in beside her and laid his hand over hers. "I'm glad you decided to come with us. I wasn't sure whether you would or not."

She removed his hand from hers and placed it firmly on the steering wheel. "I'm coming to help Joey pick out a bed for Bernie, and Becky choose a kitten. That doesn't commit me to anything else."

He suppressed a smile as he slid the key into the ignition. "Of course not."

From the backseat, Joey said, "I don't

see why Bernie can't go, too. If we're buying a bed for him, shouldn't he help pick it out?"

"Don't be silly, Joey." Becky sounded smugly big-sisterish. "Dogs can't go into stores."

"Why can't they? Besides, we're going to a pet store, aren't we? And Bernie's a pet, isn't he?"

"Oh, Joey." Becky's tone conveyed a world of long-suffering patience. "You just don't understand."

"I don't want to understand. I just want to take Bernie to the pet store with us."

Ben glanced at Joey's rebellious expression in the rearview mirror and entered the argument. "Sorry, Joey, but you'll just have to let his new bed be a surprise. Remember, we're going to have lunch, too, and poor Bernie wouldn't like waiting in the car for us."

"We could go where they have a drive-through, and eat in the car."

"With Bernie?" Ben glanced at Joanna and raised one eyebrow, as if in query. She shrank back in the seat and pantomimed exaggerated dismay. "No way," he told Joey with firm finality, and grinned again as she changed her dismay to equally exaggerated relief.

Joey's arguments gave way to a muttered remark that wasn't quite distinct enough to call for a reprimand—from Ben, anyway. Becky muttered something equally indistinct but apparently potent, and Joey lapsed into silence.

Ben took his eyes from the road long enough to glance at Joanna. The expression on her face was a blend of amusement and anticipation. He was sure she wasn't aware of it, but she looked remarkably like a doting grandmother.

Ben turned back to the road, feeling a lump form in his throat as he told himself that this was what it felt like to be part of a family. This is what he had missed—and cheated his wife and son of—by getting lost in his work. But he'd been given a second chance, and he vowed that he wouldn't make the same mistake with these children.

He glanced at Joanna, who was listening with obvious pleasure as the kids began to chatter again in the backseat. She was another kind of second chance, and he didn't intend to make that mistake with her, either.

The family feeling persisted through lunch and made Ben wonder if he'd ever again regard food as just nourishment for the body. He watched Joanna tackle her cheeseburger with as much gusto as if it had been filet mignon, and wondered if she felt the same way.

The adults had barely finished eating when the children began begging to move on to the pet store.

"What's the rush?" Ben asked. "I was thinking we might just sit here a little longer so Joanna and I can have another cup of coffee."

"Oh, Grandpa!" Becky exclaimed. "Suppose someone comes along and buys my kitten before we get there?"

"Then you'll have to pick another kitten, I suppose."

Becky's face fell, but Joanna dropped her napkin beside her empty plate and stood up. "Don't tease, Ben. They've both been very patient. Besides, I can hardly wait to meet that new kitten myself."

Becky threw her arms around Joanna and hugged her hard. "Oh, thank you, Grandma." Joey gasped and Becky's face turned bright pink as she dropped her arms and backed away from Joanna. "I'm . . . I'm sorry. I didn't mean to say that. I know you aren't really my grandmother. I was just . . . sort of . . . pretending you were."

Joanna looked stunned, and Ben held his breath waiting for her to react.

She seemed to hesitate, but so briefly it might have been only his imagination. Then she pulled Becky into her arms and returned the hug. "What a lovely compliment! And you may certainly call me Grandma if you like." She looked at Ben as she added, "There's just one problem. Nobody ever called me that before, and I might forget sometimes that you're talking to me. Would you and Joey like to call me Joanna, like my friends do? Because even if I'm not really your grandmother, I really am your friend."

Ben exhaled slowly as he understood. She wouldn't embarrass or hurt Becky, but neither would she encourage *him* by letting his children relate to her in such an intimate way. He added kind, clever, and diplomatic to the growing list of her assets.

"Is it okay, Grandpa?" Becky asked him.

"Daddy said we mustn't call grown-ups by their first names."

Ben smiled at Joanna, trying to tell her he knew what she was doing, and why she was doing it, and that he approved. "It's okay to use grown-ups' first names if they invite you to," he assured her.

The children's faces lit up, and he knew that by the end of the day, they'd have used her first name until they'd almost worn it out. He wondered if she realized that, to Becky and Joey, "Joanna" was more special and intimate than "Grandma" could ever be.

He ushered them out of the restaurant in a rosy fog that lasted all the way to the pet store.

"I hope they have a bed big enough for Bernie," Joey said.

"If they don't," Ben said cheerfully, "we'll just get one for you, and Bernie can sleep in yours."

"Can I help you, sir? Ben? Ben Walker?"

Ben glanced up at the store employee, identifiable by his red vest. "Charlie Ross! Son of a gun." They shook hands and pounded each other on the back as if they hadn't seen each other in years. Ben turned to Joanna. "Joanna, this is my old friend, Charlie Ross. We worked together until he retired about a year ago. Charlie, my neighbor, Joanna Blake, and my grandchildren, Becky and Joey. What are you doing here?" He fingered the red vest. "Don't tell me you work here!"

Charlie nodded at Joanna, grinned at the two children. "Afraid so. My wife couldn't stand having me underfoot so much. Said she married me for better or worse, but not for twenty-four hours a day, and told me to go find something to keep myself busy."

"But what about all those things you were going to do once you had the time? The trips and tours you were going to take?"

Charlie looked embarrassed. "The truth is, Ben, there's only so much fun and games a fellow can stand before it stops being fun and starts being work."

Ben turned to Joanna. "You hear that? Straight from the horse's mouth."

"Besides," Charlie added, "the wife has a lot of things going here—clubs, volunteer work, grandchildren—and doesn't like to be away from home so much, which turns out to mean she's hardly ever home. So I work part-time here for a little friendly companionship." He winked at Joey. "The customers aren't bad, either."

Becky moved closer to Joanna and asked in a soft, hesitant voice, "Joanna, do you think we could go look at the kittens while Grandpa talks to his friend?"

Joey, less discreet, announced loudly, "And I want to go pick out a bed for Bernie."

Ben grinned and ruffled Joey's hair. "Then I guess that's what we'd better do. Charlie, where—"

Charlie nodded toward one side of the store. "We don't sell animals, but the Humane Society has some pets for adoption over on the right there. And beds are this way. Cat or dog?"

"Dog," Ben said. He made a see-you-later gesture at Joanna and Becky as they headed for the adoption center, and added, "Big dog."

"Bernie's a Saint Bernard," Joey said.

Ben held his hand out about pony high. "*Very* big dog. And still growing."

Charlie laughed, and the two men followed Joey toward the dog beds. "So, Ben, how are things going at the old salt mine?"

There was a kind of desperate casualness to his voice that made Ben glance at him briefly before saying, "Going without me. I quit last month."

"A glutton for work like you? You'll go crazy!"

Ben shook his head. "I hope not. I have those two kids to take care of. Not to mention a Saint Bernard, and now a kitten." He drew a deep breath and checked to make sure Joey was out of earshot. "My son and his wife were killed recently in a car accident. I'm a single parent now, Charlie."

"God, Ben, I'm sorry. You and your son were just beginning to get to know each other, weren't you?"

"Yeah, I pretty much missed his childhood." He glanced over his shoulder at Becky, then back at Joey. "I don't intend to miss theirs."

They were silent for a minute, then Charlie shook his head. "I wish you luck, but I'll be honest, Ben. Somehow, I don't see you as full-time homemaker material." He, too, glanced toward Becky, but it was on Joanna that his eyes lingered. He grinned and added, "Unless, of course, she's part of the deal."

"I'm working on it," Ben assured him. "I'm working on it." As he hurried down the aisle to where Joey was waiting for him, he told himself that full-time home-making had to be better than clerking part-time in a pet store.

Especially if Joanna was part of the deal.

Ben and Joanna watched from the doorway of Joey's room as Bernie regarded his new bed with amiable curiosity but blithely ignored Joey's suggestion that he "get in and try it out." Joey grabbed him by the loose skin around his neck and pulled. Bernie promptly sat down and braced himself with his front paws. Joey got behind him and pushed. Bernie collapsed in a heap on the floor, as limp as overcooked spaghetti.

"Dumb dog!" Joey exclaimed. "Like this." He crawled into the bed himself and curled up at one end. Bernie immediately bounded into the bed and sat down, as much on Joey as beside him.

"That's better," Joey said. He wriggled out from under the dog and climbed over the side of the bed. Bernie bounced to his feet and followed.

"Oh, Bernie!" Joey planted his fists on his hips and glared at the dog.

"I guess Bernie isn't ready for bed yet," Ben murmured into Joanna's ear.

She could feel him shake with silent laughter, and had to work to keep her own amusement under control. "Maybe Becky's having better luck."

"Let's go see." He caught her hand and led her down the hall to Becky's room.

Becky sat on the edge of her bed, gazing blissfully down into the small cat's bed cradled on her lap. She gave Ben and Joanna a radiant smile as they came in and whispered, "She's asleep. Oh, Grandpa, isn't she just perfect?"

Ben's eyes looked suspiciously moist as he reached into the bed and gently stroked the tiny form with one finger. "If she can make you smile like that, I guess she is."

"I didn't pick her out, you know." Her hushed voice was filled with awe. "*She* picked *me*. She just came right over to me and said, "Meow. Take me. Take me.""

"What are you going to call her?" Joanna asked.

"Well . . ." Becky's forehead creased in a small frown of concentration. "I thought at first I'd call her Callie, because she's a calico cat, you know. Or maybe Patches, because of her markings. But I decided to call her Lovey, because . . ." She shrugged and flushed slightly. "You know. Just because."

"It's a perfect name," Joanna assured her, "for a perfect kitten." She put an arm around Becky and hugged her gently. "And you're the perfect little girl for her. I think you're going to make each other very happy."

She and Ben left Becky crooning a wordless lullaby to the sleeping kitten. Joanna was acutely aware of the warmth and light pressure of Ben's hand against the small of her back as he ushered her down the stairs.

"It's been a great day, hasn't it?" he asked. He turned to face her, his face alight with mischief. "I have to admit, though, I'm feeling a little bit jealous."

"Because you're the only one who doesn't have a pet? That's easily fixed."

He grinned and traced the outline of her cheek as gently as he'd stroked the kitten. "No, because I'm the only one in the family sleeping alone now. What do you think I should do about it?"

She managed what she hoped was a casual laugh, and moved out of his reach as he tried to slip an arm around her waist. "I think you'd better get used to it, because if you really want me to help you get your household in order, you'll have to agree to keep it a purely business arrangement." She clamped her mouth shut in dismay as soon as the words were out. She hadn't meant to say them. She was sure she hadn't, but she had said them and the pleased smile on Ben's face told her clearly he was going to hold her to them.

"Really? You've decided to accept my offer?"

"You were making me an offer? Funny. I could have sworn you were asking me a favor." As clever repartee, it was feeble, even to her ears, but Ben didn't seem to notice.

"I don't care what you call it," he declared, "If you'll just do it."

She drew a deep breath and tried to salvage as much as possible. "I will if you'll agree to establish a few ground rules first."

"Such as?"

She paused briefly to put her thoughts in order and to try to get her brain and tongue operating on the same track. "First, you have to understand that I have the rest of my life planned out, and it doesn't include getting involved in any kind of personal relationship with you—or anyone else. As soon as the job is finished, I get back to my own plans, my own life."

"Fine," he agreed quickly. Too quickly. "I can live with that."

"That I'm not going to get personally involved with you?" She told herself the little flutter she felt in her stomach was relief.

"No. Just that you don't intend to."

She recognized the distinction but let it pass. "Second, you won't try to turn me into a substitute grandmother for the children."

"Agreed, provided you keep your promise to be their friend."

She nodded. "Of course I will. And *you* promise to keep your distance. From me, that is. And not try to . . . to . . ." Her voice trailed off as she realized there was no way to end it without sounding either prudish or paranoid. She felt her face growing warm as he studied her thoughtfully.

"Now we're getting into a sort of gray area," he said.

"What do you mean?"

"A promise like that puts an unfair burden on me. I could make it, with every intention of keeping it, but suppose I weaken?" The corners of his lips began to creep up, as if he were trying not to smile. "Or suppose you do? If, for example, you tried to seduce me, wouldn't it be rude of me to turn you down? Assuming I had the willpower, that is."

Her jaw began to hurt and she realized she was clenching her teeth.

Ben seemed to notice it, too. The grin left his face and he told her seriously, "Joanna, I can't deny that I find you enormously attractive. Not just physically, but every other way, as well. You have a warmth and charm that have been missing from my life for a long time. And perhaps I'm only flattering myself, but I think you find me at least a little attractive, too. If you don't, it isn't because I haven't been trying.

"But I've outgrown the time in my life

when I had to bolster my ego by trying to bed every attractive single woman I met. That doesn't mean I don't *want* to, it simply means I don't *need* to. I've learned to value friendship and companionship, too.

"As much as I hope we're going to be more than just friends and neighbors, that has to be your choice, too. So I can promise you this much. I won't do anything you don't want me to do, or pressure you for anything you don't want to give. At least, not very hard. Will that do?"

She studied his face for any hint of deception, and even found herself glancing at his hands to see if his fingers were crossed, then told herself it didn't matter. She'd made her position clear. If Ben didn't take her seriously, that was his fault.

"I suppose," she said finally, "it will have to."

Five

Ben listened to Joey's prayers, gave him a good night hug, and tucked him into bed. Bernie eyed the bed hopefully, but settled into his own bed at Joey's insistence.

"He's not really a dumb dog, is he, Grandpa?"

Ben smiled at the pride in Joey's voice and reached down to ruffle the thick fur on Bernie's neck. "I believe he's the smartest dog I've ever known. We're lucky to have him."

"Yeah," Joey agreed, his voice beginning to slur with sleep. "G'night, Grandpa."

"Good night, Joey." Ben turned off the bedroom light, but lingered in the doorway, watching Joey in the dim light drifting in from the hall. The evening ritual that Joey took for granted had become one of the most important parts of Ben's day. He was still a little awed at the depth of his feelings for this small piece of himself, once removed. If he'd only known, all those years ago, what it could be like . . .

He pushed the thought aside and went to Becky's room to say good night. They had already established that she was old enough to tuck herself in, and that sometimes her prayers were private, but he didn't intend to give up the goodnight kiss until she grew up and transferred that privilege to a younger man, with whom she would share the rest of her life.

And he'd make damn sure, he promised himself, that that man knew what was important in his life and didn't throw it away, as he had done.

Becky sat on the edge of her bed, talking softly to the ball of calico fluff cuddled against her chest. "You'll like it here," she said. "Joey and Bernie can play with you, too, as soon as I teach them to be gentle, and tomorrow, I'll take you to meet Tinkerbell, Joanna's cat. And if anything ever happens to me, don't you worry. Grandpa will take real good care of you, the way he does Joey and me."

Ben swallowed hard and realized belatedly that he was eavesdropping. He cleared his throat and managed a smile as Becky looked up. "Bedtime, Becky."

"Okay, Grandpa." Becky settled the kitten into the small bed on her nightstand and swiveled to slide her legs under the covers. "You know what? Tomorrow, I'm going to unpack my things and find some toys for her to play with."

"That'll be fine, sweetheart." He bent over to claim his goodnight kiss, relishing the feel of her arms around his neck and the warmth of her lips on his cheek. "Maybe Bernie will let her share his bone."

She giggled. "Oh, Grandpa. It's bigger than she is."

He grinned and kissed her forehead. "It is, for a fact."

As he left her room, the painful thought occurred, not for the first time, that if he'd been a better father to Joel, a better husband to Fran, perhaps he'd have known what it was like to have a daughter, too.

On his way downstairs, he glanced into Joey's room again and discovered Bernie creeping into bed with Joey.

"Bernie, you rascal!" he said softly. He snapped his fingers and pointed to Bernie's bed. Bernie hesitated, as if measuring Ben's determination against his own, then heaved a sigh and retreated to his own bed.

Ben grinned and went on downstairs, knowing Bernie would be back in bed with Joey almost immediately. Well, at least he *knew* where he was supposed to sleep. Getting him to do it would have to come later.

Joanna loaded her breakfast dishes into the dishwasher and her Sunday paper, travel section and all, into the recycling bin. Robert's eyes, from the photo on the desk, seemed to follow her with disapproval.

"Don't look at me that way," she told him. "There'll be a new one next week. Meanwhile, getting Ben and the kids squared away will provide a nice transition from being a working woman to being a lady of leisure."

She reached across the desk to stroke Tinkerbell, perched as usual on the windowsill, and resisted the temptation to glance outside, at the hedge and the house beyond. "Okay," she admitted, "I said yes when I should have said no, but it's only a temporary delay. A week, two weeks at most, and I'll be back here making plans the way we used to. And he really does need help."

She pulled out the chair and sat at her desk, feeling a little guilty because she hadn't been entirely honest with Ben. She'd helped people unclutter their homes and relationships and sort out their lives before, but never people she knew and—she might as well admit it to herself—was attracted to.

Not that it was that big a deal. She would simply treat Ben like any other client. She'd already told him it was to be strictly business. Now all she had to do was remember it herself.

She picked up her pen and fanned out a stack of color-coded index cards. She'd have to have an in-depth discussion with Ben before she actually started work, but she could make some preliminary notes now.

She had become totally absorbed in her work when Tinkerbell gave a welcoming chirp, stood up and stretched prettily, then jumped down and ran to the door. Joanna pushed her chair back and went to open the door for her.

Ben stood outside, one hand raised to knock.

She stepped back, startled. "Oh, it's you."

He hesitated. "You're expecting someone else? At the back door?"

"Just Bernie. Come on in, Ben. What can I do for you this morning?"

He grinned wickedly and followed her into the kitchen. "Do you really want to know or are you just being polite?" He glanced around the kitchen, his eyes sliding tactfully over Robert's photograph, but stopping at the index cards laid out in neat rows on her desk. "I'm sorry. Am I interrupting something?"

"Just some rough notes on how I'm going to help you get your home organized."

He looked more closely at the index cards, filled with her neat, meticulous handwriting, and shook his head. "Joanna, I don't want a course in home economics. I just want a few pointers, off the top of your head."

"I don't work off the top of my head," she told him. "I organize my work the same way I organize anything else. It's easier and more efficient to plan in advance what you need to do and the best way to do it."

"Maybe," he said dubiously, "but it seems to me that by the time you get finished with all this planning, Becky will be old enough to take over the housekeeping. I thought we could just sort of . . . jump right in and *do* it."

He was talking about the help she was going to give him, she told herself sharply, and it was only her own randy thoughts making her face grow warm.

While she fought to keep her thoughts from showing on her face, Ben stared across the kitchen at the plethora of notes and memos decorating her refrigerator.

"What on earth is the matter with your refrigerator? It looks like it's molting."

He crossed the room to examine it more closely while she held her breath and prayed she hadn't posted anything personal or embarrassing there. Living alone, she'd come to expect the same privacy from the refrigerator that most people got only from a wall safe or a locked diary.

He read several items at random, then turned back to her, his expression a blend of perplexity and amusement. "Joanna, didn't it ever occur to you that in the time you've spent making these notes and reminders, you could have done all these things about twice over?"

She felt a flash of irritation, not because he was teasing her, but because his blithe good humor was stirring an emotional response in her that she hadn't felt since Robert was alive. She asked testily, "Ben, do you want something, or did you just come over to make fun of my refrigerator?"

"As a matter of fact, I do want something. Between being upset Friday evening, and excited over her kitten yesterday, Becky forgot to tell me until this morning that she promised I'd make chocolate chip cookies for the PTA open house tomorrow. I thought you might have a recipe I could use."

"You've never made chocolate chip cookies before, have you?"

He grinned ruefully. "Well, no. I was sort of hoping it might be one of the things we could just jump into, but now I'm not sure if we have time. The PTA meets tomorrow."

"It doesn't take that long to bake cookies!"

"I know it doesn't. But how long does it take to plan them and get organized?"

He cut off her indignant reply by asking seriously, "How did you know I've never made them before?"

"If you had, you'd know the recipe is printed on the chocolate chip bag."

"Oh. I see. Well then, there's only one other thing I need to say."

"And what's that?"

"About our agreement yesterday. I've changed my mind."

She stared at him in astonishment, then glanced down at her desk. Had her index cards been that lethal? Disappointment swept through her as she realized she'd been looking forward to it—more, it seemed, than she'd known.

Ben was watching her closely, obviously waiting for an answer. She took a deep breath to steady her voice, and reached down to brush the index cards into a pile. "No problem."

He put his hand over hers before she could sweep the cards off the desk and into the wastebasket. "No, not that. I'm talking about the other part of the agreement." Again, she stared at him, not sure what he meant, until he smiled slightly and said, "I promised, more or less, to keep my hands off you. It was a promise I should never have made, and I take it back. If you want to take back your half of the agreement, I'll understand, but it won't change anything."

She moved a step away from him, and said, stupidly, "I don't know what you're talking about."

His smile turned into a grin. "I'm talking about you and me. Two normal, healthy, unattached human beings who find each other attractive, and who just made a ridiculous agreement not to do anything about it."

She backed another step away from him. "You're crazy."

"Because I think you're the most attractive, desirable woman I've met in a long time? No way." He took a step toward her. "You're just what I need—in my home, in my life, and yes, in my bed, and I'm going to do my damnedest to convince you we'd *both* be crazy to just turn our backs on the pleasure we can give each other."

She retreated again. "You told me you no longer needed to bed every woman you meet."

"I also said that didn't mean I don't

want to. But not every woman, love. Just one." He took another step toward her.

This time, her backward step brought her up against the table. She began to move sideways, around it. "Ben, this is ridiculous. I'm not about to let myself get involved in a love affair at this stage of my life."

"Better late than never."

"Besides, it wouldn't work. I'm too set in my ways, too—"

"Don't be silly. If you were so set in your ways, you'd still be at work, stuck behind a desk and hating it. But you quit, because you needed a challenge, remember?" He grinned. "Believe me, love, I'm the biggest challenge you're ever likely to run into."

She didn't doubt it, or that he could also be the biggest mistake she was ever likely to make. She came to a corner of the table and began to back away from him again. "Besides, I'm not going to have time for an affair. I keep telling you, I'm going to be busy."

His grin broadened as he followed her around the table. "I promise to keep you a lot busier than you ever expected to be. Joanna, you can't deny we draw sparks from each other. Or have you forgotten those two kisses we shared? Maybe something will happen between us and maybe it won't, but can you give me even one good reason why we should stamp out those sparks before we even see what kind of fire they might start?"

This isn't happening, she told herself. *Maybe I didn't really wake up this morning, and I'm just dreaming that this madman is in my kitchen, propositioning me right in front of Robert's picture.*

Aloud, she pleaded, "Ben, please try to understand. For the last three years, since Robert died, I've been drifting, getting nowhere, just living the same day over and over again. It isn't just keeping busy that's important to me. It's controlling my life, getting back in charge and starting to move forward again."

"I don't want to stop you. I just want you to move in my direction. I need to move forward, too, you know, and I'm sure we'll both enjoy it more if we're moving together."

He rounded another corner of the table and stood so close beside her she could feel the heat of his body. She backed away again.

"What about the children? You surely don't intend to conduct this mad affair in their presence, do you?"

"The children are in school most of the day five days a week. We'll have plenty of time alone. And as soon as we get a little more settled in, and I feel a little more comfortable about leaving them at night, I'll find a babysitter so we can go out occasionally. We can spend some time with them, too. I told you, I want you in my home and in my life as well as in my bed. And we had fun with them at the pet store yesterday, didn't we?"

She had run out of arguments and could only stare helplessly at him while she faced the fact that this was the most dangerous man she'd ever met. He awakened both her body and her emotions, stirring feelings inside her that she hadn't thought would ever stir again.

He made her remember that she was a woman. She didn't have to kiss him to make sparks; just looking at him warmed her all over, and the way he looked at her made her almost sizzle. She did the only thing she could do. She backed away again.

He followed. "Joanna, I told you I wouldn't do anything you don't want me to do, or pressure you for anything you don't want to give, because it has to be your choice, too." She tried to back away again, but she had come up against the refrigerator and had no place left to go. "I meant it, so if you want me to leave, all you have to do is tell me you don't want me to do this . . ." He caught her by the shoulders and pulled her toward him.

Desperately, she turned her face away from his kiss, but the warmth of his breath against her skin as he nuzzled the side of her neck excited her more than any kiss could have done.

"Or this . . ." He cupped her breast in his palm, so that the warmth of his hand seemed to set her on fire. She opened her mouth to protest and found his lips covering hers, his tongue teasing and caressing hers while he explored her breast with strong, gentle fingers.

After a moment, he undid the buttons on her blouse and pushed the soft fabric aside. He caressed her briefly through the lace of her bra, then slipped his fingers under the strap and slid it down over her shoulder. She gave up all thought of resisting and simply leaned back against the refrigerator and shivered with pleasure as he tugged the lace down to uncover her and took her nipple into his mouth.

The motion of his lips and tongue on her breast and the warmth of his hand as he slid it slowly down the flat curve of her stomach tightened her thigh muscles and set up a sharp pulsing in her lower body. He tugged her skirt up, slipped his leg between hers, and pressed it firmly into the juncture of her thighs.

"Or this," he whispered. He splayed his fingers across her buttocks and held her so she couldn't pull away from him as he rubbed his thigh back and forth against her in a slow, irresistible rhythm.

She responded helplessly, shamelessly, letting herself move against him in eager counterpoint, welcoming the ecstasy building within her. Just a little longer, she thought, another moment or two, and her whole body would be filled with it, exploding with it. Dimly, she heard the clock in the living room begin to chime, each stroke echoing the frenzy within her.

She gasped with shock and almost fell as Ben pulled away from her suddenly.

"Damn! I've got to pick the kids up from Sunday school."

While Joanna leaned against the refrigerator, stunned and disbelieving, he bent and kissed the tip of her breast, then smoothed the lace of her bra back over her, slid the strap back over her shoulder, and rebuttoned her blouse. "Sorry, love. We'll finish this later." He gave her another quick kiss, turned away from her, and moved stiffly toward the door, pausing only long enough to call over his shoulder, "I'll pick up the chocolate chips and other ingredients while I'm out, and we can make the cookies this afternoon."

Joanna stared after him for a minute, then uttered the most potent cussword she knew. "I'll kill him," she vowed. "Unless I can think of something worse." She straightened up and persuaded her aching, frustrated body to move to the window. She nodded with vengeful satisfaction as Ben's awkward, unnatural gait confirmed what he'd tried unsuccessfully to hide as he left her.

He'd been just as aroused as she was, and was probably hurting at least as badly. "Serves him right," she exclaimed. "What makes him think he can come barging into my kitchen—into my *life*—and just take over the way he has?"

The answer was as painful as it was swift in coming. Because she had let him, that was what.

Ben made his way stiffly and painfully across Joanna's lawn to the hole in the hedge and vowed that the next time he kissed the lady, it would be at a time and place where he could follow through. He was getting too old to cope with these raging but unsatisfied hormones. He grinned, remembering the scene he had just left, and thought with considerable satisfaction that Joanna's hormones had seemed to be raging, too. That was encouraging.

He found Becky and Joey waiting for him on the church steps along with half a dozen other children. He brought the car to a stop a little distance away and watched them laughing and talking with the others. For the moment, at least, the little automatons were gone, replaced by two relaxed, happy, and blessedly normal children.

He turned into the wide, circular drive and pulled up next to the steps. They tumbled into the car, bubbling with enthusiasm and both talking at once. He gathered, from the approximately one word in three he could understand, that they'd had a good time. He offered up a quick prayer of thanks as he headed for the nearest supermarket.

The chocolate chips weren't in the candy section, where he'd expected them to be. He found them finally with the baking supplies, and made a mental note to include grocery shopping in the list of things he wanted Joanna to teach him.

"Make sure you buy enough," Joey advised.

Becky asked wistfully, "Do you remember the time Mama made chocolate chip cookies and you and Daddy ate so many she had to make more?"

Ben put another bag of chips into his cart. "I remember."

"And she pretended to be mad," Joey added. "Only she really wasn't."

"I remember that, too," Ben said, suddenly humbled by a whole flood of memories of the loving young woman who had reached out to him, treated him as if he'd been her own father, and worked to heal the rift between him and his son.

He had a vivid recollection of his visit to her in the hospital when Joey was born. He'd missed regular visiting hours and unwittingly slipped past the nurse and into Jennie's room while she was nursing Joey.

He started to apologize and back out hastily, but she cried, "Come in and see your grandson." He did, hesitantly, eyes averted, while the baby suckled at Jennie's breast and she exclaimed, "Isn't he beautiful? Joel and I think he looks just like you. He's a greedy little fellow, isn't he?"

Her voice was so natural and unembarrassed that Ben no longer felt embarrassed either but stood beside the bed and watched in awe until the nurse came in and exclaimed, "What are you doing here? Visitors aren't allowed when the babies are with their mothers!"

"It's all right," Jennie said. "He's the

baby's grandfather. And I wanted him here."

The nurse snorted her disapproval and held out her arms for Joey. Jennie handed him over, casually slid her gown and lacy bed jacket back over her bare breast, and asked Ben, "All right, where's my hug?"

As he hugged her and kissed her cheek, she said, "Joel was afraid you wouldn't be able to come, but I told him you would," and he knew that if she'd been his flesh-and-blood daughter, he couldn't have loved her more.

He located the rest of the ingredients quickly and then, both to restore their happy mood and to keep the kitchen clean for cookie making, he suggested, "Why don't we stop for fish and chips instead of making lunch at home?"

He overrode their eager request to eat in the car. "Civilized people eat at tables," he explained. "In chairs." While they waited for their order, he settled them at a table by the window, brought their food when it was ready, and glanced around for a place to put the tray.

The man lounging at the table in the

corner stood up and wiped his hands on his apron. "I'll take it."

"Thanks," Ben said, then took another look. "Tony Vincent! I almost didn't recognize you. How long has it been since we worked together?"

"About two elections ago, as I recall. Ben, it's good to see you. What are you up to these days?"

Patiently, Ben went through the explanation he had almost learned by heart now and finished by asking, "But what are you doing here? In that." He gestured toward the apron.

"Bussing tables, sweeping the floor, or whatever else needs to be done. I got caught in one of those cutbacks," he added defensively. "This is just to fill in until something else opens up."

Ben turned away to hide the sympathy in his eyes and turned back as Tony said dispiritedly, "Ah, hell, Ben. Who am I kidding? It's the young guys who get hired. The old guys, like you and me—"

"Hold it!" Ben ordered. "I don't consider myself one of the 'old guys.'"

Tony grinned faintly. "Okay, then. The 'chronologically advantaged.' The words don't matter. The result is the same. At our age, it's hard as hell to hang on to a job you already have, much less get another one worth having. Employers worry that you're going to drop dead or turn senile in the middle of a contract, so you end up doing stuff like this." He gestured around at the tables beginning to fill with the after-church crowd.

"It isn't just me, Ben. Grady Wilson is clerking over at the Quick-Shop, and Pete Donovan has signs up all over town offering to repair stereos, VCRs, and small electrical appliances. At that, I'm better off than a lot of folks. I just need something to take my mind off being out of work, but some of them really need the money."

They stood together, somber and silent, until Tony said, "Time I got to work. And forgive me for saying it, Ben, but I think you were crazy to retire when you didn't have to."

"I'm not really retired," Ben said sharply. "I just shifted to a different line of work—taking care of my family."

Tony studied him soberly then said, "Maybe. But I can't see that housework is so different from what I'm doing, except you don't get paid for it."

Ben let the children's chatter flow and ebb around him as he ate his dinner in silence. Tony was wrong. He had to be. Millions of wives and mothers had made full-time careers of caring for their homes and families. If they could do it, so could he.

At home, he set the groceries on the counter, dismally aware that Joanna might not come. She hadn't said she would.

But she did, and told him sternly, "I'm only here out of respect for the PTA. I still haven't made up my mind about the other."

"God bless the PTA," he intoned piously, and ducked when she threatened to hit him with a bag of chocolate chips.

She arranged the cookie ingredients on the counter, assembled the utensils she needed, then noticed the children staring wistfully at her from the doorway. She grinned and shook her spoon at them. "You two had better get in here and help. I'm not going to make all these cookies by myself, you know."

She soon had them sifting flour, measuring sugar, and chattering a mile a minute. Ben watched in awe and wondered how she could possibly think she wasn't grandma material. If Jennie had lived to be a grandmother, he thought unexpectedly, she'd have been a lot like Joanna.

He began cleaning up the mess while Joanna supervised the dropping of spoonfuls of cookie dough on the baking sheets. "A little less dough, Becky, or we won't have enough cookies. And Joey, you have to put them a little closer together, or we won't have enough cookie sheets."

They gave Bernie the cookies that were burned, ate the ones that were lopsided or broken, and put the rest aside for the PTA. Becky took Lovey out to meet Tinkerbell, while Joey fell asleep in Ben's recliner.

Ben bent his vow just enough to put an arm around Joanna and kiss her cheek. "God, this feels good, like being part of a family. I thought that Fran and I became a family when Joel was born, but we didn't. I gave her a child, but never the attention and intimacy that would have made us a family."

"It does feel good," she agreed, and added pensively "Robert gave me all the attention and intimacy I could ever want, but without a child, we were never a family either. We were only a couple."

Ben grinned and hugged her gently. "Stick with me, kid. I'll let you be both."

Six

Ben talked Joey out of another stomachache, promised Becky he'd take extra good care of Lovey, and packed them off to school Monday morning, then busied himself doing up the breakfast dishes while he waited for Joanna. When she hadn't come at the end of the first hour, he told himself she was probably sleeping late.

An hour later, he began to consider, that she might have changed her mind, and wasn't coming after all. An hour after that, he gave in to his mounting anxiety and went to knock on her back door. She didn't answer, and a quick check of her carport revealed that her car was not there.

She wasn't gone from his life forever, he told himself firmly. She'd simply had something else to do this morning. Shopping perhaps, or an errand to run, and she'd forgotten to tell him.

Bernie *woofed!* beside him and led him to the back of the house again, where Tinkerbell chirped at them from her perch in the window. Bernie went into spasms of joy and ran to the door, clearly expecting Ben to open it and let Tinkerbell out.

"Sorry, old boy," Ben told him. "The ladies apparently have other plans this morning." He went back home and made a pretense of cleaning up after the weekend. Lunchtime came, and he made a baloney sandwich with no lettuce and washed it down with a glass of milk. He didn't really want it, but it was the only way he knew to quiet the grumbling of his stomach.

Helen laid her spoon on the saucer beside her empty soup bowl and studied Joanna across the table with a blend of surprise and amusement. "When you said you wanted to take me to lunch today, I assumed you were just lonely for a little office gossip. I had no idea—"

She broke off and leaned back as the waiter removed her soup bowl and replaced it with the salad plate she'd ordered. "Let me see if I have this straight. This new neighbor of yours is single, attractive, fun to be with, obviously attracted to you, and makes you go to pieces every time you look at him."

"Not 'go to pieces' exactly," Joanna protested, wondering if she'd made a mistake confiding in Helen.

Helen grinned. "Approximately, then. Close enough, anyhow." She picked up her fork and speared a cherry tomato. "Forgive me if I'm a bit slow today, but I don't understand what the problem is." She glanced up at Joanna, her eyes questioning. "Unless it's the children. I never knew if you and Robert were childless by choice, or—"

Joanna shook her head. "No, of course it isn't the children. I don't know much about children, but these two seem adorable." She poked aimlessly at her own salad and added, "I would have liked children, but it just didn't work out that way. Robert never seemed very interested, so I didn't make an issue of it. Actually, I think he was more pleased than not that we never had any."

Helen nodded. "He wanted you to himself."

"Perhaps he did," Joanna admitted after a minute. "I know he was happy and satisfied with just the two of us, and he seemed to act a little . . . well . . . smug, when we could come and go as we pleased, and our friends with children couldn't. I think he believed children were a lot of work and were always getting into trouble.

"But these children aren't like that. They're quiet and well-behaved, and still hurting terribly from the loss of their parents." She smiled, remembering. "Becky called me 'Grandma' the other day, then got all flustered and told me she'd just been pretending. I can't tell you how that made me feel."

"I think I can guess," Helen said softly. "Well, if it isn't the children, what is it?"

Joanna's mouth went dry, and although she took a healthy swallow of her iced tea, her tongue wanted to stick to the roof of her mouth as she forced herself to admit, "It's how I feel about *him*. About Ben."

"And how is that?"

Joanna hesitated, then confessed, "Horny as hell."

Helen laughed—not a ladylike little ripple of amusement, but a full-throated guffaw that turned heads in their direction and made Joanna pray that her cheeks weren't as red as they felt.

Helen reached across the table and patted her hand. "I'm sorry, Jo. You took me by surprise. But you don't know how glad I am to hear you say that. I've been worried about you."

"Worried? Why?"

"Because you've been faithful to Robert's memory for three years now, and that's about two and a half years too long. Listen, if you and this Ben Walker have the hots for each other, and you're both unattached, who are you going to hurt? Go for it. Honey, this is the nineties, and although not many women our age are promiscuous—"

"Our age!" Joanna interrupted. "Helen, you're a good ten years younger than I am."

Helen grinned. "Maybe so, but I'm not the one who has a sexy grandpa panting after me. You are. And a lot of women ten years and more older than *you* are happily and sexually involved with men they aren't married to. So if that's what's holding you back . . . well, you'll never be a virgin again, so what's the point of behaving like one?"

"That isn't what's holding me back. I'm not a prude, and I never have been. But Ben . . . well, he has this uncanny ability to walk in and just take over. He started by taking over my barbecue grill and my dinner. Then he somehow talked me into organizing first his kitchen and then his whole household. And yesterday—" She stopped abruptly. How could she possibly explain what had happened yesterday?

As if reading her thoughts, Helen prodded, "What happened yesterday?"

Joanna sighed and cursed herself for not keeping her mouth shut. She'd have to explain it now, or Helen would never give her any peace. She fortified herself with a sip of tea and a deep breath.

"He came over to ask for help making chocolate chip cookies. Then . . . he, well, he . . ." Flustered, but needing to make Helen understand, she blurted, "He backed me up against the refrigerator, so I couldn't get away, and then, just when I was . . . I mean . . . he . . ."

"He *what?*" Helen demanded when Joanna faltered to a stop.

Joanna twisted her napkin between her hands and finished in one desperate gulp, "He remembered he had to go pick up the children from Sunday school, and he just left!"

Helen choked and went into a coughing fit that left her face red, her eyes moist, and her lips trying to turn up into a grin.

Joanna eyed her reproachfully, and reminded herself that Helen was not only her most valued employee, but her long-term friend and had been there with her and for her while she lived through Robert's illness and recovered from his death.

She added quietly, "I could have said no, right at the start, and I didn't. That's what bothers me. Every time he came barging in, I could have, *should* have, said no, and I didn't. That scares me. If I can't stand up to him now, when I've just met him, what would it be like if . . . if we were lovers?"

"If you were happy, what difference would it make?"

"A lot. I'm not about to hand control of my life over to someone else. Helen, I have things to do, plans to carry out, my future to manage. I'm used to being in charge, and I intend to keep it that way."

Helen was silent but the expression that crossed her face and disappeared as quickly as it had come sent a shiver of apprehension through Joanna. "What's the matter?" she asked. "Don't you think I can manage my own life?"

"Of course I do."

"Then why that look on your face? I obviously said something you don't agree with. What was it?" As Helen hesitated, she added softly, "You've never been afraid to level with me, Helen. Don't start now."

Helen hesitated, clearly uncomfortable, and fidgeted under Joanna's steady gaze. Finally, she shrugged. "Okay, but remember, you asked. And remember, I was Robert's friend, too. He was a good man, a good boss, and as far as I could tell, a good husband. I know the two of you were happy together. But I always thought it was lucky you deferred to him as much as you did, or your marriage would never have lasted."

"*Deferred* to him! What are you talking about?"

"I mean that you were never really in

charge of your life. Robert was. He was a kind, loving man, who would never have done anything to hurt you, but he was also a selfish man in many ways. He made the decisions, chose your activities, manipulated you into going along with what *he* wanted. I don't know what he'd have done if you had ever insisted on doing something your way, but you never did.

"Joanna, he ran your life as much as you're afraid Ben will, only he was more subtle about it."

Joanna stared at her, stunned at her words. "Robert didn't manipulate me," she denied. "It's true that I always let him make the decisions, but most husbands of his generation make the decisions. It's a kind of ego thing. And if I always seemed to do what he wanted, it was because I wanted the same things he did."

"Including no children?"

Joanna had a momentary recollection of a vague regret, a sense of something missing, that had touched her now and again. She brushed it aside impatiently. "If I'd wanted children badly enough, I'd have made more of an issue of it, wouldn't I?"

"I'm sure you would have," Helen agreed.

They ate their salads in silence, then splurged on sinfully rich desserts. Helen eyed hers with greedy delight and murmured, "I'll have to eat salads for another week to make up for this."

Joanna savored the first wonderful mouthful, then laughed. "I think you just solved my problem."

"Hooray for me. How did I do that?"

"So far," Joanna said, "my life has been a nice, nourishing salad. Now I'm entitled to a wonderful dessert. After that, I can get back to the salad."

"Ben's the dessert," Helen said.

"Maybe," Joanna agreed, "but only if I decide he is. And I'll be the one to decide how much dessert I want, and when I'm ready to get back to salad. My choice, not his."

She ate the rest of her dessert, her earlier doubts lessening with each bite. Life didn't have to be an either/or proposition. She could enjoy Ben's company, his friendship, and if it came to that, his sexy body, without losing control of her life or breaking her promise to Robert. She had enough room in her life for both.

But it would be on *her* terms. She promised herself that.

"I have just one question," Helen said as they finished their desserts and prepared to leave. "Did he talk you into making his chocolate chip cookies for him?"

The last of Joanna's doubts vanished as she laughed and confessed, "Yes, he did. But I emphatically declined his invitation to go to the PTA open house with him."

Ben washed his lunch dishes slowly, then wandered aimlessly from room to room.

Maybe she'd come this afternoon. Or maybe he'd come on too strong, too soon, and scared her away. So they drew sparks from each other. That didn't mean that she wanted him to light any fires. *Damn!* he thought.

Outside, Bernie *woofed,* a delighted sound that brought Ben running to the window. He felt relief wash over him at the sight of Joanna, flushed and breathless, hurrying across the yard.

"I'm sorry," she said as he opened the door for her. "I needed to talk to my office manager, so we had lunch together. I didn't realize I'd be so late."

"I was beginning to wonder if you were coming," he admitted.

She studied his face for a minute. "You thought I was backing out of our agreement?"

"Are you?"

She shook her head. "No."

Relief made him reckless. "Does that mean you're willing to drop the "business only" part of it?"

She flushed slightly, which made her look years younger and three times as desirable, and said primly, "I don't know."

"What does that mean?"

"It means I'm not making any promises, but . . ." The flush deepened. "I'm not ruling anything out either. It depends."

"On what?"

"On whether I'm willing to get involved with a man whose most visible characteristic, aside from his love for his grandchildren, is his ability to walk in and just take over."

"I don't do that," he exclaimed. "Do I?"

"You most certainly do. Feeding me hot dogs, kissing me, persuading me to organize your kitchen and then your whole life, propositioning me in my own kitchen! Ben, I spent my whole marriage letting one man make the decisions and run my life and I don't intend to do it again."

He wavered between amusement at her indignation and concern over her accusation. "Joanna, believe me, I don't *mean* to take over, and I certainly don't intend to run your life."

Some of the defiance went out of her and she sighed. "Oh, Ben, I don't believe you're really trying to run things. It's just that you're so gung-ho about everything, and I'm slower, more cautious. While I'm still thinking about something, you're already plunging into it, and sweeping me along with you."

"Don't I wish," he muttered, and had to suppress a grin when she flushed again. "Life is short," he told her. "Why waste it *thinking* about what you want to do when you could be doing it?"

"Because acting without thinking can get you into a lot of trouble."

"Granted, but it can also get you into a lot of fun. You should try it sometime."

"I might, sometime. But if I do," she

added, "it will be because *I* choose to, and not because you push me into it. And there will be some conditions regarding our agreement."

"What are they?"

She held up her fingers and ticked them off one by one. "First, I won't come over until the children have left for school in the morning, not because I don't want to see them, but because I don't want to make them think I'll always be here. I won't. And my evenings will be my own. I don't mean we can't do things with the children occasionally, but I do have a life of my own, and I want a chance to get back to some of the things Robert and I used to do together. And you'll let me move at my own pace and not try to stampede me into doing things I haven't had time to think about."

"I can live with that," he assured her.

She looked relieved. "In that case, I'll see you tomorrow morning." She turned to go.

"But you will go to the open house with us tonight, won't you? You don't want to disappoint Becky and Joey," he coaxed, as she hesitated.

"Well . . . what time?"

"Seven?"

She nodded and let herself out the back door. A few seconds later, he grinned as he heard her voice, muffled but clear, exclaim, "Damn, he did it to me again!"

Joanna set her armload of posters, folders, and leaflets on Ben's kitchen table and paused to catch her breath while he leafed through them curiously.

"What is all this stuff?" he asked, then answered his own question. "Stain removal chart. What to include in the well-stocked medicine chest. Kitchen herbs and other seasonings. Storage times for frozen foods. Poison antidotes. Table of equivalent weights and measures. Time-temperature chart for roasting meat. One hundred household tips and hints."

He shook his head, as if he couldn't quite believe what he was seeing. "Good grief, Joanna. Are we opening up a branch of the public library? I've seen encyclopedias that weren't this comprehensive. What makes you think I'm going to need all this?"

"Well, you probably won't," she conceded, "but it's better to have it and not need it than to need it and not have it."

"I suppose," he said doubtfully. He held up a thin rectangle of plastic filled with neatly arranged holes of various sizes. "I know this is a guide to screw and bolt sizes, but . . ." He held up another plastic rectangle, also with assorted holes in it. "What's this?"

"That's for measuring portions of uncooked spaghetti." As he continued to stare at it, she added, "So you cook enough spaghetti, but not too much."

He kept his face straight, but she could tell he was trying not to grin. "My, my," he murmured. "Will wonders never cease!"

"Laugh if you like," she told him with mock severity, "but someday you'll thank me for all this."

He dug through the pile a little further and found the loose leaf notebook that was her prize exhibit. "And what's this?"

"That's for keeping household records. You know, things like—"

He held his hand up, palm toward her, in the universal "stop" sign. "No, I don't know, and I don't want to know. Look, I only want my household organized, not regimented. Tell the truth, now. Do you use one of these books? Do you keep records on all these things?"

"Of course. Most of them, anyway."

The grin kept tugging at his lips. "How on earth do you ever find time to actually *do* anything?"

He was teasing her again, and she couldn't decide whether to be amused, or irritated. "Oh, come on," she exclaimed finally. "This isn't any harder than keeping accurate records on your car's mileage and servicing."

He shook his head and assumed a woeful expression. "I hope I don't make you lose all respect for me, but I don't do that either." He riffled through the pile of papers again and told her, "I believe the only bit of useful information you don't have here is a diagram of the neighborhood and a dossier on each of the neighbors."

She stared at him for a minute. "No, I don't. I'm sorry. It never occurred to me—"

"Hey, I'm teasing," he exclaimed. "I can get to know my neighbors the old-fashioned way—when they come to complain about the noise. Or you can just tell me about them. I should start getting acquainted with them, I suppose."

"I don't know how much help I'll be," she said regretfully. "I really don't know the neighbors too well. Oh, it isn't that they aren't friendly, or anything like that. It's just that, well, when Robert and I first moved here, we were pretty busy getting the business going, and didn't have a lot of time for socializing. By the time we did have, it seemed a little late to finally start getting acquainted."

It had seemed that way at the time, she thought, but now that she had put it into words, she realized that it had been because Robert didn't want to give up their privacy and togetherness.

"You must have had other friends, though."

"Not many," she admitted. "We never did really have much free time, and what we did have, we pretty much spent alone together."

"I can understand that," Ben said. "I'd have felt the same way. But how did you feel about it?"

He'd obviously jumped to the conclusion that being alone was Robert's idea, which irritated her, probably because she had just reached the same conclusion.

"I felt fine about it," she said shortly,

then added with painful honesty, "At least, I did while Robert was alive. Afterwards . . . it might have been nice to have friends to rally around me, keep me company, maybe include me in some of their activities, at least until I got used to the idea of going places and doing things alone."

She paused, dealing with the memory of the few times she'd ventured out since Robert's death. She'd loved going to dinner or the theater on his arm, enjoying his company, sharing his pleasure in whatever they were doing, knowing that people were watching and thinking what a handsome couple they made.

Doing the same things by herself had been the pits.

As if sensing her feelings, Ben caught her hand in his. "You don't have to go places or do things alone anymore. I'm going to step up my search for a babysitter, and then we can—"

She snapped back to the present abruptly and tugged her hand free. "Ben," she warned him, "you're trying to take charge again."

"Oh. Sorry."

She gathered her scattered papers and

charts into a neat pile and turned the conversation in a different direction. "What
about you? Your friends?"

He shrugged. "Well, there are my old
work buddies. I suppose I'll be seeing
some of them once in a while. Or were
you talking about women friends?"

Her face grew warm. "Oh. No, I . . ."

His voice turned serious as he told her,
"I told you, my wife left me because I was
too busy to have time for her and my son.
I found out pretty quickly that most women
feel the same way." The teasing note came
back. "That's another reason I'm glad I'm
retired now."

The grin came back, too, when she
cleared her throat and told him, "If we're
going to get anything done today, we'd better get started."

Saturday morning, Joey pushed his chair
back from the breakfast table and asked,
"Can I go see Joanna?"

"*May* I," Becky corrected, then added,
"Can we, Grandpa? Lovey wants to see
Tinkerbell again."

"Not this morning, kids. Joanna has a

life of her own, you know, and she said she had errands to run this weekend."

They looked so crestfallen he relented and broke one of his unbreakable rules. "I tell you what. Just this once, you can watch cartoons on television for a while."

He watched them disappear into the living room, and told himself this was something else he needed to learn from Joanna—how to keep the kids entertained and happy when they really wanted to do something else.

As he loaded the breakfast dishes into the dishwasher and generally tidied the kitchen, he thought back over the week just passed, mentally reviewing the things Joanna had already taught him.

They'd stocked the medicine chest with first aid supplies and posted a list of remedies for minor ailments, a poison control chart, and a list of emergency telephone numbers on the inside of the linen closet door. They'd outfitted his broom closet with everything he'd ever need to clean anything, a chart showing what to use where, and a list of cleaning and other household hints. Even his admittedly sketchy assortment of tools had been supplemented with items Joanna assured him all homeowners needed sooner or later. He fervently hoped it would be later.

She'd educated him on the finer points of laundry, and he could now sort, spot, presoak, fold, and put away with the best of them. He had learned how to plan meals around supermarket specials, read labels, compare prices, and pick ripe cantaloupes—along with half a dozen other men and a new bride who'd happened by the produce section and stopped to take advantage of Joanna's know-how.

He couldn't imagine what might be left for next week. Rotate and balance his tires, maybe?

It had been a wonderful week, filled with rich emotional pleasure and enormous physical frustration. He wouldn't have missed a moment of either, but as he finished the kitchen and hung his apron on the hook behind the door—another of Joanna's refinements—he decided he was suffering from cabin fever.

He followed the children into the living room and said, "Hey, how'd you like to go for a walk and take a look at our new neighborhood?"

Joey popped up from the rug where he'd been sitting cross-legged. "Sure. Can Bernie come?"

Becky glanced down at the kitten cradled in her arms. "Can I take Lovey? I can carry her."

"I think we'd better leave the animals at home this time," Ben said. "Maybe we can take them later."

He'd checked the neighborhood briefly before he bought the house, and liked its blend of older houses and newer ones, clear signs that it was no developer's project, but a place where people moved in because they liked it. He examined it more closely as they strolled around the block, decided his neighbors were also a blend of young and old—retirees enjoying their leisure years and younger couples raising families, with children ranging from babies to babysitters.

Halfway around the block, they discovered that Joanna's next-door neighbor was having a yard sale. "Look, Grandpa," Becky exclaimed. "There's a croquet set like the one we used to have."

"Oh, boy!" Joey cried. "Can we have it, Grandpa?"

The set was well used, but in good shape, surprisingly cheap, and a wonderful alternative to Saturday morning cartoons. Ben paused and studied it deliberately while the children watched anxiously.

"I don't know," he said, pretending to think it over. "It seems to me Bernie's penchant for reverse paleontology has pretty much ruined our yard for croquet."

"What's reverse pale . . . pale . . . that stuff you said?" Joey demanded.

Ben exchanged grins with the woman who seemed to be in charge. *"Burying* bones," he explained.

Becky said wistfully, "Mama said Bernie's bones made croquet the most challenging game she'd ever played."

"Challenging, huh?" Ben reached into his pocket for his billfold. "Then I guess we'd better buy it."

The woman tucked the money into her pocket and asked pleasantly, "Do you see anything else you like?"

"No," Ben said, and grinned again as a thought struck him. "But do you know if there's a good babysitter in the neighborhood?"

Seven

Ben spent his second week as a home-maker-in-training learning the finer points of housecleaning. He became intimately acquainted with brooms, mops, dust cloths, furniture polish, and detergents, and mastered the most efficient ways of using them.

It was the vacuum cleaner that thwarted him at every turn. It locked its wheels when he wanted it to follow him and tipped on its side when he yanked on its hose. It steadfastly refused to touch the dog and cat hair thick on carpets and upholstery but sucked up safety pins, paper clips, plastic twist-it ties, and the remnants of Bernie's last bone, then choked on a crumpled paper towel that had missed the wastebasket, and required a machine's version of the Heimlich maneuver to unclog its windpipe.

Or rather, Ben thought, watching Joanna

hook the hose up backward to eject the offending towel, a mechanical emetic. Or possibly enema.

In the bedroom, it knocked over the wastebasket, jammed itself into a corner, and while he was trying to pull it loose, swallowed a good portion of his bedspread. "That's it," he snarled finally as he watched it ingest one of his favorite cuff links for dessert. He yanked the cord from the wall and was about to commit assault and battery on the machine when Joanna deftly maneuvered it out of his reach, opened it, and fished his cuff link from the dust and lint that now filled its innards.

"Get that damned thing out of my sight," he snapped. "Stuff it back into the closet. Use that hammer we bought last week and nail the door shut."

"Now, Ben." Her voice held a hint of suppressed laughter. "You don't want to put it away until you're through using it."

"I am through," he swore. "Probably forever. That infernal machine is out to get me!"

Joanna sobered enough to assure him, "You can lick it, Ben. You're bigger than it is."

"I don't want to lick it, I want to get rid of it." He fidgeted under Joanna's steady gaze, then felt his anger deflate suddenly. "Oh, hell, Joanna, it isn't the vacuum cleaner. It's me. I thought—I really thought—that if I put my mind to it, I could make it as a full time parent and homemaker, but I just don't have what it takes. I've put my heart and soul into mastering these things—"

"And you're doing just fine," she interjected.

"Maybe," he said grimly, "but it's just beginning to soak through my thick head that as soon as I finish, I'm going to have to turn around and do them all again. And again. For the rest of my natural born days, I'm going to be locked into this never-ending cycle. Boy, do I understand now why so many wives and mothers rebel! If this is what women have been enduring all these years, no wonder they want to be liberated."

Joanna shoved the vacuum cleaner into a corner and took his arm. "Let's take a break," she suggested, and led him downstairs to the kitchen, where she seated him at the table, poured him a tall glass of freshly brewed iced tea, and sat down opposite him.

"It's not that I mind doing the work," he said. "I know it has to be done, and I'm not so arrogant I think some woman or some servant should be doing it for me. It's just that I'm a mover and a shaker who doesn't have anything to move or shake anymore. There's just this big hole in my life. I've been telling myself that raising the children would be enough of a challenge for me, but I have no right to lay that burden on them. It's up to me to make their lives happy and satisfying, not the other way around."

He swirled his glass and watched the ice spinning in the liquid, trying to find the words that would make her understand. "I used to work with the most sophisticated, state-of-the-art electronic equipment. Last week, my most exciting moment was operating the washer."

He set the glass down and reached across the table to take her hands in his. "I'll never be a workaholic again, or let my work come between me and the things that really matter, but I need something else to challenge me, to keep my brain from rusting out. Do you understand what I mean? I love the children with all my heart, but I need something else, too, something just for *me*, something to fill this awful hole in my life. Is that so terrible?"

She shook her head. "Not terrible at all. It's what we all need. And you're right. This is exactly why women rebel. Ben, you've just figured out precisely what the women's movement is all about, and it isn't really just a woman's thing at all, is it?"

He released her hands and leaned back in his chair. "Oh," he said. It was little enough to say, but somehow, it seemed adequate. After a moment, he thought to add, "I see." And then, after that, "But what can I *do* about it? No matter how *I* feel, it's the kids who matter, and they need me here, not off somewhere satisfying my own wants and pretending I'm doing it for them, the way I did with Fran and Joel." He grinned wryly. "At least, Fran had the option of leaving me and finding someone else. Becky and Joey don't."

Joanna smoothed her thumb over her glass, making patterns in the moisture that covered it. "Have you considered working part-time?"

"Doing what? Sweeping out cages at the pet store? Sacking groceries at the supermarket? No. If I just needed something to pass the time, I'd build model airplanes or collect stamps." He drained his glass and set it back down, then rubbed his fingers across his forehead to savor their coolness.

"Joanna, not long before I retired from my job, I prepared a proposal for a bid on a multimillion-dollar contract." He managed to grin at her. "You'd love proposals—analyzing, planning, estimating. You have to decide what the project involves. How many man-hours it will take. How many writers. Illustrators. Typists. How much computer time. Then you make your best educated guess, and if you're too low, the company will lose money, and if you're too high, someone else will underbid you and you lose the job. Miss too many times, and you lose *your* job. It's like high-stakes gambling."

"A natural high," she said softly.

He nodded. "Exactly. And now I'm studying the grocery ads for the best price on ground beef. I know feeding the kids is a lot more important, but it isn't nearly as exciting."

"Have you given any thought to going back to work when the children are a little older and more self-reliant?"

He sighed and shook his head. "It isn't really an option. As a friend pointed out recently, at our age it's hard as hell to hang on to a job you already have, much less get another one worth having. It isn't fair and it doesn't make sense. People live longer today, stay healthier longer, and don't lose either their ability or their need to be useful and productive just because they're . . ." He paused. What was it Tony Vincent had called it? "Chronologically advantaged," he finished.

He took his glass to the freezer for ice, then refilled it with tea. "No, when I took early retirement, I pretty much closed that door behind me." He leaned back against the counter, feeling the years settle on him, press him down. "Damned if I know what I'm going to do."

Joanna studied him thoughtfully. "You could always start your own business."

She meant it as a joke, of course. He smiled dutifully and said, "Maybe I should at that. I could hire all my friends who've had to retire, or been caught in layoffs, and we could . . ." He paused, feeling as if the heavens had suddenly opened up and poured sunlight and inspiration into him. "We could do it," he said, more to himself than to Joanna. "We really could. Not just our own company, but . . ."

He glanced down at Joanna. "Do you know what a job shop is?"

She shook her head.

He pushed himself away from the counter so that he could move freely around the kitchen. "It's usually feast or famine in the defense industry," he told her. "When it's feast, there's usually more work than a company can handle, but it's only temporary. There's no point in hiring people who would only have to be laid off in a few weeks or months. So what do you think they do instead?"

"Temps?"

"Not quite. Job shops. Companies that don't just supply people to do the work, but handle the whole job. Subcontractors, in other words, and nobody cares if the people they supply are young or old, as long as the job gets done right and on time. And *I* know where to find people who can do the work and would almost sell their souls for the chance."

"It sounds great. What kind of money would you need up front?"

He shrugged. "Start-up costs would be minimal. All we'd need would be business cards, résumés, and plenty of chutzpa. I've got all three."

"I believe it. But what about equipment, office space—"

"Wouldn't need much. Most of our work would be done on-site. Anything else could be handled out of my dining room." He grinned. "I've been wondering what to do with that dining room. Equipment? Couple of typewriters. Maybe a computer or two."

He'd been getting more and more excited as he talked, pacing around the kitchen so that Joanna had to keep twisting and turning in her chair to keep him in sight. Now he stopped in front of her, caught her hands in his, and pulled her to her feet. "It'll work. I know it will."

"Of course it will."

"We can take on only as much work as we want to, work the hours we want to, have plenty of free time for our families or whatever else we want to do . . ."

He knew he was as out of control as the vacuum cleaner had been, and Joanna was laughing at him, but that was all right. He felt like laughing at himself. He forced himself to stop and take a deep breath to calm down, and added, "There's just one major problem, as far as I can see."

"What's that?"

He circled her waist with his arms, half afraid she would pull away. "I don't know anything about starting a business or running one. But you do. What do you say, Joanna? Will you help me 'get it up and running'? Not just for me, but for all of us who still have productive, useful years left?"

She leaned back so she could look at him and exclaimed, "You don't think I'd let you keep all the fun to yourself, do you? Of course I will."

It was only coincidence, he told himself, that she had moved just far enough away that the tips of her breasts lightly grazed his chest. She couldn't possibly know that the excitement he felt over the thought of working again was kindling another kind of excitement in him, or that the soft pressure of her body against his sent ripples of desire through him. Or that her shining eyes and parted lips invited, almost commanded, him to kiss her. His own lips parted and he leaned forward.

She made no effort to resist him this time, but met him halfway or maybe more than halfway, with an eagerness that matched his and told him this wasn't going to be the slow, gentle seduction he had intended, but quick and hot and passionate, with Joanna backed up against the refrigerator again—his refrigerator this time—and joining fiercely in the battle of the hormones.

He felt the heat building where his thighs and pelvis pressed against hers, felt it rise into the thermonuclear range as she responded with a subtle, erotic motion of her hips. He shivered with anticipation as she unbuttoned his shirt and threaded her fingers sensuously through the mat of hair on his chest, raked his skin lightly with her fingernails, then sent shock waves through him as she massaged his nipples gently with her thumbs.

He tugged her shirt up and unhooked her bra, reached under it and cupped her breasts in his hands. Fine tremors swept her as she pressed her hands over his, coaxing his fingers to explore and caress her. After a moment, he pushed the bra out of the way and took first one breast and then the other into his mouth, exulting in his power to coax her nipples into warmth and firmness with his lips and tongue.

The movements of her hips against his had brought him almost to full arousal when she pulled away from him, slipped her leg between his and drove him into an even greater frenzy by rubbing it gently against his growing erection. He pulled her skirt up and reached into the sweet space between her thighs, felt them tighten briefly around his hand, then relax and separate as he caressed her through the smooth nylon of her panties, delightfully damp with the proof of her desire for him.

With his own arousal becoming more urgent, he slid the scrap of lace down over her hips until she could kick it off, then brought his hand up the inside of her thigh to the warmth and moisture waiting for him. She gasped and her hands clenched and unclenched on his shoulders as he explored her with uninhibited thoroughness, his fingers seeking out and caressing her most sensitive spots until he was certain she was as aroused and eager as he was.

She gasped then wordlessly reached down between them to guide him into her welcoming warmth, and then they were moving together as smoothly and expertly as if they'd been doing it all their lives.

Ben tried to delay his climax as Joanna clung to him and matched him thrust for thrust, but he'd waited for her too long, wanted her too badly. He reached the crest and tumbled over as his body convulsed with an exquisite agony more shattering and satisfying than anything he'd ever felt before, but too soon, too soon. He felt a sharp surge of anger at himself, knowing Joanna hadn't had time—but even as he berated himself, she shuddered, cried out softly and trembled against him for a long, wonderful moment, then slowly went limp in his arms.

They clung together, warm, quivering flesh still sheathed in warm, quivering flesh, until Joanna stirred in his arms and they slipped apart. She kissed the side of his neck, the line of his jaw, finally his lips, and asked him, "Ben, do you have some sort of thing about refrigerators?"

He sucked in enough breath to answer, "No, just about you." She laughed and put her arms around his neck, which brought her nipples, still swollen from his suckling, against his chest—not as arousing now that the frenzy was over, but nice to feel, just the same.

She laughed softly as he spread his fingers against her buttocks and held her close. "Haven't you had enough yet?"

He pressed his leg between her thighs again. "Have you?"

"What will you do if I haven't?"

He grinned and started to make her an offer, then sobered and told her, "Joanna, I didn't mean for it to happen this way. I was planning a leisurely, romantic seduction, with soft music, and champagne, and clean sheets on the bed. We can still go up and have that romantic seduction for our second time."

"I wish we could, Ben, but it's getting late." There was no mistaking the regret in her voice. "We don't want the children to come home and catch us." She eased herself out of his arms and began to straighten her disarrayed clothing.

He sighed and started to do the same.

Joanna restored her bra and blouse to respectability, retrieved her lace bikinis from the floor, and tucked them into her pocket. No way was she going to step into them and pull them up while Ben looked on. He was already watching her with good-natured lechery that made her wish they had all afternoon before the children came home. She turned to the counter quickly and made a show of pouring herself a glass of tea.

Ben moved close behind her, put his arms around her waist, and murmured in her ear, "We may have a problem here. When you've just made wild, passionate love in the kitchen, in the middle of the day, and the kids will be coming home soon, what do you do for an encore?"

She leaned back against him, marveling that despite the intensity of their passion and the depth of her response to it, she still hadn't had enough of him. She wanted him again almost as badly as she had the first time. She cleared her throat.

"You could always tackle that vacuum cleaner again."

"Believe me, it isn't the vacuum cleaner that I want to tackle again." He reached under her blouse and curved his fingers gently but firmly around her breasts.

She surrendered briefly to the sensual pleasure of his fondling, then regretfully pressed her hands over his and held them still.

"Ben, we aren't going to come down off this high as long as we're together, and I don't want to put either of us through the kind of frustration I've suffered all week. I think it would be wise for me to go home now."

"Wise, perhaps, but terribly frustrating."

"I know, but there's always next week."

He kissed the back of her neck. "Next week is a lifetime away."

"And the school bus is only a few minutes away."

He sighed, and when she released his hands, he tweaked her nipples gently through her bra, then let her go. "Next week, then."

She turned to face him and they shared one more kiss, not fueled by passion this time, but slow, and gentle, and lingering, and then Joanna slipped out the door and headed for home.

Back in her own kitchen, she sat at her desk and absently stroked Tinkerbell while she sorted through her thoughts and feelings.

She'd expected Ben's lovemaking to be something special, but the reality had exceeded her expectations. She couldn't help comparing him to Robert. Robert, too, had been an eager lover, with a powerful sex drive that had soon banished any inhibitions she'd brought to their marriage bed. They had conducted a prim and proper marriage during the day, but in bed at night, shyness and propriety had vanished.

No, not just in bed, or at night. They'd made love in the kitchen while dinner cooked, on the living room rug on lazy Sunday mornings, on the office sofa after everyone else had gone home, and once, standing in the garage at high noon, with only her station wagon between them and the open door.

It was probably another reason why Robert hadn't really wanted children and perhaps one of the reasons she hadn't insisted.

They had been deeply into the delights of each other's bodies. Robert was completely uninhibited about exploring, fondling, and arousing every square inch of her. She delighted in his erotic handling, and eagerly learned from him how to bring him to the same immoderate level of arousal. Sometimes, as she basked in the sweet afterglow of their lovemaking, she thought that completion of the act, as glorious as it was, was almost an anticlimax, and laughed at herself for the unintended pun.

She sobered, hurting with the memory of how Robert's illness had robbed him of his joy and passion, and how she, in her shock and grief, had somehow forgotten, until today, how deeply her body could respond to a masculine touch. Mother Nature, she thought, protecting her from needs that could no longer be satisfied.

But today that protection had ended, and she could only hope that the next time she and Ben made love, they'd have time to explore each other longer, more thoroughly. She wasn't complaining, because hot and passionate and intense was wonderful, too, but she hoped Ben could slow down long enough that they could at least get undressed.

She grinned as she got up to see what she could fix for a light supper. For that matter, she hoped *she* could.

Ben picked up the glass of tea Joanna had poured and drank deeply. The icy liquid slaked the dryness in his throat, but did nothing to quench the fire that still burned in his loins. He shook his head in awe. He'd been sure that when he and Joanna finally made love, it would be wild and wonderful, but he hadn't been prepared for anything like what had just happened between them.

He'd never experienced anything so fantastic in his life—not with the first fumbling encounters in his teens, nor with Fran, and certainly not with any of the brief affairs or one-night stands he'd had since.

He hoped—believed—that Joanna had been as satisfied as he had. He was aware that his sexual experience was probably not as varied as most men's, but he'd had enough to know that frustrated or disappointed women didn't act the way she had when it was over, or indicate their willingness for an encore.

Most women didn't act the way she had while it was happening either. She'd had him in such a frenzy he'd hardly known which way was up. Although, he reflected smugly, he hadn't had any problem knowing which way was *in*. His thoughts skidded to a stop as his body took over.

Damn! A lot of good it had done for her to go home. He was just as hot for her now as he had been at the beginning. With grim determination, he went back upstairs and battled the vacuum cleaner until he heard the children come home.

He hurried downstairs to meet them and found Becky, her dress torn and dirty, standing in the living room blinking back tears.

"Sweetheart, what's wrong?"

Joey started to answer, but Becky hushed him quickly. "I tore my dress," she said. "I'm sorry, Grandpa. I didn't mean to."

He put his arm around her shoulders.

"Never mind the dress. How did it happen? Did you get hurt?"

"I fell down, and I skinned my knee."

His newly developing parent's instinct told him there was more to it than that, but didn't tell him what to do about it. He tabled the problem for later and turned his attention to Becky's injury, wincing as he examined the scraped and bloody knee. It probably hurt like hell, but Becky clenched her teeth and held her breath while he cleaned and applied soothing ointment to the injury. He made a mental note to thank Joanna again for her first aid chart and his well-stocked medicine chest.

He had almost finished when the doorbell rang. Joey ran to answer it, and immediately backed away, his face and posture triggering Ben's parental alarms again. Ben couldn't see who was on the other side of the door, but heard an angry voice cry, "Is this the kid who gave you the black eye?"

He followed Joey to the door and pulled it open the rest of the way to find himself facing a beefy, red-faced man and a boy, the man clearly angry and spoiling for a fight, the boy about Becky's age, but considerably larger, and sporting what was obviously going to be a beautiful shiner, as if he'd already been in a fight.

"Is this the kid who gave you the black eye?" the man repeated. "Christ, Danny, you ought to be ashamed. He's only half your size!"

Danny shook his head. "No," he said with obvious reluctance. "It was her." He pointed to Becky, half hidden behind Ben.

Astonished, Ben turned to question Becky, but Joey exclaimed indignantly, "He knocked me off the bus steps, trying to get off first, and Becky told him to leave me alone, so he knocked Becky down, too, and that's when she tore her dress and got it all dirty. And he told her to shut up or he'd knock me down again, so she got up and hit him and made him run away crying."

The man grabbed Danny by the shoulder and shook him. "You let a *girl* beat you up?"

Danny cringed and tried to pull away.

Ben was torn between pride that Becky had decked Danny and an urgent desire to do the same to the little monster's father, realized in time he'd be setting a bad example, and settled for a soft answer with a touch of malice. "We appreciate your coming by to apologize, but—"

"Hey! We weren't apol—"

Ben raised his voice and continued speaking, "But maybe if you teach your son not to pick on girls or kids half his size, he won't get beaten up again."

The man's face grew redder and he poked Ben in the chest with his forefinger. "Now, look here—"

"No," Ben said. He brushed the hand aside and did some chest poking of his own. "*You* look here. If your boy lays a hand on either one of my kids again, you'll both wish he hadn't. Now if you're still looking for a fight, you'd better look for it someplace else, because if you tangle with me, it won't be a fight, it'll be a massacre—yours." He put enough menace into his voice to balance the five inches, fifty pounds, and twenty or more years the man had on him.

Apparently, it was enough. Father and son stared at him for a minute, then backed down the steps and retreated down the walk.

Joey stepped in front of Ben and called after them, "Yeah, you better not pick on me anymore, or my sister will beat you up again!"

Ben suppressed his laughter and pulled Joey back inside with him. "No need to gild the lily," he told him.

"Grandpa?" Becky's voice was soft and apprehensive. "I'm sorry I didn't tell you the truth. I was afraid you'd be mad at me for fighting."

He hugged her gently. "Not this time, sweetheart. I'm proud of the way you stuck up for your brother."

"Yeah," Joey agreed. "Me, too."

Eight

Joanna lingered over her breakfast, leafing through the Saturday morning paper and entertaining joyous memories of yesterday's lovemaking. She'd been afraid she'd be a little sore or at least tender after more than three years of abstinence, but she felt fine this morning. More than fine. She felt fulfilled and complete, feminine, sensual, earthy, carnal, and—she grinned at herself—horny as hell again. Ben had been right. Next week was a lifetime away.

After a few minutes, she folded the newspaper and laid it aside. There wasn't anything in its pages half as exciting as what was dancing through her head. She leaned back in her chair and stretched luxuriously. God, she felt good this morning! She hadn't felt this good since—

She turned to face her desk—and

Robert's photograph. "Don't look at me that way," she said softly. "It's been over three years. Three years of being only half alive and not even realizing it. Half alive? Half dead. And I'd still be half dead if it weren't for Ben.

"Besides, you were the one who taught me how important physical intimacy can be, and made it such a wonderful part of our lives. Well, you did a better job than you knew. I've missed it terribly, and I don't intend to be half dead ever again.

"You don't really mind, do you? He's a good man, Robert. Open, honest, loving. You'd like him. And it wasn't just . . . physical. It was warmth, and intimacy, and just . . . just being with someone." But even as she said it, she knew it wasn't the wonderful lovemaking she had shared with Ben and intended to go on sharing with him that bothered her. Robert wouldn't have begrudged her that, any more than he would have denied it to himself, if she had been the one to go first. In fact, he'd probably have agreed with Helen that three years was too long—much too long.

It was the other thing she felt guilty about—her promise to help Ben start his own company. Once again, she'd put her plans, Robert's plans, on hold.

"But it's different this time," she insisted, as much to herself as to Robert. "I'm not letting Ben take over my life. I *want* to do this, *need* to do it. It wasn't just my sex life that died when you did, you know. Everything went to pieces. All the joy went out of my life, all the excitement, the challenge. Now I have a chance to get it back.

"But it won't be forever. As soon as I can, I'll turn everything over to Ben, and then, I promise, I'll . . ."

She forgot what she was going to promise as Bernie *woofed* and Tinkerbell ran to the door to greet him. Joanna opened the door for her and found Ben and the children outside.

"Joanna!" Joey cried. "Grandpa's going to have a party, and you're invited."

"Oh, Joey," Becky exclaimed. "You always get things wrong. It isn't a party, it's a *meeting.*"

"What kind of meeting?" *And is it important enough*, she asked silently, *for you to bring your sexy body over here where I can see it but can't do anything about it?*

"It's a kind of business meeting," Ben said, as coolly as if he'd forgotten all about yesterday—until he grinned and winked at her, and she knew his memories were as clear and vivid as hers.

"I've been on the phone this morning," he explained. "Talking to some of my old work buddies. I didn't tell them in any detail what we have in mind, but I asked four of them to come over this evening to talk about the employment problem. I know your weekends are your own, but I'm hoping you'll want to be there, partly to lend your business expertise, and partly to make sure that I'm the perfect host."

She hesitated, wondering how she could possibly spend a whole evening with Ben and not give away some of what was churning inside her. She wanted to be there, but—

"Grady's divorced and Tony's a widower, but Charlie and Pete are bringing their wives," he added. "I thought you might like to meet them."

She made up her mind. "I would," she told him. "What time do you want me?"

She cursed her choice of words as a slow

grin spread over his face, but all he said was, "How about right after lunch?"

"Right after lunch? I thought you said this evening."

"This evening is for the meeting. Right after lunch is for some more chocolate chip cookies."

She stared at him, her mouth open and her tongue poised to deliver the scorching retort that would no doubt occur to her any minute.

"The whole PTA went crazy over your chocolate chip cookies," he reminded her.

"Yeah!" Joey seconded.

Becky asked eagerly. "Can we help you make them again?"

Joanna's protest died before it reached her lips. "Of course you can." She gave Ben her best "wait till I get you alone" look. The problem was, he gave it right back, and she didn't have to be a mind reader to know that his look didn't mean quite the same thing hers did.

Joanna wiped crumbs from the last cookie sheet and put it away while Joey studied the cookies cooling on the table and shook his head. "Ole Bernie isn't going to like this," he predicted. "We didn't burn as many cookies for him this time."

"He'll survive," Ben said cheerfully. He broke a cookie in half and offered Joanna one piece.

"What about Lovey?" Becky asked. "She doesn't like cookies."

"There's a hamburger patty left from lunch. Give her a little piece of that."

"Oh, thanks, Grandpa."

The children ran outside with their cookies and hamburger, and Joanna turned to the cupboard to find a container for the cookies.

Ben came up behind her, wrapped his arms around her, and sent warm tingles through her as he kissed the side of her neck. Affection had also been missing from her life lately, and she felt a long absent sense of contentment well up in her.

He reached up to her breasts, molding and shaping them in his hands, and that felt wonderful, too, but even as the insidious warmth began to build inside her, she caught his hands in hers and pulled them away from her. "Ben, no."

"It's okay," he told her. "I'm not planning to repeat yesterday's performance. Not right now, anyway. I only want to touch you a little. If the kids come back in, we'll hear them in plenty of time for me to get my hands back where they belong and put some space between us."

"It isn't the children I was thinking of." She turned to face him and laid her hands on his chest, not in a caress, but to keep distance between them. "Ben, we unleashed something pretty powerful yesterday, something we can't indulge every time we'd like to, and something we may have trouble controlling."

"Tell me about it," he murmured. The distance between them was from the waist up only. Below that, they were pressed firmly together, and she could feel the beginnings of his arousal—and hers.

She knew trying to pull away would only make it worse. She kept her body absolutely still and told him, "I'm not playing coy or hard to get. Whenever we have the time and the privacy, you can do whatever you like and I'll enjoy every moment of it, but the rest of the time, there's no point making it harder on ourselves than we have to.

"The children will be coming in soon, and then your friends will be here. Now, if you want to spend the rest of the day keeping something between you and anybody who might happen to glance in your direction, that's up to you, but please don't make me feel the same way. I get very bad-tempered when I'm frustrated."

"So do I," he admitted. After a minute, he stepped away from her and laughed softly when she couldn't help glancing down at him. "Yes, I'm feeling a little frustrated right now, but I'll get over it in a few minutes. And you're right. I know you're right. I just have trouble keeping my hands off you."

She laid her hand on his cheek. "And I have trouble wanting you to, but for the rest of the day, we're business associates only."

He caught her hand in his and pressed his lips into the palm. "Okay. Business associates it is, but . . ." He grinned wickedly and reached up to pinch her nipples lightly between his thumbs and forefingers. "Business associates with the hots for each other."

She glanced down at her tingling nipples, showing firm and erect through her lacy bra and soft cotton blouse, and turned Ben's grin into laughter as she exclaimed, "Damn it, Ben. Now I'll have to go into hiding."

Like any other proud parent, Ben let the children stay downstairs to meet and be admired by his friends, then sent them to get ready for bed with the promise that they could stay up and do whatever they wanted to until he came upstairs to tuck them in.

He watched as they scampered up the stairs, then turned to study the men and women gathered in his living room. Excitement and apprehension swept him by turns as he mentally rehearsed what he wanted to say. He had a good idea; he knew he did. And he had Joanna's business expertise to back up the idea. But suppose they didn't go for it? Suppose he couldn't make them see it the way he did?

He rubbed his hands together, realized that made him look nervous, and stuck them in his pockets instead.

"Well?" Pete Donovan prompted. "You

called us all over here. So what is it you wanted to say?''

Ben glanced around the room again, caught an encouraging look from Joanna, and realized he couldn't stall any longer. "It occurs to me . . ." He stopped to clear his throat, then began again. "It occurs to me that we have gathered here in this room a tremendous quantity of expertise, brain power, and just plain ability. So what are we doing with it?"

"Not much," Grady Wilson admitted.

"You're darned right, not much," Ben agreed. "Sacking groceries, bussing tables, even"—he wryly indicated himself—"keeping house." He grinned at the women. "No offense to the ladies. They probably know better than any of us how quickly that gets to be an old story. And how lousy the pay is."

The women smiled dutifully, and Tony Vincent said, "We've talked about this before, Ben. None of us likes what we're doing, but you know what we're up against."

"I know. But I propose to do something about it."

Charlie Ross raised one eyebrow. "Like what?"

Ben hesitated, then plunged in. "I've been thinking about a job shop."

"Oh, come on, Ben," Tony exclaimed. "What makes you think a job shop will want us any more than the companies that retired us or laid us off did?"

"I don't mean go to work for a job shop," Ben said quietly. "I mean form one. Of our own."

"Oh, sure," Grady scoffed after a minute. "They won't hire one of us because we're too old, so you think they'll hire a whole bunch of us?"

Ben had anticipated that reaction, and had an answer prepared, but it was Pete Donovan who said thoughtfully, "You know, it could work."

"How?"

Pete shrugged. "Listen, most companies know damned well older people can do the work and do it a sight better than younger, less experienced workers. The reasons they give for not hiring older workers are that they're afraid their insurance rates will go up, that they'll have more absenteeism, or that somebody will drop dead in the middle of a job."

"And the younger guys work cheaper," Tony added. "So?"

"So they won't be hiring us," Pete said. "We'll be independent contractors. Not their responsibility. And they won't worry about our pay scale as long as we submit the lowest bids."

Ben felt his confidence begin to rise. If he had Pete Donovan on his side, the battle was half won.

Charlie cleared his throat. "There are job shops out there already. What makes you think we can compete with them?"

Again, it was Pete who answered, grinning. "I just told you. We submit the lowest bids."

"You can go broke in a hurry that way," Grady objected. "We wouldn't have the financing to survive even a small miscalculation."

"So, we don't miscalculate." Pete leaned forward in his chair. "Ben's right. We've got the brains, ability, and expertise to handle almost any job we might come across, and we've all had experience submitting proposals. When's the last time one of us made a bid that lost money?"

"Made a few that lost us the job," Tony said.

"Yeah," Charlie agreed, "but on most of those, the company that underbid us lost money. We were right, they weren't. Another point in our favor."

"So we know what we're doing," Tony said. "And we could afford to take a lower profit, until we'd built up some reserves." He grinned wryly. "It wouldn't take much to make my present income look puny. Hell, it *is* puny."

"Shouldn't have much overhead," Charlie added. "Just the four of us."

"To begin with," Ben said, "if we're as good as I think we are, as I think we'll *be,* this thing is likely to take off and grow. Before you know it, *we'll* be hiring."

"I have a question," Betty Donovan said. "Who will you be hiring? I mean, is all this just to get you four back to work, or are you going to bat for others who are in the same boat you are?"

Ben stared at her for a minute, his thoughts doing wheelies somewhere in the back of his head. "That idea crossed my mind briefly," he admitted, "but I haven't really given it a lot of thought yet."

"You should," Ginger Ross put in. "You guys feel sorry for yourselves, but you're the lucky ones. For every one of you who has even a crummy part-time job, there are a lot of others who don't have anything, and some of them need the money."

"You're right," Ben told her. "And they all need to know they've still got some productive, useful years left."

"Besides," Tony put in, "if we start taking in some of these young go-getters, pretty soon, they'll be pushing us out of the way again. I vote we keep it older people only."

Grady shook his head. "You're talking like it's already settled."

Charlie reached over and thumped him on the shoulder. "Aw, hell, Grady. Ben had it all settled before we even got here. Divided, we sack groceries and repair toasters. United, we get back into tech pubs. All we have to do now is thrash out the details."

"Now wait just a minute," Grady protested. "I'm not saying this isn't a good idea, but what do any of us know about running our own company, much less starting one?"

Tony cleared his throat. "Grady's got a point."

"Joanna knows," Ben said. "She's already started one company and got it so successful and running so well there wasn't anything left for her to do. I've persuaded her to provide the business expertise for ours."

Grady eyed Joanna with good-natured lechery, and Ben belatedly remembered his reputation as a hit-and-run Romeo. "Great. And what are we going to do for her?"

"Not what you're probably hoping," Ben said, more sharply than he'd meant to. The other men grinned, and the women glanced first at Joanna, then at him. "I promised the children I'd tuck them in," he said abruptly. As he started up the stairs, he called over his shoulder, "Joanna will answer any questions you have about running a business. I'll be back down in a few minutes."

Damn! he thought. So much for being discreet, for waiting until he and Joanna had had time to get used to their new relationship before they acknowledged it to anyone else. *One wrong word,* he thought, *one wink or knowing leer, and she'll kill me.*

He lingered with the children longer

than he needed to, and when he went back downstairs, the men were, as Charlie had put it, "thrashing out details," and the women were not there at all.

"In the kitchen making coffee," one of the men answered his question, then plunged back into the debate. Ben relaxed. Maybe he hadn't blown it after all, either about the job shop, or with Joanna.

Ben closed the door behind the last of his departing guests and grinned triumphantly at Joanna. "I think the meeting was a big success. That was a great sales pitch I gave them, wasn't it?"

"Yes, it was," Joanna agreed. "You had them eating out of the palm of your hand."

"That was when I was passing out your chocolate chip cookies. But they did seem pretty positive about the idea. Actually, the moment of truth will be when Charlie and Pete get home and discuss it with their wives. If they didn't like it, we're sunk." He hesitated. "Uh, how did you like Ginger and Betty?"

"I liked them fine." She grinned and

added, "And you can relax. They're both in favor of the job shop. Ginger said she hasn't seen Charlie so excited since he retired, and Betty said she doesn't care if the job shop is a success or not, if it just stops Pete from moping around the house for a while. And she wants her kitchen table back."

"Her kitchen table?"

"That's where Pete works on those old TVs and toasters he's been repairing."

"Oh."

She began to move gracefully around the room, gathering up cups and saucers and crumpled paper napkins. He watched her, his pleasure in the part of the evening just passed blending with anticipation of the part still to come. "I should be helping you do that, shouldn't I?"

"Now that you mention it, yes. Why aren't you?"

"Because it's so much more fun to watch you." He took time to turn off all the lights except one on the end table in the corner, and followed her to the kitchen. "Now I know why I never entertained much."

She grinned. "No one to clean up for you?"

"No." He caught her as she turned away from the sink and put his arms around her. "Because it was always so lonely when everyone went home. I'd rattle around afterward, knowing something was missing, but not knowing what." He leaned forward to brush her lips with his. "Now I do."

She slipped her arms around his neck and returned the kiss with a casual affection that had also been missing. "But I have to go home, too."

"Not just yet. Not when we're finally alone and the lights are low in the living room, where there's a wonderful sofa and not a refrigerator in sight." He savored the light pressure of her breasts against his chest for a minute, then caught her by the hips and pulled the rest of her against him. He felt his body respond as they came together, and from the way her eyes widened, he knew she felt it too.

She pulled away from him—not far, but far enough that they were no longer touching. They didn't have to be, he thought. Just being close was enough.

"You have a short memory." He thought—hoped—she sounded a little breathless. "I told you—"

He kissed her again, deeply and persuasively this time, and brought his hand up to rub her breast gently. She returned the kiss and allowed him to tease her nipples into firmness. He undid the top buttons of her blouse and slipped his hand inside. "I know what you told me, but my friends have gone home, and my children are asleep, and—"

She pulled away, but he caught her hand in both of his. "And I'm going home, too."

"—and I'll walk you home afterward, so you can stay as late as you like, and we can—"

"No," she said firmly. "We *can't*. Not with the children asleep upstairs. Suppose one of them wakes and needs you, or comes downstairs and finds us on that wonderful sofa?"

His mind acknowledged that she was right, but his body refused to be convinced. "All right then," he said. "I'll go home with you. The children will be all right for a little while."

"No," she repeated. "What if Joey has another of his nightmares?"

He slipped one finger into the open neck of her blouse and traced a line down the warmth and softness of her cleavage. "How about a blanket on the grass out by the hedge? I could still hear Joey if he cried out, and I've always wanted to make love under a full moon."

"No!" She removed his hand again and kissed the palm, causing an instant reaction in quite another part of him. "Ben, I promise you, Monday, when they're in school . . ."

He groaned. "Monday is a lifetime away."

She grinned and patted his cheek. "It'll give you something to look forward to. Now I really am going home. Good night, Ben." She leaned forward to kiss him, lips only, no body contact, and started for the door.

He followed. "I'm going to walk you home, whether I get to stay or not."

"Thanks. I'd like that."

He lingered at her door for a good night kiss, using his lips and hands in a way that brought first a sigh and then a gasp from her and made her pull away from him abruptly.

He said hopefully, "The kids will be in Sunday school again tomorrow."

"And how long will you have between

the time you get back from taking them and the time you have to leave to go get them? Thirty minutes?"

"Well, forty, if I hurry."

Her laughter was warm and intimate and teasing. "Ben, if you have to hurry, just forget it."

He exclaimed indignantly, "That isn't what I . . ." But she'd already slipped inside and closed the door. He sighed and started for home, hoping desperately that Joey wouldn't have another stomachache and stay home from school Monday.

Joanna let herself in the back door and dropped her purse on the desk. The day had been a washout from beginning to end. Despite a morning dedicated to total self-indulgence—lingering over breakfast with the Sunday paper, a leisurely bubble bath, facial, manicure, pedicure—she'd been bored to death by noon. Clean and well-groomed, but bored to death.

The afternoon had been worse. The author reading from his latest book at an Atlanta bookstore had been as pompous and dull as his material. The waiter at the fashionable restaurant where she'd eaten a sinfully expensive but unimpressive dinner had parked her at a table in the corner, and then forgotten her while he catered to the male diners in the room.

Worst of all, after a month of casual dressing, she'd felt stiff and awkward in a dress she'd once loved, and might have today, she admitted to herself, if she'd had someone to admire her in it.

She poured herself a glass of milk in lieu of the dessert she'd skipped and stared out the window at the house beyond the hedge while she drank it. It hadn't helped that she'd spent the entire day wondering what Ben and the children were doing, and knowing that whatever it was, she'd have been welcome to do it with them. Or that she felt lonelier tonight than she had in months.

But that, she told herself hastily, wasn't because of Ben and the kids. It was because, if going out alone was the pits, coming home alone was even worse. She'd begun to suspect a long time ago that she and Robert didn't go out for the fun of going out, but for the pleasure of coming home.

"Oh, Robert," she whispered. "Do you remember how it used to be, when we'd spend the whole evening so aware of each other that we missed most of the play or concert, and were so eager for each other when we came home that you wouldn't even take time to close the garage door before you followed me inside."

She laughed softly, remembering. "Sometimes we made it up the stairs, and sometimes we made it *on* the stairs, but either way, coming home was always the best part of the evening. Oh, God, I miss you."

She blinked back the coming tears and went upstairs. She was half tempted to spend the night in the guest room, where the memories were not as thick, but knew she'd have trouble sleeping in the unaccustomed bed.

She had trouble enough sleeping in her own bed. She tossed and turned for what seemed like hours, and finally fell asleep to erotic dreams in which she wasn't sure if the man in her arms was Robert, or Ben.

She woke, finally, depressed, headachy, and farther from sleep than she had been when she first went to bed. She rolled over on her back and stared up at the ceiling while she debated the relative merits of a cup of warm milk and a cold shower. After a few minutes, she rejected them both in favor of a more direct remedy.

She reached under the covers, slid her hand slowly down her taut stomach muscles and under the hem of her short gown, to the aching emptiness there. It wasn't what she wanted, and it wasn't what she needed for the loneliness tormenting her, but it was what she had, and for now, it would have to do.

Nine

Despite her restless night, Joanna woke early Monday morning. Knowing there was no point in trying to go back to sleep, she went down to the kitchen for breakfast, then sat at her desk and filled another set of index cards with the mental notes she'd made at the meeting Saturday evening.

It seemed forever before the sounds of the school bus told her the children were gone and Ben was alone. She gathered up her notes, then took time to finish her coffee and rinse out the cup, so she wouldn't seem too eager, and headed for the hole in the hedge.

Ben apparently wasn't worried about looking eager. He'd already pushed his way through. They met in the middle of the yard and she had only a brief second to be grateful for the privacy the hedge gave. Then she was in his arms, with all the sensual, earthy, carnal sensations sweeping through her again as their bodies and then their lips came together.

When their lips finally separated and he began to unbutton her blouse, she asked, "You in a hurry or something?"

"Of course not. I waited all weekend, didn't I?"

She explored his broad chest, causing him to draw in his breath sharply as she found and massaged his nipples through the soft fabric of his shirt. "Good, because Friday you promised me a leisurely, romantic seduction, and I intend to hold you to it."

He unhooked her bra and slid his hands under it. "In that case, I have just one question."

She reached down and found his zipper tab. "What?"

His voice sounded half strangled as he asked, "Your place, or mine?"

She lowered the zipper tab a couple of inches. "Mine's closer, and my living room has a wonderful sofa in it, too."

He caught her hand and held it. "Your place it is, and you'd better stop that if you expect me to be able to walk."

She laughed softly. "Oh, I expect you to do a lot more than just walk."

Somehow, they managed to make it to the living room, where Joanna lowered the blinds and pulled the cushions from the back of the sofa to make more room.

Ben began his leisurely seduction by undressing her slowly, pausing to kiss and caress every step of the way. Her blouse and bra went first, then her skirt and half slip. Finally, he eased his hands inside her panties, sending shivers of anticipation through her as he slid them down to join the pile of clothing at her feet.

She kicked the clothing aside, stepped out of her shoes, and presented herself for his approval. She felt no inhibitions about showing herself to him. Her body might not be as young and firm as it had once been, but it had continued to stir and arouse Robert right up to the time he had become too ill to make love.

It seemed to affect Ben the same way. He drew in his breath and licked his lips lightly while his gaze swept over her. Her body responded, bringing the familiar, welcome warmth to her breasts and that other, secret, place that waited for him, but when he moved closer and would have touched her, she stopped him.

"My turn," she whispered. She unbuttoned his shirt and slid her fingers slowly down his chest until her fingers reached his belt buckle.

The buckle resisted her efforts. He unfastened it for her, then dropped his hands to his sides and watched, his lips curved in a lazy, contented smile, as she undressed him. He shivered once, and once he sucked his breath in sharply as she let her hands stray from their self-appointed task, and once he whispered urgently, "Joanna, *hurry!*"

When she'd finally removed everything but his unbuttoned shirt, she moved closer to him, so that their bodies touched—lightly, but everywhere it mattered—and slid the shirt off his shoulders. He groaned and reached for her, but she backed away. "Not yet," she told him. "I want to see you, too."

She studied him, as thoroughly and completely as he had studied her, amazed as always at how beautiful a man's body could be—especially when aroused. Although Ben was clearly self-conscious, either about being naked in her living room or because of the way she was looking at him, it didn't affect his very visible desire for her, and that, she thought, made him twice as beautiful. She felt her own body quicken in response.

And then there was no more time for love play and they tumbled onto the sofa. Ben knelt between her thighs and caressed her briefly, then slid eagerly into her as she arched up to meet him.

Once again, it was quick and hot and overwhelming. She was afraid for a minute that she'd teased Ben too long, weakened his control too much, but it didn't really matter. There'd be another time, perhaps even today, and if she didn't make it all the way to her destination this time, the trip alone would be worth the effort.

She surrendered to the exquisite pleasure of his body moving inside hers, then gasped as his cry of triumph unexpectedly triggered her own release. She pressed herself against him while the sweet agony swept through her, leaving her shaken and breathless.

Ben kissed her once, his lips firm and warm on hers, his tongue thrusting deep into her mouth, before he braced himself with a hand on either side of her and grinned down at her. "Lady, has anyone ever told you you have *two* areas of expertise?"

"So have you." She returned his grin, then glanced down between them, to the place where they were still delightfully joined together. "Not to mention some pretty sophisticated, state-of-the-art equipment."

His quick laughter jostled them apart. "Can't say I ever heard it called *that* before." He lay beside her and pulled her close. "I still haven't had enough of you, but it's going to be a little while until I can do anything about it."

"There's time," she murmured. "Meanwhile, I still have some expertise I haven't used yet." She began a leisurely, teasing exploration of his body, not from sexual need, but just for the sheer pleasure of touching him, pleasing him.

He lay still for a few minutes, welcoming her erotic love play, then began to return it, joining her in touching, stroking, exploring, until Joanna was sure she knew Ben's body as thoroughly as she knew her own, and he had made her aware of hers as she hadn't been aware of it since Robert had loved her this way.

Between deep, delicious kisses, Ben murmured, "You're just overflowing with expertise, aren't you? I wish I'd met you a long time ago. I wouldn't have wasted so much of my life rolling over and going to sleep." He trailed a line of kisses from her lips to her right breast, across to her left breast, and back up to her lips, then lifted his head and studied her soberly.

"Nothing like this has ever happened to me before. I didn't realize . . ." He paused and his voice was thick with regret when he continued, "No wonder Fran left me. With her, I was always too busy, or too tired, or just didn't understand her needs. I cheated her in more ways than I ever knew. I hope to God her second husband made it up to her for my failures."

"She remarried?"

He nodded. "A hot-blooded Italian. They live in Europe. I've never been quite sure what her husband does, but it seems to leave him plenty of free time for her."

"What about the women in your life since then?"

"First, there haven't been all that many.

Second, they didn't have a lot of time for me. Like me, they were mostly after something quick and uncomplicated, and afterwards, they were always in a hurry to leave and go back to their children, or work, or whatever."

She couldn't help teasing him a little. "Or husbands?"

He grinned and shook his head. "A boyfriend or two, maybe, but I never knowingly bedded another man's wife."

"No," she agreed softly, "I don't think you're the kind of man who would." She pulled his head down and kissed him, cutting off anything else he might have said.

Gradually, the intent of their love play shifted, became urgent and arousing. Her nipples grew hard and full and the warm, throbbing place between her thighs ached with the need to hold him inside her again. She arched her back and pulled his head down, wordlessly urging him to cool the heat in her breasts with his lips and tongue while she slid her fingers down to capture and arouse him, and found him already ripe and eager.

Their first urgency had been softened by their surrender to it. This time, they took each other slowly and deliberately, savoring and prolonging the pleasure they were giving each other. They surrendered finally to the need for completion, and were swept at last into an ecstasy of fulfillment that wasn't quick and hot and fierce, but deep and full and lingering, like the distant thunder of a summer storm.

Ben watched through the window as Becky, Joey, and Bernie energetically pursued two croquet balls, while Lovey and Tinkerbell watched from the security of the patio. "They seem to be making up their own rules as they go along," he told Joanna, "but they're obviously having fun. I do appreciate the use of your backyard."

She laughed and came to watch with him. "I can just imagine the set of ground rules you'd need if you tried to play in Bernie's bone yard."

"I have been told it's quite a challenge," he admitted.

"I'll bet. I wonder why Bernie hasn't expanded into my yard. Not enough bones?"

"No, he probably figures this is Tinkerbell's yard, and if he buries his bones here, she'll get them." He slipped his arm around her waist and pulled her closer, rejoicing in the knowledge that it wasn't just sex he enjoyed with this woman, but everything. "Want to go out and join them? I used to play a mean game of croquet."

"I'd love to, but a little later. First, we have some business things to discuss." She picked up a stack of colored index cards from her desk and handed them to him.

He glanced at them, then grinned at her. "Do you get a discount on these things for buying in quantity?"

"Laugh if you like, but those cards are tremendous time and work savers. And never mind how I buy them, just read what's on them. I've been busy this week."

He leered good-naturedly. "I know. I was there."

She patted his cheek. "I remember. But take a minute to look over the cards. These are things we need to talk about at the next meeting."

He sat down at her desk and thumbed through the cards. Once again, he was astonished at the things she'd written down in detail that he would never even have thought of. He whistled in disbelief. "Do we really have to go through all this just to write a few technical manuals?"

"No, to organize a business."

He studied the cards again. "By the time we get through here, Becky and Joey will be old enough to retire. I thought—I guess we all thought—all we had to do was go out and find some work to do, and do it."

She shook her head. "I'm afraid not. You have a lot of questions to answer and decisions to make first."

"Like what?"

She reached down to spread the cards out, her other hand resting lightly on his shoulder as if it belonged there. He liked the feeling. "First of all, do you want to form a partnership, or a corporation? What about start-up costs? Will you all ante up equally? Suppose someone can't afford his share? And how will you divvy up the income? Pay yourselves salaries? Share the profits equally? Pay each person according to the amount of work he's done? Does someone working at a higher-paying job get more than someone who works as many hours at something less profitable? And how will you decide who does what? You can't run a business if you're busy fighting over things like this."

"Joanna, we're friends, buddies. We'll be fair with each other."

"A business isn't like a croquet game." Her voice was gentle, but firm, "You can't make up the rules as you go along, the way the kids are doing. You have to decide this in advance, and put it in writing. Actually, you'll need a lawyer to put it in writing for you, and not just for the good of the business, but for the sake of those friendships."

He stared at the cards in dismay. "I still can't believe we need to do all this stuff just to write a few technical manuals."

"Ben, with all this 'stuff,' as you call it, you're a business, a company, a force to be reckoned with and listened to. Without it, you're still the same individuals who were retired or laid off. You have no standing, no clout, nothing to offer that you didn't have as individuals."

He sighed. "Okay. I believe you, but you may have a problem convincing the other guys, much less making them understand all this stuff."

"I've already thought about that. Tomorrow, I'm going in to the office and pick up copies of some of our early paperwork, so I can show them." She leaned over and kissed his cheek. "Your friends believe in you, Ben. They'll listen to you. You do the convincing, and I'll do the explaining."

He caught her hand and kissed the palm. "Business or pleasure," he said, "we make a great team, don't we?"

Joanna paused outside the familiar door and brushed her fingers lightly over the words on the frosted glass. She remembered the day Robert had painted them there—EFFICIENCY, INCORPORATED—and how excited he'd been that they finally had a home for their fledgling business.

The letters had faded and chipped over the years, and should have been repainted long ago, but they'd represented a small part of Robert and she hadn't wanted to lose them.

She reached for the doorknob and hesitated. She'd passed through that door so many times over the years, but now, she felt almost like an intruder. Or, she thought unexpectedly, like a parent trying to interfere in a grown child's life.

She shook off the feeling and opened the door. Trudy sat at her desk, reading a magazine. Joanna stepped inside and closed the door quietly. "You'd better put that magazine away and get busy before the boss comes in and catches you goofing off," she said.

Trudy dropped the magazine and jumped up. "Joanna! What are you doing here?" She circled the desk and caught Joanna in an enthusiastic hug.

"I'm watching you goof off," Joanna said as soon as she could get her breath back.

Trudy shook her head. "I'm on my lunch break. Why aren't you off on an ocean cruise, or a trip somewhere?"

The inner office door opened and Helen stuck her head out. "Yes, why aren't you, instead of here checking on us?"

Joanna grinned and held out her arms for another hug. "I'm not checking on you. I just came to hunt through the files for some papers I need. I seem to have become a little sidetracked on my way to the ocean. Would you believe I'm neck deep in getting another business started? That's why I need the papers—to prove to a roomful of men who know nothing about running a business that there's a little more to it than just putting an ad in the paper or hanging out a shingle."

"Men!" Trudy exclaimed. "I knew you'd find some out there, if you'd only look."

"There are wives out there, too," Joanna retorted, "and I didn't have to look for them. Anyway, that doesn't matter. The important thing is, I'm back in harness again, feeling useful and productive, and having the time of my life."

"You certainly look wonderful," Helen said. "Color in your cheeks, sparkle in your eyes, and I think you've gained back a little of the weight you lost while Robert was ill. Look, why don't you tell Trudy what you need and let her get it for you. There are a couple of things I need to talk to you about."

Obediently, Joanna handed Trudy her list and followed Helen into the office that, until a few weeks ago, had been hers. Helen would need a little while to settle in and make it totally her own, but already, it had begun to take on bits of her personality. Joanna searched her inner self for twinges of jealousy or regret, and was pleased when she found none.

She settled herself in the visitor's chair while Helen sat behind the desk, and was pleased again when it felt comfortable and right. "Don't tell me you're having problems already."

Helen shook her head. "Not at all. I just want to hear some of the details of your new life that probably aren't fit for Trudy's innocent little ears."

Joanna grinned. "First, Trudy's ears probably aren't as innocent as you may think, and second, if any details in my life are that X-rated, you're not likely to hear them."

Helen returned the grin. "Maybe not, but I can see for myself that you're taking my advice."

"What advice?"

"About your sexy neighbor."

"What makes you think—"

"Oh, come on, Joanna. The last time I saw you glowing like this was before Robert got sick, and you can't make me believe it's because you're starting a new business. You obviously have something else new and wonderful in your life, and I'd be willing to bet in your bed as well."

For half a second, Joanna considered denying it, but Helen would simply laugh in her face if she did, and besides, she didn't want to deny it. "You'd win your bet," she admitted. "Oh, Helen, he's fantastic. This last week has been . . ." She tried to find the right words and could only repeat, "Fantastic. It isn't just . . ." She felt her cheeks grow warm but finished gamely, "It isn't just the sex, as wild and wonderful as that is. It's having someone there, not being alone anymore. It's having a purpose in life, and a reason to get up in the morning."

"I'm so happy for you," Helen said softly. "I always felt that when Robert died, part of you died, too. I'm glad to find out it was only sleeping and that your prince has finally come to wake you. If anyone ever deserved to live happily ever after, it's you."

Joanna shivered suddenly, as if a cold draft had blown across her. "That's the one thing that bothers me. The 'happily ever after' part. I didn't think that far ahead. The truth is, I didn't really *think* at all.

"You had it right when you said we have the hots for each other. Boy, do we! And it was so easy to let him into my bed without realizing I was letting him into my life as well. And I didn't stop to wonder, then, how you get out of something like this afterwards, without regrets or hard feelings."

"Joanna, that's terrible! Your relationship with this man is hardly begun, and you're already wondering how to get out of it? Are you crazy?"

"Of course not. But I still have my own life to live, my own plans to carry out, just as Ben has his. What we have now is a pleasant interlude, but it isn't going to last forever. And wondering when it's going to end, and how, is scary as hell."

"And it should be!" Helen said sharply. "Joanna, you've been given a second chance to . . ." She broke off as Trudy knocked, then came in with a sheaf of papers in her hand.

"Here you are, Joanna. Copies of your original incorporation papers, payroll records, tax returns, all the stuff on your list. It wasn't all that hard to find. You must have organized those files yourself."

"I did," Joanna said, just as happy to change the subject. She stood up and took the papers from Trudy. "Thanks for collecting these for me. I wish I could stay and visit for a while, but I have a million other things to do today. The minute I get a little free time, though, we'll order up a big Chinese dinner and eat it here at the desk, the way we used to do."

She drove home, wondering how Ben would react when the time came for her to get out of their relationship and on with her own life, and then, unexpectedly, how she would react if he wanted out first.

Ben made use of Joanna's absence to get caught up on things he'd been neglecting. One of them was the stack of mail which Becky had brought in for him every day and put on his desk, but which he hadn't bothered to look at all week.

He paused beside the desk and riffled through the stack, throwing out the obvious junk mall, setting the light and telephone bills aside to pay in a day or two.

The last item was obviously and unexpectedly a personal letter. He felt a ripple of apprehension at the sight of the envelope with its foreign stamp and graceful, curved handwriting. He heard from Fran so seldom that he couldn't shake off the superstitious feeling he and Joanna had somehow conjured up the letter by talking about the writer.

He picked the envelope up and studied it, turning it over and over as if he expected to find some clue as to what was in it. He had no reason to expect bad news, but neither could he think of anything good Fran might have to tell him.

Finally, he inserted his finger under the flap and tore it open, took out the elegant, cream-colored stationary, and began to read.

Dear Ben,

I still can't quite believe that Joel and Jennie are gone. If I could get hold of that drunk driver, I'm sure I could strangle him with my bare hands. If only it had happened the other way, and he had died hor-

ribly while Joel and Jennie were unhurt. I know it's terribly wrong of me, but I hope with all my heart that someday, he'll be hurt as badly as he hurt us.

"You don't hope it half as much as I do," Ben said fervently.

It grieves me that Carlo and I were traveling when it happened, and you couldn't reach us immediately. It was horrible enough to learn of their deaths, but finding out too late to attend their funeral was almost more than I could stand. I'm so glad you were able to be there for the children. I'm sure Jennie's parents are lovely people, but they've always struck me as being a little—well, strange.

Ben grinned. *Amen to that!* It was the first time he and Fran had agreed about anything in years.

Ben, I don't know any way to say this except to come right out and say it. Carlo and I have discussed it at some length, and we think the children ought to come live with us.

Ben's hand clenched on the stationery and he sank into the desk chair. It didn't ease his shock any to realize that he should have expected this. Somehow, he hadn't. Give the children up to Fran and Carlo? His children? No way. For their sake as well as his. He smoothed out the wrinkles in the paper and read further.

I know you'd do your best for them, but I also know how difficult it is to raise children alone (how well I know!), and it would be even harder for you after your years of being foot-loose and fancy free.

He grinned without humor. Trust Fran to find a diplomatic way to remind him he'd been selfish and neglectful.

But Carlo and I are used to children, having raised three others of our own, and Joey and Becky would be a blessing, not a burden to us.

He shook his head and scowled at the letter. He didn't care how many other children they had raised. Becky and Joey were *his* blessing, Joel and Jennie had left a legal paper saying so, and as long as there was life in his body, he wasn't going to give them up to anyone.

I can see you now, shaking your head and scowling at even the hint that there's something you might not be able to do, but before you get all fired up about meeting this new challenge, please remember that the children are not a challenge; they're two small human beings who need comfort and reassurance and stability now, preferably in a home with two loving parents.

Please don't say no until you've had a chance to think about it, and to consider how much we can do for them. The chance to travel and to be educated in Europe would be such a wonderful experience for them, as it was for their father. Of course, you'll be able to see them whenever we get back to the States, or anytime you're able to visit us.

Ben remembered with tightly controlled anger and sorrow the loneliness of those years Joel had spent in Europe, years that had created an almost total break between them. When Joel had finally returned to the States, it was to attend college, and his efforts to spend time together were as minimal as Ben's had been when Joel was young. And maybe he wouldn't have grown any closer to Joel during those years apart, but dammit! Fran hadn't given him the chance. There was no way he was going to let her take Becky and Joey away as well.

There was only a little of the letter left. He forced himself to finish it.

> *I'll be looking forward to hearing from you. If we work together, we should be able to arrange things with a minimum of fuss and bother for everyone.*
>
> > *Affectionately,*
> > *Fran*

There wasn't going to be any fuss or bother, he thought, because the children were staying right where they were, where they belonged, with him.

He jerked open the desk drawer, found pen and paper, and began a blunt, angry reply. After a few sentences, he faltered to a stop and laid his pen aside. Fran had plenty of reason for everything she'd said, and he had no right to be angry with her. She only wanted what was best for the children, just as he did. With a sigh, he crumpled the letter and began again.

Dear Fran,

It was good to hear from you, after all these years. I only wish it could have been under happier circumstances.

The children are well, and adjusting to their loss better than I had expected them to, thanks in part to a wonderful neighbor—a widow who understands what the children are going through and has already helped us over some rough spots. Both the children and I have become quite fond of her.

As to the children coming to live with you, I appreciate your concern, but I feel that at this point it wouldn't be in their best interest. They've already had one upheaval in their lives, and I don't think they should have to face another one.

I'm sure Europe would be a wonderful experience for them, but I doubt that they're quite up to wonderful experiences just yet. What they need at the moment is to keep everything as normal as possible, as much like what they're used to, as possible.

I understand your concerns about my ability to care for them adequately, but you needn't worry. I'm not quite the self-centered workaholic you used to know. In fact, I've taken early retirement to make sure that Becky and Joey won't be in the least neglected, or take second place in my life. I assure you, they are no burdens, but as big a blessing to me as they would be to you.

In addition, Joel and Jennie not only asked me to be the children's guardian if it was ever necessary, but drew up legal papers to ensure it. I think we should honor their wishes.

He thought for a minute, then succumbed to the temptation to add a few more lines.

It goes without saying that anytime you and your husband are in the States, you're more than welcome to come visit the children. I know they'd love to see you.

He couldn't quite bring himself to profess affection, and closed instead with

"Sincerely." He had no idea how much postage to put on it, but plastered it with enough to send an elephant around the world three times, and put it out in the box before the mailman came.

He knew better than to hope he'd convinced Fran, but perhaps her husband had sense enough to realize there was no way in the world Ben was going to let anyone take his children from him.

Ten

Joanna and Holly Taylor, her next-door neighbor's seventeen-year-old daughter, arrived at Ben's together. Joanna watched with amusement as Ben blundered through his first encounter with a sitter. "The number where I'll be is by the telephone," he told her, "and a list of everything I could think of that you might need to know. Help yourself to anything you want from the refrigerator. After Joey goes to sleep, you'll have to go chase Bernie into his own bed, maybe more than once, but—"

"We'll be fine, Mr. Walker," she assured him. "Don't worry about us. If I need anything, I'll call, and if I need something in a hurry, I'll call Mom."

"Well then, I guess we'll be going." He paused, then added, "Uh, Joey sometimes has nightmares, and—"

"So does my little brother. I can handle

it. You and Mrs. Blake just go on and have a good time."

Ben flushed faintly and explained, "It's a business meeting. We aren't planning to have a good time. Oh, I mean . . ." The flush deepened as Holly and Joanna fought back smiles.

Becky came to his rescue. "Grandpa, you're going to be late for your meeting. We'll be okay. We've been with sitters before, you know. And you told Holly all about us the day we bought the croquet set. Remember?"

Holly laid her hand on Becky's shoulder and smiled at her. "And we do plan to have a good time, don't we?"

Joanna caught Ben by the arm and tugged gently. "Come on, Ben, or I'll go by myself."

She let him help her into the car, waited until he slid in under the wheel, and told him, "I guess we forgot to cover sitters in our homemaking lessons. Ben, I know you feel uneasy about leaving the kids for the first time, but Holly is an intelligent, level-headed girl. The kids will be all right, and perhaps being in someone else's care for a little while will be good for them."

He reached over to squeeze her hand gently. "I know, I know." He backed out of his drive and pulled into the street before he added, "But I worry about them. Sometimes I think they're adjusting to the loss of Joel and Jennie, and other times, I worry that they're just keeping it all inside. And they haven't made any friends in the neighborhood yet. The school bus comes in the afternoon, the other kids pile out and run off chattering and playing, and my children come home. If it weren't for Bernie and Lovey—and you—I don't know what they'd do."

The sober tone of his voice and the tense line of his jaw told her he was more uptight than she'd realized. She tried to think of some way to ease his worry—and her own. "Perhaps they aren't ready to make friends yet, Ben, and the other children sense this. When they heal a little more, and are ready to try trusting the world again, they'll reach out and I'm sure the others will respond."

"You're probably right. And maybe Holly can help. They seemed to respond to her, didn't they?" He glanced at her and grinned. "That's something else you can do for me, if you will."

"What?"

"Go places with me, so I have an excuse to leave them with Holly more often."

She gave thanks that it was a comment, not a question, and didn't need an answer. She had no idea what it would feel like to come home with Ben and say good night at the door because he had to go take the sitter home, and she wasn't sure she was ready to find out.

Ben drove in silence for a few minutes, then told her, "I'm probably supersensitive just now anyway. The truth is, I got a letter from Fran yesterday."

Fran? Oh. The ex-wife. She kept her voice casual as she asked, "Is anything wrong?"

"That depends on your point of view, I guess. She thinks the children should go live with her and her husband, since she knows how hard it is to raise children alone, and it will be so much harder for me after my years of being 'foot-loose and fancy free.' "

His tone of voice told her he was quoting directly from the letter. She fought down an instinctive stab of panic and managed to say, "Oh, Ben. I'm sorry. Is there any chance—I mean, do you think . . ."

"Oh, she isn't going to get them," he assured her. "Joel and Jennie wanted me to have them, and unless I really mess up, no court is going to take them from me so she can haul them off to Europe. But she might try, and I don't think the children need to be dragged through that kind of hassle just now."

"Neither do I," she agreed.

They drove in silence for a few minutes, then he added, "I was angry at first, but then I realized she only wants what's best for the children, just as I do. And remembering the kind of father I was to Joel, I can see her point."

"Surely you can explain to her that you aren't the man she remembers, that the children come first in your life now."

"I did. I sent off an answer explaining why I didn't think handing the kids over to her was a good idea." He glanced at Joanna and grinned. "Don't worry. I was tactful and polite. That alone should tell her I've changed. Of course, I don't know if she'll take my word for it or not. Joanna, if she doesn't believe me, or if she actually shows up and tries to take the children, I wondered if you . . . if you . . ."

"Oh, Ben! Of course. I'll be glad to put in a good word for you. In fact, I'll give you such a great testimonial you won't recognize yourself. I know how lucky those children are to belong to you, and I'll do everything I can to make sure she knows it too."

"Bless you." His voice was husky, and he cleared his throat. "Actually, I was sort of hoping . . . maybe you might pretend we're . . . engaged, or something . . . so Fran will think I can also give the children a home with '*two* loving parents.' "

Once again, she could hear the quotation marks around the words. She sat in stunned silence, knowing she couldn't do as he asked, but not knowing how to tell him so.

Finally, she drew a deep breath and said, "I don't think that would be such a good idea, Ben. it would be hard to carry off convincingly. The children would likely give us away if they knew we were lying, and be terribly upset if they thought we meant it. And with as little experience as I have with children, I'm not sure being engaged to me would be a point in your favor anyway. I'll speak up in your defense, but that's all, absolutely all, I'm qualified to do."

He braked the car gently and turned into a broad driveway already filled with cars. As he came to a stop and turned off the ignition, he slipped his arm around her and pulled her toward him for a warm, lingering kiss. "Not *absolutely* all," he corrected.

She made him wait while she found a mirror and checked her lipstick for smears, scrubbed his mouth briefly with a tissue, then walked with him across the lawn and up the porch steps.

Betty Donovan met them at the door and ushered them into a room already filled with a dozen or so people engrossed in animated conversation. Joanna nudged Ben and murmured, "Well, you may not be planning to have a good time, but it looks like everyone else is."

"You say one word about that," he warned her, "and I'll buy Bernie so many bones he'll *have* to bury them in your yard."

Pete waved at them from across the room. "Ben, I think you already know everyone. Joanna, the new faces belong to Jim and Sandy Bagwell, Carl and Margaret Dennison, Jake and Esther Gold. Guys, this is Joanna Blake, the lady with the business expertise."

Joanna acknowledged their greetings with a smile and a nod, feeling a little out of place as she realized that the others all knew each other, and she was the only newcomer to the group.

She gripped the handle of her briefcase more tightly, grateful for the carefully prepared presentation inside to remind her that she wasn't here socially, but in the more comfortable and familiar role of planning consultant.

"Glad to see you all," Ben said. "Jim, I didn't know you were retired."

"He's not," Sandy Bagwell answered for her husband, "but he will be soon, and I don't intend to have him mooning around the house telling me every two minutes that he has nothing to do. He's bad enough on weekends. I don't think I could take it seven days a week."

"Gee, thanks," Jim said.

Charlie Ross clapped him on the shoulder. "Meanwhile, Jim has brought us a hot lead on what may be our first job. We've already agreed that since Ben is the most recently retired and has had the most experience with writing proposals, he should be the one to at least lay the groundwork here."

Ben's face lit up and he seemed to grow inches taller and years younger. "Not to mention that this whole thing was my idea. I'll be glad to—"

"Hold on a minute," Pete Donovan interrupted. "Begging your pardon, Ben, but we've got a long way to go before we're ready to start writing proposals. Sure, we all agree you're the expert on proposals, but what about the rest of us? What do we do?"

"We write," someone said.

"Aren't we getting a little ahead of ourselves?" Jake Gold asked. "I don't care how great a proposal Ben writes, nobody is going to take us seriously unless we can prove that we know what we're doing. We have to show some kind of work experience, job histories, expertise."

"So we'll all update our résumés," Tony Vincent said.

Grady Wilson added pensively, "And

we'd better settle, right at the start, who makes the decisions."

"You mean, who's going to be boss," Charlie Ross put in.

Carl Dennison asked plaintively, "Why do we have to go through all this fuss and bother? Why can't we just see if we can get the damned job and decide all this stuff then?"

"I'm afraid it isn't that simple," Joanna said, and realized a moment later that no one had heard her. The discussion had degenerated into a general free-for-all with everyone talking at once and no one listening.

She suddenly lost her sense of being a stranger in a strange land. This was something she knew how to handle. She carried her briefcase to the oversized desk on one side of the room, set it down with a thump, and turned to face the arguing men and the amused, irritated, or long-suffering wives.

She raised her voice. "Hold on a minute. Hold on! Let's have a little order here." From the corner of her eye, she saw one of the women—Margaret Dennison, she thought—take a pencil and steno pad from her purse and prepare to take notes.

Bright lady, she thought. *She knows when the good stuff is about to begin.*

As the rumble of male voices died away, she snapped her briefcase open and took out a sheaf of papers. "It's neither as simple or as complicated as you're trying to make it," she told them. "For one thing, you have to realize that there's no way we're going to find all the answers tonight, but if we approach it systematically, we'll get a lot more of the questions asked." She waited until they were all quiet and attentive. "Now here are some of the things we need to consider."

She asked them, briefly but completely, the same questions she'd asked Ben. They looked as dubious and impatient as he had, but they listened to her. She had to give them credit for that. They squirmed impatiently now and again, they frowned and shook their heads a lot, and several times they looked as if they wanted to protest, but they listened.

"That's about it," she said finally. "Any questions?"

The question they all seemed to have was the one Ben had asked. "Do we really have to go through all this just to write a few technical manuals?"

She gave them the answer she'd given him. "No. To start a business. These points may not seem important now, but if you neglect them, they can cause you trouble later."

They were silent briefly, then Esther Gold asked her, "Did you and your husband do all these things when you were setting up your business?"

Bless you! Joanna thought. Aloud, she said, "No, we didn't, but later, we often wished we had."

Ginger Ross spoke for the first time. "That's good enough for me. I really think, if you're going to all the trouble to set up this business, you ought to do it right."

"If you really believe in it," Esther added, "you'll *want* to do it right."

The men began to speak again, one at a time, at first, and then simultaneously, one voice cutting across another as they debated, discussed, and disputed.

Betty Donovan listened as the masculine voices became louder and more combative. "Let's go make coffee and slice the cake," she murmured to the woman nearest her.

"We may need it to quiet them back down."

As they disappeared into the kitchen, the other women followed them. Joanna hesitated, not certain whether the invitation included her or not. Maybe she was expected to stay here and argue with the men. After all, the other women all seemed to know each other, while she was a stranger.

She told herself she was being silly. Whether she'd been specifically invited or not, she certainly hadn't been excluded, and although her experience with groups like this was limited, she remembered that, normally, the sexes separated at some point in the proceedings, with the women usually ending up in the kitchen.

A particularly vehement male voice made up her mind for her. *If you can't stand the heat,* she thought, *get out of the living room.* She followed the other women into the kitchen.

They didn't bother to welcome her, but accepted her presence so casually that she knew she'd been right. This was where she belonged.

She was a little surprised to find that the others weren't indulging in "girl talk," or discussing the three "C's"—cooking, cleaning, and children. They were carrying on their own version of the discussion she'd just left behind.

"Crazy idea or not, I think they can make a go of it," Esther Gold was saying. "Joanna, what do you think?"

Joanna nodded. "They obviously have the skills and expertise they need. If the work is there to be done, and if they'll take the time and effort to set this company up right instead of going off half-cocked, and don't bite off more than they can chew, then yes, I think they can make a go of it."

Ginny Ross looked up from the cake she was slicing. "I'm sure Joanna is right. Our men are really good at what they do—or used to do. I'll admit, I thought the whole thing was just a pipe dream at first because, let's face it, ladies, our men are *not* very good at being practical. But Joanna sure is. She not only knows what needs to be done, but did you notice? She knows how to make them shut up and listen."

"Maybe she can teach us," Margaret Dennison said.

"Don't count on it," Joanna advised. "I

was never able to make my own husband shut up and listen."

Sandy Bagwell loaded a tray with paper plates, napkins, and plastic forks. "Well, I for one sure hope they make it work. Jim keeps talking about how he wants me to retire when he does, and even if I am getting a little tired of adding columns of figures and trying to make them balance, it sure beats staying at home picking up his dirty socks."

"While he moons around the house telling you every two minutes that he has nothing to do," Ginny and Betty chorused. It was obviously an old joke.

"Isn't that the truth!" Esther said. "I always looked forward to Jake's retirement. I thought we'd finally have time to do things together, but Jake never learned how to just relax and have fun. He races through everything as if he still had a deadline to meet and a penalty to pay if he didn't, and that's no fun for me."

"I have mixed feelings," Margaret Dennison admitted. "Carl begged me to retire when he did, so he wouldn't have to sit at home alone. Now, it looks as if I'm the one who's going to be at home alone, and

I don't mind telling you, I don't look forward to it."

Betty Donovan finished measuring coffee and water into the coffeemaker and plugged it in. "Believe me, it's better than sitting at home listening to Pete gripe because he has nothing to do but repair toasters. Whether they make this thing work or not, I'll be delirious with joy if it just gives him something to keep him busy and interested for a little while."

"Don't get me wrong," Margaret said hastily. "I certainly don't begrudge Carl this chance to feel needed and useful again. I just wish I had something new and exciting to look forward to while Carl is out conquering new frontiers."

Betty sighed. "I think we all feel that way. Now that the kids are grown, and Pete doesn't need me to pack his lunch and get him off to work every morning, I rattle around the house as badly as he does."

She glanced at the kitchen door, toward the sound of men's voices from the living room at the other end of the hall. "Listen to them. They're busy discussing their futures—*our* futures—and we're in here making coffee and slicing cake."

Esther shrugged. "They're all having midlife crises."

Ginny sliced through the last piece of cake and dropped the knife on the table with a clatter. "Well, damn it, so are we!"

"Midlife crisis," Joanna repeated thoughtfully. "You know, I thought my life was falling apart because I lost my husband three years ago, but maybe I'd have gone through these bad times anyway."

"Why not?" Sandy asked. "The rest of us are. We just didn't realize it until now."

"Right," Margaret exclaimed. "We all thought our midlife crisis was menopause, or maybe the empty nest. But it isn't. It's the time when we—just like the men—take a look at what we've accomplished and where we are, and it doesn't matter if we're satisfied with it or not, we still have the rest of our lives to worry about."

Ginny drew a deep, shaky breath. "I don't want to spend the rest of my life sitting in my rocker in some corner telling my grandchildren what it was like in 'the good old days.'"

"Or doing the equivalent of fixing toasters," Betty added.

"Me, either," Sandy said. "God, Joanna, you're lucky. You and the men. They're getting ready to—what did you call it, Margaret?—conquer new frontiers, and you're right there in the middle of it."

"Conquering new frontiers isn't exclusively for men," Joanna said. "It's for anyone who has the gumption to decide what he—or she—wants, and go after it."

"I suppose you mean go looking for another job," Margaret said, "but it isn't that easy getting back into the job market once you're out of it."

Esther laughed, a brittle, humorless sound. "Particularly if you're fifty-plus and haven't worked since before you were married."

"That's right," Ginny agreed. "We're up against the same age barrier the men are."

Joanna felt the skin on the back of her neck tingle as she understood suddenly how Ben had felt on that marvelous morning in his kitchen. She paused a minute, testing the feeling, and found it right and good. "The men are finding a way around the barrier," she said softly. "We can, too."

They stared at her in silence, and she

watched as understanding and then incredulity dawned on one face after another.

"You mean, start our own company, too?"

"Doing what?"

"We wouldn't know how."

"We have no job skills, nothing to offer."

She waited for the clamor to die away. "You have plenty of skills."

"Well, Margaret and Sandy do, of course, but the rest of us . . ."

"All of you," she said firmly. "The kind of skills that can't be taught, usually can't be bought, and are learned only through years of living, years of taking care of homes and families."

"You mean, *homemaking?*" Esther's normally low-pitched voice rose to a squeak on the last syllable.

"Well, you have those, all right, but I'm talking about organizational ability, relationship skills, being able to plan and juggle and accomplish a dozen things at one time, and qualities like honesty, integrity, loyalty. Ladies, we fifty-plus women, homemakers or working women, married, single, widowed, or divorced, are the most skilled and talented people on the face of this earth, and don't you forget it!"

She came to an abrupt halt, partly because she was out of breath, and partly because she was embarrassed by her own vehemence. "Sorry," she said. "I didn't mean to preach a sermon."

"But it was such a wonderful sermon," Betty said. "And you're right. We can be anything we want to be, do anything we want to do."

"Except form our own business," Esther said mournfully. "I don't know about the rest of you, but I wouldn't have the slightest idea where to even start."

Joanna laughed and picked up Margaret's steno pad from the table where she'd laid it. "You start right here. With this, you know everything about it the men know."

They stared at each other, sharing thoughts with the mind-reading skill of old friends, while Joanna wondered what it must be like to be part of a group like this.

They apparently reached a decision, and all of them turned simultaneously to stare at her.

"Will you help us? The way you're helping the men?" It was Ginny who spoke, but she clearly spoke for the group.

Pete stuck his head through the kitchen door. "Hey, what's the holdup in here? You all waiting for the coffee beans to finish growing?"

"We'll be there in a minute," Joanna told him. She looked back at the women, still watching her expectantly. "Next week," she said. "We'll meet at my place while the men meet at Ben's. Wear comfortable clothes, and bring pencil and paper."

Ben watched Joanna covertly as they drove home, wondering if the meeting had made as big a difference in her as it had in him.

He'd known most of the people they'd been with tonight for years, worked with the men on a dozen different jobs in this city and in others, been part of their social functions and get-togethers time after time, but tonight had been different from those other times.

Joanna had made the difference.

For the first time, he hadn't been that anomaly, the unattached male. Oh, he had taken women with him to their get-togethers before, but they'd been temporary, transient, and everyone had known it. Joanna wasn't. He had a feeling everybody knew that, too—except, possibly, Joanna. He glanced at her and smiled. No problem. She'd realize it, too, soon enough.

She returned his smile. "Penny for your thoughts."

He patted her knee. "I was thinking what a good meeting it was, and how they hung on your every word. We got a lot done, I think."

"We did. Maybe more than you realize."

"What do you mean?"

She turned to look at him, her face half in shadow, half limned by the lights from the dash. "I got to talking with some of the women in the kitchen. They aren't very happy at the prospect of sitting at home doing nothing while their men are off working again."

"Damn. I was afraid some of them might feel like that, but I was hoping—"

"Ben, I didn't say they weren't happy about their men working again. I said they weren't happy at the prospect of being left behind. Only Sandy Bagwell is working now, and she's about as bored with it as I was. Margaret Dennison retired when her husband did. The others were full-time homemakers. They stuck with it until their kids were grown, but now they feel the same way about it you do. No excitement, no challenge, just monotony."

"I see. It makes sense, I suppose. It just never occurred to me that women would feel that way." He grinned wryly. "Women with husbands, anyway. I always thought most women wanted to be full-time home-makers and women who had to work could hardly wait to retire."

"Not likely! I mean, a lot of women are happy and contented as homemakers, and I say more power to them. The world would be a sad place without them. But just as many do it for the same reason you do. They're needed. Either way, life can become pretty empty when the job is finished."

"I guess so." He took advantage of a straight stretch of road and no oncoming traffic to study her briefly. "Why do I get the idea you aren't just making idle conversation?"

"Probably because you're intelligent, clever, understanding—"

"Flattery will get you almost anywhere," he interrupted cheerfully, "but not while I'm driving. Why don't you just get to the part where I'm so understanding, and tell me what it is I'm going to be understanding about."

She leaned back against the seat and watched the road ahead. "I'm going to help the women find some new frontiers of their own to conquer."

After a brief moment of dismay, he wondered irritably why he hadn't seen it coming. He should have realized that Joanna wasn't the only woman bored with life, looking for something to take the place of the house, the kids, the job, or whatever. But . . .

"New frontiers to conquer? You mean jobs? Working? At what?" She frowned and he realized, too late, that he'd said the wrong thing. He hurried to correct his blunder. "No, don't get angry. I'm not speaking as a male chauvinist now. I mean, we men know we have a skill we can sell once we get past the age barrier. What do the women have that's comparable? Or even marketable?"

He wasn't sure, but he thought her voice held a faint note of annoyance. "A lot more than you—or they—realize. Ben, you'd be surprised at the number of skills a woman develops during years of caring for a home and family."

"No, I wouldn't. Not after the last couple of weeks, anyway, but it never occurred to me that anyone would pay me to do them." He thought back over the dull, boring, and often physically exhausting homemaking chores he'd learned and added, "Or that there was enough money in the world to make me do them for pay."

"Oh, Ben, I'm not talking about housework. Anybody can do housework. But managing a home and family, not to mention a marriage, is at least as difficult as managing a successful company, and calls for many of the same skills and abilities."

"I don't mean to be a wet blanket," he persisted, "but what makes you think you can compete with the people who are already running successful companies?"

"What makes you think you can compete with the people who are already writing technical manuals?"

This time, he was sure that she was annoyed. It was time to back off. Besides, it occurred to him belatedly that he had zeroed in on the lesser implication and ignored the larger one. "Won't it take a big chunk of your time?"

"Don't worry, I'm not abandoning you and the job shop, but that won't take all my time."

"I'm not worrying about the job shop," he admitted. "I was sort of planning to take the rest of your time myself."

"Well, don't worry about that either." She reached over and squeezed his knee, sending tingles of anticipation to places that didn't need to tingle while he was driving. "I intend to keep plenty of time free for you."

He should have felt better, but he had firsthand knowledge of what could happen to a relationship when one person became obsessed with something else. He didn't want it happening to them. He didn't want to fight about it either. Time to change the subject.

He slipped his hand under the hem of

her skirt and stroked the inside of her thigh in a way that he hoped would start her tingling, too. "It's still early and I have a babysitter, so let's take you home and use some of that free time right now."

"And make the neighbors wonder why your car is parked in my drive for so long?" He couldn't be sure, in the dim light, but he thought she was smiling. "You wouldn't want them to think we're having a good time, would you?"

"I suppose not," he said glumly, then brightened. "I can take you home, park around the corner, and walk back."

"Holly's mother will be listening for your car. She'll know what time you brought me home and what time you drove away. I'm sure you don't want her wondering why you brought me home, then presumably went home yourself, but Holly hasn't come home yet."

He groaned. "You think of everything, don't you? I don't suppose you'd consider letting me park around the corner and both of us walk back?"

"No, I wouldn't. What I want you to do is park in your own garage so I can go in and see how the children made out with

Holly. Then I'll walk her home so you won't have to leave the children alone."

"That way, I won't even have time for a proper good night kiss," he complained.

She snickered. "Oh, yes, you will. You just won't have time for an *im*proper kiss."

Eleven

Over Sunday morning breakfast, Joanna forced herself to face what she had decided must be a midlife crisis. She felt slightly astonished that she was having one. She'd made it through menopause without any problems, and her nest had always been empty, so she hadn't had to cope with that. And she had, to her great surprise, survived Robert's death. After all that, if she'd thought about it at all, she'd have assumed she wasn't going to have any more crises.

If it hadn't been for Margaret's comment last night, she wouldn't have realized she was having one now.

Midlife crisis, Margaret had said, was when you took a look at what you'd accomplished and where you were, and it didn't matter whether you were satisfied with it or not, because you still had the rest of your life to worry about.

Joanna had already looked at the last three unsatisfying, unproductive, empty years. Now, she wandered through the house, because her desk seemed too confining for a job of this scope, and sent her memory burrowing through the earlier years.

She'd had a happy childhood, loving parents, a better education than many women of her generation, a good marriage, a satisfying career, and a business that still produced a comfortable income.

She had a few regrets, a few things she'd done and wished she hadn't, and some she hadn't and wished she had, but on the whole, she was satisfied with her life. There was very little in it that she regretted, a great deal that she was pleased with or proud of.

The future she and Robert had planned so carefully should be equally satisfying, with dozens, perhaps hundreds, of things to do and enjoy: She could travel—go on tours, safaris, expeditions, or just explore on her own. She could rest and relax on an ocean voyage, at a warm, sunny beach resort, or at a bed-and-breakfast in some cool mountain area. If she chose to stay at home, she could enjoy or even become involved in a variety of entertainments and cultural events in nearby Atlanta.

So, where was the crisis? And why did she have this feeling that something was missing, that there was a gap of some kind between the past and the future, so that they didn't quite meet in the here and now?

She certainly didn't want to resume her old life. That had already reached a dead end. But neither was she ready to step into the future, no matter how attractive it might seem.

There *was* a gap, she thought suddenly, and it was made up of all the things she hadn't done yet but wanted to, things which weren't included in that preplanned future. If she wanted to do them at all, she had to do them now, in the present.

If? She shook her head. There was no "if" about it. If she didn't do them, she'd regret it for the rest of her life.

Her wandering had brought her back to the kitchen. She stared down at Robert's picture and made up her mind with uncharacteristic abruptness. "Trips and tours and good times are for when your life is settled and you're finished with everything else you want to do, but I'm not finished yet. Besides, I'm having a midlife crisis, and I want to see how it turns out."

She brushed her fingers lightly over the picture. "You don't mind, do you, if I put our plans on hold for a little while? Ben is right, you know. I'm not ready to put myself out to pasture just yet. Remember, you were ten years older than I was. You'd already taken stock of your life, and were ready to move into the future. And I would have gone with you, willingly and joyfully, as I always did. But I'm not ready to do it by myself. There are these other things I want to do first, and then, I'll update those plans we made and start moving into the future we planned together, just as I promised."

She pulled out her desk chair and sat down, but instead of reaching for pen and paper, she folded her hands on the desk and stared out the window, trying to decide what it was, exactly, that she wasn't finished with. What were the things she'd missed in her life, and wanted now, before she moved into the future?

The first one was easy. She wanted to be

herself, to be in charge of herself and her life. Looking back, she realized she never had been. Her life had always been managed by someone else, first by her parents and then—Helen had been right—by Robert, but never by her. For the most part, she hadn't minded, but now, suddenly and fiercely, she did. She'd been her parents' child, her husband's wife, but never just herself, never just Joanna. It was time she tried it. She might like it, might like "just Joanna."

She wanted to help make Ben's job shop successful. It might be the last chance she ever had to face this kind of challenge, or to bask in the kind of respect and admiration she'd felt at the meeting last night—not to mention the look of pride and pleasure on Ben's face when his friends "hung on her every word."

She wanted even more to help Margaret and Esther and the other women make a success of their venture. Older women had been ignored and undervalued long enough. They, even more than men, needed to know they were still useful, still needed. She wanted them to prove to the world and to themselves that they really were the most skilled and capable people on the face of the earth. Maybe she even needed to know that she was, too.

The next thing was harder to put into words. She wanted . . . The word came to her slowly and surprisingly. She wanted friends, people who knew more about each other than the visible, superficial things, people who had interests in common, who did things together, accepted each other, shared with each other. She wanted to be part of something that was bigger than just two people.

She hadn't felt this need when Robert was alive, but now she did. Maybe it was because she was alone now, or maybe because, through sheer luck—and Ben's help—she'd stumbled onto the kind of people she wanted as her friends. Would they feel the same way about her? Accept her into the group? She thought about the night before and had the comforting feeling that they already had.

The last thing was easy, too. Even more than she wanted friends, she wanted to know what it might have been like if she and Robert had had children, had been a family. She wanted a chance to find out what children were like, what it might have felt like to be a mother, and then a grandmother. She could never be the surrogate grandmother Ben wanted for Becky and Joey, but she could at least be their friend and get to know them better. She could pretend, as Becky had done.

These were the things she wanted, the things that had been missing from her life, and through some kind of miracle she surely didn't deserve, these were the things she had. She could satisfy her hunger for them, and then move on.

But what about Ben? she thought abruptly. Could she satisfy her hunger for him so easily? Be as willing to leave him behind when it was time to move on?

She drew a deep breath and reminded herself that there were other reasons why Ben was only a temporary part of her life, so it didn't matter anyway. She wasn't going to have a choice. The day would come, inevitably, when he would move into her past and she would move into her future, but until then—

She jumped up and ran to the door at the sound of Bernie's cheerful *"Woof!"*

Her stipulation to Ben that her weekends were her own seemed silly now. She had no intention of spending another horrible Sunday like the last one when she could join Ben and the kids for hot dogs and french fries, and beat Ben at croquet afterward.

Ben turned out the light in Becky's room, pulled her door part way shut, and followed Joanna down the hallway and stairs. "You play a mean game of croquet, lady. I'll bet they sleep well tonight." At the foot of the stairs, he stopped and turned her to face him. "This has been the best day they've had—*we've* had—since . . . since they came to live with me. I don't know how to thank you properly, but if you ever want me to walk barefoot over red-hot coals . . ."

"No thanks necessary. It was a good day for me, too, hot dogs and all."

He put his arm around her and they walked together into the kitchen. "What was wrong with the hot dogs? I thought they were the best part of the day."

"Yeah, sure they were."

He laughed. "Okay, so you're not the

hot dog lover the rest of us are. But how would you feel about a cup of coffee and another piece of that cake before you go?"

She hooked her thumb into the waistband of her slacks and tugged. "Coffee, yes, but I'd better pass on the cake." She didn't bustle around trying to help, but sat quietly at the table and watched while he measured the water and coffee into the pot and plugged it in.

It was one of her better qualities, he thought, that she knew when to take the lead, and when to relax and let him be in charge. He felt a quick stirring in his loins as he realized she had the same talent in bed.

He squelched the thought, before it got out of hand, and sat at the table opposite her. "You know, when Joel and Jennie died, and I quit work to take care of the children, I thought my whole life had turned upside down."

"Well, hadn't it?"

He shook his head. "No, I realize now it had only tipped a little. It wasn't until I met you that it turned upside down. Not to mention topsy-turvy, front-to-back, and inside out. If anyone had ever told me it was possible to cram as much into four weeks as we have and have as much fun doing it, I'd have said he was crazy."

"It has been fun," Joanna admitted, "in a wild sort of way. Before I met you and the children, I felt as if my whole life had just stopped moving."

"And now?"

"I feel as if I'm on an out-of-control merry-go-round."

He grinned. "Hanging on for dear life?"

She nodded. "And getting dizzier by the second."

"Not wanting to stop and get off, are you?"

"No. Not yet, anyway." She hesitated, then added, "But I do want to talk to you about something."

He felt a flicker of unease. "Sounds serious."

"It's about the children," she said.

"Oh-oh. I'm not sure I like the sound of that. Is there a problem?"

"I'm not sure." She drew her thumbnail lightly along the wood grain pattern of the table, then looked back up at him. "There may be one developing. Holly and I had a chance to talk when I walked her home last night." She grinned wryly. "Holly probably has more experience with children than both of us put together."

"And she thinks there's a problem?"

Joanna nodded. "She thinks Becky and Joey are playing together too much."

She waved him to silence as he started to protest. "No, she didn't mean that, exactly. What she said was that they both need to make other friends, be less dependent on each other. She thinks Becky is both too bossy and too protective, and Joey is too submissive. You haven't noticed it because you're too close to them, and I haven't because I don't have that much experience with children, but I watched them today, as much as I could, and she's right."

He drew a deep breath and let it out in a gusty, cheek-puffing sigh. "Oh, I think I've noticed. I just didn't know what to do about it. I still don't. Sure, they need other friends and playmates, but I can't go out and make friends for them. I thought they'd meet kids at school and on the bus, but the only one who's taken any notice of them so far was teasing Joey, and Becky decked him."

Joanna stared at him for a minute, eyes wide, then burst into laughter. "You're kidding."

He shook his head. "Nope. The kid's father was pretty steamed about it, too, especially when he found out it was a girl who had done it."

"Good for her."

Behind him, the coffeemaker stopped making little clucking sounds, and he got up to pour them each a cup. "That's what I said, but maybe I was wrong. Damn it, Joanna, I know you and Holly are right, but like I say, I don't know what to do about it."

"Holly had a suggestion. Her little brother is only a couple of months younger than Joey, and would be in the first grade with him if his birthday had been a little earlier. He missed the cutoff date by less than a week. He's bright, and smart, and almost as much in need of playmates as Joey is."

"Sounds good," Ben agreed. He ran his fingers through his hair, a nervous gesture he'd been trying for years to break, and had the distinct feeling that his hair had become noticeably thinner since the last time he'd done it. "But would it be fair to Becky? If Joey has a friend, and she doesn't . . . I can't help remembering the way she reacted when I told Joey that Bernie could sleep in his room. Uh, I don't suppose Holly has a little sister, too?"

Joanna shook her head. "No, but her best friend does. The two girls study together, and when they get stuck taking care of the younger ones, they usually do that together, too. So Holly wondered if the next time she sits with Joey and Becky, she could bring the whole mob and let the kids play together."

He thought about it. It sounded good, but . . . "What do you think?" he asked.

"I think it's a good idea. I don't see how it can do any harm, and if it doesn't work out, they don't have to do it again."

He grinned and lifted her hand to his lips. "And if it does, we'll just have to make the sacrifice and go out as often as we can."

She raised one eyebrow. "We?"

He raised both of his. "You don't think I'm going out by myself, do you?"

* * *

Ben watched Joanna spread frosting on her devil's food cake and licked his lips in anticipation. "Now there's a third reason I'm glad we're meeting tonight instead of waiting for Saturday. Do I get the mixer beaters to lick when you're through?"

She shook her head. "Becky and Joey asked first, but you can have the spatula. I know the main reason you're glad we moved the meeting to the first of the week is that you're all in a hurry to get moving. What's the other one?"

"Now I can take you out to dinner Saturday, and maybe dancing afterward. And Holly and her friend can bring their little brother and sister over to meet Becky and Joey."

She paused in her attentions to the cake and frowned at him. "You've already made arrangements with Holly? Aren't you taking a lot for granted?"

He shrugged. "If dancing's not your thing, maybe we can find a play or something you'd like to see."

She shook her head. "That isn't what I mean. You're trying to take charge again."

"No, I'm not. We'll eat dinner wherever

you want to, and do whatever you like afterwards. Your choice, all the way."

"Except that you've already decided we're going out."

"We don't have to. We can stay home if you'd rather. I just thought—"

"What I'd *rather*," she told him, "is that you'd consult me before you go making plans that involve me."

"Okay," he said with brusque impatience. "I'm consulting you now."

She turned back to the cake, and all he could see was the back of her head and the set of her shoulders. They looked annoyed. "Only because I'm making a fuss about it." She sounded annoyed, too.

"Look, if you don't want to go out with me, just say so. I can tell Holly I don't need her after all." He also sounded annoyed, and was. "You don't have to stay home with me either. I can watch TV or play Old Maid with the kids."

The spatula clattered against the mixer beaters as she dropped it back into the frosting bowl. She turned to face him. "Ben, you don't have to play Old Maid with the kids. I'm not refusing to go out with you."

"Then what are we arguing about?"

"I'm not arguing. I'm just telling you that I prefer to be asked, not told."

He ran his fingers through his hair. Definitely, it was getting thinner. "Well, then, I'm asking you. Joanna, will you have dinner with me Saturday evening, and maybe do something special afterward?"

"Yes," she said. "I will, and thank you. It's thoughtful of you to ask." She turned away from him and went to the door to call Becky and Joey.

His common sense told him it was time to be conciliatory and avoid irritating her further. His male ego wanted to put her in her place—just a little.

Ego won.

"The thing I *don't* like about this Monday night session is that instead of being over there with me, you'll be over here with the women. I still don't see why you scheduled your meeting for the same time as mine."

She handed Becky and Joey each a beater from the mixer and gave Ben the spatula. "Because it's easier to hold two meetings at the same time than to hold them at different times."

He hadn't had a frosting spatula to lick in years, and was delighted to find it tasted just as good now as it had half a century and more ago. "I was really counting on having you there tonight. Besides, you promised to stick with us until we got this business up and running."

She pushed the cake to the back of the counter and wiped up a few stray icing spatters. "Good Heavens, Ben, I'm not abandoning you. I'll be there anytime you need me, but you don't need me tonight. Tonight, you need to go over what we discussed last week and answer some of the questions we raised."

"I'd still feel better if you were there to make sure we get the right answers, and to see that we don't forget anything."

She shook her head. "You have Margaret's notes from last week. You'll manage just fine without me. I'd be more of a hindrance than a help. And we'll all get together at your place afterwards to compare notes and eat the cake."

He finished the spatula and dropped it into the sink to be washed. "Well, if that's the way it has to be, I guess that's the way it has to be. But I don't have to like it."

"You don't have to sulk about it either," she told him.

He winced at the sharp tone of her voice, but knew he'd brought it on himself. "Sorry," he muttered. "I guess I've gotten a little spoiled."

Joanna accepted the well-polished beaters that Becky and Joey handed her. "You've gotten a *lot* spoiled," she corrected.

"Can we have a piece of cake, too?" Joey asked.

"No," Ben said. "We'll save you some. Joanna doesn't want to cut the cake now."

"Why not?"

"Right," Joanna said. "Why not? Ben, if they ate a good dinner, and you don't mind, there's no reason why they can't have some now. Nobody's going to care if there are a couple of pieces missing."

"Oh, all right, then."

He watched while she cut the cake and gave each child a slice. "Uh, you don't suppose—"

"No," she said firmly. "You're a grown-up. You can wait."

Becky nudged Joey and they both burst out laughing.

"What's so funny?" Ben demanded.

Becky swallowed her giggles and regarded Joanna with affection. "That's just what Mama used to tell Daddy."

Joanna put her arm around Becky and bent to drop a light kiss on the top of her head. "Your mama sounds like a very smart lady."

Ben waited for the children to eat their cake, then told them, "You kids run on home in case anybody comes to the meeting early. I'll be along in a minute."

When they were gone, he told Joanna, "That's the first time I've heard her mention her mother without a quiver in her voice. You've been good for those children, Joanna—almost as good as you've been for me."

"They've been good for me, too, Ben. I've just begun to realize how much I missed by not having children. I intend to enjoy yours as much as you'll let me."

He caught her face between his palms and kissed her gently. "As much as you want to, anytime you want to." He slipped his arms around her and held her delightfully close. "And it goes without saying, you have my permission to enjoy *me* as much as you want to, and anytime you want to."

"Mm." She returned his kiss. "I'll keep it in mind. Now you'd better get on home. You don't want to leave the kids alone too long."

"I suppose you're right. I'll see you after the meeting then, for cake and coffee. And with any luck, maybe I can see you for a little while after the cake and coffee, when everyone else has gone home." He kissed her again and started for the door, but stopped beside her desk to pick up a stack of colored index cards. "Joanna, do you own stock in the company or something?" He held the cards out of reach as she snatched at them. "Ah-ah. Not until you pay the ransom."

She was still paying it a few minutes later when the front doorbell rang.

She ran into the living room to answer the door, and he went home to his kids and his own meeting, marveling at the difference between kissing Joanna and kissing an ordinary woman. But then, everything about Joanna was different from ordinary women, for which he was profoundly grateful.

* * *

Joanna paused in front of the door, clutching her index cards and suffering from a sudden attack of stage fright. She'd felt cool, collected, and professional talking to the men, but now, remembering everything she'd practically promised these women, women she hoped would become her friends, she found her palms sweaty and her mouth dry.

She wiped her hands against her thighs, one at a time, told herself sternly this was no time for a lapse in self-confidence, and opened the door. "Come in. You're right on time."

They came in talking, laughing, and so obviously glad to see her that her stage fright disappeared.

"I'm so glad you could all come."

"Wild horses couldn't have kept us away," Sandy Bagwell assured her.

"Or cranky husbands," Margaret Dennison added.

"Oh, dear," Joanna said, remembering Ben's reaction. "Just one, or did they all—"

"Carl was unhappy at the idea of having to take his own notes," Margaret explained. "Where do men get the idea the whole world should revolve around them?"

"From us, probably," Betty Donovan said. "When the kids leave home, we start spoiling our husbands."

"Enough about husbands," Sandy declared. "We have work to do."

"Right," Joanna agreed. "Do you want to make yourselves comfortable in the living room, or sit at the dining room table where it's easier to take notes?"

"Since it's a business meeting," Esther said, "I think we should be businesslike. I vote for the dining room table."

It was a good beginning, Joanna thought. As she watched them settle in at the table, she felt a sense of exhilaration and adventure that had been missing too long from her life. She had stopped drifting and taken charge.

"Tonight," she said, "we're going to identify the things *you* can do."

"That shouldn't take a whole session," Betty said.

"A whole session and more," Joanna assured her. "You know a lot more than you think you do. We just have to dig it out and recognize it. So get out your pencils and paper and put your thinking caps on."

She fanned out her index cards, glanced

at them, and realized she didn't need them. She knew exactly what she wanted to say. "If you can cook a meal and get it all ready for the table at the same time, you know how to plan and organize. If you can keep the kitchen clean as you work and still have dinner ready on time, you're efficient and use time well. If you can do it with kids and a husband interrupting you every two minutes, you have the ability to concentrate and ignore distractions. As important and basic as these skills are, many otherwise trained and educated people never acquire them."

"I never thought of it that way," Ginger said. She sounded awed.

"Of course you didn't," Joanna agreed, "but from now on, you will. You're going to examine everything you can remember doing in your whole life and ask yourself what skills were involved and in what other ways you could use those skills, that experience. For example, what kind of volunteer work have you done? If you belong to any clubs or organizations, have you held office? Worked on or chaired committees?"

She gave them a minute to think about it, then continued, "Have you ever helped to organize and carry out some complex project—cake sales, flea markets, banquets, Halloween carnivals, your church's Christmas pageant?"

She paused again, listening to the scratch of pens across paper as they scrawled hasty notes.

Betty glanced up. "My kids always claimed I threw the best birthday parties in the neighborhood. That ought to be good for something."

"You bet it is," Joanna said. "Probably several somethings when we have time to analyze it."

"I used to work one day a week at our neighborhood thrift shop," Ginger exclaimed.

"And I used to help my son with his newspaper route," Esther confessed.

"I've worked as a secretary for years," Margaret said, "but on the home front, I've packed up and moved more times than I can count, helped my kids make friends in a new neighborhood, and squeezed six rooms of furniture into five rooms, or stretched it out to fill seven or eight. As mobile as our society is these days, I'll bet a lot of families—younger ones, especially—

could use some help getting ready for a move or settling in after one.''

"Wonderful!" Joanna said. "That's just the kind of thinking I want to hear. But think even bigger. You've developed good work habits and learned to accept responsibility. You're self-starters, and you can work without supervision. What other skills and expertise have you 'helpless little homemakers' developed over the years?"

They laughed, then set to work to answer the question while she sat quietly and listened. This was what she liked best—starting something and then sitting back to watch while it ran itself. She grinned wryly. It was also what had made her so unnecessary in her own company that she'd resigned, and would sooner or later do the same thing here.

They were still at it when Ben called and wanted to know, "What's keeping you? We have the coffee made and are ready for you to bring the cake over. I knew I should have brought it with me."

"And I knew you shouldn't. There wouldn't be a crumb left for us if you had. We'll be over shortly."

She went back to the dining room and announced, "The men are through with their meeting and want to know what's keeping us."

Esther looked surprised and glanced at her watch. "I had no idea it was so late. I wonder if the men got as much done as we did?"

Joanna grinned. "That's a silly idea. When do they ever?"

Twelve

Ben poured two glasses of orange juice and set them on the table, then stepped into the hall to call up the stairs, "Breakfast is ready, kids. Come on down."

Joey came clattering down immediately with Becky following more slowly—and quietly. They sat at the table while Ben served up oatmeal sprinkled with the smallest amount of brown sugar the kids would tolerate. Joey grabbed his spoon and dived in as soon as Ben poured the milk, but Becky stared at hers and told Ben, "I guess I'm not very hungry this morning, Grandpa."

Her voice was subdued and shaky. He glanced at her sharply and felt a quick pang of alarm at the sight of her flushed face and too-bright eyes. It was obvious, even to a novice parent like him, that she didn't feel well.

He laid his hand against her forehead,

the way he remembered his mother doing to him, but his maternal instincts failed him until he felt Joey's head for comparison and found it considerably cooler than Becky's.

He tried to remember if any of the charts and lists Joanna had posted inside the linen closet said anything about what to do for a fever, but could only come up with a garbled list of stain removal methods. He settled finally for telling Becky, "No school for you today, sweetheart. Go on back up to bed. I'll come up as soon as I get Joey off."

Becky sat up straighter and reached for her orange juice. "I'm not sick, Grandpa, really. I can go to school."

He shook his head. "Not today. You're running a fever, and I can tell you don't feel well. Just let me get Joey ready for school, and—"

"No!" Joey knocked over his empty juice glass as he pushed his chair back from the table. Ben grabbed it before it fell to the floor. "I don't want to go to school if Becky doesn't."

"There's no reason for you to stay

home. You're not sick," Ben said, then added with belated concern, "Are you?"

Joey shook his head, but added stubbornly, "But I don't want to go to school by myself."

"I can go, Grandpa," Becky added.

"No, you can't," Ben said, more sharply than he'd intended. He softened his voice and added, "There's no reason why Joey can't go to school alone, and every reason why you can't go at all. Now I want you to go upstairs and get back into bed. Joey, you finish your breakfast and get ready to go out to the bus stop."

Joey's lower lip trembled, and Becky began to cry. "Grandpa, please let me go to school, or let Joey stay at home. Don't make him go to school by himself."

Damn! Ben thought, his concerns for Becky's health momentarily set aside. He'd accepted Joanna and Holly's pronouncement that the children were too dependent on each other, but had thought they were doing better. He tabled the problem for later. "Children, I'm sorry. Becky, you're sick and need to go back up to bed. Joey, you're old enough to go to school by yourself."

Joey eyes filled with tears and Becky cried, "He can't go to school by himself, Grandpa. I have to go with him and look after him."

Ben ran his fingers through his hair. "You don't have to look after him, Becky."

"Yes, I do," she insisted. "Grandma and Grandpa Spencer said so. I'm a big girl now, and Joey is still a little boy, so it's my job to look after him."

The Spencers again. He held back his anger at this further proof that no matter how sweet Jenny was, her family was nuts, and filed the information away to discuss with Joanna.

"No, sweetheart," he said quietly. "You're a big girl, all right, but not big enough to be saddled with a responsibility like that. Looking after Joey—looking after both of you—is my job. Your job is just to have fun and be happy."

"But you can't look after him at school," she protested.

"When he's at school, it's the teacher's job." Over her weakening protests, he sent her back up to bed, then packed Joey off to the bus stop. He stood in the doorway for a minute or two, feeling like an ogre as he watched the boy trudge forlornly down the walk to the corner. He almost relented and called him back, but managed to go back into the house instead.

Before he went upstairs to Becky, he took a minute to call Joanna and tell her not to expect him this morning, then added, "It probably isn't anything serious, but when your women get there, maybe you could send one of them over? I'd feel better if someone who knows kids could take a look at her."

With a sigh of satisfaction, Ben pushed his plate away and leaned back in his chair. Two of man's most basic needs, he thought, were food and sex. With his belly and taste buds still rejoicing from Joanna's excellent cooking and his body still vibrant and alive from their earlier lovemaking, he couldn't think of anything else a man might want.

Then Joanna poured him a cup of freshly brewed coffee and set a piece of cherry pie in front of him.

He caught her hand in his and smiled up at her. "Every time I think life is perfect, you do something to make it better."

She bent over and kissed him lightly. "It has been a good morning, hasn't it? In fact, except for Becky being sick yesterday, it's been a wonderful week. I'm glad she felt well enough to go back to school today."

"Not as glad as I am," Ben declared. "Esther was right. She said it was most likely one of those twenty-four-hour things. But it scared me half to death just the same, particularly when all she did was sleep most of the day. When Joey had his 'stomachaches,' he kept me so busy I knew he wasn't seriously ill. I was mighty relieved when Becky was her old self this morning.

"But you're right. Except for that, it was a wonderful week—an absolute workaholic's heaven. I don't remember working so long or so hard at so many things when I really was a workaholic." He picked up his fork, but looked up at her instead of at the pie. "The difference is, this time I also made time for the kids, and for you. I got just as much done and had a helluva lot more fun. I guess that's another one I owe you for."

She slipped back into her chair and picked up her own fork. "I owe you one, too, for introducing me to your friends."

"You're a real glutton for punishment, wanting to get two new companies started at one time."

She shook her head. "It isn't just that. It's . . . well, it's the way they make me feel I'm one of them. I think I told you, Robert and I pretty much kept to ourselves, so I've never really had any close friendships with women, except for Helen, my office manager. I never really missed them when Robert was alive, but now . . ." She paused. "What's wrong? You look unhappy about something."

He had three choices. He could lie; he could try to change the subject; he could tell her the truth. "No, not at all." The minute the words left his mouth, he realized he'd made the wrong choice. "Well, maybe a little. I've enjoyed having you all to myself, and not having to share you with anyone but the kids."

She frowned. "You make me feel like the last slice of cake. I should think you'd be glad I'm getting along so well with your friends."

He ran his fingers through his hair, vaguely aware that he was never going to kick the habit at this rate. "They aren't really my friends, exactly. The only thing we actually have in common is that I've worked with the men from time to time. I mean, they're polite enough to include me in their social activities now and again, but we've never been what you could really consider *friends*. Not close friends, anyway. And I'm not sure it's wise to get *too* friendly with them if we're all going to be working together."

"That's ridiculous. I wouldn't want to work with people I couldn't be friends with." She stabbed a cherry with her fork, studied it for a minute, then looked back up at him. "And I wouldn't like to be part of another relationship that excluded everyone else."

"I'm sorry. I didn't mean . . ." He couldn't think what else to say, and shoved cherries and pastry around on his plate until enough time had passed that he could reasonably change the subject. "Did I tell you we've got this job shop organized almost to the point where we can put something in writing to show a lawyer?"

"That's wonderful."

"And Jim has a hot tip on a contract

that's going to be up for grabs shortly. We think we'll be ready to go after it."

"That's even better." There was no mistaking the genuine pleasure in her voice.

He sighed with relief and finished the shambles he'd made of his pie. "Wonderful pie," he told Joanna. "Wonderful meal. Wonderful woman."

She dropped her napkin beside her plate and stood up. "Thank you kindly, sir."

He circled the table and caught her in his arms for a brief but potent kiss, then let her go. "I guess we'd better get these dishes out of the way before the mob starts arriving."

She measured detergent into the sink and turned on the water while Ben rolled up his sleeves. "What's your group working on today?"

"Résumés. Not a pretty subject, but a necessary one. Will your ladies need some help with theirs?"

She shook her head. "I'm not even sure we'll need résumés. If we do, they'll be very different from yours. But thanks for the offer." She helped him clear the dishes from the table, then leaned against the counter and watched while he washed them.

"How are your ladies coming, by the way?"

"Still exploring their strengths and weaknesses, and realizing they know a lot more than they ever thought they did."

"I always thought 'woman's work' was pretty clearly defined."

"Well, you thought wrong. They aren't talking about the obvious things, like selling cosmetics, or baby-sitting, or catering. Believe me, if they wanted to do those things, they'd already be doing them. What they're trying to do is create *new* opportunities, using their own unique experiences and expertise."

"Such as?"

"Margaret's an expert at following her husband from job to job. She thinks she could provide a valuable service helping other families relocate. Sandy's had to find a new job every time she and Jim moved. She'd like to help other women organize effective job searches. The others haven't made up their minds yet, but believe me, they aren't going to be just gray-haired temps. Whatever they choose, they'll be hired and paid by the job, not the hour, just like your job shoppers."

He emptied the sink, and dried his hands, grinning a little at her vehemence. "Did I just strike a vein of feminism?"

"Well . . . maybe just a little one," she admitted.

He draped the towel over the towel bar, but before he could roll his sleeves down, she slipped her arms around his waist and kissed his chin. "Do you know how incredibly sexy you look with your sleeves rolled up?"

He pulled her close and returned the kiss, not on the chin. "I do?"

"Oh my, yes. You ought to wash dishes all the time."

He released her, turned her around, and swatted her rump gently. "You women are all alike." He put his arms around her and kissed the back of her neck. "All you really want from a man is help with the housework."

"Not *all,*" she murmured. "There are a few other things."

"You mean, things like this?" He reached up to cup and fondle her breasts, relishing their weight and warmth against his palms. They were one of her best features, he thought, shapely and attractive when she was dressed, exciting and responsive when she was not. They were neither too big nor too small, but just right for his hands, firm enough to send shivers through him when they were pressed against his chest and soft enough to yield to his gentle kneading and shaping.

"Like that," she agreed. She leaned back against him while he stroked and caressed her, clearly enjoying it as much as he did. He marveled again at her honesty and lack of pretense. She liked sex, she liked sex with him, and she didn't lessen their pleasure in each other by pretending otherwise. He wondered if she could possibly know how much he treasured that.

Despite their wonderful before-lunch lovemaking, upstairs in the bedroom because she didn't want to mess up the living room, he felt himself becoming aroused again, and wondered if they had time—

But the clock in the living room chimed, and she turned in his arms to kiss him quickly and then slip away from him. "They'll be coming any minute now."

"Then my bunch will be, too. I'd better go." At the door he paused and glanced back at her. "If we can't get loose at a reasonable hour today, I'll see you in the morning."

She shook her head. "No. Tomorrow we have a dinner date, and I intend to spend the whole day getting ready for it."

He grinned. "I have a feeling this is going to be an evening to remember."

She returned the grin. "You'd better believe it."

Joanna had a few bad moments, dressing for dinner with Ben. It seemed strange to be alone as she pampered herself with a bubble bath, shampoo, and manicure. She half expected to hear Robert's good-natured complaint about the steamy bathroom mirror as he shaved, or bump into him as they both tried to get into the closet at once. And when she was finally dressed and checking her makeup in the mirror, the room seemed cold and empty without Robert peering over her shoulder as he knotted his tie.

She shook the feeling off and told herself firmly she was only dressing alone, not going out alone. More to the point, and more important than a vague case of "the lonelies," was the fact that she was going out because she wanted to and not because Ben had pressured her into it.

Besides, even if Robert wasn't present in the flesh, he was surely here in spirit, enjoying the sight of her in what he always called her "Sunday-go-to-meeting clothes."

She took one last look at herself as she heard Ben's car turn into her driveway and decided she looked elegant enough for anyplace he could possibly take her.

Ben clearly thought so, too. He stood in the open doorway for a minute, and simply looked at her. "Oh my," he murmured finally. "I knew this was going to be an evening to remember."

He had also taken extra pains with his appearance. He'd obviously visited a barber recently, and his suit looked freshly pressed. His cheeks were pink and glowing from a recent shave, and the faint, elusive scent of his aftershave made her want to nuzzle the side of his neck to smell it more clearly.

She wasn't sure which of them moved or if they both did, only that they came together and she had only a moment to think how warm his lips were before the warmth spread and her whole body seemed to glow with it.

She pulled away from him finally. "Didn't you say you'd made reservations? We don't want to be late."

He helped her into her coat, then turned her around and set her whole body tingling as he smoothed the collar around her neck and slid his hands inside the coat for an uninhibited exploration of what lay beneath.

She put her arms around his neck and pressed closer to him. "You're getting good at that," she murmured.

"Mmm, practice makes perfect. Are you sure you really want to go out? Maybe we should just stay in tonight."

Reluctantly, she pulled away from the warmth of his hands. "No, you promised me dinner in a fancy restaurant, and I intend to hold you to it."

He sighed and let her go. "All right. I suppose we have to eat, too. And don't forget, I promised that, after dinner, we could do whatever you want to do."

"I haven't forgotten."

"Well?"

"I want you to enjoy your dinner. I'll tell you later."

"That bad, huh?"

She brushed his lips with hers and moved away before he could get hold of her again. "No, silly. That good."

He escorted her out to his car, helped her in, then circled to the driver's side and slipped in beside her.

"How did Becky and Joey react to the other children?" she asked.

"Pretty well, I think. Good old Bernie took to Matt right away, knocked him down, stood on his chest, and gave his face a couple of quick slurps. That pretty well broke the ice."

"I should think so!"

He grinned at her tone. "Don't worry. Little boys like that sort of thing."

"What about the girls?"

"Well, that was a lot more refined and genteel, but before I left, they were taking turns feeding Lovey bits of leftover roast beef and planning to fix up her basket with a new cushion and some velvet bows."

She smiled at the picture his words conjured up. "Little girls like *that* sort of thing," she murmured.

He reached over and took her hand in his. "And what do big girls like?"

She grinned and squeezed his hand. "Pretty much the same things big boys like."

"Hallelujah!" he murmured.

They rode in satisfying silence until they reached the restaurant, a fancy new place she'd read about but never visited. It had a reputation for good food, a relaxed but luxurious ambience, and a growing list of regulars.

She was pleased with his choice, but although she was anticipating a wonderful meal, it was what would come afterward, her part of the evening, that she was really looking forward to.

Ben knew he'd picked his restaurant wisely the moment they stepped inside, where the smell of good food and the spicy-scented candles on the tables complemented the murmur of good conversation and the muted click of silverware on china.

They were greeted immediately by an attractive hostess, who checked their reservations, told them their table would be ready in a few minutes, and led them past a series of intimate, softly lit dining areas on either side of a wide hall to a simple but elegant lounge at the far end.

She found them a secluded corner, partly shielded from the rest of the room by a potted tree of some kind—whether real or fake Ben had no idea. From another corner, the soft notes of a piano blurred the buzz of voices, creating a further illusion of privacy.

They sat together on a small sofa, or perhaps a love seat, so close together that Ben was sharply aware of the warmth of Joanna's thigh against his and the way the décolletage of her dress swung an inch or so away from her body each time she leaned forward to pick up her before-dinner drink or set it back down on the small table in front of them.

It wasn't much, but it was enough to give him a breathtaking view of the creamy mounds of her breasts swelling above a lacy bra as ivory as her skin, so low cut that the tops of her breasts were almost totally exposed, and so sheer that the rosy brown of her nipples was clearly visible.

He licked his lips, remembering the feel

of those creamy breasts in his mouth and the taste of the nipples as he stroked them with his tongue.

The room seemed suddenly warmer and smaller. He tried to think of some simple, commonplace thing to say, and blurted instead, "Uh, maybe this wasn't such a good idea, after all."

She paused in the act of reaching again for her drink and glanced at him with mischief in her eyes. He realized with a happy shock that she knew perfectly well what her low-cut neckline was doing to him.

"Why not?"

"I had no idea how erotic a simple before-dinner drink and quiet piano music could be," he confessed. "But then, I had no idea how erotic *anything* could be until I met you."

She smiled, a private sort of smile as if she'd looked inside herself and found something she liked. "We do have something pretty extraordinary going, don't we?"

"More than extraordinary," he said. "Much more. Joanna, every time we make love, you shatter me into a million pieces, and then you make me whole again. Every time we make love, I think this is it, this is the time when I'll finally get enough of you to last until the next time. But it never is. Sex with you involves my whole mind, and soul, and body, not just that little cylinder of flesh I used to be satisfied with. We barely pull apart before I want you again, and even if that little cylinder isn't ready again, the rest of me is."

"I know," she said, her voice soft and somehow vulnerable. "Ben, do you have any idea what a tiny distance separates *wife* from *widow,* or what an enormous distance it is from *widow* back to *woman?* You helped me across that distance, not just in bed, but in the rest of my life, and I thank you with all my heart."

Her words made his eyes sting and his throat close up, so that the sip of his drink he'd just taken didn't want to go down. He swallowed hard and said lightly, "Let's give credit where it's due. I knew, from the night Bernie stole your steak and I invited us to dinner and then kissed you afterwards, that you were the sexiest woman I'd ever met, and that making love to you would be the greatest adventure of my life."

The solemn look left her face and she grinned. "Well, don't sell yourself short. Sex is a lot like dancing and bridge. It goes better if you have a good partner."

He laid his hand discreetly on her knee. "You'd better believe it."

She lifted his hand from her knee and held it in both of hers. "You have the most exciting hands. I love the way you always seem to know exactly when and where and how to touch me."

He lifted her hands to his lips and kissed first one and then the other, belatedly aware this was still another kind of lovemaking she'd taught him. What they were doing was purely emotional, purely cerebral, but it was as powerfully arousing in its way as any physical foreplay he'd ever experienced. His cylinder of flesh, thank the Lord, was still quiescent, but the rest of him was totally and vibrantly alive.

"And I love the way you love to be touched," he told her, "but if you keep talking this way, you're going to make me embarrass myself. And let me tell you, if I have to settle for a chaste good night kiss at your door, I'm going to be in big trouble."

Her smile was sweet and demure as she murmured, "We'll see."

The hostess appeared suddenly from the other side of the potted tree and told him, "Your table is ready, sir."

They ate what Ben supposed was an excellent dinner. Afterward, he wasn't sure what he'd eaten or how it tasted. It was the taste and smell and feel of Joanna that possessed him, obsessed him.

He waited until they'd eaten the last bite of dessert, drunk the last sip of coffee, then asked her, "So what do you want to do with the rest of the evening?"

She set her small evening purse on the table and unzipped it, fumbled inside it for a minute, then held up a small plastic square from which dangled—

His breath caught in his throat. "What's that?"

"That," she answered softly, "is the key to room nine at the Quiet Rest Motel."

He left twice as big a tip as he'd meant to, paid the bill, and led her out to the car. They didn't speak as he pulled out of the restaurant parking lot, but at the first stoplight, he reached over to trace the line of her chin and jaw, then dropped his hand to rub lightly up and down her thigh.

She moved close to him and he put his arm around her shoulders, reflecting that it had been a long time since he'd driven one-handed, and thank God for automatic transmissions.

After a moment, she moved closer still and slid down in the seat beside him, so that he could reach into the low-cut neck of her dress and free one breast from the lace of her bra. Her nipple hardened almost instantly under the gentle kneading of his fingers.

She turned slightly to give him better access to the breast and trailed her fingers up the inside of his thigh. "Oh my," she murmured.

The motion of her hand against him sent shock waves of lust through his whole body.

They reached the motel and parked in front of room nine, but he found himself reluctant to interrupt their love play. He shifted position so that he could give her other breast the attention it deserved. After a moment, that wasn't enough, and he relinquished her breasts in favor of reaching under her skirt in search of other treasure.

"We don't have to do this in the car, you know," she told him. "The room is already paid for." But instead of moving away from him, she shifted on the seat, straightening one leg, bending the other and pressing it toward him, making it easier for him to move his hand to the moist warmth he sought, and creating sweet havoc where her knee moved against the heat building between his own legs.

He hadn't made out in a car, he realized, since he'd been dating Fran, and he'd forgotten how wildly exciting it could be. "Shh," he told her. "I'm having too much fun to stop now, and the room will still be there when we want it."

She tipped her head back and he lowered his face to the soft swell of her breasts where they disappeared into her dress, flicking his tongue in and out of her cleavage, wishing the dress buttoned—or unbuttoned—down the front so he could taste more of her.

She began to use her hands, too, reaching under his coat and exciting his nipples into tingling hardness. He had a moment to wonder why he hadn't known until now how sensitive they were before she slid her hand down to his crotch and murmured approvingly as she felt the fullness there, then reached for his zipper.

She slid it down slowly, tantalizingly, and reached inside to pull him free of his clothing. The warmth of her hand contrasted sharply with the cool night air, and his whole body twitched as she drew her fingers slowly along the naked length of him. He shivered and thrust his body upward to expose more of himself to her touch.

He barely noticed the sound of a car turning into the entrance of the motel, until headlights poured through the window and splashed over them. He jerked upright, feeling his face flame, but the headlights moved away as the car passed, and Joanna laughed softly, but with obvious amusement.

"You're right," he said. "We don't have to do this in the car. It's been a helluva lot of fun . . ."

"It still is," she said, leaning forward to trail kisses along his jaw, while her fingers continued to threaten his self-control.

"Yes, but I think we'd better go inside now."

"Well . . . if you really want to."

"I want to," he said fervently, becoming aware that not only was he less uninhibited than he'd thought, but less limber as well. His back had begun to give him hell.

"You're probably right," she agreed. She pulled away from him and straightened her disarranged clothing, while he discovered to his dismay that there was no way he was going to get his zipper closed again, or even cover the evidence of Joanna's ministrations. He had the choice of sitting here for God only knew how long, with Joanna no doubt continuing to tease him, or walking across the sidewalk to their room fully erect and exposed to the world.

He compromised by praying that no other cars would turn in and walking as close behind Joanna as he could.

He breathed a sigh of relief as they finally stepped inside the room and Joanna closed the drapes before turning on the lights. He fought again for control when she turned and glanced at him—glanced *down* at him—and grinned.

"Are you in that big a hurry?" she asked. "Or were you just not ready to put it away yet?"

"Come here, woman, and I'll show you where I'm going to put it." He pulled her skirt up and pressed himself against her, aware that he was about to lose it, but past caring.

She pulled away. "Oh, no. We're not going to ruin my dress. Or my pantyhose."

"Then take them off," he said. "And don't be all day about it."

But after they'd hastily undressed each other and she started for the bed, he stopped her and turned her away from him, so that she was facing the mirror, and they could watch as he molded and shaped her naked breasts. She pressed herself back against him, keeping him fully aroused with the slight motion of her buttocks.

After a minute, she moved her feet a little apart, caught his hand and urged it downward, into the space between her legs. She drew in a deep, ragged breath as he worked his palm back and forth against her, and gasped sharply when he slipped one finger between the warm folds of flesh to stroke the sensitive nubbin beneath.

After a moment, he looked away from

what his hands were doing and watched the ecstasy on her face. As he did, she reached behind her, to where he was pressed hard against her buttocks. She wrapped her fingers around him and moved her hand back and forth with quick, firm strokes, giving him the same kind of ecstasy he was giving her, and now it wasn't his hands she was watching, but his face, just as he was watching hers.

She gasped suddenly as her body jerked, and her hand tightened spasmodically around him, bringing his explosive climax to coincide with hers.

Their pleasure was powerful and prolonged. It was some time before the echoes died away and they could stand together quietly while he stroked her breasts and belly and thighs, smooth and satiny now with a soft sheen of perspiration, and she continued to fondle him, moving a little to the side after a moment so they could watch that, too.

Afterward, they showered together, reveling in the feel of the cool water on their heated bodies and the creamy lather of the sweet-scented soap, exploring and delighting each other with hands, lips, whole bodies, until they were so frantic for each other again that they barely had time to rinse off the soap and tumble, still dripping wet, into the bed, to come together in another explosion as shattering as the first one.

Thirteen

Joanna woke Sunday morning feeling young and beautiful and vibrantly alive. She inhaled deeply and opened her eyes, a cheerful "Good morning" on her lips, and found herself staring at emptiness beside her and feeling a matching emptiness inside her, as if she'd tried to put her weight on a step that wasn't there.

Then memory returned. Of course. How could she have forgotten? It wasn't Robert who had made such wild, wonderful love to her last night, but Ben.

She rolled over onto her back and stared up at the ceiling, shaken by the sudden doubt that swept her. It had never occurred to her, after Robert's death, that she'd ever feel this way again, but as much as she'd loved Robert, as powerful as the sex between them had been, this thing she shared with Ben was something new. He wasn't the

smooth and polished lover Robert had
been, not as aware of her special needs and
nuances, but the urgency, the explosiveness
she felt with him wasn't like anything she'd
ever felt before, not even with Robert. As
wonderful as it was, it was a little scary, too,
that any man could have such power over
her.

She was reasonably sure that it was the
same for Ben. Certainly he responded to
her with a readiness that men years younger
than he would have envied, and that was
also scary. She'd never expected to have
such power over a man again, and now that
she had it, she wasn't sure she wanted it.
She had things to do, promises to keep, but
every time she and Ben made love, her
plans seemed to become a little more tenu-
ous, a little more distant.

She finally persuaded herself that she
was seeing problems where none existed.
She had no intention of throwing away her
whole future for one man, no matter how
good he was in bed, or how good she was
with him. She was responding to three years
of abstinence, and the thrill of being with
someone new and exciting, that was all, and
Ben— She grinned. Any man would be

turned on, the shameless way she'd been throwing herself at him.

So she could relax and stop fretting. The novelty would wear off after a while, and they'd settle down into a more normal relationship, one that would leave room in her life for some of the other things she'd promised herself.

By the time Ben came over for the second cup of coffee that had become their habit while the children were in Sunday school, she had put her worries aside and felt only pleasure at the way her body quickened against his when he held her close for a good morning kiss.

"You look wonderful this morning," he told her. "About sixteen years old and as if you didn't have a care in the world."

She studied him with approval, wondering if she had the same glow of contentment and satisfaction that radiated from him. "You look pretty great yourself."

"I feel great," he admitted. "Fresh and rested and ready to tackle the world. I don't know where all this energy is coming from."

"I do." She kissed him lightly, then slipped out of his arms to pour them each a cup of coffee. "Sex in the morning is wonderful, but sex at night, even when you have to get dressed and go home afterwards, makes for a wonderful night's sleep."

"Doesn't it, though? In fact, the only thing better would be *not* to have to get dressed and go home." He slid his palm in a slow caress across her cheek and down her throat, then stroked her breasts lightly but effectively with his fingertips. "I have this recurring fantasy that sometime when we sleep together, we'll really sleep together, and I'll wake in the morning to find you still beside me. Joanna, we need to—"

She knew instinctively that she didn't want to hear the rest of what he was going to say, and pulled away from him abruptly. "Sit down," she said. "Your coffee will get cold."

He hesitated, then took his place at the table.

She sat opposite him and told him firmly, "I want to hear how the children made out with their new playmates." It was an obvious move to change the subject, and she was afraid he might not let her get away with it, but after a minute, he grinned.

"I'm sure they'll want to tell you all about it themselves, but they seem to have had a great time, particularly Joey, Matt, and Bernie. I suspect that, from now on, wherever you see one, you're going to see all three."

"And Becky?"

"She wasn't quite as vocal about it as Joey was, but I think she had a good time, too. I hope so, because I've just realized that it would be good for *me* to have some other children around, so I can see how normal children are supposed to behave, and get some idea of when or whether to worry about mine."

"Makes sense."

"Glad you agree." He grinned. "Now I have something for *you* to worry about."

"What's that?"

"Holly and her friend are giving a Halloween party for the kids on the block. Becky and Joey are invited, and I think they plan to consult you on the subject of costumes. I ought to warn you, they're expecting you to come up with something pretty spectacular. This wouldn't happen to be another of your areas of expertise, would it?"

She'd never made a Halloween costume before, and knew immediately that she'd missed something important. She felt a quick surge of pleasure that the children wanted her help, and a keen sense of anticipation as she considered the challenge. "I might have an idea or two," she admitted.

"Great. And while they're at the children's party, why don't we have an adult party for just the two of us?"

"Sounds good. Am I supposed to choose costumes for that, too?"

He shook his head. "I've already decided. I thought we could come as Adam and Eve."

She leaned back in her chair and grinned at him. "With or without fig leaves?"

He returned the grin. "What do you think?"

Ben held the door while Joanna slid behind the wheel of her car, then circled to climb in on the passenger side. As he settled himself and closed the door, he asked plaintively, "Do we really have to go through with this?"

Joanna paused with her key halfway into the ignition and glanced at him, surprised. "Of course not. It's just a couple of typewriters I'm picking up. I can manage by myself if you don't want to go."

"That isn't what I'm talking about. Of course I want to go. I'm looking forward to seeing your office and meeting the ladies who are running your business since you retired."

The motor purred into life as she turned the key. "Then what—"

He sighed. "It's those grumpy men who'll be sitting in your dining room next week pecking away at those typewriters and getting all your attention that sort of takes the edge off the day for me."

She let the clutch out and backed smoothly out of the drive. "Oh, come on now. Admit it. What's really bothering you is that you're going to be one of them. Ben, I don't see how you men—you electronics engineers—made it this far into the twentieth century without learning to type or use computers."

"We know how to use computers," he protested. "At least, I do—but with a mouse, not a keyboard."

"Well, a mouse doesn't enter text. A keyboard does. And not knowing how to type—excuse me, use a keyboard—is a luxury you really can't afford right now."

"I know. I just hate losing our afternoons together."

"So do I," she admitted, "but we'll still have our mornings."

"For which I'm profoundly grateful, but I enjoy doing other things with you, too, you know."

She reached over to pat his hand. "I know. I enjoy them, too."

"And I really am looking forward to meeting Helen, and, ah, Trudy—is that her name?"

"Yes," she told him. "Trudy." She lapsed into silence and let him think she was concentrating on her driving while she brooded over the fact that he was probably looking forward to it more than she was. She really wasn't ready to run Ben past the Helen-Trudy gauntlet. She wasn't sure she ever would be. But they needed the two perfectly good Selectrics that had been relegated to the storeroom when the computer replaced them, and Ben had insisted on coming along to carry them for her.

But she knew, as surely as she knew her name, that if Helen or Trudy didn't do or say something to embarrass her, Ben would.

By the time they pulled into the parking lot, she'd become philosophical—or maybe just resigned. He had to meet them sometime; it might as well be today.

For the first time in three years, she barely noticed the lettering on the glass as Ben held the door for her and she preceded him into the office.

The typewriters had already been retrieved from the storeroom and sat side by side on the counter that separated the small reception area from Trudy's office while Trudy bent over them, using a small brush to flick away accumulated dust and flecks of ribbon carbon.

She glanced up as they came in, her eyes widening as she spotted Ben behind Joanna. "Oh, wow!" she murmured, then flushed. "I mean, is this your new neighbor, Joanna? The one who needs the typewriters?"

Joanna nodded. "Good to see you, too,

Trudy. Yes, this is my neighbor, Mr. Walker. Ben, this is Trudy, the best girl Friday and typewriter cleaner anyone ever had.''

Trudy laid the brush down, offered Ben a slightly dusty and carbon-smeared hand, withdrew it abruptly as he reached for it, wiped it vigorously on her skirt, and held it out again. Instead of shaking it, Ben flashed Joanna a brief grin, took the hand in his, and raised it to his lips.

''Hello, Trudy,'' he murmured. ''I've heard wonderful things about you.''

Trudy drew a deep breath. ''I've barely heard anything about *you*,'' she answered, ''but it was all good.'' She seemed to realize that her hand was still hovering in midair where he'd released it and snatched it abruptly back to her side. As she did, her elbow hit a stack of boxed ribbon cartridges and sent them skittering across the counter. She grabbed for them, sent several of them spinning to the floor, gave Joanna an anguished look, and bent to pick them up.

Joanna grinned and murmured, too low for Trudy to hear, ''Don't give yourself too much credit. She's young and impressionable.''

Ben scooped up a box that had fallen on their side of the counter and murmured back, "Don't be silly. When you've got it, you've got it, and apparently, I've got it." He straightened up, found himself face to face with Trudy, and turned pink. He thrust the box at her, and repeated, "I've got it."

Trudy accepted the box. "Thank you," she managed to say, seemed to draw courage from the sound of her voice, and added, "I've been cleaning these up a little bit. They were awfully dusty. Let me plug one in and you can try it out, Mr. Walker."

Ben stopped her as she found the end of an electric cord and started to duck under the counter with it. "No need to do that. The only thing I know about typewriters at the moment is that I don't know anything about them. Joanna is going to have to teach me."

Trudy gazed at Joanna with a look that said clearly, "Lucky you!"

The door to Helen's office opened. "I thought I heard voices out here," Helen said. "Hello, Joanna." She took one step into the room and stopped. At least, her body did. Her eyes kept moving and her lips curved in an approving smile as she looked Ben up and down.

Joanna held her breath, waiting for Helen's version of "Oh, wow," and winced when Helen murmured, "If this is a sample of life after retirement, you'll have my resignation in the morning."

"I'll have your head on a platter if you aren't careful," Joanna warned under her breath.

Helen ignored her and offered Ben her hand and her rapt attention. "You must be the famous—or should I say, infamous?—Ben Walker."

Ben took her hand. He didn't kiss it as he had Trudy's, but only held it between both of his. "Oh, infamous, please," he said, "and working on notorious."

Helen flashed Joanna a quick grin, then turned back to Ben. "When Joanna retired, we really thought she'd spend a lot of time hanging around the office. I see now why she hasn't."

"I have kept her pretty busy," Ben agreed. "And vice versa."

"I'm glad to hear it," Helen said, turning serious. "Joanna doesn't handle leisure very well."

"As it turns out," Ben told her, "neither do I, which is probably good, since it looks like I'm not going to have any. Not if I'm going to have to learn how to operate one of these infernal machines." He gestured toward the typewriters.

Joanna grinned at him and spoke in the tone Becky used when Joey tried her patience. "Ben, I keep telling you, it isn't going to hurt a bit." She went back to her normal voice and added, "But it may give you a little more respect for the women who type for men who can't."

"I have all the respect in the world for them," he assured her. "I just never wanted to be one of them."

Helen gestured toward the sofa and chairs in the reception area. "Why don't we sit down and visit for a little while? I want to hear about all the ways you've been keeping Joanna busy."

Joanna shook her head. "I wish we had the time, but we really are going to be busy this afternoon." She quashed any protests by adding, "If you know what's good for you, you'd better be, too."

"We will be," Trudy assured her. "Starting right after lunch, my appointment book is almost full.''

"Then we'll take these typewriters and get out of your way.''

Trudy ran ahead of Ben to hold the door for him while Helen clutched Joanna's arm and whispered, "Joanna, if he's as good in bed as he is *gorgeous*—''

"He is,'' Joanna whispered back. "And more.''

"How did you get so lucky?''

"Clean living, a pure heart, and incredibly good timing.''

Ben came back for the other typewriter and they said their goodbyes. Helen and Trudy stood in the office doorway and waved as Joanna drove away.

"What was all that stuff about clean living, a pure heart, and good timing?'' Ben asked.

She gave him her most innocent look. "Those are the qualities you need to be a good typist.''

"Oh.'' He grinned. "I thought maybe you were talking about sex.''

She returned the grin. "Well, in a way, I suppose we were.''

He was silent for a few minutes, then

asked, "Do they know what's happening between us?"

She glanced at him briefly. "Trudy doesn't," she said. "Helen does." She negotiated the next red light, then added, "I'm not one to kiss and tell, but Helen knows me very well. She figured it out."

He nodded. "That's about what I thought. Joanna . . . are you embarrassed about it? That Helen knows, I mean."

She reached over and laid her hand on the inside of his thigh, just above the knee. "No way." After a minute, she asked slyly, "Are you?"

He caught her hand and slid it higher. "Let's go home," he told her, "and I'll show you how embarrassed I am, and while I'm at it, I'll show you what clean living, a pure heart, and incredible timing are really good for."

Ben carried the mail inside, thumbed through the inevitable junk mail, and stopped at the envelope with the familiar handwriting and foreign stamp. He had a finger halfway under the flap before he realized it was addressed to the children, and not to him. He held it flat on his palm for a minute, as if weighing it, then took it into the kitchen where the children were enjoying an after-school snack.

"You have a letter," he told them. "From your grandmother." They glanced at each other in a way that made him add hastily, "Not your Grandmother Spencer. Your father's mother. Do you remember her?"

Joey screwed up his face in concentration, then shook his head.

"Maybe just a little," Becky said.

Joey looked puzzled. "If you're our daddy's father, and she's Daddy's mother, why isn't she your wife?"

"Uh, well . . . it's a long story, Joey."

"They're divorced, Joey," Becky said.

"Oh." Her brief explanation seemed to satisfy him. "What does the letter say?"

"I don't know," Ben said. "It's addressed to you children." He handed it to Becky.

She opened the envelope, took the letter out, and unfolded it. Several photographs fell from it. She put them aside and held the letter in her hand, running her fingers over the flowing script. "I can't read writing yet," she told him. "I only can read printing." She handed the letter back to him. "You read it, Grandpa."

He carried the letter to the window, where the light was better, cleared his throat, and began to read:

Dear Children,

I've been thinking a lot about you lately, and wondering how you are.

It's been a long time since I last saw you. I'll bet you've both grown so much I'd hardly recognize you. I hope you remember me, but if you don't, the enclosed pictures will show you what I look like, and where I live.

I'm sorry I can only send you my love in this letter and can't be there to give you a real hug. Perhaps you can give each other a hug for me.

Please write to me and tell me all about your new life. Send me some pictures if you have some.

Love and kisses, Grandmother.

The children were quiet a minute when he'd finished, then Joey said, "That was a nice letter. Is she a nice lady, Grandpa?"

"Yes," Ben said after a brief pause. "She's a very nice lady."

"Then why did you divorce her?"

"Joey!" Becky's tone indicated both exasperation and disapproval. "That's not polite." She picked up the pictures and studied them, then handed them to Joey. "She looks like a nice lady."

"Are you going to write to her?" Ben asked.

"I guess so," Becky said, "only I don't know what to say."

"I'm sure you'll think of something," Ben told her. "Joey can help."

He supplied pencil and paper, and listened to them as they worked over the letter, spelling an occasional word as needed, while he started dinner. By the time he was ready to lower the flame under his beef stew and let it simmer for a while, Becky brought him the letter.

The daylight was fading fast. He turned on the light over the sink and took the letter there to read it. Becky's handwriting—printing, he corrected himself—was firm and clear, the letters well shaped, and mostly all the same size. He smiled at her and began to read:

Dear Grandma,

It was nice of you to write to Joey and me. We are fine. We hope you are fine, too. We miss Mama and Daddy very much, but Grandpa takes good care of us, and he takes care of Bernie, our dog, and Lovey, our kitten. Joanna takes good care of us, too. She is our neighbor and our friend and she has a cat named Tinkerbell. We don't have any pictures right now, but Grandpa says we will send you some when we get some. Love, Becky and Joey.

They went into the living room, where Ben sat at the desk and addressed an envelope while Becky folded the letter and Joey waited to glue on the stamps Ben had given him. He still didn't know how much the postage was, and could only hope Joey didn't run out of spit before he ran out of stamps.

He didn't, but seemed happy enough to let Becky lick the envelope flap.

As he watched Becky carry the letter outside and place it carefully in the mailbox to be picked up in the morning, Ben decided that, on the whole, he was glad Fran had written. After a couple more letters like the one the kids had written to-night, she'd begin to realize how much he'd changed, and how well off the children were with him. He owed her that much—and a lot more besides.

Joanna wasn't sure who was happier when her living room clock chimed three o'clock—the men fitfully poking at the typewriter keys, or the women listening to them complain about it.

Ben leaned back in his chair with a sigh of relief. "This is the hardest work I've ever done."

"And then some," Grady Wilson agreed. "I haven't stirred from this chair in an hour, and I'm as wrung out as if I'd been digging ditches." He laced his fingers together and pulled until the joints popped.

Ginger Ross winced. "You do that again and you'll be digging a grave—your own."

Grady grinned at her, but unlaced his fingers. "Party poop," he accused.

Sandy Bagwell glanced up from the end of the table, where she was loading résumés into a computer donated by the Donovans' oldest son. "The more you learn, the easier it will get," she predicted. "The problem now, Grady, is that you're putting pressure on a part of yourself that hasn't been used much lately."

He studied his hands. "My fingers?"

Ben laughed, "I think she means your brain." He pushed his chair back from the table and stood up. "The kids will be coming in soon. Time for me to get on home. You'd better come, too, Grady. I think the ladies have had all they want of us for one day."

"Amen to that," Esther Gold muttered, just loud enough to be heard.

Ben grinned and beckoned for Joanna to follow them. At the kitchen door he stepped aside to let Grady through first, kissed Joanna quickly, and went out before Grady could come back and see what was keeping him.

Joanna turned to go back to the dining room and discovered Margaret Dennison watching from the doorway. "It's hard to believe that's the same Ben Walker we've known all these years. I've never seen anyone change so much in such a short time."

"Change? How?"

Esther followed Margaret into the

kitchen and poured herself a cup of the coffee Joanna had made earlier. "He's warmer, friendlier. More open. I don't mean he was unfriendly before, but he was always . . . oh, I don't know. Aloof, I suppose."

"Sexy as hell," Margaret added, "but closed in on himself. Not cold, exactly, but detached, uninvolved."

"You must be talking about Ben." Sandy came in with Ginger Ross and Betty Donovan right behind her, and poured coffee for all three of them. "Personally, I was never really sure the man was human, until lately. Enormously attractive, of course, but not quite human. What's your secret, Joanna?"

"It's not my secret," Joanna denied. "It's the children. For the first time in his life, Ben has found something more important to him than his work. He's making up for lost time, that's all."

"Oh, sure," Betty scoffed. "That's what you'd like us to believe."

Esther smiled over the rim of her coffee cup. "I'm sure the children are a big part of it. I don't know what it is about grandchildren, but even a man who's been the best of all possible fathers, or the worst, turns into a total softie when the next generation starts arriving."

"They're not the only ones," Ginger said. "I never had a bit of trouble telling my kids no when they wanted something they shouldn't have, but the grandchildren can make the most outrageous demands, and I don't even put up a token resistance."

"None of us do," Margaret said. "We don't have to. We can spoil them all we want to and not have to live with the consequences. After we've indulged them until they aren't fit to live with, we can send them home to drive their parents wild."

"Right," Sandy agreed. "I enjoyed raising my family, but there are some distinct advantages to having the nest empty, too."

"Such as privacy," Margaret said.

"True," Betty agreed. "As much as I love to have my children and grandchildren visit, I'm just as glad when it's time for them to go home again. I don't really mind the extra housework and noise, or having to keep them out of assorted television and toaster parts, but . . . Pete and I aren't used to sharing the house with anyone anymore. It . . . it sort of cramps our style."

Esther set her empty cup on the counter. "That it does. And no matter how much the men love the grandchildren, they do get grumpy when they're frustrated."

"Tell me about it," Sandy exclaimed. "Jim is bad enough now. I can hardly imagine what it's going to be like when we're both retired."

Ginger grinned at Joanna. "I hope we aren't shocking you, Joanna. What they're trying to say is, once you're able to bring sex out of the bedroom, it's hard to put it back."

"I'm not shocked," Joanna denied. "It's just that, since Robert and I never had any children, we never had to face that particular problem. We always had the freedom of the whole house." She couldn't resist the chance to boast a little. "And the garage, and the patio." She smiled as memories flooded over her and added softly, "Anytime, anyplace, as long as the drapes were closed."

The others were silent for a minute, either respecting her memories or indulging in a few of their own.

"What I want to know," Sandy said finally, "Is how you and Ben manage, having his grandchildren full time and not even living together."

"Sandy!" Esther gasped.

Sandy's jaw snapped shut with an audible click and her face turned crimson. Joanna could sympathize. Her own face felt like a furnace.

"Oh, Joanna, I'm so sorry," Sandy cried. "I had no right to say such a thing. Or even think such a thing. I mean, it's none of my business how—or even if—"

Esther laid a hand on Sandy's shoulder and told Joanna, "Don't be too upset with her. We've all been friends for so long, and know each other so well, we don't have any secrets left. We tend to forget that you haven't had time to get used to our particular brand of togetherness—or nosiness, I guess you could call it."

Sandy caught her breath and managed to say, "I just meant, we're all over here most afternoons, and the kids are here in the evenings, and . . . of course, maybe you don't— I mean, you aren't . . . that is, you and Ben seem so perfect for each—I just assumed—I mean, I guess we *all* assumed . . ."

"Shut up, Sandy," Margaret said, not unkindly. "You're only making it worse."

"It's all right," Joanna managed to say. "In Sandy's place, I'd probably be wondering, too. All I can say is, now you know why we only meet after lunch."

Margaret grinned at her. "That's it? No juicy details?"

"There are plenty of juicy details, but they're none of your business," Joanna said firmly. "Now, ladies, the men are over at Ben's trying to put together a proposal for their first job, and I think we'd better get back to work, too."

But as they cleaned up the men's typing clutter to make room for their own work, she found herself basking in an unaccustomed glow—first, because they had accepted her into the group so completely that they felt free to make such personal comments, and second, because they had thought it was perfectly reasonable for her, the outwardly staid and proper widow Blake, to be in the middle of a blazing love affair with a man they found enormously attractive and sexy as hell, and that they credited her with making a tremendous change in the man they had originally thought was cold and aloof.

Later, as she and Ben said good night, it occurred to her that it worked both ways. He and the children had made some tremendous changes in her, too. A vague sense of unease stirred inside her, then was lost in the warmth of Ben's good night kiss.

Fourteen

Joanna paused in the doorway and grinned at the expression on Ben's face as Joey scampered into the living room on all fours, barking and growling in a way that brought the fur up on the back of Bernie's neck. Bernie took refuge behind Ben, watched for a minute, then seemed to decide it was a new game. With a window-rattling woof of his own, he bounded across the room and leaped on Joey, knocking him flat on the carpet.

Joey screamed with delight, grabbed Bernie around the neck, and the two of them wrestled their way across the room in a flurry of arms and legs and plumy tails that made it hard to tell where the real dog ended and the boy in the dog's costume began.

Ben moved hastily out of the way, then surrendered to his own helpless mirth.

The tumult on the floor subsided after a few minutes. Bernie sat back with his tongue lolling from his mouth and his tail thumping on the floor while Joey sat up and tugged at his mask until the eyes lined up more or less with his own.

"Boy, this is some great costume, isn't it, Grandpa? It even fooled old Bernie."

"It sure did," Ben agreed. "I'm glad Bernie's wearing a collar. Otherwise, I might have trouble telling the two of you apart." He grinned at Joanna. "Joey's right. That's some great costume."

"The children did most of the work," she protested, but she had to agree with them. The costume was sensational. It had started life as white cotton pajamas, but now sported large brown patches which Joey had painstakingly drawn and colored to approximate Bernie's lush coat. She'd added a fluffy tall of yarn and they'd bought a brown and white dog's mask to complete the costume.

"Where's Becky?" Ben asked. I want to see her costume, too."

"I'm right here." Becky stepped into the doorway beside Joanna. She was also wearing what had once been white pajamas, now marked with black and orange patches to match the calico kitten snuggled against her chest.

"That's a great costume, too," he exclaimed. "You look as if you really are Lovey's mama."

"Thank you, Grandpa. Now you know why we needed all those Magic Markers."

"I'm very relieved. I thought maybe you were eating them or something."

Both children giggled, and Joey exclaimed, "I'll bet we win a prize at the party."

"I wouldn't be at all surprised," Ben said.

"Grandpa," Becky said, "don't forget. You said you'd take some pictures to send to Grandma."

"So I did." He took a camera—brand new, from the looks of it—from the desk drawer, and looked it over dubiously. "I hope I can remember what the instructions said about using this."

Joanna watched him fumble with it for a minute, then took it from him. "Allow me."

"Thanks. I don't know the first thing about photography," Ben admitted, and proved it with a barrage of advice and suggestions as she framed shot after shot in the viewfinder—of the children alone, with Bernie and Lovey, and with Ben.

Then, at the children's insistence, she gave the camera to Ben, showed him which button to push, and posed with them herself, finding herself misty-eyed as she suddenly felt every inch the grandmother she'd never been.

Ben called a halt when Becky wanted to go find Tinkerbell. "Maybe some other time," he said. "Right now, I think we'd better get you to the party, or they'll be starting without you."

They took the shortcut through the hedge, Becky and Joel running on ahead, Ben and Joanna following at a more sedate pace. "Look at them," Ben said. "Normal, happy children, excited about going to a party with other normal, happy children. That's something I was afraid I might not ever see. I owe you again, Joanna, anything you want, anytime you want it."

"Don't be silly. All I did was help them a little with their costumes."

He shook his head. "I don't mean for the costumes. I mean, for doing for Jennie's children what she would be doing for them if she could. The children and I are eternally grateful, and I think somehow, somewhere, Jennie is, too." He was quiet for a minute, and when he spoke again, his voice was rough with emotion.

"I thought I was handling things so well. My own grief, the children's loss. But tonight I realized for the first time how much Joel and Jennie lost. Not just their own lives, but their children's lives, too, and that's the worst hurt of all. They're the ones who should be here, admiring the costumes, loving the children, caring for them, watching them grow up."

She caught his hand in hers and said softly, "You said it yourself, Ben. Somehow, somewhere, they are. And it's you they're grateful to."

He lifted her hand to his lips and kissed it, and they walked the rest of the way in silence.

They watched from the front walk as the children ran up the steps and Holly opened the door for them. Before they disappeared inside, Becky turned and waved. "Good night, Grandpa and Joanna. We'll see you tomorrow."

"Tomorrow?" Joanna asked.

"Oh, didn't I tell you?" Ben asked, his quick grin making it clear that he knew perfectly well he hadn't. "Holly's parents thought it would be easier to hold a sleep-over than to take all the kids home tonight." He took her arm and gently urged her back the way they had come. "So we have the whole night to ourselves. Now, about that adult party you promised me . . ."

She pulled away from him in mock indignation. "*I* promised *you*? I thought it was the other way around."

"Whichever. Why don't we go home, get into our costumes, and—"

"Our costumes? Oh, you mean our fig leaves."

"No fig leaves."

"All right," she agreed. "No fig leaves. Where are we holding this party? Your place, or mine?"

"Mine." They had reached the privacy of her backyard. He caught her face between his hands for a warm, lingering kiss that made her hungry for more. "For once, I want to make love to you in my own bed, and spend the whole night with you, and find you still there beside me when I wake in the morning."

She returned his kiss, savoring the warmth of his body in the cool night air. "Sounds like my kind of party," she told him. She thought unexpectedly of Sandy Bagwell saying, "What I want to know is, how you and Ben manage . . ."

She took Ben's arm and they started across the yard to the hole in the hedge. *We manage just fine, Sandy,* she thought. *We manage just fine.*

It had been his kind of party, too, Ben thought. He savored the memory of Joanna's nude body in the flickering light of the jack-o'-lanterns he'd placed at either end of the dresser, and the memory of Joanna, warm and vibrant beneath him. But as wonderful as their lovemaking had been, he cherished even more the joyous intimacy of sharing his own bed with her, of falling asleep beside her, and of waking this morning to find her still there.

He propped up on one elbow to study her sleeping form in the daylight that streamed through the window. Snuggled under the covers, one hand tucked beneath her cheek, she looked as innocent and vulnerable as Becky. He let his gaze move lower, over the full breasts, shapely and exciting even under the thin blanket, the slender waist, the curve of her hip. Now she looked like the sex goddess she'd been last night.

Most of all, she looked as if she belonged there, in his bed. In his life. Completely and permanently. It was an idea he'd given a lot of thought lately. Maybe it was time to do something about it.

Then she opened her eyes and smiled at him, a wicked, inviting smile, and the subtle but definite stirring in his loins told him there was something else he wanted to do first.

The special feeling of intimacy continued as they dressed and went downstairs together, grew as they cooked and ate breakfast, and almost overwhelmed him through the simple domesticity of cleaning the kitchen together. Definitely, it was time to do something about it. Joanna was probably wondering what was taking him so long.

He waited until she'd emptied the dishwater and dried her hands, then slid his arms around her while he nuzzled the side of her neck and kissed the curve where it joined her shoulder. "Did you enjoy last night and this morning as much as I did?"

"You need to ask?" She glanced over her shoulder at him and grinned. "Don't tell me you're suffering from performance anxiety at this stage of the game!"

He shook his head. "No. Separation anxiety. After that wonderful night we just spent—sleeping together, *really* sleeping together, all night, waking up together, having breakfast together—I don't want it all to come to an end when you go home."

She turned to face him and put her arms around his neck. "Silly. It isn't going to come to an end. We'll still have our mornings together, and an occasional dinner out and motel afterwards."

"You'd better believe it," he agreed, "but that's not what I mean. We could have so much more. I *want* so much more. I want—oh, damn." He stared toward the living room and the sound of his front door bell. "Don't go away," he told her. "I'll get rid of whoever it is and be right back."

He yanked open the front door, prepared to deliver a blistering lecture to whatever eager-beaver salesman or religious fanatic dared to disturb what would have been, if he'd been allowed to finish it, a proposal of marriage.

Instead, he stared goggle-eyed and open-mouthed at the handsome, dark-haired woman who stood on his porch and smiled faintly at his consternation.

"Fran?" the word came out a hoarse croak.

"Hello, Ben. I came to find out for myself how you and the children are managing. May I see them, please?"

Her voice was pitched a little lower than he remembered it, her words a little slower and more precise, but the rhythm and cadence of her Southern upbringing were still there, still as attractive as the first time he'd heard them.

With an effort, he dragged his jaw back up into place and found his own voice. "They aren't here right now."

Her brows slanted together in a faint but unmistakably skeptical frown. "Where are they?"

"They were invited to a Halloween party and sleepover at a friend's house."

"Will they be home fairly soon? I've come a long way to see them, Ben."

"Anytime now."

"Then I'd like to wait, if you don't mind." She hesitated, then asked, "Aren't you going to ask me in?"

"Oh, of course. Please, come in, Fran."

She stepped inside, waiting patiently while he pulled the door shut and turned to study her. He hadn't seen her in years, and the image he carried in his mind was of the Fran he'd known then. Somehow, he'd forgotten that she would grow older, even as he had. She hadn't changed much, otherwise, only traded the youthful prettiness he remembered for the same kind of graceful poise and maturity Joanna had. It made her enormously attractive. He wondered unexpectedly what she saw when she looked at him. He'd changed a lot more than she had.

He took her coat and started to ask her to sit down, remembered Joanna, waiting in the kitchen, and asked instead, "Have you had breakfast, Fran? Or can I offer you a cup of coffee?"

"Coffee would be nice."

She followed him into the kitchen and

came to a sudden halt at the sight of
Joanna, still sitting at the table. Joanna's
eyes widened briefly, and her lips curved in
a smile that was warm without being effu-
sive. Then they both turned to look at Ben.

He remembered his manners abruptly.
"Uh, Joanna, this is Fran. Fran, Joanna."
In his stupefaction, he couldn't remember
either woman's last name.

He watched while the two women examined each other briefly, sizing each other up
like two stray dogs. *Only,* he thought, fighting a sudden urge to giggle, *with a lot more
class.*

They seemed to reach a decision about
each other. Fran stepped forward and offered her hand.

"Joanna," Fran said. "The children
wrote to me about you. I'm glad to meet
you at last."

Joanna flicked a quick glance at Ben,
then extended her own hand. "I'm glad
to meet you, too."

"Well," Ben said, and winced at the false
heartiness in his voice. "I'll have that coffee for you in a minute, Fran."

He managed to measure water and coffee into the pot without spilling either,

and turned back to the women just as Fran sat down and grinned at Joanna. "This is something I never expected to see—Ben Walker, homemaker."

Joanna returned the grin. "I don't think he ever expected to see it either, but he's doing very well at it."

"With Joanna's help," Ben said. "She started by helping me organize the kitchen, and ended by giving me a crash course in cooking, cleaning, laundry, first aid. You just name it, and somewhere around here, you'll find a chart that tells you how to do it." He realized he was babbling and changed the subject quickly.

"Fran, what brings you back to the good old U.S.A., and how long do you plan to stay?"

"We're here for a combination of business and visiting old friends," she said. "We plan to stay through Christmas and go back to Rome around the first of the year. Carlo is going to be busy all this week, so it seemed like a good time for me to come and check on the children."

"They're doing very well," he said. "They're turning from sad little robots back into normal, happy children. Joanna's helped a lot."

"Not that much," Joanna denied. "It's Ben who's made them feel secure and loved and safe again. He adores them, and they think he's the greatest grandpa in the world. I suspect they're right."

"I try," Ben said, his voice gruff. He took cups and saucers from the cupboard and set them on the table.

Joanna shook her head and pushed her chair back. "None for me, thanks. It's time I went home and tended to my own home-making. Fran, it was so nice to meet you. I hope we'll have a chance to visit again before you leave."

"You can count on it," Fran murmured.

Before Ben could ask her to stay, Joanna was gone. They watched the kitchen door swing shut, then Fran said, "She's afraid I'm going to make trouble for you and the children."

"So am I," Ben said frankly. "Fran, if you have any idea of taking the children back to Europe with you, forget it. They've been through a terrible experience, and they're just beginning to feel safe again. I'm not going to let anything threaten that."

"I agree with you. I'm not at all convinced they should stay with you permanently, but they aren't ready for another change just yet. So, as much as I'd like to have them, I'm not here to try to take them from you. I just want to make sure you're doing right by them."

"I'm doing the best I can." He hadn't meant to sound so defensive, and added quickly, "I told you, Joanna gave me a crash course in the basics of homemaking, and the kids are giving me a crash course in parenthood. I don't know it all yet, but I'm learning more every day."

Fran smiled faintly. "No one ever knows it all. Ben, I know how hard you're trying, but I also know, probably a lot better than you do, what an enormous burden you've taken on yourself."

"I don't consider it a burden," he said gruffly. "Fran, I've changed since you last knew me. Those children have become the most important part of my life. I'd do anything in the world for them, and consider it a privilege."

"Of course you would. Now. But what about next month? Or next year? Sooner or later, the novelty is going to wear off, and you'll want to be off looking for the next challenge."

He shook his head. "No. You have every reason to feel that way, and once upon a time, you'd have been right. But things are different now. Fran, when I found out I was going to have the children, I didn't just take some time off from work. I *retired*. I'm not the same man who used to neglect his wife and family. I've changed."

"Into a full-time homemaker and single parent? That's hard to believe."

"No," he admitted. "Not full-time." He grinned as a new thought hit him. "I'm not sure the children could stand me full-time. Besides, they go to school, they visit their friends. Those are the times I use for myself."

"Use? How?" She glanced quickly out the window, toward the house on the other side of the hedge.

"Yes, Joanna's part of it, but I'll be working part-time, too. Some of us who've reached retirement age are forming a job shop. I'll be my own boss. I'll work only as much as I want to, and only when I want to." He forced himself to meet her eyes. "I'll be working again, but

I'll never again be a workaholic. I've finally come to understand how much I cheated myself and everyone around me by letting my work become more important to me than the people I loved, the people who loved me."

"I hope you're right, but . . ." She shrugged, and he knew what she was thinking. It didn't matter. He and Joanna knew the truth, and Fran would learn it, in time.

He took a deep breath and glanced, as she had done, out the window and toward Joanna's house. "And as for the single part, I'm hoping to change that, too."

"I don't blame you. She's not only very attractive, but she seems like a nice person, and she obviously has pretty strong feelings about you, too."

"Strong feelings?"

Fran nodded. "Protective. I think she'd probably tear me limb from limb if she thought I was going to harm you or the children in any way."

"Really?" Ben realized he was grinning like an idiot and added hastily, "Let's hope it doesn't come to that."

Fran started to answer and broke off as

the kitchen door swung open, and Becky stood silhouetted in the opening.

"Bye, Holly," she called over her shoulder. "We had a wonderful time. Thanks for walking us home." She turned to come in and was nearly knocked off her feet as Joey and Bernie scrambled past her.

"Grandpa," Joey exclaimed, "It was the best party, and I did win a prize. And so did Becky."

"Oh, Joey," Becky cried. "I wanted to tell him myself. Holly said we had the best costumes she'd ever—" She broke off as she caught sight of Fran.

"Children," Ben told them gently, "This is your Daddy's mother, your grandmother. She's come all the way from Europe to see you."

They immediately turned shy and silent, staring down at their feet as if they were afraid Fran would break if they looked at her directly.

Bernie had no such inhibitions. He bounded around the table, plopped his front feet in Fran's lap, and greeted her with a lopsided, tongue-lolling grin.

"Bernie!" Becky's voice held an agony of embarrassment.

Fran laughed, grabbed a handful of fur on either side of Bernie's head, and tugged on it the way Joey did. "Hello, Bernie. I'm glad to meet you, too."

Joey's eyes widened. "Do you like dogs?"

"Yes, I do, and I like boys who dress like dogs. That's some costume."

"Joanna helped me make it."

"Well, I think you and Joanna are both very clever. What about you, Becky? Are you dressed to look like your kitten? If so, she must be a pretty one."

"Oh, yes!" Becky exclaimed. "I'll go get her." She ran from the room and returned almost immediately with Lovey cradled in her arms.

Ben watched in awe as the children blossomed under Fran's gentle charm. Relief washed over him as one of his deepest fears—the one he tried to keep so far in the back of his mind that it wouldn't control his life—began to ease. He would never give the children up while there was breath in his body, but if anything ever happened to him . . . He drew a ragged breath. They wouldn't have to be alone again. He blinked fiercely, hoping no one would notice that his eyes were moist, then realized that

Fran's had grown moist, too, and her voice had become higher pitched and a little wavery.

"Kids, why don't you go upstairs and put on some regular clothes, then you can come back down and visit with your grandmother some more."

"Okay," Joey said. "Come on, Bernie." Dog and boy squeezed through the door together.

Becky started to follow, then came back and handed Lovey to Fran. "You can hold her while I change my clothes, Grandma."

Fran held the kitten close while her eyes filled with tears. "Oh God, Ben," she whispered. "They're gone. They're really gone, aren't they? I don't think I actually believed it until I saw the children. Somehow, I expected to find Joel and Jennie here with you and the whole thing just some silly mistake. But . . ." Her tears spilled over and she turned her face away from him.

"I know," he murmured. "I know. Every so often, it hits me all over again, and even though I know it's true, some little, irrational, part of me keeps insisting that maybe it isn't. Maybe I'll wake up, and it will just be a dream."

He thumped his fist with controlled violence against the table. "And I get so angry. Not just for the children, or even for myself, but for *them*. I miss them so much, but it's worse, wondering if somehow, somewhere, they're missing us, missing the life and happiness they should have had."

She jerked her head up and stared at him. "You really have changed. The old Ben would never have thought a thing like that, much less have said it aloud."

He grinned wryly. "The old Ben was an idiot." He took a paper napkin from the holder on the table and handed it to her. "The kids will be back down in a couple of minutes. I've assured them that grown-ups cry, too, but I'm not sure they quite believe it yet."

She smiled through her tears, accepted the napkin, and wiped her face. "Well, I certainly don't want to shatter their illusions. Ben, may I spend the day with them? I mean, take them out to lunch, maybe to a movie afterward, or just someplace where we can talk and get acquainted. They've grown so much since the last time I saw them, I hardly know them now. And I'm sure they barely remember me."

He hesitated, and she added, "I promise, I won't kidnap them and take them back to Europe with me. You tell me what time you want them back, and I'll have them here."

"I'm not worried about that. I was just thinking, there aren't many places you can go to just talk, and it's too chilly to spend the day in the park or at the playground. If you'd like, you can take them to lunch, and then bring them back here."

He forestalled her protest by adding quickly, "I'd enjoy the chance to take Joanna out to lunch and spend the afternoon with her. I'm due for another typing lesson anyway."

"You're learning to type?"

He grinned. "There seem to be conflicting opinions on that, but I'm trying."

She crumpled the napkin and threw it into the trash as the children came back in. "Ben, I think parenthood is doing you a world of good."

"You're right," he said soberly. "I should have tried it years ago."

Fifteen

Somehow, Joanna made it across what seemed like miles of her backyard and braced herself against the kitchen door for a few minutes, gulping in deep breaths of the chilly November air as if her lungs were starved for oxygen. Her face felt flushed and the breakfast she had so lightheartedly helped Ben prepare and eat seemed to have taken up residence in her throat.

She felt like a total idiot, behaving this way. She had known Fran existed in Ben's past. She should have been prepared to face her in Ben's present and in the children's present. Besides, Fran seemed to be a lovely woman, not the type to make trouble for Ben, or to put the children through a custody battle she had almost no chance of winning. Surely she would leave them with Ben and content herself with visiting them and perhaps letting them visit her now and again. There was no reason to be so upset.

A shiver swept over her and she hurried into the warmth of the kitchen before she became any more chilled. Once inside, she rummaged through the vitamins and cosmetics in the bathroom medicine chest, looking for an antacid tablet, then admitted to herself that the pain in her chest wasn't indigestion. It was plain old green-eyed jealousy, not because of Ben, but because of the children. Why would they need a substitute grandmother when a real one was available? And why hadn't she kept her original vow not to get involved with this sexy grandpa and his adorable children?

She sighed. Might as well ask why she and Robert hadn't had a family, so she'd have grandchildren of her own, and not need Ben's. Or ask why Robert hadn't lived, so she wouldn't need Ben.

But she didn't need Ben, she told herself fiercely. She only wanted him.

The sound of the back door opening and closing sent her back to find him standing in the kitchen.

He grinned at her. "The bad news is,

you're stuck with me for the rest of the day. The good news is, I'll take you anywhere you want to go for lunch."

"Lunch?" She didn't want lunch; she was having enough trouble with breakfast. Then the other thing he'd said registered. "The rest of the day?"

"Fran wants to spend a little time alone with the kids, have a chance to get acquainted. There aren't many places you can go, this time of year, so I said I'd spend the day with you and let them stay at home." When she didn't answer, he added uncomfortably, "Unless, of course, you don't feel like putting up with me."

She came out of her stupor abruptly, pulled out a chair, and sat at the table. "Of course not. I'm glad you came over. I've been sitting here wondering what was going on over there. Now that I have the chance to be nosy, I'm not going to blow it. Did she really just come to visit, or . . ."

He moved a chair close to hers and sat beside her. "She came to check on me," he admitted. "So far, she seems agreeably surprised at the way I'm handling things, but doubtful that I can keep it up for long." He drew a deep breath and let it out slowly.

"She still doesn't believe I won't get tired of the children sooner or later, and go back to my old habits. I can't blame her. She only knows what I was like before. It's going to take a while before she realizes I'm not the same man she used to know. '

"The children will set her straight," Joanna predicted, then couldn't help adding, "I suppose they were excited to see her."

"I think 'stunned' might be a better word. At least, at first. They hadn't seen her in awhile, and I don't think they really remembered her. But after she'd admired their costumes, made friends with the animals, and shaken Joey's hand instead of kissing him, she had them pretty well won over."

"I should think so!" She hesitated, then glanced away and added, "She sounds like top-notch grandmother material."

Ben studied her profile briefly, then caught her chin in one hand and turned face toward him. "Hey, do I detect a bit of 'performance anxiety' there?"

"Of course not," she snapped, then added with reluctant honesty, "It's just that she's a real grandmother, and knows all about children, and . . ."

"And the children know all about you, and no one, real grandmother or not, will ever take your place. Trust me." He released her chin and added, "And with that settled, do you suppose you could spend the afternoon teaching me to cook something really classy and gourmet?"

She stared at him, bewildered by the abrupt change of subject. "Classy and gourmet? Why?"

"Because I invited Fran to have dinner with us tomorrow—you're supposed to come, too—and I want to impress her."

She laughed helplessly and put her arms around him. "Doesn't she like hot dogs?"

"Joanna!"

"Sorry. Ben, make your famous beef stew and a tossed salad. We'll all enjoy that, and if you like, I'll show you how to make dumplings for the stew."

"I'd like. Meanwhile . . ." He hesitated, clearly not as relaxed as he was pretending to be. "There's just one other thing I need to tell you. She wants them to spend Thanksgiving with her."

She fought off another pang of jealousy,

but couldn't help asking, "Will you let them?"

"I don't think I have much choice. I want her and the children to know each other, now, while they're young. I want her to see them growing up, not miss years out of their childhoods." He paused, then added, "And I don't want to put Fran through the same thing with the kids that I went through with Joel. I blamed her for that for a long time, before I realized it wasn't really her fault."

"You blamed Fran? I thought you said you missed out on his childhood because you were too busy with your work."

"Maybe I was, but maybe, if I'd had the chance—but I didn't." He stared down at the table, one thumbnail tracing the design of the plastic tabletop.

"Want to tell me about it? I'm not being nosy this time," she added quickly, "But if it would help to talk about it . . ."

"I don't know if it will help or not. There isn't really a whole lot to tell." He lifted his gaze to the window over her desk, as if he might see through the hedge and into his own kitchen, then stared back down at the table as he spoke.

"Joel wasn't much older than Joey, when Fran got fed up with me—or maybe I should say without me—and decided to call it quits. She married again within a couple of years, and she and her new husband moved to Europe. They took Joel with them, of course."

"That must have been rough—for both of you."

"Rougher on me than on him, I expect. He had his mother and his new stepfather, and an exciting new life; I had . . . my work, and somehow, it didn't seem as important or fulfilling as it had been.

"Joel finished school in Europe, and I only saw him a couple of times before he came home to attend college. We tried to get together now and again, but by then we were strangers and it was just too uncomfortable.

"Then he met Jennie and became engaged to marry her. He at least invited me to his wedding, although I suspect that was mostly Jennie's doing. For some strange reason, she liked me." He grinned wryly. "Or maybe she just felt sorry for me. Whatever it was, she made up her mind that Joel and I were going to get to know each other, and because of her determination, we did."

His voice had grown rough, and he stopped to clear his throat. "We were just starting to be close, for the first time in our lives, when the accident happened." His voice betrayed him utterly, and he sat mute, his eyes closed as if to keep Joanna from seeing what he was feeling.

She reached out anyway, laid her hand over his, and waited patiently until he was able to speak again.

"Fran visited them, of course, but thanks to Jennie, she and Joel and the children were closer to me than to Fran for the last few years. I think that's why they named me as the children's guardian."

This time, when he paused, she said softly, "You loved Jennie very much, didn't you?"

He nodded. "She was the daughter I never had—not one who came to me by an accident of birth, but one who chose me." He looked up at her and smiled faintly. "The way the children have chosen you."

Her inadequacies surfaced again and she glanced away quickly.

He sighed gustily. "So, that's why I'll

most likely let the children spend Thanksgiving with her, if they want to. But I want you to know, I'm going to miss them like hell."

"So am I. Maybe we can do something special for Thanksgiving, something to keep us busy while they're away. Perhaps we could go somewhere together, or have a special celebration at home, just the two of us."

He took her hand and pressed it to his lips, first the back, then the palm. "Sounds wonderful, and I think I know the perfect thing to celebrate."

"And what's that?"

"I'll tell you later," he promised, "when I have all the details worked out."

Ben spent Sunday watching Fran and Joanna get acquainted. If either of them felt any insecurity or sense of rivalry, he couldn't detect it. They seemed as casual and comfortable with each other as if they'd been friends for years. He relaxed finally and enjoyed the day as much as Becky and Joel did.

When Fran went upstairs to say good

night to the children, Joanna decided it was time for her to say good night, too. Ben followed her down the steps into the garage and took her in his arms as she turned to face him.

"I'm glad you were here today, and that you and Fran had the chance to get to know each other."

"So am I. She seems to be a wonderful person, and I think you were crazy to let her get away from you."

"You're right, but at least I learned something important from it."

"And what's that?"

He nuzzled the pulse point just below her left ear, hoping to catch a lingering whiff of her perfume, then inched his lips down the line of her jaw and kissed the corner of her mouth. "I won't make that particular mistake again."

She turned her head so that their lips met, and returned his kiss as eagerly as he gave it.

"Are you sure you can't stay just a little longer?"

She shook her head and slipped out of his arms. "Fran will be ready to leave as soon as the kids are in bed, and the two of you will probably want to talk a little more before she goes. You don't need me for that. Say good night to her for me."

He watched until she disappeared through the hedge, then went back inside.

Fran came down the stairs a moment later. "I expect they'll be asleep in about five minutes. Ben, thank you for giving me this weekend with them. I hope I'll be welcome again soon."

"Of course you will. For their sake as well as for yours."

She glanced into the kitchen, and then into the living room. "Where's Joanna?"

"She went home."

"Oh, I'm sorry. I wanted to speak to her again. Well, perhaps next time." She opened the storm closet where he'd hung her coat.

"She wanted to give us a few minutes alone, in case we wanted to talk a little more."

Fran smiled. "Do we?"

He took the coat from her but instead of helping her put it on, carried it into the living room and laid it over the back of a chair. "We do."

"Then your lady is not only considerate, but perceptive. I hope you appreciate her."

"Believe me, I do. But what I wanted to say is that I've learned to appreciate you, too. Fran, Joanna's taught me about a lot more than housekeeping. Between her and the children, I've finally come to understand just how badly I cheated you and Joel—and myself.

"I won't go into the details of how and why I was such a jackass. I'm sure you know them as well as I do. I just want to ask if you can ever forgive me for the hell I put you and Joel through." His voice felt unsteady, and he paused to clear his throat. "I missed both of you terribly, but I'm glad you had the sense to leave me. It would have been a pity to waste your life and Joel's, too, just because I was such a fool."

"Ben . . ." Fran reached out to touch his cheek in a gesture of affection that had never meant more to him than it did now. "I forgave you years ago. I'm sure I was as much to blame as you were. If I'd been less demanding and a little more patient and understanding, like Joanna, maybe things would have been different for us."

She dropped her hand and laughed

softly. "But of course, if they had, I wouldn't have had these wonderful years with Carlo, and you wouldn't have met Joanna." Before he could think of an answer to that, she leaned forward and kissed him lightly on the lips.

"I've been totally happy and fulfilled in my marriage to Carlo, but if anything ever happens to him, Joanna had better watch out, because I'll be back here giving her some competition." She took her coat from the back of the chair and handed it to him.

He couldn't seem to get his tongue working again, and his ears were burning, and probably glowing, too, but he helped her with the coat, and hugged her warmly before they said goodbye.

At the door, she paused. "Do I get the children for Thanksgiving?"

He nodded. "Of course, and any other time you want them. Just not for keeps."

"Not for keeps," she agreed, and then she was gone again, but this time, he knew he'd gained something wonderful, not lost it.

Joanna sat at her desk, trying not to look across the hedge toward the house where

Ben and Fran were saying good night. She'd turned Robert's picture to face away from her, because she was still battling twinges of jealousy and felt ashamed of herself.

She knew Ben was right. She and the children loved each other, and she'd always have her own place in their lives. But her years with Robert, as rich and wonderful as they'd been, hadn't taught her much about sharing. It was hard to know that Fran also had a place.

Her conscience stabbed her painfully again and she thought—hoped—it was winning. She loved the children. She wanted them to have everything they needed, and after the day she'd just spent with them, she knew they needed Fran.

Besides, Fran was a lovely woman, who deserved the love of her grandchildren. Joanna was glad she'd met her, glad for the relief of knowing Fran held no ill will toward Ben, and also wanted only the best for the children.

And Fran certainly had too much class to try to push Joanna aside. It was just that she also had all those grandmother skills that Joanna did not.

The ringing of the front door bell startled her. She almost never had visitors this late at night, except for Ben, and he came in by the back door.

Not alarmed, but prudent, she kept the chain on as she opened the door and peered through the crack, then took the chain off and opened the door wide. "Fran! I wasn't expecting you."

"I know. I'm sorry if I startled you. I just wanted to talk to you for a few minutes before I leave."

"Oh, of course. Please, come in." She closed the door behind Fran and offered to take her coat.

"Thank you, but what I have to say won't take that long."

Joanna's conscience stabbed her again. "If you're worried about my relationship with Ben, I swear to you, the children are always our first concern. We've been very careful never to—"

Fran hushed her with a wave of her hand. "I know that. It isn't what I want to talk about, anyway. I mean, this is the nineties, after all, and you and Ben are both adults, and it really isn't any of my business."

Joanna gave her conscience a silent

sneer and told it not to jump to any more conclusions.

"Besides," Fran added, "you're good for him, Joanna. I don't ever think I've seen him looking so happy and contented."

Prodded either by modesty or the need to atone for her jealousy, Joanna protested, "Most of that is because of the children. It hurts him so badly that he missed his son's childhood. He feels the children are a second chance, and he swears he isn't going to blow it."

"And I believe him. But it's you I came here to talk about, not Ben. I'll admit, I was concerned at first about your relationship with the children, but after seeing you with them today, I'm not worried anymore."

"Maybe you should be. I never had children of my own. I don't know the first thing about them, or about taking care of them. The only thing I can do is muddle through and try not to make too many mistakes."

"You know how to be warm and loving, don't you? What more do you need to know?" Fran wrapped her coat a little more warmly around her and moved closer to the door. "Anyway, I just wanted to tell you I'm glad, both for Ben's sake and for the children's, that he found you, and I want to wish you all much happiness together."

"Oh . . . Fran, maybe before you're too free with your approval, you ought to know that although I'm very fond of Ben, and all that, there isn't anything permanent between us."

Fran looked surprised, then grinned. "Maybe not now, but it won't be long. He always was a little slow at some things, but—"

"No," Joanna denied. "That isn't what I mean. I have plans that were made long before I met Ben. I put them aside when he asked me to help him get this job shop started, but one of these days, I have to get on with them."

"Perhaps," Fran said. "But don't be surprised if Ben has other ideas. And don't be surprised if you find yourself changing those plans. He has a way about him."

She opened the door, stepped out, and pulled it shut behind her, leaving Joanna with no one to hear her exclaim, "Now tell me something I don't already know."

* * *

Joanna turned off the vacuum cleaner and surveyed the dining room with satisfaction. It still looked more like an office than a dining room, but at least it looked like a clean office. She normally detested housework as much as any woman did, but with the men busy researching a contract they hoped to bid on, the women had decided to spend the time catching up on their domestic duties. She took comfort from the knowledge that she wasn't the only one pushing a broom and mop this week.

She unplugged the vacuum and wheeled it into the closet, laughing softly as she remembered Ben's fervent declaration that vacuum cleaners were aliens from outer space who had declared war on earthlings— and were winning.

In the kitchen, she put a pot roast in the Dutch oven to brown while she tried to decide how many potatoes and carrots to scrub. She'd always known exactly how much she and Robert would eat, but cooking for a family was a new experience. She wanted to make sure there was enough, but for one meal, not several.

"One apiece and one for the pot" had been her mother's rule of thumb. She shrugged and took out five carrots, five potatoes, then added a couple more of each, just to make sure. If there were leftovers, she'd freeze them or make beef stew for lunch.

Having a man come home to dinner was a new experience for her, too. She and Robert had always come home together. Often, instead of cooking, they had dinner first, or brought in some kind of fast food or a meal from the deli. But food in those days had been simply nourishment. What she was planning today was sharing and companionship, and it was infinitely more satisfying.

The chimes of the Seth Thomas clock in the living room reminded her that the children would be coming home in a few minutes. That was a new experience for her, too. She hoped Becky and Joey were enjoying their time together as much as she was.

She set the scrubbed vegetables aside and started a pot of hot chocolate to have ready when they came in. The bus stop was only a block away, but the November afternoons had turned chilly. Besides, dinner was a long time off for healthy young appetites.

Maybe, after they finished their chocolate, they could—

The thought went unfinished as she enjoyed a good laugh at her own expense. Was this the Joanna who was not going to get involved? Who was going to be so independent, so in charge? Taking care of Ben's children while he worked, fixing Ben's dinner because he'd be tired and hungry when he got home?

Yes, she told herself firmly. It was. She was doing it because she wanted to, had freely chosen to, and not because she had to, or because someone had pressured her into it. This was her way of dealing with her midlife crisis, and of experiencing the things that had been missing from her life.

If it was possible to be more in charge than that, she didn't know how.

Ah, but there was, she realized suddenly. She turned the fire down under the chocolate, reached for the telephone, and called Sandy Bagwell.

By the time Sandy had eagerly accepted Joanna's invitation to a thank-God-it's-Friday lunch the next day, the chocolate was ready to drink and the children were tumbling through the back door. She gave them each a hug and took their jackets.

"Goodness, Becky, what happened to your dress?"

Becky's smile disappeared as she glanced down at the dirt and grass stains on her skirt. "I fell down," she said, after a minute. She ducked her head and her next words were barely audible, "I tore my dress."

At a loss for words to ease her obvious distress, Joanna could only say cheerfully, "I hate to think how many dresses I tore when I was your age."

Becky looked up, her eyes wide and somehow hopeful. "Really?"

Joanna nodded. "Really. Let me see. Maybe we can fix it." She bent over to examine the gap between skirt and bodice and exclaimed, "Good news, sweetheart. You didn't tear it at all. The seam just came apart. Tell your grandpa to bring it over after he washes it, and I'll fix it for you. And tell him if he can't find instructions for removing grass stains, to call me."

Becky sighed with relief. "Oh, thank you, Joanna. I'll be sure to tell him."

Joanna hugged her again, then said, "Go wash your hands, and when you finish your chocolate, you can help me make dessert."

"Oh, good," Joey exclaimed. "Can we make chocolate chip cookies?"

Joanna ruffled his hair. "It's easy to tell whose grandson you are. But I thought we'd do something different tonight. How would you like to make gingerbread men?"

It was completely dark by the time Ben got home, tired from a week of putting his nose back to the old grindstone, but happily confident that this small but lucrative contract was in the bag. Even at this preliminary stage, he could estimate, almost to the penny, how much the job would cost, and how high they could go to make the most profit and still submit the winning bid. God, it felt good to be back in harness again!

He dropped his briefcase on the dining

room table, picked up the flashlight hanging by the kitchen door, and hurried across the familiar route to the hole in the hedge and Joanna's house. The lights streaming from her kitchen windows seem to exude a special kind of hospitality that made him pause for a moment just to prolong the pleasure of it, until a chilly breeze puffed around the corner of the house.

He hurried inside, into the welcoming warmth and the wonderful aroma of pot roast simmering on the stove, and a sweet, spicy scent that promised something special for dessert. Joanna and the children were laughing and talking in the living room, and he had to fight off an almost overwhelming desire to call out, "Honey, I'm home."

He didn't have to. The children had heard the door open and close and came boiling into the kitchen to greet him. Joanna followed, and while he hugged Becky and Joey, she took the lid off the pan on the stove, releasing a cloud of steam and a fragrance that made him realize suddenly how ravenous he was.

"Take off your coat and stay awhile,"

Joanna said. "Dinner will be ready in a minute. I just have to thicken the gravy."

Obediently, he hung his coat in the closet, sharply aware that it wasn't just food he was ravenous for, but Joanna. He fought the urge to take her in his arms and greet her properly, knowing she expected him to observe certain minimum standards of decorum in front of the children.

It was another reason, if he'd needed one, why he had to find a way to get her alone and finish his interrupted proposal. Once they were properly married, the children would expect him to kiss her when he came home at night—or any other time the notion occurred to him. And they'd expect her to share his bedroom, a thought that moved directly from his brain to his loins and sent sweet shivers through his whole body. It had been a week since they'd had a morning alone together, and he was suffering.

Blithely unaware of his discomfort, Joanna set plates and silverware on the table for Becky and Joey to distribute and asked, "How was your day?"

With an effort, he put the needs of his body out of his mind and told her, "Great.

But my evening promises to be even better. Dinner smells wonderful."

He managed to keep his randier thoughts and reactions under control and concentrate on the food and the children's cheerful chatter as they ate. *If Fran could see us now!* he thought. He ate slowly, trying to make the moment last, until Becky exclaimed impatiently, "Oh, hurry up and finish, Grandpa, so we can have dessert."

"We made something special, "Joey said. "It's a surprise."

Ben put his fork down and pushed his plate back. "Okay, I'm finished."

Joanna cleared the dishes away quickly, then produced a tray full of cookies.

"Gingerbread people," Joey exclaimed. "I made the men, and Becky made the ladies."

Ben studied the tray and the cookies with their raisin eyes, candy buttons, and skirts or trousers outlined somewhat erratically with cake icing. "They're wonderful," he said. "They look almost too good to eat, and I'm already pretty full. Maybe I should save mine and just admire them for a while."

The children glanced at each other, and Becky announced, with great dignity, "It's okay, Grandpa. We washed our hands first."

Meekly, he chose one gingerbread man and one gingerbread lady and ate them down to the last crumbs, while Joanna turned quickly to the dishes in the sink, hiding her grin but not her amusement.

After dinner, while the children reveled in an unaccustomed half hour of television and Ben helped clean the kitchen, he told Joanna, "I saved the best part of my news for last. We finished up a little earlier than we'd expected, and I have tomorrow free. We can spend the whole day together."

Unexpectedly, she frowned. "Oh, Ben, I'm sorry. Sandy Bagwell and I are having lunch together tomorrow."

"Can't you put it off until later? She'll understand."

"I could, but I don't want to. I'm looking forward to a little female companionship for a change. Besides, she might understand, but she'd be terribly disappointed. I remember what a treat it used to be, when I was working, to toss my brown bag in the trash and go out somewhere nice."

Great, he thought. *The first time in a week I have some free time, and she's going to spend it with someone else.*

As if she had read his mind, Joanna added, "I really am sorry, Ben, but I had no way of knowing you'd be free tomorrow. Besides, it will only be for an hour or so. Sandy's a working woman; she can't spend all day on lunch."

There was an edge to her voice that warned him not to push it. He stifled his irritation and told her as cheerfully as he could, "Well, then, have a good time."

"Thanks." She sounded mildly surprised, but pleased. "I will."

It seemed a propitious time to finish his interrupted marriage proposal. He debated briefly whether to make it romantic or practical, and settled for asking, "How would you like to give Sandy some really great news tomorrow?"

She opened the door to let Tinkerbell in. "I'd like it fine. What kind of news?"

Before he could answer, Tinkerbell and Lovey bounded in, with Bernie behind them, his joyous *woof!* summoning Joey and Becky from the living room.

By the time the hubbub died away and the

room was quiet again, it was time to take the children home and put them to bed. He'd missed his chance again. He shrugged. He was disappointed, but there'd be another.

It was one of the rare days that Ben and Joanna had to themselves. Nothing was scheduled, and no one was coming.

Except, Ben thought, *the two of us. Any minute now.* Then he pushed the thought away and concentrated only on Joanna beneath him and the heat building in him as they moved rhythmically and magically together. He studied her face, glowing with the pleasure they were giving each other, and realized suddenly that when he thought of making love to Joanna, it wasn't her luscious body that he saw—the warm, full breasts, the slender thighs spread in eager invitation—but her face as it was now, her lips slightly parted, her eyes closed, and her golden brown lashes resting on cheeks flushed from a combination of exertion and sexual excitement.

His own excitement grew now as she opened her eyes and studied his face as avidly as he studied hers. Slowly, he thought. Slowly. Hold back until her body quickened around his and her face filled with the ecstasy that told him she had reached fulfillment. Then he could give in to his own pleasure.

It came quickly and wonderfully, with the intensity he had learned to expect from her. He relaxed his control and surrendered to the explosion that started in that part of him that Joanna held within herself, and then spread to fill his whole body—maybe the whole world, for all he knew—and left him weak and limp and filled with gratitude. He'd had more and better sex these past few weeks with Joanna than most men had in a lifetime.

He waited for her to grow relaxed and still, then reluctantly withdrew from her and lay down beside her. The room was cool, and he pulled the blanket over both of them, then nestled her close.

"It just keeps getting better, doesn't it?" he asked

She laughed and slipped her arm around his waist. "Well, you know the old saying: Practice makes perfect."

"It's always perfect with you." He

reached between them to caress her breasts and nipples, still full and firm from their lovemaking. "I'm only sorry we have so little time to ourselves lately. And if the bid we just submitted wins us that contract, we'll have even less time together."

"And if you don't get the contract, you'll be a full-time homemaker again, and totally miserable."

"Maybe so," he admitted, "but I sure hate having to go down and pound on that typewriter when I'd rather be up here hitting on you."

She made a sound that might have been a suppressed giggle. "Ben! You're terrible."

"Well, it's true. Maybe someday the novelty will wear off, but for now, I still can't get enough of you."

"Or I you," she admitted softly. "There are times when I'd like to call everyone and tell them not to come, then pack a picnic lunch and spend the whole day up here, not having to do anything but just be together and enjoy each other's company, not even making love, if we didn't want to."

"I think we'd probably want to." He lay quietly for a few minutes, luxuriating in the soft warmth of her breasts beneath his fingers, the exciting pressure of her thigh that was slowly but surely arousing him again, and her words echoing through his mind. Maybe it was time to try his proposal again. The longer he waited, the harder it was going to be to take care of all the pre-wedding details in time for the Thanksgiving honeymoon he wanted.

"Ben . . ." Joanna's voice, soft and thoughtful, interrupted his musing. "I can't help noticing that the closer we get to Thanksgiving, the edgier you get."

"Sorry about that, but I have a good reason."

"I know. You're not looking forward to being separated from the children, even for a few days."

"Well, that, too," he agreed.

"When you first said Fran could have them, I said maybe we could do something special for the holiday."

"Something *really* special."

"I've been giving it some thought, and I have a wonderful idea. Why don't we have Thanksgiving dinner here?"

A long weekend alone with Joanna? That would probably reconcile him to the children's absence, if anything could, but his own plans were much grander. He shook his head. "The truth is, I was thinking more of some place with a heart-shaped bed, a hot tub, and room service."

"A heart-shaped bed?" The idea seemed to amuse her. "It's Thanksgiving, not Valentine's Day."

"Okay, a turkey-shaped bed then, and the hot tub is negotiable, but I refuse to budge on the room service."

"Oh, Ben, be serious!"

"Room service is serious."

"So am I, and I'd really like to cook and serve Thanksgiving dinner here."

"It sounds tempting," he agreed, "but it also sounds like a lot of work for just the two of us."

She shook her head. "No, just the fourteen of us. Or sixteen, if Grady and Tony want to bring dates."

"Sixteen! Dates? Joanna, what are you talking about?"

"Thanksgiving dinner," she said patiently. "I want to ask everyone to have dinner here with us."

Ben held back his exclamation of dismay with an effort and tried to think of a way to quash the idea gently. Diplomatically. Totally.

"Oh, it still sounds like . . . well, like an awful lot of work."

"Not really. It just takes planning and a bit of advance preparation. I mean, I've never actually prepared and served a dinner to that many people, but I know how. I'm sure I can do it."

He was willing to bet she'd plan and prepare to the nth degree, and it would be the finest Thanksgiving dinner any of them had ever had, but he had no intention of spending his holiday—holiday? His *honeymoon!*—helping to entertain a dozen or more other people. He tried again. "I'm sure you can. But do you have to do it *this* Thanksgiving?"

"Why not?

"Because . . ." He struggled to find a reason she'd accept. "Because it's our first Thanksgiving together, and we'll be *alone* together, and . . . and there are better things to do than to knock yourself out to entertain people we see almost every day anyway."

"That's silly. I'd hardly knock myself out for strangers. And I'm not planning to knock myself out. I just want to fix a nice meal and enjoy it with my new friends and business associates. You can look at it as a sort of office party, if you want."

"I hate office parties." A horrible thought occurred. "You haven't already invited them, have you?"

"Not yet. I wanted to check with you first, but if I'd known what a fuss you were going to . . ."

Relief washed over him. "Good. Let's forget the whole idea and go with *my* plan."

She pulled away from him and sat up, clutching the blanket around herself. "I don't want to forget the whole idea. I want to have a big, old-fashioned Thanksgiving dinner with the lace tablecloth, and both leaves in the table, and all the other trimmings. What can you possibly have in mind better than that?"

It was the wrong time now, the wrong mood, the wrong everything, but he'd set out to ask her to marry him, and he'd be damned if he was going to fail again. He sat up beside her and took her hand in his.

"What I have in mind is a quiet wedding Wednesday evening before Fran takes the kids, and a four-day honeymoon in some sinfully opulent lovers' hideaway."

Her eyes widened and her mouth opened—not enough for her to say anything, just far enough to let her draw a quick, astonished breath.

"I know it's short notice," he admitted, "but if I let you think about it very long, there won't be enough colored index cards in the world to—"

"I don't need any index cards," she exclaimed, "because there isn't going to be any wedding. I'm sorry, Ben, but I'm not going to marry you."

He thought at first that he had misunderstood her. Or that she'd misunderstood him. He'd expected her response to be happy, excited, eager. It had never occurred to him that she might say no.

"Don't look at me that way," she exclaimed. "I told you up front that I already had a future planned, a future that didn't include getting involved in any kind of personal relationship, not even with a 'sober, solvent, sexy, single senior citizen' like you.''

He winced as she repeated the words he had so casually and flippantly used to introduce himself. ''But you are involved with me, and I don't know how *you'd* define it, but it seems pretty personal to me.''

She reached up to touch his cheek. ''Personal, and very wonderful. Ben, don't misunderstand me. We have a wonderful relationship, and I've loved every minute of it. I have absolutely no regrets. But . . . you once told me that you didn't think I was ready to put myself out to pasture yet, and you were right. But neither am I ready to . . . to . . .''

''Is it the children? You said you didn't have any maternal instincts, that you wouldn't be a surrogate grandmother—''

''Ben! Of course not. This has nothing to do with my maternal instincts, or your children. You know I love them almost as much as you do.''

''Then what is it? What can you possibly want that I—the children and I—can't give you?''

''Myself,'' she said quietly. ''Ben, this is

the first time I've ever had the chance to run my own life, make my own decisions, please myself for a change instead of someone else. I know that sounds selfish, and maybe it is, but I've spent my whole life as someone's child, or someone's wife. Now, I have a tremendous need to be just myself, to find out who I am, what I am."

"My God!" His voice came out barely louder than a whisper. He cleared his throat and added, "I wouldn't take that away from you, Joanna. You know I wouldn't."

"You wouldn't mean to," she agreed, "but with your energy, and determination, and enthusiasm, you wouldn't be able to help it." She drew a deep breath and let it out slowly, then gave him a shaky grin. "Besides, sex—even the fantastic sex we have—isn't enough to build a marriage on."

"We have a hell of a lot more than sex," he exclaimed. "Joanna, we're friends, companions. We enjoy doing things together, being together. We should *be* together, not living two separate lives in two different houses, having to fit our times together into whatever is left over after everything else is taken care of.

"I'd like to make love to you after dinner once in awhile, instead of after breakfast, or wake in the middle of the night and know you're there beside me. I want you to share your life with me, not just your bed. I want us to do *together* all the things that come between us now.

"And as for finding out who you are, or what you are . . . isn't that what you've been helping *me* do, these past weeks? Maybe now it's my turn to do the same for you."

She moved her hand across his cheek so that her fingertips rested lightly on his lips. "It's no use, Ben. I'm not going to let you stampede me into marrying you, the way you did into baking cookies and going to the PTA."

He moved her hand aside. "I've never tried to stampede you."

"All right. Call it what you like. But the fact is that I never intended to get involved with you at all, but you didn't give me any choice! First, you wanted me to help you get your household organized. Then you asked me to visit Joey when he was sick, and help Becky pick out a kitten. And then there was the job shop you wanted me to help you start.

"And there was you, yourself. I was so lonely, and there hadn't been anyone in my life—or in my bed—since Robert died. You were so much fun to be with, so attractive and so persistent—and such a wonderful lover! So I put my plans on hold and went along with you.

"But each time, I told myself it was just for a little while. I wasn't abandoning my plans and my future, I was only setting them aside for a little while. But if I marry you, I will be abandoning them, and you'll continue to plunge full steam ahead, making decisions for both of us and giving me no choice but to trail along in your wake, and that's a rotten basis for a marriage. Besides, Robert and I spent too many years making these plans for me to give them up now."

God! he thought, he had plans for the two of them that made her plans—her dead husband's plans—seem pitiful. But all he said was, "Okay. Maybe I do get a little carried away sometimes, but that's just my natural enthusiasm. I'm not a tyrant. Anytime you think I'm trying to stampede you into something, all you have to do is tell me no."

"All right. I'm telling you no. I won't marry you and I won't spend Thanksgiving honeymooning with you. I'm going to cook a wonderful dinner and invite all our friends to come share it. I hope you'll come, too, but if not, I'm going to do it anyway."

"I'll come," he told her. "You know I'll come. I'll even be civil to everyone, if it'll make you happy."

"It will," she assured him. "It will."

He'd lost one battle, Ben thought, but not the war. Somehow, he'd manage to make her see that they belonged together, forever, and if the only way to hold her until then was with sex, he'd take vitamin E, eat oysters, and watch dirty movies if he had to.

The subtle stirring between his legs told him he wouldn't have to just yet.

As if on cue, she raked her fingernails lightly across his chest, sending tingles of anticipation through his whole body. "You're not angry, are you, Ben?"

He caught her hand in his and kissed it, then slid it down his belly and pressed it against the heat growing below. "No, I'm not angry."

Joanna closed the door quietly behind Ben and watched through the window as he trudged across her backyard and went home to meet the children as they came in from school. When he disappeared through the hedge, she drew a deep breath and sank into her desk chair, wondering if things would ever be the same between them again, and knowing that they would not—could not—be.

Robert's picture still faced the wall. She'd forgotten to turn it back after Fran's visit. She turned it now with a murmured, "Sorry. It's been a mite hectic around here this week." His expression seemed reproachful, and she couldn't decide if it was because of the week he'd spent facing the wall, or because of what had happened between her and Ben.

"Oh, Robert. I really botched things today, didn't I? I should have been more diplomatic, not so blunt. But he took me by surprise. It isn't my fault. I told him, right at the start . . ." But she knew it was her fault. She'd taken the easy way again, drifting into a relationship with Ben when she should have been taking charge of her life.

She'd told Helen that Ben was like a sinfully rich dessert in the salad of her life. Now, it was time to get back to the salad, for his sake as well as hers.

"But not right now," she told Robert. "Not with Thanksgiving and then Christmas coming up. I couldn't bear not sharing Christmas with the children. And it would be cruel, leaving Ben to cope with the holidays by himself, when I've let him come to depend on me for so much.

"Besides, December is a terrible month for turning your life around. After Christmas . . . January . . . yes, that would be good. The first of the year is the best time for making changes and going in new directions. I'll do it then."

The clock chimed in the living room, reminding her that it was time to start dinner, but the house seemed cold and empty without the children, and she had no appetite for a dinner cooked for one and eaten alone. Maybe she'd be hungry later. For now . . .

She unwrapped a new package of index

cards and tried to remember if there was
any country in the world that had decent
weather in January and wasn't in the grip
of civil unrest, war, terrorism, or other
pandemonium.

Sixteen

Joanna was unusually quiet as they drove to the Dennisons'—not in any kind of withdrawn way, Ben thought, but as if she had better things to concern herself with than casual conversation. He glanced at her now and again. Her eyes sparkled in the glow of the panel lights, and her lips curved upward in a soft, expectant smile that gave her face its own kind of glow.

"You're really looking forward to this affair tonight, aren't you?" he asked her.

"Yes, I am. Aren't you?"

"Not that much. I mean, we've been seeing these same people every couple of days for weeks. I'd think some of the novelty would have worn off by now."

"That's business, Ben. This is a party. I haven't been to a party in a long time."

He reached over to squeeze her hand.

"Then I'll look forward to watching you enjoy it."

At the Dennisons', he helped her from the car, then retrieved her broccoli and rice casserole and his own more modest basket of assorted dinner rolls from the back seat. He kissed her lightly before they started down the walk to the house. This casual, taken-for-granted affection had become almost as important to him as the wonderful sex they enjoyed, and was one more reason why he wanted them married and living under the same roof.

He wondered whether it would help to point out that learning about this kind of relationship between a man and a woman was one more thing the children had lost when they lost their parents—

He shook his head ruefully as he followed her up the porch steps. He might stoop to such emotional blackmail eventually, but he wasn't quite desperate enough yet.

Inside, they surrendered the food to Margaret, who disappeared into the dining room with it, and their coats to Carl, who hung them in the closet, gave Ben a hearty clap on the back, then put his arm around Joanna's shoulders for a quick hug. "Can you believe it's been only six weeks since our first meeting, and here we are tonight, celebrating our first bid on a contract?"

"When Ben makes up his mind to do something, he doesn't waste any time," Joanna said.

Ben removed Carl's arm from Joanna's shoulders and replaced it with his own. "And when Joanna plans and organizes something, she does a great job."

"*If* you two can stop patting each other on the back for a minute," Ginger Ross put in, as Margaret came back from the dining room, "we have something else to celebrate tonight. Tell them, Esther."

"Well, I don't like to brag," Esther said, "but while you men are bidding on a contract, I already have one. Our next-door neighbor just got a promotion that means having to relocate immediately. He thought at first he'd have to go ahead and leave his wife behind to manage the moving details and follow him later with the kids.

"I remembered something Margaret said at that first meeting of ours, about using her experience to help people who had to move, so I told her about these people. But she said I have as much moving experience as she has, and they're my neighbors, my hot tip, *my* job." She paused, glanced around the room, and finished proudly, "So they'll all go together, and *I'll* handle the moving details."

Joanna gave Esther a warm hug. "Congratulations. We're proud of you."

"We certainly are," Carl exclaimed. "But we're also hungry." He appealed to Margaret. "Honey, now that Ben and Joanna are here, can't we go ahead and eat? My stomach thinks my throat's been cut."

The women glanced at each other with an air of patient resignation that made Ben laugh.

"So much for your moment of glory, Esther," Margaret said. "I guess we'd better feed them."

They filled their plates from the array of foods in the dining room and carried them back into the living room, where an assortment of TV trays and small folding tables had been placed in strategic locations to hold drinks and side dishes. Ben had planned to sit next to Joanna, but found that the men had gathered on one side of the room, and the women were clustered together on the other.

He watched her for a while, as she took part in a lively conversation with the other women. He heard her voice, pleased and excited, rise above the rest.

"What a marvelous idea. I'd love to! I always put a load of canned goods in the bin at the supermarket every Thanksgiving and Christmas, of course, but that always seems so impersonal."

"Well, this is certainly personal," Esther Gold said. "We get a list of families with information about their needs and tastes, and then we tailor each basket for a particular family. We try to include everything they need for a big Thanksgiving dinner with lots of leftovers, and we usually include whatever else we think they may need."

"Goodies for the children," Betty Donovan said. "Fruit juice, milk, formula for a new baby, canned baby food, whatever they seem to need most."

"Sounds like a tremendous amount of work," Ben said, dismayed by visions of Joanna cooking not just one Thanksgiving dinner, but several.

"Not so much," Betty said. "We make a master shopping list, then each of us takes part of it, so no one has to do it all. And we buy the staples and nonperishables early, and arrange for the supermarket to keep the turkeys in the store freezer until we're ready for them."

"You don't cook them yourselves then," Ben said, already feeling relieved, but wanting to make sure.

"No," Betty said. "The idea is not to deliver a cooked meal, but to let the families do it themselves. We want them to have the *experience* of Thanksgiving, as well as the food."

"Besides," Pete said, "can you imagine missing out on the wonderful smell of turkey roasting in the oven? Or pumpkin pies and biscuits baking?"

"I can," Joanna said. "Thanks for inviting me to take part. You said you've been doing this for several years. How did you get started?"

"It was an election year," Charlie Ross said soberly. "With no new contracts, there were a lot of cutbacks, and a lot of people we knew—our friends—got laid off that summer."

"Including us," Betty said. "Jobs were pretty tight for a while. We'd probably have had beans that year if someone hadn't rung our doorbell and left a basket of food on our doorstep. I can't tell you what a difference it made—not just in our Thanksgiving dinner, but in our morale."

She paused, blinked hard, and cleared her throat. "We always figured there was some good fortune in that box besides the food, because Pete found work just a few days later. It was several years before we found out who we had to thank. By then, we were doing well enough to join in and feed not only our own family, but another family as well."

"That's a nice story," Joanna said. "I feel honored to be included in such a wonderful project."

"I'd like to help, too," Ben said. "What do the men contribute?"

Charlie laughed. "Cash, what else?"

"Cash is good," Ben agreed. He thought about it a minute, then added, "But what I'd really like to do is supply the ingredients for every family to have at least a double recipe of chocolate chip cookies."

"That's my Ben," Joanna exclaimed.

Those two words, "my Ben," kept him grinning like an idiot for the rest of the evening.

Ginger deposited a stack of plastic plates and paper napkins in the trash and asked, "Why do we always get stuck with the cleaning up?"

"Cheap labor," Betty told her.

"But we don't get paid for this," Sandy objected.

Joanna disposed of a handful of plastic tableware. "You can't get much cheaper than that."

Esther emptied foam coffee cups into the sink before adding them to the trash. "You know something? The greatest thing about this moving job is that I'm getting paid for it. Not because the money matters so much, but just that something I'm doing is worth money. A couple of months ago, I'd either have been embarrassed to accept payment at all, or I'd have figured my work was worth so little that I'd still have been embarrassed to charge for it."

"You're not alone," Margaret said.

"Studies show that women are not only less likely to put a reasonable cash value on their services than men, they're much less likely to ask for raises at work, too."

"That's one advantage to being in business with a man," Joanna informed them. "He can make the money decisions. If I hadn't had Robert to answer to, I might never have learned how much I was worth."

"I used that formula you gave us," Esther said. "Figured the hours it would take, multiplied by a decent hourly rate, added my estimated expenses, plus a percentage to cover miscalculations. I came up with a figure that took the starch out of my backbone, but I squared my shoulders, quoted it without explaining or apologizing, and she never even blinked, just said thank God I was there to help."

She held her hands out, palms up, in a gesture of wonder. "And right then, I stopped feeling like a housewife earning butter and egg money, and saw myself as a businesswoman, an entrepreneur, who wasn't afraid—much!—to believe in herself and ask for what she was worth. God! No wonder men are so cocky."

The other women burst into laughter.

She waited until they were quiet, then said, "Joanna, I owe it all to you. I don't know how I'll ever thank you."

"You just did," Joanna said. "Now you can do something for me. All of you."

"You know we'll do anything we can," Sandy assured her.

"Well, it's pretty simple, really. Ben is already having withdrawal symptoms over letting the children spend Thanksgiving with their grandmother, and it's been so long since I enjoyed a good old-fashioned Thanksgiving get-together that I've almost forgotten what it feels like. I'd be more pleased than I can tell you if you'd help me kill two birds with one stone, and join Ben and me for Thanksgiving dinner at my place."

The other women exchanged glances in one of the moments of wordless communications she'd observed before, then Margaret spoke. "We'd love to, Joanna, but we've already made plans."

"Actually," Ginger said, "we have a sort of group tradition we've developed over the last few years."

Joanna forced her face muscles into a bright smile, astonished at how sharp her disappointment was. "Well, I'm the last one to interfere with tradition."

"But we want you to," Esther exclaimed. "We were going to talk to you about it tonight, see if you and Ben would like to join us, only you beat us to it."

Margaret held up a warning hand. "Before you make up your mind, we'd better tell you what we're going to do. You might not want to come with us."

Joanna couldn't imagine anything they could do that she wouldn't want to take part in—or perhaps she could, but she was certain this group wasn't into anything like *that* any more than she and Ben were.

"A few years ago," Betty said, "we found this great bed-and-breakfast inn about an hour's drive north of here. The owner likes to spend Thanksgiving with her daughter in Florida, but hates to lose money by shutting down, so she gives us a bargain rate on the whole place, and we do our own cooking and housekeeping."

Margaret took a roll of plastic food wrap from a cupboard and stole a generous pinch of icing from the remains of Ginger's devil's food cake before she began to cover it. "This isn't one of those rustic cabins with two-bedrooms-men-in-one-women-in-the-other deals but a really nice old farmhouse that's been spruced up and decorated for guests. There's no hot tub, I'm afraid, but there's a wonderful fireplace in the living room, and handmade quilts and comforters on the old-fashioned four-poster beds.''

"There's a new gas range in the kitchen," Sandy added, "as well as an old-fashioned wood cookstove. The kitchen and the dining room were originally built for feeding farmhands at planting or harvest time, so there's plenty of room for all of us."

"We usually go up Wednesday evening, get a good night's sleep, then get up early and collaborate on fixing a couple of turkeys with all the trimmings," Esther added. "And although we take everything for Thanksgiving dinner, it's still a working farm, with the owner's son and daughter-in-law living on the place, so there's plenty of fresh milk and eggs, and a larder full of ham, cider, vegetables, and other goodies to feast on."

"The rest of the time," Ginger explained, "we just sit around and visit, relax, or . . ." She rolled her eyes expressively and the other women laughed.

Joanna grinned at them, joyously aware that they had made her as much a part of the group as they were. "I can't imagine any reason why Ben and I wouldn't want to come with you," she exclaimed.

They shared glances again. "Well," Sandy admitted, "there is one small drawback, or something you might think is a drawback."

"What's that?"

"There are only six bedrooms. If you and Ben come, you'll have to share one."

Joanna didn't even have to think about it. "That's no problem for me," she assured them, "and I'm sure it won't be for Ben, but of course, I'll have to ask him before I can give you an answer. Is there anything we should bring?"

"All you and Ben have to bring is yourselves," Esther said. "Next year is time enough for you to contribute. This year, you're just guests."

They went on then with the after-dinner cleanup, but although she listened to the others laughing and chattering, Joanna was quiet, dealing with both the pleasure of knowing that she would be welcome in the group next year, and fear that she wouldn't be there to take advantage of it.

Ben and Joanna left the party in a flurry of goodbyes and let's-do-it-again-soons and hurried through the brisk November night to get into the barely less chilly car. Seeing how Joanna wrapped her coat more snugly around herself and ducked her head, turtle-fashion, into the collar of her coat, he told her, "I'll turn on the heater as soon as the engine warms up."

"I'm all right. It's just a good night for feeling cozy."

"You really enjoyed yourself tonight, didn't you?"

"Yes, I did. The food was great, the people were friendly, and Esther! I was so proud of Esther. I guess we all were."

"I was proud of *you*. You made it possible for her, you know, and for the rest of us." He glanced at her, snuggled down in her coat, her contented smile just visible above the collar, and felt a rush of affection toward her and a need to touch her, be close to her. He leaned toward her, slid his arm around her shoulders, and tugged gently. "Come over here, woman."

Obligingly, she slid across the seat and cuddled next to him. He spent a minute regretting the bulk of her coat, then realized it wasn't wrapped around her as securely as he'd thought it was. With a little maneuvering, he was able to slip his hand inside the coat, and then inside her dress and under her bra.

As his fingers cupped her breast, she gave a little squeak and protested, "Your hand is cold."

He laughed, feeling contentment well up inside him. "It'll warm up in a minute."

"My hands are cold, too," she said. "How would you like it if I . . ." She laid her hand on his knee and started to slide it upward.

"I'd like it just fine."

She immediately slipped her hand back into her coat pocket. "You just think you would."

He laughed to himself and took advantage of a deserted stretch of road to nuzzle her cheek.

"Eyes on the road, sir," she told him sternly.

Yes, ma'am," he said meekly, and gave her breast a gentle squeeze. After a moment, he asked, "Did you have a chance to invite everyone to Thanksgiving dinner?"

"Yes, but it turns out they already have plans."

He felt a surge of gratitude for people who made their plans early, and then she added, "They want us to join them. I said I'd have to ask you."

He pushed aside a touch of apprehension. He could give up one day out of four. "What are their plans?"

"They're going to spend the entire holiday at a lovely bed-and-breakfast inn about an hour north of here. The owner will be spending her Thanksgiving in Florida, so we'll have to do our own cooking and cleaning, but I gather that the privacy is worth it."

"Privacy! With five other couples?"

"And six bedrooms."

"It sounds like a helluva poor substitute for what I wanted to do."

"Well, it sounds marvelous to me. A wonderful change of scenery, Thanksgiving dinner prepared and shared with good friends."

"Why do we have to start socializing *now*? Why can't we wait until after Thanksgiving? Or Christmas? Maybe the first of the year. Isn't January the time you're supposed to make changes in your life?"

"I'm not asking you to change your life," she snapped. "I'm just asking you to share Thanksgiving with me and some people who are rapidly becoming good and dear friends. For most of the time we've known each other, we've done pretty much what you want to do. Well, just this once, I want to do what *I* want to do. This is very important to me, Ben, important enough for me to tell you that you can either spend Thanksgiving up at that inn with me and the others, or you can spend it alone."

Her vehemence shocked him into silence. It wasn't until she reached for the door handle and he realized she was going to get out that he found his voice.

"Joanna, I'm sorry. Really I am. I had no idea it meant that much to you. Of course we'll go, and we'll have a wonderful time. I promise you." He paused, then added, "Maybe we could compromise a little, though."

She let go of the door handle and turned back to face him. "Maybe. How?"

"We go ahead and get married first and make it a honeymoon."

She stared at him as if he'd suddenly lost his mind, then grinned. "Oh, Ben! A honeymoon with five other couples?"

He shrugged. "I don't think it's worse than being the only single couple among five married ones."

She didn't answer, just kept grinning.

He sighed. "Well, you can't say I didn't try. But I do need to ask you something. Are you sure it won't bother you, that everyone will know we're sleeping together?"

She shook her head. "No. For one thing, they already know, or they wouldn't have asked us to come." Her grin grew wider. "And for another thing, there's a certain status to sleeping with a man the other women all agree is sexy as hell."

He felt his ears grow hot again. *"What?"* His voice came out a rusty croak.

"Never mind. That just slipped out. I think we'd better say good night now. It's late, and Holly will need to be getting home."

He walked her to the front door. Knowing that she wasn't going to invite or even let him in, and he had to say good night here, he slipped his hands inside her coat and did a thorough job of it, delighting in the warm, familiar curves and feeling a touch of smug satisfaction at the knowledge that she was becoming aroused, even as he was, and would probably also have trouble getting to sleep that night.

When she finally murmured in protest and started to pull away from him, he ran his hands firmly over her body one more time, then nestled her snugly against him and murmured, "I know there's no point in asking if I can come in for a little while, and make love on the sofa, but have you ever made love on a porch rocker?"

She moved away from him and caught his hands in hers as he started to reach under her coat again. "Of course I have, but not in this kind of weather."

She slipped inside, closed the door quickly, and turned the lock with what he thought was unnecessary firmness. He shrugged, grinned, and started back down the steps toward his car.

The grin faded as he drove home and found himself pondering that "Of course

I have," and wondering if she really meant it.

Joanna knew it would be a waste of time to go to bed right away. She wouldn't sleep until she had come down from the evening's wonderful high and settled down a bit from Ben's exuberant good night. She decided a cup of hot chocolate might help.

She heated a cup of water in the microwave, emptied a packet of instant cocoa mix into it, then sat at the desk and studied Robert's picture as she sipped it.

"I know why Ben is antisocial," she told him. "He just never had the time to find out how much fun friends can be. But why were you? Was it really because you wanted to keep me to yourself? I think Ben has a touch of that, too, and that's why it was important to stand up to him tonight."

She sipped the chocolate and added thoughtfully, "I wonder what our lives might have been like if I'd stood up to you like that." She shivered suddenly, although the room was warm. "Or what would have happened if I'd ever realized that I *wanted* to?"

Seventeen

Becky blinked back tears and told Lovey, "I'll be back real soon. You be good while I'm gone." She surrendered the kitten to the kennel attendant with the sorrowful air of a mother sacrificing her first-born and asked Joanna, "Do you think she knows I'll come back for her?"

"I'm sure she does," Joanna said. "She knows how much you love her. Besides, she'll be with Tinkerbell, and Tinkerbell's been here before, you know. She'll tell Lovey not to worry." She looked down into the drawn little face, trying to find words of comfort, and settled finally for a quick hug. "She'll be fine, Becky, really she will. Now let's go see how Joey and Bernie are making out."

They went outside and around the building to the dog runs where Ben and Joey were saying goodbye to Bernie. Joey stood clutching the fence with both hands, his face pressed against the wire while Bernie sat inside the run, tipping his head first one way and then the other as Joey asked, "You won't forget me while I'm gone, will you, Bern?"

"You won't be gone that long, Joey," Ben told him, amusement and sympathy battling for control of his voice.

"But I'm going to miss old Bern something awful," Joey said, "and I'll bet he's going to miss me, too."

Ben flashed a quick grin at Joanna. "Well, if he's missing you, he won't be forgetting you, will he? Besides, Holly promised to bring her little brother and come visit Bernie and Lovey both while we're gone. Now, hurry and finish saying goodbye. You're keeping your grandmother waiting."

Joey and Becky both reached through the fence to stroke Bernie and tug at his fur, then trudged with Ben and Joanna back to the parking lot, where Fran and her husband, Carlo, waited for them.

"I'm sorry we're running so late," Ben told them. "I'd have taken care of this earlier today, but the children begged me to wait until they were home from school and could come say goodbye. I didn't realize it was going to be such a lengthy or traumatic event."

"But of course it is," Carlo said. His voice was a husky tenor with only a trace of accent. "Pets are part of the family; you can't just go away and leave them. But we do have to be on our way soon."

"That's right," Fran said. "You children have some aunts and uncles who are dying to meet you, not to mention some cousins."

"We have aunts and uncles?" Joey sounded incredulous.

Fran nodded. "My two daughters, who are your father's half-sisters, and their husbands, and my other son, your father's half-brother."

"And cousins?" Becky asked. "How old are they? Are they boys or girls?"

"There's a boy just a little younger than Joey. I'm afraid we don't have a girl your age, but there's a precious little girl only three years old, and a baby not quite a year old."

"Oh, I'm glad," Becky exclaimed. "I love babies."

Fran opened the car door and the children climbed into the backseat, their anguish over parting with Bernie and Lovey eased by the promise of aunts and uncles and cousins waiting to meet them.

"I'll bring them back before bedtime Sunday," Fran told Ben. "You have the phone number where we can be reached?" At his nod, she added, "And I have your number if I should need anything." She smiled warmly at Joanna. "You two have a good holiday, too."

She made sure the children's seat belts were buckled, then slid in beside her husband and they drove away.

Joanna watched them go, fighting the totally irrational feeling that Fran wasn't playing quite fair. She told herself that it wasn't her fault she didn't have a readymade family stashed away somewhere for the kids, or Fran's fault that she did.

Besides, it was only because the kids were going to be with Fran that she and Ben were free to spend their Thanksgiving at the inn. And they were only going to be separated for a few days. The children wouldn't forget her, any more than they'd forget Bernie and Lovey.

She glanced at Ben and found him staring at the place where the car had disappeared, looking so much like Joey clutching the fence that she forgot her own distress. "Ben, they'll be all right."

"I know, it's just . . . I forgot to tell her about Joey's nightmares, and—"

"She's a natural-born grandmother. If he has nightmares, or any other problems, she'll know exactly what to do."

Ben put his arm around her shoulders and they walked together to his car, already packed for the trip. "You have an absolute gift for saying the right thing. Now let's see how good you are at reading a map."

She grinned and kissed his cheek. "What's to read? Just take I-75 north. I won't need Margaret's map until we're almost there."

"Good enough. But I wish I'd remembered to ask Fran—"

"Ben!" She laughed at the sheepish look on his face and added, "The kids will be fine with her, they won't be gone long enough to forget you, and I'm going to keep you so busy you won't have time to miss them."

He cleared his throat and said gruffly, "You'd better."

They drove in friendly silence, sharing the wordless intimacy of people who didn't need the buffer of words to be comfortable with each other.

Almost like an old married couple, Joanna thought, and felt the comfort evaporate as she remembered her pledge to cool things a little between her and Ben. A four-day retreat in the country, even with five other couples, wasn't going to cool anything. At best, it would only make it harder to pull back from Ben when the time came. At worst, she was leading him on, making him expect more from her than she was free to give.

She sighed. It was too late to change their plans now, even if she'd wanted to. And she didn't. There was more involved here than just her obligation to Ben. She had obligations to herself, too. To make new friends. To be a part of something bigger than she was. To take charge of her life and be "just Joanna."

She didn't want to ruin Ben's weekend either. But, she promised herself, as soon as the holiday was over and they were home again, she'd start putting some distance between them. Until then, she'd try to give him the best Thanksgiving he'd ever had.

Ben fumbled in his pocket for a slip of paper and handed it to her. "Better check the map," he said. "It can't be much farther."

It wasn't. A mile or two later they pulled into a long winding drive that curved around behind an old-fashioned farmhouse, and parked next to the row of cars already there. Jake and Pete came out to welcome them and assure them they were in the right place.

"Everybody's here now," Jake said. "As soon as the ladies finish stowing the food away in the kitchen, we'll be ready to head out and get some dinner." He held the door while Ben and Pete carried the luggage inside.

Sandy appeared and took their coats, adding them to those already hanging on the long row of hooks on one side of the hall.

"Let's just take your stuff upstairs and leave it in your room for now," Pete said. "You can get settled in later."

"Which—"

"You've got the best room in the house," Jim declared. "Not the biggest or the most luxurious, but the one closest to the stairs. No long trudge down the hall when you're in a hurry."

"Jim!" Sandy's nudge to his ribs this time was hard enough to make him grunt. "I'm sorry, Joanna. The minute we get these men out in the country, they forget how to be civilized."

Pete laughed and carried Joanna's suitcase up the stairs. Ben, his lips pressed together in a way that Joanna knew meant he was irritated, followed with his own.

Joanna paused long enough to reassure Sandy, and hurried after them.

The room might not have been large or luxurious by Jim's standards, but from the handmade quilt on the bed to the braided rugs on the polished hardwood floor, it possessed an old-fashioned charm and elegance that made Joanna exclaim, "How lovely!"

She studied the room with growing appreciation. It had clearly never been "decorated," but had simply grown as the people who used it added things they needed, or simply liked—starched white priscillas and an old-fashioned roll-up shade at the window, a well-used easy chair on one side of the room, a cane-bottomed rocker on the other, a bulky cedar chest at the foot of the bed, hobnailed glass lamps on the bedside stands.

She inhaled deeply, relishing the just-right blend of aromas—lemon oil, floor wax, lavender sachet, moth crystals.

"Oh, Ben! I think this is the most romantic room I've ever seen in my life."

He grinned wryly. "Glad you think so, but don't say it where anyone else can hear you." The grin disappeared, and he added soberly, "I'm sorry about the jokes. As soon as I can get those so-and-so's alone, I'll read 'em the riot act."

She slipped her arms around his neck. "They don't mean any harm. And it doesn't really bother me."

"It bothers me," he said. His voice was grumpy, but he put his arms around her and pulled her into a warm embrace.

"Then just ignore them, or you'll only make it worse." She kissed him lightly.

He kissed her back, not so lightly, and then with growing enthusiasm.

They were interrupted by a brisk knock at the door and a male voice, she wasn't sure whose, called, "Hey, in there. It's time to go eat. You can get back to . . . whatever it is you're doing . . . after dinner."

Ben released her. "Damn! I knew a romantic weekend with five other couples would never work."

She caught his face between her hands and kissed him again, lightly but effectively. "Well, it won't be the first time you've been wrong."

The bed was everything Ben had hoped it would be—the mattress firm, the quilts warm and cozy, the springs blessedly and, considering the workout they were given, miraculously silent. Joanna had been right. The weekend was going to be a success—was already a success—after all. He allowed himself a smug smile as Joanna murmured contentedly, "Maybe it's the moth crystals. Do you suppose they're really some sort of aphrodisiac?"

He fell asleep with her cuddled warmly against him, and woke in the morning to a blast of cold air under the covers where she had been. He opened his eyes to find her standing beside the bed, dressing as quickly as possible.

"What are you doing? It's too cold to get up just yet. Come on, slip back under the covers with me." He shivered in another blast of cold air as he lifted the blanket invitingly for a fraction of a second, then clutched it around himself again.

She pulled on the sweater she'd worn the day before, ran a comb through her hair, and put on a touch of lipstick. "Come on, lazybones. Everyone else is up already."

"Not lazybones," he grumbled. *"Cold* bones. How do you know everyone else is already up?"

"I heard them going past our door and down the stairs."

"They're crazy, and so are you, but that doesn't mean *I'm* going to freeze my tail off at this hour of the morning."

Before he could protest, she reached over and twitched the covers away from him. "Yes, it does. Besides, it's probably warmer downstairs, and anyway, it'll soon be time for breakfast."

She had a point. She also had the covers. Shivering and reluctant, he rolled out of bed and climbed into his clothes in record time.

It was warmer downstairs, but only marginally. Everyone was huddled around the big wood-burning range in the kitchen, which was barely beginning to put out heat. Ben nudged Charlie and Jake apart to make room for Joanna, then stood close behind her with his arms around her waist, enjoying the warmth from the stove on his face, and the warmth from Joanna everywhere else.

"Sorry about the big chill," Charlie said cheerfully. "It was warm last night, so we didn't turn up the thermostat. Then the temperature dropped during the night, and it's going to take the furnace a while to catch up."

"No problem," Ben said. "At least, it wasn't while I was still snuggled under those warm blankets, which is where I'd still be if Joanna hadn't heard you all coming downstairs and decided to join you."

"You didn't have to come down with me," she told him. "You could have slept late."

He kissed the side of her neck and was pleased when she didn't act embarrassed or pull away. "After you snatched the covers off the bed? Not likely!"

"The kitchen will be warm in a little while," Margaret promised. She opened the firebox door, stirred up a flurry of sparks with the poker, and reached for another piece of firewood.

"Hey, easy on that wood," Carl protested. "We'll have to replace whatever we use, and I've never known you women to go out and chop wood."

Ginger stuck her tongue out at him. "Maybe that's because we're so busy feeding you bottomless pits."

"Maybe we wouldn't be so bottomless if we didn't work up such an appetite chopping wood," Jake said.

"I'm not being wasteful," Margaret said. "We'll need a good fire for cooking breakfast, and then dinner."

"You're actually going to cook on this?" Ben asked.

Sandy waved at the electric range on the other side of the room. "You don't really think we'd get a twenty-five pound turkey, four pumpkin pies, a dozen big sweet potatoes, and assorted dinner rolls in that oven, do you?"

"That's hours away," Pete complained. "When do we get breakfast?"

"As soon as the stove is hot enough to cook it," Margaret said.

Jim spat on the stove top and produced a hearty sizzle. "It's hot enough now."

"Jim!" Sandy exclaimed. "You *barbarian.*"

Ben laughed at the outrage in her voice, then pantomimed an abject apology when she turned her glare on him.

"Let's feed them and get them out of here," Betty suggested. "Then we can eat our own breakfast in peace while they chop firewood."

"We can't do heavy labor for at least an hour after eating," Charlie objected.

"That's for swimming," Joanna told him.

"Besides," Esther said, "farmers do it all the time."

"Well," Jim said, "engineering writers don't."

Margaret put another piece of wood on the fire and ended the argument by announcing firmly, "They do if they want Thanksgiving dinner."

Ben joined in the collective masculine groan that went up, but his heart wasn't in it. He couldn't remember when he'd last taken part in this kind of good-natured battle between the sexes, or if he ever had, but he was surprised at how much fun it was, and at how much Joanna seemed to be enjoying it.

He'd been wrong about this weekend in more ways than one. Being with these people was probably the best thing that could happen to them just now.

Joanna had never talked much about her marriage or her late husband. He was sure she'd loved him and been happy with him, but he was becoming equally sure something about the marriage had left Joanna leery of committing to another one.

Whatever it was, he had to make her see that it didn't have to happen again, and what better way to do that than to let five happily married couples show her what a good marriage was really all about?

Joanna ate the last bite of her pumpkin pie, shoved her plate back, and sighed with pleasure. "I thought dinner was the best meal I'd ever eaten, but this supper was even better."

"It always is," Pete agreed. "I wonder why?"

Carl scraped up the last trace of whipped cream from his plate and regarded it with pleasure. "Because that's when you get to eat double helpings of the dessert you were too full to eat at dinner." He licked the whipped cream off his fork and added, "I thought everybody knew that."

"Not everybody pigs out at dinner the way you do," Margaret told him.

"Not everyone has spent a lifetime developing my expertise," he said.

Sandy laughed. " 'Expertise,' in this case, being a fancy term for plain old-fashioned gluttony."

Jim pushed his plate back and patted his stomach with satisfaction. "Speaking of full, I really am, and it's getting late, so what about that movie we're planning to watch?"

"What do you mean, 'we'?" Betty demanded. "You men are going to watch it while we poor women clean the kitchen again."

Pete reached over and tousled her hair.

"Our turn will come Saturday, when we provide not only the meal, but the entertainment."

"I'm a pretty good cook," Ben said, "but I hope you don't expect me to get up and sing or tell funny stories."

"We hope you don't intend to," Jake said. "No, we already have something planned. Tell you about it later; it's supposed to be a surprise for the women."

"It had better not be another bucket of carry-out chicken and an X-rated movie," Ginger warned, "or you're the ones who may end up being surprised."

"Maybe they'll take us out this year," Margaret said. She stood up and began stacking the dirty dishes nearest her. The other women joined in.

The men poured fresh coffee and disappeared into the living room—all but Ben, who waited while Joanna carried an armful of dirty dishes into the kitchen and came back for another load.

"Wonderful meal," he said. "Wonderful day." He put his arms around her. "I hate to admit it, but you were right. I'm glad we came. I never realized how much fun friends could be. These guys are great." He brushed her lips lightly with a kiss that tasted of spices and whipped cream and murmured into her ear, *"You're* great, and tonight, upstairs in that romantic bedroom, *I'm* going to be great."

He kissed her again, then tipped an imaginary hat to the whistles and applause from the kitchen doorway.

"Ben," Ginger exclaimed, "why can't you set a good example for our husbands and pay Joanna that kind of attention when they're around to see it?"

He hugged Joanna again and let her go. "Maybe we can work out a deal. You keep feeding me like that, and I will. In fact, if you keep feeding me like that, I'll pay *you* that kind of attention when your husbands are around to see it."

Joanna hit his chest lightly with the back of her hand. "Not while *I'm* around to see it, you won't."

"Yes, ma'am," he said meekly.

She kissed him quickly and gave him a gentle push toward the living room, where the other men were gathered, thinking how glad she was that they had come. Ben had missed out on the friendships and male bonding most men enjoyed. What better way for him to catch up than among these five men who seemed as willing to accept him as their wives were to accept her?

And she'd feel a lot better knowing Ben wasn't going to be left alone when she got back to her own agenda. With this group around, she assured herself, he'd hardly have time to feel lonely.

Margaret grinned at her as she joined the cleanup detail in the kitchen. "I certainly never thought I'd see the day when we'd be holding Ben up as a good example for the other men. You're one lucky lady, Joanna."

"Seems to me Ben's the lucky one," Esther said. "Look at all Joanna has done for him and the children. I don't know how they'd ever get along without her."

"They'll soon have to," Joanna said, more sharply than she'd intended. "After the first of the year, there are some things I intend to do for myself, starting with a nice, long ocean trip to someplace in the tropics, where I don't have anything to do all day but loll in the sun, sip piña coladas, and ogle handsome young natives in loincloths."

The silence that followed made her glance up, then look over her shoulder to see what the other women were all staring at.

Ben stood in the doorway. The expression on his face left no doubt that he'd heard every word she'd said. He stared at her wordlessly for one long, heart-stopping moment, then turned and disappeared before she could even speak his name.

Ben strode through the dining room and into the hall, with its banistered stairway on one side and the long row of coats hanging on the other. He ignored the coats, jerked open the front door, and plunged out into cold night air not half as chilling as the weight settling in his chest.

Ripples of shock swept over him—shock, and a deep sense of betrayal. One minute, Joanna had been warm, responsive, everything he wanted her to be. The next, she was talking about—

The door opened and closed behind him. "Ben?"

At the sound of her voice, soft and somehow vulnerable, perhaps even . . .

guilty . . . his shock began to turn to anger. *How dare she!* he thought. *How dare she bring me out here for this wonderful weekend, then spring something like that on me?*

She took a step closer and reached out to touch him. He shrugged her hand from his shoulder and moved away from her, down the steps and along the side of the house, stopping just outside the pool of light spilling from the living room where the other men were.

She hadn't actually sprung anything on him, he admitted. He'd overheard it. His anger increased. Why couldn't she have had the decency to tell him of her plans first, before she shared them with the women? Bad enough that she was going; worse that she had chosen this way to let him know.

He heard her soft footsteps in the dry grass and knew she was standing behind him again. "Don't worry," he told her bitterly. "I'm not going to make a scene in front of all your new friends." He kept his voice low so those inside wouldn't hear.

"Ben, I'm sorry. It just slipped out. I hadn't intended to say anything yet."

"What were you going to do? Just let

me come over some morning and find you gone?''

"Of course not!" She kept her voice low, too, and sounded all the more vehement for it.

"Maybe leave a note on the back door for me? 'Dear Ben, Surprise! I've decided to take an ocean cruise. See you later. Joanna.' "

"That isn't fair." She seemed more defensive than guilty this time. "You've known all along that I have things I plan to do, places I want to go."

"Knowing you have places you want to go is a lot different from knowing you're planning a trip to the tropics to 'ogle young natives in loincloths' next month!"

"Ben, you're making this very difficult for me."

"You don't think it's difficult for me, finding out that the kids and I are about to be dumped? Damn it, Joanna, things were going so well between us. I thought—"

"I'm not dumping anyone." Now she was plainly irritated. "I'm not leaving forever, you know. I'll only be gone a few weeks. Then I'll be back."

"Maybe, and maybe not. Either way, if

you go, it'll never be the same between us again."

"And if I don't go, it won't be the same either, because I'll always feel it was by your decision, not mine. And I'll be angry with you, and disappointed in myself."

"You won't like it," he warned. "A ship full of man-hunting women, a few gigolos dancing attendance on them."

"It isn't really any of your concern whether I like it or not."

She'd shifted gradually as they'd argued until she was standing beside him. He turned away from her again, ashamed to let her see the emotions he knew were plain on his face. Something inside him insisted frantically that it wasn't fair. He'd deserved to lose Fran, but this time, he'd tried to do everything right, and he was losing Joanna, too.

The cold he felt was no longer just inside him. The night air had sucked the heat from his body, leaving him painfully chilled. He glanced at Joanna, saw that she had her arms wrapped around herself and was shivering hard.

"Go back inside before you freeze," he

told her. "We can finish talking later, if there's anything left to say."

She continued to stand beside him, long enough that he thought she hadn't heard him, or had decided to be stubborn, then she turned and started back for the house. She stopped after a step or two and told him, without turning around, "You'd better come inside, too."

He waited until the sound of her footsteps died away and he heard the front door open and close again, then followed her.

She'd gone back to the kitchen with the other women. When they joined the men in the living room, she made an obvious effort to take part in whatever the others were doing and look as if she were having a good time. It might have fooled them; it didn't fool him.

After a few minutes, he turned away and threw himself feverishly into the men's activities. He told himself he was simply following the lead of the other men, who were also ignoring the women to pursue their own interests, but he knew it wasn't true. What he was doing was deliberate and cruel, and was hurting Joanna. He felt ashamed of himself, but his own hurt had hold of him and wouldn't let him behave any differently.

When they finally went upstairs together, and he silently crawled into bed with Joanna and turned his back to her, he was ashamed of that, too.

Eighteen

Joanna lay awake for a long time, fighting back tears and feeling both physically and emotionally chilled without Ben's warmth against her. Her body finally rebelled and succumbed to the effects of a long and busy day, but her mind remained active, interrupting her sleep with a restless jumble of dreams, memories, and emotions. The dominant theme seemed to be: she'd really messed things up this time.

She woke in the morning to find that, sometime during the night, she and Ben had rolled toward each other and were snuggled together now as if they'd never had a quarrel, but she could tell by looking at him that he hadn't slept any better than she had.

While she watched, he opened his eyes, looked for a minute as if he wasn't sure where he was, then let his breath out in a long, slow sigh. "I feel as if I'd been run over by a bulldozer," he said finally.

"Oh, Ben." She laid one hand against his cheek. "I'm so sorry. I didn't mean for any of this to happen. I hadn't even made up my mind for sure that I was going, and then, all of a sudden, I was blurting it out as if I'd been planning it for months. No wonder you—"

He shook his head. "No, it was my fault. You have every right to come and go as you please, whether I like it or not. It's just that I—the children and I—have gotten used to having you around, and when I heard you say . . . it felt like we were losing you."

"Never! I told you, I'm only taking a short vacation—something I haven't done in longer than I can remember. I'll be back before you even have time to miss me."

"I'll miss you. And the whole time you're gone, I'll be wondering where you are, and what you're doing, and if you'll still be alone when you come home, or if—"

She clapped her hand over his mouth. "Don't even think such a thing. Ben, I'm not going looking for someone. I *have* someone. And even if I can't make you the center of my existence the way you seem to want me to, that doesn't mean that anyone could ever take your place. It just means I need a little room for myself. That's not so unreasonable, is it?"

He studied her soberly, his eyes moving over her face as if he were searching for answers to questions he hadn't even asked. Finally, he sighed. "No, I guess that's not unreasonable. It isn't what I want, but it isn't unreasonable. Uh, are we still going to spend Christmas together?"

She slipped her arms around him and hugged him fiercely. "Of course we are. I wouldn't miss it for the world. Now, it's getting late. Shall we go downstairs and join the others?"

He returned the hug, then kissed her, a fervent, hungry kiss that stirred an answering hunger in her. "Not just yet," he whispered.

Saturday afternoon, the men disappeared for a couple of hours and returned laden with grocery sacks. They banished the women from the kitchen and sent them upstairs to "put on those party dresses you packed but didn't expect to wear."

"We can't be going out if they brought food in," Margaret commented, halfway up the stairs.

"Then why are we supposed to dress up?" Betty asked.

"Who knows?" Ginger said. "Maybe it's fancy food. I didn't smell any hot Styrofoam."

They came back down to find the table set with a buffet of deli goodies and assorted rich desserts, the dining room decorated with streamers and balloons, and the men waiting with a corsage for each of them.

"This year's theme," Carl announced. "Prom night."

They ate dinner to a taped assortment of music from the forties and fifties, remembering, reminiscing, living for a few hours in the years they remembered as golden, joyous, carefree.

It was a wonderfully nostalgic evening that soon turned romantic, as the men moved the big table to one side of the room and they began to dance.

They changed partners until each one

had danced once with every member of the opposite sex, then danced the rest of the evening with their own mates. As the hour grew later, the music grew more romantic, the dancing slower and dreamier, until at last, they began to drift up the stairs, couple by couple.

"What a wonderful night!" Joanna told Ben, when they were alone in their room. "It was almost like going to the senior prom all over again."

"Almost," Ben agreed, "but with one big improvement."

"What's that?"

He caught her hands in his and grinned at her. "I'm willing to bet you didn't sleep with your prom date."

"No," she agreed. "I didn't."

"Neither did I," he admitted, and added quickly, "but it wasn't for lack of trying."

She moved closer to him and slid her arms around his neck. "Don't worry about it. I have a hunch you're going to get lucky this time."

They were quiet on the ride home, wrapped in their own thoughts, until

Joanna told Ben, "Don't forget to stop at the kennel so we can pick up the animals."

"There'll be someone there on a Sunday?"

She laughed. "You'd be surprised what a well-placed bribe can do. Besides, the attendant has to be there anyway, to feed and water the animals."

They put the carrier with Tinkerbell and Lovey in it on the seat behind Joanna, leaving Bernie to sit behind Ben and drape his muzzle lovingly over Ben's shoulder.

They drove home with the cats loudly protesting their confinement and Ben slapping ineffectively over his shoulder at Bernie, and demanding, "Damn it, dog, quit drooling down my neck. I swear, Joanna, I'm not taking another vacation until I find a kennel that picks up and delivers. *Aiee!*" he added as Bernie's tongue slurped across his ear.

Joanna reached over the back of the seat to tug on Bernie's head until he was facing her. "Behave yourself," she scolded.

"We should have left them at the kennel until Joey gets home from school tomorrow," he muttered.

"And explain to the children when they get home why their animals aren't there to greet them?"

"You have a point, I guess."

At home, the animals followed them into the house, Tinkerbell to curl up on Joanna's lap, Bernie and Lovey to conduct a room-to-room search for the children.

"All right," Ben said, with vengeful satisfaction, as they raced up the stairs and tumbled back down for the third time. "Would you care to explain to the animals why their owners aren't here to greet them?"

"They will be in a minute," Joanna said. "I think I just heard a car in the driveway."

Ben opened the door and almost got knocked on his back as the children flew into his arms, then nearly fell on his face as Bernie rushed past to greet the children.

"Where's Lovey?" Becky exclaimed. She found the kitten and carried her over to Joanna so she could cuddle Lovey with one hand and pet Tinkerbell with the other.

Ben untangled himself from the commotion at his feet and looked out at Fran and Carlo, grinning at him from the safety of the porch. "Abandon hope," he said in his gloomiest tone, "all ye who enter here."

They came in, but refused to let him take their coats. "We can only stay a minute," Carlo said.

"Just long enough to thank you for letting us take the children," Fran added. "We had a wonderful time, and I think the children did, too. I'm sure they'll be talking your ears off about it for the next week."

"We hope you'll let us take them again sometime," Carlo said.

Ben nodded. "I'm sure they'd like that, and I would, too. I think it's important for them to form close ties with everyone, not just Joanna and me."

"You're very wise," Carlo said.

He glanced at Fran, who hesitated, then added, "We hope you'll even think about letting us take them home for a month or so next summer."

"Home? You mean Europe?" For a second, all he could think of was the years he and Joel had lost because Joel was in

Europe with Fran. He pushed the thought away. This was different. *He* was different. "I don't know if I can part with them that long," he said honestly, "but I'll consider it."

"Perhaps you and Joanna could come, too," Fran said. "We have plenty of room, and we'd love to have you."

He glanced at Joanna, Joey on one side of her, Becky and Lovey on the other, Tinkerbell on her lap, and Bernie's head on her knee. "Maybe we can," he agreed. "I'm sure she'd miss them as much as I would."

Maybe Joanna's upcoming trip would turn out to be a good thing after all, he thought. If absence really did make the heart grow fonder, a few weeks away from him and the children might make Joanna miss them enough to realize she belonged with them—full time.

The days until Christmas flew by at an almost frightening pace. For once, Joanna's expertise deserted her. Blithely unaware of the facts of Christmas shopping, she'd naively planned to start right after Thanksgiving, and was astonished to learn that by then most of the good stuff was already gone from the shelves. It didn't matter. They still found enough to fill her spare bedroom to overflowing.

Ben brought in a last armload of packages from the car and dumped them on the bed. He studied them, along with the accumulated heaps from earlier shopping trips, and asked Joanna, "You don't suppose we overdid it a bit?"

"Probably," she admitted, "but we're allowed to. Besides, I can't remember when I've had so much fun."

He slipped off his coat and dropped it on the bed beside hers. "I can," he said. He nestled her against him, marveling again at how well they fit together. "Perhaps you need a little reminder," he suggested. Then, as she slid her arms around his neck and pressed close to him, he cleared his throat and added, "Then again, maybe you don't."

After a few moments in which they established that neither of them needed a reminder, but both would like one, they moved by mutual consent into the other bedroom.

They had barely begun to undress each other when the phone rang. Joanna made an exasperated sound and pulled away from him. He let her move far enough away to answer it, and prayed it was a wrong number.

But it wasn't. Joanna listened for a moment, said, "He's right here," and handed Ben the phone. "It's the school."

He fought off an instant wave of panic and took the phone, holding it against his head with a pressure that turned his ear numb almost immediately. "Benjamin Walker here. What's wrong?"

"This is Mrs. Luden, Becky's school counselor." Her voice was calm and soothing. "Don't worry, Mr. Turner; the children are all right." His relief was so sudden and overwhelming he almost missed her next words. "It's just that we have a small problem. Becky's been in a fight with one of the boys, and—"

"Is she all right?"

"Except for a skinned knee and a bloody nose, she's fine. The problem is, this isn't the first time. Mr. Walker, is it possible for you to come by the school for a small conference this afternoon? Something seems to be troubling Becky, and I think we need to find out what it is."

"I'll be there as soon as I can make it." He put the phone down and turned to Joanna, standing tensely beside him.

"Becky's been in a fight at school," he managed to say, "and apparently it's happened before. They want me there. You'll come with me?"

"Of course."

They were mostly silent as Ben drove them to the school, but as they started up the school steps, Joanna paused. "Ben, when she came in that day with her dress torn and dirty . . . do you suppose she was fighting then? And why didn't she tell us?"

Two memories flashed through his head: A bully with a black eye and Joey, saying, "He told her to shut up or he'd knock me down again, so she hit him and made him run away crying." And Becky, too sick to go to school, and begging him, "Please don't make Joey go to school alone."

"I think she tried," he said bleakly, "and I didn't pay attention." He pulled the door open and held it while Joanna preceded him inside.

Schools hadn't changed much, he thought, since he was being sent to the principal's office on a pretty regular basis. Same old cinder block walls painted with some glossy, neutral-colored paint, same scuffed floors, bulletin boards, and trophy cabinets spaced along the walls. The only thing missing was the pervasive aroma of dirty sneakers and sweaty gym clothes. But then, he reminded himself, this was an elementary school. The kids had recess, not PE.

The only other difference he noted was that there hadn't been counselors when he was in elementary school, and he had no idea where to look for them.

"Over there," Joanna said, her voice hushed as if she, too, might have had more than a nodding acquaintance with the principal's office. Even in the midst of his worry, Ben had to suppress a grin, wondering what kind of misbehavior had been her undoing. Talking, he decided. Most likely talking and giggling.

Mrs. Luden, young, petite, reassuring, welcomed them and introduced them to Mrs. Martin, the school principal, an older woman who outwardly resembled a WAC drill sergeant Ben had run afoul of during his army days, but who had a firm, no-nonsense handshake, a warm smile, and a soft voice that banished the WAC image and made Ben think unexpectedly of his mother.

"Mr. Walker," she murmured, "Mrs. Blake. I appreciate your coming on such short notice. Won't you sit down, please?"

"How is Becky?" Ben asked. "Where is she? Can I see her?"

"She's fine," Mrs. Martin assured him, "and you can see her in a few minutes. Mrs. Luden and I would like to talk a bit first."

The soft voice held a firmness that turned even the adult Ben meek and submissive. He glanced at Joanna, and they both sat down, Joanna perching stiffly on the edge of her chair while he leaned back and tried to look as relaxed and at ease as possible.

"I'm sorry we have to meet like this," Mrs. Luden said. "But we were on the verge of calling you anyway. Becky seems to have some problems we need to discuss. They may not be serious—yet—but we want to make sure."

She opened a folder on her desk and glanced down at it, most likely for effect, Ben thought. He was sure she knew the contents by heart.

"Becky's a good student. She pays attention, does her work, does it right, and generally turns it in on time. She's well behaved—almost *too* well behaved, her teacher says—and seems to get along with her classmates. She works well with them on class projects, and they seem to like her. But out on the playground . . ."

"She fights," Ben said.

"She fights," Mrs. Luden agreed, "but that's only a symptom. Her real problem is that instead of playing with her own classmates, she spends recess hanging around the area where Joey and his classmates are playing, which isn't good for either her or Joey. It's prevented her from making friends her own age, and it's keeping Joey from adjusting to school and becoming self-sufficient."

Relief washed over Ben. "I think I can explain that. I didn't realize until recently that, in addition to all the other adjustments the children have had to make, Becky's maternal grandparents taught her that it was her job to look after Joey. I'm sure that's what happened today."

"Probably so," Mrs. Martin said, "and it's to Becky's credit that she's so conscientious, but she went too far today, when 'looking after' Joey took the form of attacking another boy and giving him a bloody nose."

Ben suppressed a grin and refrained from glancing at Joanna. "Becky and I talked about this the other day, and I thought I'd made it clear . . ." He drew a deep breath and admitted, "I guess I didn't do as good a job as I'd thought. I'll have another talk with her this afternoon. Can I see her now?"

Mrs. Martin said, "Of course."

Mrs. Luden left the room and came back a minute later with Becky.

Becky's dress was torn and dirty, her cheeks streaked with tears. She had the beginning of a bruise just under her eye and assorted scrapes on knees and elbows. She looked so small and scared and vulnerable that Ben couldn't trust himself to speak. Instead, he simply held out his arms to her and hugged her hard when she flew into them.

"Oh, Grandpa . . ." Her voice was as small and scared as the rest of her. "Are you very mad at me?"

Joanna plucked a tissue from the box on Mrs. Luden's desk and handed it to him. He blotted Becky's tears, careful not to hurt the bruise on her cheek.

He handed her the tissue to blow on, and smoothed her hair back from her face. "Why should I be mad at you?"

"Because I was fighting."

"Why were you fighting?" He thought he already knew. He wanted Mrs. Luden and Mrs. Martin to know, too.

Becky rolled the tissue into a little ball and stared down at it as she reminded him, "You told me that at school, the teacher was supposed to look after Joey, but, Grandpa, she *doesn't.*"

"How do you mean, Becky?"

She unrolled enough of the tissue to blow her nose once more and glanced timidly at Mrs. Martin, who said gently, "It's all right, Becky. Just tell us the truth."

"Well . . ." She wadded the tissue up again. "When the other kids tease him and pick on him and make him cry, she just tells him to act like a big boy and not to be such a baby. Only he's *not* a big boy, and he's not a baby either."

Mrs. Martin took one look at Ben, seemed to sense the anger building in him—at the boys who teased Joey, at the teacher who let it happen, at himself, for not understanding what Becky had tried to tell him—and said quickly, "Mrs. Luden, please take Becky to the library and give her some books to look at, then go take over Miss Warren's class so she can come to the office for a few minutes."

Miss Warren turned out to be young and pretty, with an air of confidence that didn't quite hide her uneasiness at being summoned to the principal's office.

In spite of himself, Ben felt a twinge of amusement. *So,* he thought, *even teachers aren't immune.*

Mrs. Martin waved her to an empty chair. "Miss Warren, are you aware that the incident on the playground today was part of an ongoing problem?"

"Well, yes, although I don't think it's really a prob—"

"How did you handle it?"

"Well—I—that is, there really wasn't anything to handle." She paused to shake a halo of short dark curls back from her face, and straightened her shoulders. "It's true that Joey isn't adjusting to school as well as he should, but a lot of first graders have trouble. It's nothing to worry about. I'm sure he'll get over it soon, particularly if his sister will just stop hovering over him all the time."

Joanna laid her hand on Ben's arm in silent warning. He choked back his first reply, substituting, "Did it ever occur to you that she wouldn't have to hover over him if you did your job properly?"

"I'm doing my job!" she protested. "I know the boys do tease Joey a bit, but they don't mean any harm, and they'll stop as soon as Joey stops getting so upset about it. Really, Mr. Walker, Joey is very immature for his age. Have you considered that perhaps he needs professional help?"

Before Ben could answer her, Joanna jerked her hand from his arm and jumped to her feet. "Miss Warren, what Joey needs is a teacher who can keep order on the playground and not let the other children exploit the grief and distress of a little boy who has just had his whole world turned upside down by the death of both parents and the loss of almost everything he's ever known."

Miss Warren's self-confidence deserted her suddenly. "His parents died recently?" She appealed to Mrs. Martin. "Nobody told me—"

Ben jerked a thumb toward the folder on Mrs. Luden's desk. "It's right there in his records."

"I—I've been so busy. I haven't had time—"

Mrs. Martin explained hastily, "Miss Warren wasn't here when you enrolled Joey. She came in several weeks later to replace Mrs. Briggs, who's on extended leave of absence because of illness in her family. It's created a lot of extra work for all of us."

"I don't see that it matters," Joanna said coldly. "No one with an ounce of human compassion, much less a teacher, should have to study records to know when a child is hurt or has special needs. Becky's right. Joey isn't a big boy. He's just a little boy bearing a bigger burden than any little boy should ever have to. He doesn't need professional help, he needs someone who'll understand and care and help him instead of just telling him to grow up."

Miss Warren looked almost as small and vulnerable as Becky. "But I do care. I just didn't—"

"It's all right, Miss Warren," Mrs. Martin said. "Go back to your class now. We'll finish talking later."

As soon as the door closed behind her, Ben stood up. "I'd like to see Becky again, please, and Joey, too. I'm going to take them home with me. I'll let you know later whether I'm going to leave them here, or withdraw them and find a school where they'll be treated as children deserve to be treated."

"Please, Mr. Walker. I don't think such a course of action would be good for either the children or Miss Warren."

"I don't give a fig for—"

"Miss Warren is young and inexperienced," Mrs. Martin continued, suddenly every inch the WAC sergeant, "and working under the handicap of taking over another teacher's class with very little time to prepare for it. But I've watched her work and I can assure you that, with a little seasoning, she's going to make a fine, caring teacher.

Today's experience will help her tremendously, if you let it.

"And taking the children out of school will make the experience bigger and more important in their minds than it needs to be. Given the chance, they'll forget it over Christmas vacation. Miss Warren will remember, and when they come back to school, things will be different." When Ben hesitated, she added, "You have my word."

"She's right, Ben," Joanna said. "The sooner we put this out of our minds, the sooner the children will. Let's say goodbye to Becky and reassure her, but don't call Joey from his class, and don't take either one home. Miss Warren made a mistake, that's all. Give her a chance to set it right."

Mrs. Martin regarded her with approval. "You aren't a former teacher by any chance? No, well, that's too bad. I suspect you'd have been a good one."

On the drive home, Joanna told Ben, "I don't know how she could say such a thing, the way I lost my temper. And after trying so hard to keep you from blowing up! Ben, I'm sorry."

He caught her hand and held it for a minute. "I was proud as hell of you. Fran herself couldn't have done better."

She smiled and relaxed.

So did he. He wasn't sure what it was she was hoping to find, down there in the tropics, but he was willing to bet she wouldn't find anything she cared about half as much as she cared about his children.

And maybe, he thought, half hoping, half praying, *me*.

Most of the group met in Joanna's dining room one last time before Christmas, not because they needed to, but because, like the holiday at the inn, it was something they'd never do again in the same way, or for the same reasons.

They had changed, Joanna thought, from the first time she'd met them. No longer drifting, bored, taking life for granted, they had goals, direction, a new knowledge of their own abilities and importance in the world. They still looked to her for guidance but, like children growing up, depended on her less and less. That was the way it should be, she told herself firmly. She needed her freedom, too, whether she wanted it or not.

And that was a stupid thought, if she'd ever had one. Of course she wanted it. Hadn't it been her whole reason for retiring? So she could add a little pizzazz to her life?

Ginger came in beaming and scattered Joanna's thoughts with her triumphant announcement, "Well, the score now is: men, nothing; women, two. I've just found a market for some of my hard-earned expertise."

Ben looked up from the Christmas present he was wrapping. "If you're expecting me to be jealous, you're out of luck. I'm truly happy for you, and even if we don't get this contract, we'll have plenty of chances at others. What's the expertise?"

"Well, the market where I shop just hired a new bag boy. When I started unpacking my groceries, you wouldn't believe the mess he'd made. The roast was leaking all over the sugar, the bread was flattened under the canned goods, and I won't even tell you what he'd done with the tomatoes.

"I marched myself right back to the store and complained to the manager, and guess what? He wants me to teach everyone in the store—including him—how to bag groceries." She paused to catch her breath, and added, "It's not a very big or important job, I admit, but it's a start."

"It's a wonderful start," Joanna said. "I'll bet you can promote the same job at half the markets in the area. Maybe more."

"I hadn't thought of that," Ginger admitted.

Grady directed a potent cussword at the typewriter he was using and ripped the paper from it. "It's thinking about things like that that's going to make the difference between finding a few odd jobs, and building a successful business."

Ben glanced at Ginger's crestfallen face and laughed. "She'd have thought of it in a few minutes, Grady, as soon as she came back down to earth." He set the wrapped package aside and started on another.

Betty picked up the finished package and examined it critically. "Ben, that's beautiful. Where did you learn to wrap packages like that?"

"In the army."

"The army!"

He grinned. "Well, that's where I learned

to put hospital corners on my bunk mattress. Same principal, more or less."

"He's great with square packages," Joanna explained, "and completely helpless with anything else."

"So, we'll put the wrapped presents under the tree now, and hide the others until the kids go to bed Christmas Eve. *If* they go to bed, that is."

"Let 'em stay up late the night before and get 'em up early Christmas Eve morning." Jim advised. "They'll not only go to bed, they'll go to sleep."

"Thanks. I'll remember that." He finished wrapping the package, stuck a ribbon on it, added a name tag, then sat back and sighed with satisfaction. "There," he said. "I think that's the end of it. And just in time. Today is the last day of school before Christmas vacation starts." He shook his head. "I love my kids, but I sure hope the weather stays fair. I'd hate to be cooped up inside with them until they go back to school."

"Have you put your tree up yet?" Pete asked.

"We've put it up and Bernie's taken it

down about three times. We're going to wait until Christmas Eve to put it back up."

"Kids and pets," Jim said. "It wouldn't be Christmas without them."

"I've had Tinkerbell for years," Joanna said, "but this is the first time I've shared Christmas with children since I was a child myself. I think I'm as excited about it as they are."

"Me, too," Ben admitted.

By mutual agreement and established custom, the meeting broke up shortly after the children came home. The men carried the typewriters and computer over to Ben's living room, their new base of operations. The women stayed behind to help Joanna clean up the dining room, then exchanged hugs and a chorus of Merry Christmases.

"By the time we get back from visiting all our children and grandchildren, you'll probably be somewhere relaxing and building a terrific tan," Margaret said.

"We hope you have a wonderful time," Ginger said, "but not *too* wonderful."

"We don't want you to be gone too long," Esther added. "We love you and we'll miss you."

"I'll miss you, too."

After they left, she went to the dining room door and looked in. It was neat and clean, with no sign that it had ever been an office. She couldn't believe how empty it looked. She swallowed hard and admitted that what it looked was *lonely.*

She closed the door, quietly but firmly, and went to the kitchen, where she poured herself the last cup of coffee and cradled it between her hands, hoping its warmth would ease the chill she felt, while she studied Robert's picture soberly.

"I've come a long way, haven't I?" she asked him. "I've filled my present with friends, work, children, pets, a wonderful lover. I'm going to have a great Christmas, then get started on our plans, the way I've been promising you. I've done just about everything I set out to do, haven't I? I should really be proud of myself, shouldn't I?"

She sat down at the desk, rested her head in her hands, and choked back a sob.

"So why do I feel as if the bottom just dropped out of the whole world?"

Nineteen

Joanna studied the array of gifts critically, moved one or two to make a more pleasing arrangement, and sat back on her knees to enjoy the effect. "Well, I think that about does it, Ben. The children are going to have a good Christmas."

He moved close enough to kiss her. "With special thanks to you, not just for the gifts you've bought them, but for these last months of loving them and caring about them. You've helped me give them back some of what they lost."

She felt flustered by the warmth of his words and reached for the switch that would turn the tree lights on. "Let's see how it looks."

"Wait," he said. He stood up and turned off the room lights, then came back and knelt beside her. "Now," he said, and the lights played over them in a rainbow of pastel colors as she flipped the switch.

She drew in a deep, happy breath. "I always loved this part of Christmas more than anything else, at least, once I got old enough to stay up and help put the gifts under the tree on Christmas Eve."

"Me, too, when I was home to help. I'm ashamed to admit that, even on Christmas Eve, I was sometimes too wrapped up in work to take time off. I was always there for Christmas morning, but sometimes, I was too tired to enjoy it."

"You won't be too tired for this one," she said, "because I think we ought to go to bed early ourselves and get a good night's sleep."

She started to get up, but he caught her and pulled her back down. "Stay a little while longer," he begged. "It's too fine a moment to cut short." He slid back until he was leaning against the sofa, and she moved back until she could lean against him and he could slide his arm around her waist.

"For a little while," she agreed.

The flickering lights and the warmth of Ben's body beside her cast a hypnotic spell. Tired after a busy day, she let herself fall into a relaxed state that was half waking, half sleeping. When Ben began touching her intimately, she didn't stop him, but surrendered to the pleasure of his touch and let him do whatever he wanted.

At first, he only touched her breasts lightly, his fingers tracing random patterns across them. It felt wonderful. She moved a little, so he could reach them more easily. In a few minutes, he unbuttoned her blouse and opened it, undid the front opening of her bra and pushed it out of the way so the tree lights cast colored patterns on her bare breasts, and on his hand when he stroked and fondled them, and that felt even better.

His hands were as skilled as ever, and excitingly warm against her skin. She knew it was time for both of them to get some rest before the kids got them up in the morning, but it felt so good to lie there, feeling her breasts grow full and heavy, her nipples firm and sensitive under Ben's knowledgeable touch.

Drowsy and contented, she made no protest when he moved her so that they were lying side by side, or when he pulled her skirt up to her waist, and when he slid his hand inside the elastic and lace of her panties, her only thought was to open her legs enough to let him pleasure her with the warmth and gentle movement of his hand against her.

After a few minutes, she heard the sound of his zipper and felt him fumble with his pants, but even when he caught her hand in his and moved it to his crotch, her dreamy thought was that it was only fair for her to please him as he was pleasing her. She caressed him luxuriously, feeling and exploring him with her fingers, liking the weight and warmth of him in her hand, liking even more the feel of him as he stiffened and grew under her touch.

She held him lightly but firmly, stroking him as gently as he was stroking her, but knowing that soon, very soon, she would have given him the ultimate pleasure, even as he was about to give it to her. She smiled, anticipating his enjoyment as much as her own.

She protested sleepily as he pulled away and rose to his knees beside her, but when he eased her legs apart and knelt between them, she came to her senses abruptly.

"Ben," she gasped. "We can't. The children—"

He hadn't entered her yet, but she could feel him, hard and hot, trembling against her. Wide awake now, she fought to keep from arching up to him, to keep from taking him inside herself and plunging with him into the consummation they both lusted for.

"Joanna, it's all right. The door is closed and this is the one night of the year when the children would rather die than come in here. If the house caught fire, they still wouldn't peek in here until morning. Please." His voice was thick with desire. "Don't stop me."

She knew he was right, although it no longer mattered. It was she who was on fire, unable to quench the blaze he had kindled inside her. She surrendered, as much to her own needs as to Ben's plea. "Do it," she whispered.

He surprised her, slipping into her slowly, riding her with a gentle, unhurried rhythm that slowed her own eager response, so that they moved together in a sweet, joyous cadence that was different from anything they'd done before—slower, more lingering, but infinitely more exhilarating, more intoxicating, and—the thought flashed into her head before she could stop it—more loving.

The warmth of the room, the multicolored lights from the tree, the fresh pine scent, all combined to create an atmosphere of magic, a languorous sensuality in their coupling that she had never felt before.

For once, they hadn't undressed completely. She was sharply and erotically aware of her open blouse and her skirt, rucked up about her waist, making her feel sexier and more exposed than if she'd been fully nude. She relished the smooth pile of the carpet under her bare buttocks, the rough texture of Ben's pants against her thighs. And above and beyond all of that, she was completely and totally aware of every warm, pulsing inch of Ben, sliding powerfully back and forth against her and inside her.

As they had built their desire slowly, they satisfied it slowly, moving without urgency as Ben brought her again and again to the brink of release without quite pushing her over. Now and again, he lowered his head, and she caught her breasts in her hands to shape and lift them for his sweet suckling.

Finally, when she felt she must reach completion or die of wanting it, he quickened his movement inside her, deepened it, until his joyful thrusting sent wave after wave of sensation through her, spreading from the eagerly responding center of her being throughout her whole body, so that she shuddered and trembled helplessly, and thought she might shatter from the sheer strength of it.

Ben's breath came in quick gasps and he pressed deeper and deeper into her as powerful spasms shook him. She rocked her hips against his, careful not to lose him, but wanting to give him every last bit of pleasure she could. She knew she had succeeded when he moaned, low in his throat, gave one last shuddering thrust, then relaxed against her.

They lay together for a long time afterward, while Joanna held him inside her and exulted in feeling his body still pulsing with the aftershocks, even as hers was. When they were finally quiet, and she was storing away memories to last her a lifetime, she murmured, "I wonder if we'll ever manage anything like this again."

Ben withdrew from her slowly and lay on the carpet beside her, his "cylinder of flesh" limp and relaxed now, resting damply and comfortingly against her thigh. "Oh, I don't know." He smoothed his hand down her stomach and into the crevice below, letting it rest warmly and wonderfully against her. "What are you planning for the Fourth of July?"

Ben tiptoed down the stairs before daylight Christmas morning to make the coffee he and Joanna were going to need. It was still dark when Joanna tapped at the back door a few minutes later. Even so, they barely had time to pour the coffee before Joey called from the top of the stairs, "Grandpa! Grandpa, is it time to get up? Did Santa come yet?"

"You plug the tree lights in," Ben told Joanna. "I'll get the kids."

He let them come downstairs in their robes and slippers, then he and Joanna sat back to watch them. Joanna proved to be as much fun to watch as the children. Eyes sparkling, cheeks flushed with excitement, she seemed to be enjoying Christmas as much as they were.

Before long, she slipped out of her chair and joined them on the floor, helping to pull packages from under the tree, gathering up the ribbons and torn wrapping paper they handed her, admiring and exclaiming over each gift as if she'd never seen it before.

The white sweater she wore picked up the color from the tree lights, bringing back memories of the previous night. Maybe tonight he could persuade her that the children were far too tired to come downstairs, and she'd let him make love to her with those same lights playing once more over her bare breasts.

He wondered with a touch of panic how many more chances they'd have to make love before she left on her tropical cruise, or whether things could possibly be the same between them when she came back. It wasn't likely. He understood, perhaps better than she did, that she didn't care about lazing in the sun. The trip was only an excuse to get away, whether from him or from her own feelings he didn't know.

Either way, he knew better than to argue with her. She'd just accuse him of trying to take charge again. The only thing he could do was let her go and pray that when she came back—

Becky's voice broke into his thoughts. "Grandpa, you and Joanna have to open your presents now."

Obediently, Ben handed Joanna a small, rectangular box wrapped in white tissue. "You first."

They all watched, hardly breathing, as she unwrapped and opened it, then lifted out a charm bracelet and examined the charms one by one: a dog, a cat, a kitten, birthstones set in silver for each of the children, a key.

"To our hearts," Becky explained.

"It's from all of us," Joey said.

"It's wonderful," Joanna said. "You couldn't have given me anything I'd love more." She slipped the bracelet around her wrist and held it out to Ben. "Can you fasten it for me, please?"

Instead, he reached into his pocket and handed her a tiny box. "There's one more charm. I didn't have time to put it on the bracelet for you."

Joanna opened the box and burst out laughing at the sight of the tiny silver refrigerator he'd had such trouble finding.

"What is it?" Becky asked.

"It's a private joke between Joanna and me," Ben said.

"Will you 'splain it to us when we get older?" Joey asked.

"Oh, Joey!" Becky exclaimed. "If he explains it, it won't be private anymore, will it Grandpa?"

"You're absolutely right. Let's see that big package now, the one with my name on it."

It turned out to be the biggest cookie jar he'd ever seen.

"Look inside," Becky told him.

He lifted the lid and discovered that the jar was filled to the brim with chocolate chip cookies and gingerbread people. He looked up at Joanna and licked his lips. "I can't think of anything I'd rather have."

She grinned. "Neither could we."

"We helped make 'em," Joey said, "and we washed our hands first."

"Thank you," Ben said gravely, "both for helping to make them, and for washing your hands first."

"Can we have one?" Joey asked.

"Just one," Joanna warned. "At least until after brunch."

"What's brunch?"

"Brunch is what we're going to eat so that Joanna and I don't have to spend the whole day in the kitchen cooking a fancy meal everyone is too excited to eat anyway," Ben told him.

Excited or not, the kids ate heartily, then returned to the presents in the living room, where Ben found Joey a little while later asleep under the Christmas tree using Bernie for a pillow, and Becky curled up in his recliner with Lovey cuddled beside her.

He filled his nose and lungs with the piney scent of the Christmas tree, then returned to the kitchen's lingering aromas of bacon, biscuits, spiced applesauce, and hot coffee, and the welcome sight of Joanna, working as comfortably in his kitchen as she did in hers.

She smiled at him, with a warmth and intimacy that made him hope for a minute she'd changed her mind about— But he knew she hadn't.

"How are the kids doing?" she asked.

"Sound asleep."

"I'm not surprised. It's been a wonderful Christmas, hasn't it?"

"Wonderful," he repeated mechanically, and then his good sense disappeared and his vow not to put any pressure on her deserted him as if he'd never made it. "No," he said. "No, it isn't wonderful, and I can't keep acting as if it is, when I know that in a couple of weeks, you'll be off somewhere forgetting all about us."

"Ben! I'm not going to forget—"

"Yes, you are. That's the whole purpose of the trip, isn't it? Not to sip piña coladas and flirt with the native boys, but to get away from us."

She hesitated before she answered, not much but enough for him to know he was right. "That's ridiculous."

"Is it? Because if it's travel you really want, you don't have to do it this way, you know. Wait until summer, when the children are out of school, and we'll come with you. If you don't want to travel with the children, Fran has already asked me to let her have them for part of the summer. We can leave them with her and go anywhere in the world, just the two of us."

She turned away from him, picked up a

towel, and began to polish the already spotless counter. "Ben, my mind is made up. For once, I'm going to do what *I* want to do. Can't we just leave it at that?"

"No, we can't leave it at that, because I don't for one damned minute believe it's what you want to do." He caught her by the arm and turned her to face him. "Look at me," he demanded. "Can you look me in the eye and tell me you'd really rather traipse around the world by yourself than stay here where you're loved, wanted, needed? Can you look at me and tell me honestly that you aren't really running away? Away from me, and the children, and the way you've begun to feel about us?"

She jerked her arm loose. "Of course I'm running away, you idiot. You haven't left me any choice. If I don't go now, I never will." She caught her breath in a half sob and exclaimed, "Last week, I found myself looking out the kitchen window and thinking how nice it would be to have a vegetable garden next summer."

His mental gears spun at the abrupt change of subject. "A garden! What does that have to do with—"

"Don't you see? I've begun to think

about long-term things, things I can't do and still do the other things I've planned. I have to go *now*, or give it up."

"What would be so wrong about that? Joanna, the kids and I love you, and I think you love us. The months since we met have been the happiest of my life. What is there about this hypothetical future of yours that is so much better than the reality we have *now*, that we can keep on having for the rest of our lives?"

She turned away again and stared out the window, toward her own house, but not before he saw the tears glinting in her eyes. "You don't understand, Ben. I promised."

"Promised? What? Who?"

"I promised Robert. He said he couldn't bear to think of me sitting at home in a darkened room, grieving for him while life passed me by, and he made me promise that I would do the things we'd planned."

"Did he say you had to do them alone?"

"No," she admitted. "He said to find someone to do them with, if I could, but if not, to do them anyway." She turned away from the window. "I know what you're thinking. But it won't work. You aren't the one to do them with me. You have the children to think about. They need you, and you love them too much to give them less than your best." She was crying openly now.

"My best includes you." He tried to think of some way to comfort her, but all he could come up with was, "Joanna, you spent your whole marriage doing what he wanted you to do, but you don't have to let him go on running your life now that he's gone."

"Yes, I *do!*" she cried. "You don't understand. It wasn't just an ordinary promise. It was a *deathbed* promise—the last thing I said to him before he died. I can't break a promise like that."

She drew a deep, sobbing breath and then, while he was still groping for something else to say, she grabbed her sweater from the hook beside the door and was gone.

Joanna pushed her way blindly through the hedge, heedless of the dry twigs that caught at her clothes and scratched her skin. Once inside her own kitchen, she stood with her arms wrapped around herself, shivering as if she'd never be warm again, while the tears she had begun to shed in Ben's kitchen poured down her cheeks.

Ben was right. She loved him, loved his children, loved his exuberant Saint Bernard and calico kitten. She wanted to spend the rest of her life with them, being Ben's wife, the children's grandmother, but how could she?

She straightened up and turned toward the desk, clutching the back of the chair for support, and faced Robert's picture. "You gave me everything I ever wanted," she whispered, "except for one thing. You never gave me the chance to run things, to be in charge, not even of myself. And I've been so worried that Ben would do the same thing that I didn't even *realize* you're still doing it, still trying to run things, run *me*, with that damned promise."

On the windowsill, Tinkerbell woke, saw that Joanna was upset, and stood up to pat her face with one outstretched paw. Joanna picked her up and pressed her wet cheek against the cat's soft fur.

"I meant to keep that promise. Truly,

I did. And I've felt so guilty and miserable because I kept putting it off and putting it off. I did try to keep it once, but . . . you saw what happened when I went out by myself that Sunday. It was the most miserable time I've had in years. All the trips and tours and cruises in the world wouldn't be any better, just longer.

"Oh, Robert, how can I make you understand? You didn't want me sitting in a darkened room while life passed me by. Can't you see that, without you, all the things you planned for us *are* a darkened room?

"Do you have any idea how lonely and empty my life would be today if I hadn't met Ben and the children? If I hadn't put off your plans so I could get to know the children, and help him start his job shop, and meet all his wonderful friends? You had no right to ask that promise of me. I almost hate you for it."

But she didn't want to hate him. She wanted to go on loving him, the way she had before Helen had made her see— "Oh, Tinkerbell, why didn't I learn to dig in my heels and say no to *him* when I had the chance? Did I think the earth would open up and swallow me if I ever asserted myself? Do I think the earth will open up and swallow me if I assert myself now?''

She shivered again, with a cold that had nothing to do with temperature. Maybe she did. Maybe she'd always done as Robert wanted not because she agreed with him and wanted what he wanted, but because it was easier . . . safer.

Tinkerbell protested as Joanna's grip on her tightened. Safer? Where had that come from? Had she been afraid? Was that why she'd never stood up to Robert? Why she wasn't standing up to him now? She was afraid?

Afraid of what? Of Robert? No. Never. Robert hadn't been some kind of tyrannical monster. He'd been a good man, a kind man, who'd loved her and wanted her to be happy.

Afraid of Ben? Of course not. He loved her, too, wanted only the best for her—for both of them.

Of what, then?

Of herself, she realized bleakly. Of making the wrong choices. Of failing.

She let Tinkerbell pour through her fingers back onto the windowsill and felt her anger at Robert dissolve as she faced another truth about her marriage, and about herself.

It wasn't Robert, but her own inadequacies that had caused the gap between her past and her future. She hadn't deferred to him, she'd leaned on him, used him as a shield between her and all the things she hadn't been sure she could do—making friends, having the responsibility of children, even being "just Joanna." And she was still leaning on him, using the promise she should never have made as an excuse to hide from her inadequacies, her fear of failing, her fear of making a new life with Ben.

Because Ben wouldn't protect and shield her. Ben would always be a step ahead of her, demanding that she keep up. Ben would always ask the most from her that she could give, blithely assuming that she had the "expertise" for whatever he wanted them to do.

But Ben would also help her reach out in new directions, fill her life with all the things she had missed the first time around. He'd already begun—by catching her up in his life, sharing his children with her, introducing her to his friends—only she hadn't realized it.

For all that she'd thought she was taking charge of her own life, she hadn't done it yet, and if she ran from Ben, she never would. He was right. If she kept seeking the protection of a future that no longer existed for her, she'd never be able to have the glorious, wonderful *now* that he offered her.

She picked up Robert's picture and stroked it gently. "I love you," she told him. "I'll always love you. But you're my past, and it's time for me to move into the future now. It won't be the future we planned together, but it won't be sitting in a darkened room letting life pass me by either. I'm not sure yet what it will be, except that I have to find my own kind of happiness. Mine, and Ben's."

He seemed to smile at her, and she learned the third and most important thing about her marriage.

Robert hadn't been trying to control her through her promise. He'd known about her fears and inadequacies, and he'd only been trying to protect her from what she'd almost done—let life pass her by. Her own kind of happiness was what he had always wanted for her.

Ben stood in the middle of the kitchen, his mind playing over and over again the soft click the latch had made as the door closed behind Joanna. With each repetition, his anger grew. He'd slowly come to realize, from hints and clues he'd pieced together, that Joanna's husband had pretty much kept her under his thumb, making the decisions, running her life.

He didn't know whether Joanna really felt honor-bound to keep that cockamamie promise, or if she was just afraid that he, Ben, would also take away her freedom, her right to run her own life, but either way, that SOB still had her under his thumb, and now he was interfering in Ben's life as well.

And there was nothing Ben could do about it. If he let her go, let her take that cruise and try to carry out whatever other plans her husband had made for her, he risked losing her. If he tried to make her see what was happening, she'd only believe he was trying to "stampede" her into doing what *he* wanted her to do.

He balanced on the balls of his feet, fists clenched at his sides, while he tried to decide what to do, then realized the decision was out of his hands. He was an action person. Given the only two choices he had, he wasn't going to stand around and wait for Joanna to come to her senses. Maybe he couldn't do anything, but he had to try.

He tiptoed to the living room door. The children were still sleeping soundly. It wasn't likely they'd wake for hours. In the face of an emergency the size of this one, he could leave them alone for a few minutes.

He started across his backyard at a brisk pace, but by the time he reached the hedge, he was running. He barely slowed as he pushed through, then skidded to a stop on the other side at the sight of Joanna running toward him.

He didn't stop to wonder what she was doing there, but caught her by the shoulders and held her at arms' length so he could look into her eyes as he spoke, and so that she could look into his eyes and know he was telling the truth. "Joanna, I'm not trying to run your life, and I'm not trying to stampede you into anything, but you have to listen to me."

She shook her head. "No, you have to listen to me. Ben, I dug in my heels and told him no."

He gawked at her, trying to switch his brain from "send" to "receive." "You what?"

"I dug in my heels and told him no, that I wasn't going to keep my promise, because he had no right to ask me to make a promise like that. And then I found out that I hadn't really promised him what I thought I had, so . . ."

His brain still refused to make sense of what she was saying. "I don't know what you're talking about."

She caught his face between her hands and kissed him soundly. "Of course you don't. I'll explain it all to you someday when we don't have anything else to do. For now, all you have to know is that I love you, and I love your precious grandchildren, and your overgrown Saint Bernard, and your calico kitten. And if you'll all have me—and Tinkerbell . . ."

"We will," he assured her. It would be a while before he figured out what had happened, but he knew a miracle when he saw one, and he wasn't about to turn one down—not this one anyway. "We will."

"Then I'm asking you to marry me and let me spend the rest of my life loving and taking care of you—all of you. I really think, given half a chance, I could develop a totally new field of expertise. What do you think?"

He pulled her close, relishing the way they fit together and feeling sorry all over again for tall men and short women. "I think we ought to go inside and tell the children we saved the best Christmas present for last."

She laughed softly and then kissed him, a kiss that blended passion, affection, and a promise for the new future that beckoned to them.

When they finally separated, he cleared his throat and managed to say, "Joanna Blake, you're my kind of woman."

She tightened her arms around him and laughed again, a tiny ripple of pure happiness that sent tingles of joy and anticipation up and down his spine. "Yes, I am, and you, Benjamin Walker, are my kind of man."

WATCH AS THESE WOMEN LEARN
TO LOVE AGAIN

HELLO LOVE   (4094, $4.50/$5.50)
by Joan Shapiro

Family tragedy leaves Barbara Sinclair alone with her success. The fight to gain custody of her young granddaughter brings a confrontation with the determined rancher Sam Douglass. Also widowed, Sam has been caring for Emily alone, guided by his own ideas of childrearing. Barbara challenges his ideas. And that's not all she challenges . . . Long-buried desires surface, then gentle affection. Sam and Barbara cannot ignore the chance to love again.

THE BEST MEDICINE   (4220, $4.50/$5.50)
by Janet Lane Walters

Her late husband's expenses push Maggie Carr back to nursing, the career she left almost thirty years ago. The night shift is difficult, but it's harder still to ignore the way handsome Dr. Jason Knight soothes his patients. When she lends a hand to help his daughter, Jason and Maggie grow closer than simply doctor and nurse. Obstacles to romance seem insurmountable, but Maggie knows that love is always the best medicine.

AND BE MY LOVE   (4291, $4.50/$5.50)
by Joyce C. Ware

Selflessly catering first to husband, then children, grandchildren, and her aging, though imperious mother, leaves Beth Volmar little time for her own adventures or passions. Then, the handsome archaeologist Karim Donovan arrives and campaigns to widen the boundaries of her narrow life. Beth finds new freedom when Karim insists that she accompany him to Turkey on an archaeological dig . . . and a journey towards loving again.

OVER THE RAINBOW   (4032, $4.50/$5.50)
by Marjorie Eatock

Fifty-something, divorced for years, courted by more than one attractive man, and thoroughly enjoying her job with a large insurance company, Marian's sudden restlessness confuses her. She welcomes the chance to travel on business to a small Mississippi town. Full of good humor and words of love, Don Worth makes her feel needed, and not just to assess property damage. Marian takes the risk.

A KISS AT SUNRISE   (4260, $4.50/$5.50)
by Charlotte Sherman

Beginning widowhood and retirement, Ruth Nichols has her first taste of freedom. Against the advice of her mother and daughter, Ruth heads for an adventure in the motor home that has sat unused since her husband's death. Long days and lonely campgrounds start to dampen the excitement of traveling alone. That is, until a dapper widower named Jack parks next door and invites her for dinner. On the road, Ruth and Jack find the chance to love again.

Available wherever paperbacks are sold, or order direct from the Publisher. Send cover price plus 50¢ per copy for mailing and handling to Penguin USA, P.O. Box 999, c/o Dept. 17109, Bergenfield, NJ 07621. Residents of New York and Tennessee must include sales tax. DO NOT SEND CASH.

IT'S NEVER TOO LATE
TO FALL IN LOVE!

MAYBE LATER, LOVE   (3903, $4.50/$5.50)
by Claire Bocardo
Dorrie Greene was astonished! After thirty-five years of being
"George Greene's lovely wife" she was now a whole new person. She
could take things at her own pace, and she could choose the man she
wanted. Life and love were better than ever!

MRS. PERFECT   (3789, $4.50/$5.50)
by Peggy Roberts
Devastated by the loss of her husband and son, Ginny Logan worked
longer and longer hours at her job in an ad agency. Just when she had
decided she could live without love, a warm, wonderful man noticed
her and brought love back into her life.

OUT OF THE BLUE   (3798, $4.50/$5.50)
by Garda Parker
Recently widowed, besieged by debt, and stuck in a dead-end job,
Majesty Wilde was taking life one day at a time. Then fate stepped in,
and the opportunity to restore a small hotel seemed like a dream come
true . . . especially when a rugged pilot offered to help!

THE TIME OF HER LIFE   (3739, $4.50/$5.50)
by Marjorie Eatock
Evelyn Cass's old friends whispered about her behind her back. They
felt sorry for poor Evelyn—alone at fifty-five, having to sell her
house, and go to work! Funny how she was looking ten years younger
and for the first time in years, Evelyn was having the time of her life!

TOMORROW'S PROMISE   (3894, $4.50/$5.50)
by Clara Wimberly
It takes a lot of courage for a woman to leave a thirty-three year marriage. But when Margaret Avery's aged father died and left her a
small house in Florida, she knew that the moment had come. The
change was far more difficult than she had anticipated. Then things
started looking up. Happiness had been there all the time, just waiting for her.

*Available wherever paperbacks are sold, or order direct from the
Publisher. Send cover price plus 50¢ per copy for mailing and
handling to Penguin USA, P.O. Box 999, c/o Dept. 17109,
Bergenfield, NJ 07621. Residents of New York and Tennessee
must include sales tax. DO NOT SEND CASH.*